# FOOL THEM ONCE

KYRA PARSI

Fool Them Once



Cover Design: GR Book Covers

Editing: One Love Editing

## CONTENT NOTE

A list of content warnings for all my books can be found on my website at https://kyraparsi.com/content-warnings/.

# 1

# kylar

*This... can't be right. There's no way this can be right... right?*

I wasn't sure how long I'd been sitting there, staring out the window in a state of mild disbelief. But judging by the tone of the driver's voice when he addressed me, it exceeded the appropriate length of time for someone to still be in the cab after arriving at their destination.

"Miss?" he said, eyeing me through the rearview mirror.

"Oh, sorry, um, this—I mean, we're sure this is the right place?" I pulled my phone out to confirm the address again. Maybe I'd gotten it wrong? Accidentally transposed the street numbers or something?

"Yep, this is definitely it," he said, squinting down at the screen. "Nice buildin', too."

I looked back out at the two massive glass doors of the pale grey stone building, each one adorned with gold framing, frozen vines, and its own uniformed doorman waiting on the other side.

"You need help with the bags?" the driver asked in yet another attempt to get me out of his damn car.

"Oh, no, that's okay. But thank you." I reached for my wallet before my nerves could take over and ask him to drive me back to the airport. "How much do I owe you?"

I was standing out on the sidewalk thirty seconds later, deeply regretting not having worn a thicker sweater under my winter jacket. How was Toronto this much colder than New York? They weren't that far apart on the map.

Hesitation shifted my weight from one foot to the other and back again. Then, as though it could smell my fear, a door swung open and summoned its designated human to figure out what the weirdo with a scuffed-up duffle bag and suitcase lingering outside was doing. Probably.

"Miss Gaige?" the man said, offering me a bearded smile as he approached.

He knew my name?

"That would be me."

His grin widened. "It's excellent to meet you, Miss Gaige. I'm George. Miss Milani has been expecting you. I'll take you up to the suite if you are ready?" He gestured for my suitcase with a gloved hand.

"Oh, that's okay, I got it." It wasn't very heavy. No need to bother him with it. "Thank you, though."

"Very well. This way, please."

I followed him into the warmth of the massive foyer, where two suited women seated behind a concierge desk stood and greeted us as we walked past.

The space was impressive, to say the least. The entire room was lavishly decorated with red roses in asymmetrical black-and-gold vases, and the black marble tiles were kept in such pristine shape that they perfectly mirrored the giant cascading crystal chandeliers above. And I do mean *perfectly*. I almost felt bad walking on them.

"Miss Milani says you'll be staying with us for three months?" George asked politely when we reached the elevators. He'd led us to the smallest one at the end of the hallway. It opened up right away.

"That's right. I'm here for an internship at—" I froze midsentence, watching as his hand pulled away from the button he'd just pressed. Number 44. The only one on the board. "What—sorry, there's just the one floor?" Where were the buttons for the other forty-three?

"Yes, that is generally how private elevators work." He smiled as though that were a perfectly good explanation. As though using a private elevator was a normal, everyday occurrence and *I* was the weird one for having asked. "It's reserved for the two penthouse units," he clarified.

*Um. What.*

George, absolutely oblivious to my state of confusion, continued on with the small talk. Something about the weather and an incoming storm. Wasn't entirely sure. I was too busy going over my conversation with Alexis, trying to figure out where in the *"Oh, oh, oh! I have a spare apartment you can use!"* part of the talk I was supposed to have picked up on the fact that there would be a private elevator involved. *Or a penthouse.*

"Here we are," George said, just as the elevator greeted our arrival with a small *ding*. "It'll be the unit to your left. Miss Milani did inform us that she was home and would be waiting for you, but please do not hesitate to reach out with any questions or concerns."

"Great, thank you," I mumbled, trailing into the hallway with my luggage in tow.

I walked over to the white double doors and knocked, very much convinced at this point that either this was a prank, or I'd accidentally stepped into the matrix. Was that how the matrix worked? I didn't know. Hadn't seen the movie. Wasn't important right now.

"Come in! It's open!"

It *sounded* like Alexis, at least.

I opened the door, holding my breath. A wasted effort since all the air spilled out of my lungs the second I stepped inside.

It was *huge*. And beautiful. Oh, so beautiful.

The majority of the furnishings were neutral toned, with random pops of deep blues, greens, and golds in the form of throw pillows, centerpieces, and plants spread across the living space in front of me. To my right was a massive contemporary kitchen, separated from the living area by a long, white marble island, and to my left was a floating staircase.

This place had multiple floors.

"Skylar!" The sweet, familiar voice tore through my daze, followed closely by hurried steps as Alexis ran down the stairs, a graceful flurry of long, dark-chocolate waves and excitement.

"Alexis! Hey!" I dropped the bags I was holding when she flung her arms around me and hugged her back. She was ten inches shorter than me, standing at an even five feet, and yet she still somehow managed to knock me back a few steps.

"I've missed you," she said, giving me a tight squeeze of her arms before we parted. "How are you? How was the flight?"

"Flight was good. No screaming babies, chair kickers, or engine failures, which is always nice."

"No engine failures? Like, at all?"

"Nope."

"No wings falling off midflight? Snakes hiding under the seats?"

"None of that, either, unfortunately."

She rolled her eyes. "How boring," she said, starting to turn away from me. But then she stopped, and I knew the second it hit her. "Or should I say, *Boeing*."

I tried not to laugh. I really did. But the wide, open-mouthed grin she wore was so proud it broke me.

"It was a good one! Admit it!" Alexis demanded as soon as the defeated huff escaped me.

"It was pretty good."

"Thank you for your honesty." She was still grinning, extremely pleased with herself. "Speaking of honesty, whatchya think?" she asked, walking farther into the apartment and gesturing around. "Do you like it?"

Did I *like* it?

I had to take a second before answering, not entirely sure where to start with this one. "Alexis, when you said you had a 'spare apartment' that I could stay at after the other place fell through, I was expecting like a five-hundred-square-foot one bedroom, not a *penthouse* in a gigantic skyscraper located smack in the middle of downtown Toronto."

Disappointment dampened her smile. "I thought it'd be a nice little surprise. You don't like it?"

The only thing I could do was stand there and gape back at her. I'd known Alexis for four years, having met her at a fashion photography seminar during my first year at college. So, I was aware of the fact that she was well-off, especially for someone her age. But she was also a pretty successful photographer, booking shoots with major designers before she'd even graduated, so I'd never questioned any of the high-end clothes or lavish trips. But this... this was a whole other level. The girl obviously also came from money.

"No, that's not what I meant. It's lovely, Alexis. And I really do appreciate it, so please don't take this the wrong way, but I don't think I can stay here."

"What? Why not?" She sounded a little offended.

I'd thought this part would be pretty self-explanatory. "Because it's way, *way* too much."

"I wouldn't go that far. I know it's not exactly what you were expecting, but it's only for a few months, right?" she tried to reason. "Plus, it's not like anyone else is using it since I moved in with Joel. Kind of a waste to let it just sit here all empty, don't you think?"

I shifted uncomfortably on my feet, unsure of what to say. She smiled and walked over to grab my arm when I didn't answer. "Come on, I'll show you around first, and if you still really hate it, we'll figure something else out for you."

It felt like I was walking through an interior designer's wet dream or an *Architectural Digest* article. Four bedrooms, four and a half baths, a small wine room, and a rooftop terrace with a built-in firepit, bar, and pool. An actual private rooftop pool. *And* a hot tub.

"Last but not least, this one right here is your room!" Alexis said when we entered the last bedroom on the second floor, ending the tour.

It was lovely, of course, and the approximate size of the small apartment I had been expecting when she told me about the place. It came with its own en suite bathroom and walk-in closet and featured the same floor-to-ceiling windows that surrounded the rest of the apartment, providing a breath-taking view of the city skyline.

"It's incredible," I admitted. "But seriously, Alexis, are you really sure this is okay...?"

"*Yes*! I am a hundred percent sure it's okay."

I looked around again before answering. "Okay. But I'm not staying here for free. You'll have to accept rent." Not that I could afford even a fraction of what this place would actually cost, but there was no way my conscience would allow me to stay here for free. No matter how much Alexis had initially insisted.

"Okay, then how about this. I don't want rent, *but* I do have a couple of shoots lined up over the next few weeks that I would love to work with you on. I know you've scaled back on all that, but you do those with me, and we'll call it even." The subtle, playful narrowing of her eyes was the giveaway. This wasn't something she'd just thought of on the spot.

*Ah.*

I'd always felt that people didn't give Alexis enough credit. She was smarter than she usually let on. Sometimes, I wondered if that was on purpose.

"Fine. You win," I caved with a little laugh, just as she knew I would. "You get as many shoots as you want for this one. Just name the time and place."

"Deal!" She practically hopped over to shake my hand.

"...IN addition to the multiple snow warnings, temperatures in Toronto are expected to continue dipping well below their normal averages over the next two weeks, making this the coldest winter the city has seen in over a decade," the perfectly postured man claimed as soon as I turned on the TV. "Stay safe out there, folks."

I settled into bed, flipping through the streaming catalogue before deciding on a tenth rewatch of *The Office*.

It was the right decision. Michael Scott was a whole new experience on a one-hundred-inch high-definition TV. It was awesome.

I closed my eyes for what felt like a second, four or five

episodes in, but was evidently more than that because when I opened them again, the show had paused, asking me if I was still alive.

The mattress was to blame. I was starting to understand why people splurged on them. I'd slept better over the last two days than I had... well, ever.

I stretched out on the bed, igniting a string of relieved snaps and crackles from my spine, and then lay there for a few minutes, contemplating whether my need for a glass of water outweighed the laziness that would have me glued to the magic mattress for the foreseeable future.

Eventually, the thirst won. I rolled out from under the covers and onto my feet, regretting leaving the warmth almost immediately. A light snowstorm had started outside, and though my view of the flurries against the black sky wasn't one to complain about, it sent a new wave of shivers down my body.

I pulled up the hood of my oversized sweater and slipped my hands into its pockets before sauntering out of the room. I didn't bother turning on the lights since the view of the lit-up city illuminated the apartment just enough to allow me to navigate my way through it without a problem.

That was my first mistake.

I was halfway down the stairs when I thought I heard something. A shuffle or a whisper of movement. I paused midstep, scanning the room and listening.

*It's probably nothing*, I thought after a few seconds, continuing to walk in the dark. Just like every single unsuspecting idiot in every single scary movie that's the first one out of the group to get murdered.

Then, I heard it again just as I was about to reach the kitchen. This time it was louder, and I was sure it came from behind me. I stilled, a shot of adrenaline firing up my spine.

A small part of my brain tried to calm me down with logic and reason. The chances of a break-in happening on a private floor of a building this secure were slim.

*But not zero*, the other, less reasonable but much larger voice in my head noted.

Then something moved. I was sure of it this time. *Oh god.*

I was frozen, trying to listen and figure out where the noise was coming from, which would have been a lot easier had all the blood in my body not been roaring in my ears.

Then it happened. The unmistakable sound of someone taking a step right behind me.

I jumped straight out of my skin and into another dimension, whipping around instinctively with my heart attempting to pound out of my rib cage so it could abandon me and *thump* its way to hidden safety. The traitor.

But also fair, because I was straight up about to be murdered by the towering, dark figure that was standing not two feet away from me, holding something that strongly resembled a baseball bat.

*Oh, sh—*

My heel caught the edge of a rug when I tried to take a step back, flipping my view in the dark before I could even finish the thought, let alone scream. I landed right on my tailbone, and just as I was mentally preparing myself for the inevitable shot of pain that would follow, the back of my head hit the wall with a dull, distinctive *thud.*

*Ow... just, ow.*

It took a couple of beats to recover enough from the impact that I could breathe and open my eyes again.

"How the fuck did you get in here?" The source of the deep, aggressive growl was closer than I was expecting, reigniting my panic.

I blinked frantically, like that would help magically rid the stars speckling my vision and allow for a clearer view of the shadowed features of my soon-to-be murderer.

"*Why* are you in my apartment?" he demanded again unreasonably, as though my voice wasn't hiding somewhere I couldn't reach.

I opened my mouth to try and explain, but the only word I managed to rasp out was "Alexis."

Silence echoed against the ringing in my ears before he spoke again. "What?" he said, more evenly, less growly this time.

"Alexis," I repeated, my voice akin to that of a person who'd smoked ten packs a day for the last seven hundred years. But, by some inconceivable miracle, that seemed to be a sufficient answer because he took a step back and dropped the weapon.

Before I could make sense of what the hell was happening, a small lamp in the corner of the room snapped on, and the tall figure began pacing in front of me.

"Don't move," he bit out, and then I heard the faint sound of an outgoing call ringing in between his steps.

Thinking that I might actually have an opportunity to escape, I took a sleeve to my face, quickly wiping at the tears brought on by the pain of nearly breaking my tailbone and skull all in one go, and glanced up once my vision had semi-cleared. I didn't have a weapon, and my phone was upstairs, but having him in my line of sight also meant that I would at least be slightly better prepared to defend myself if he came at me. Not *very well*, mind you, taking into consideration his massive frame, but better. I could also maybe dive for the bat.

Apparently, though, hitting my head on the wall had killed off my last functioning brain cell, rendering the whole thing utterly useless. It had to have. Because that was the only logical explanation as to why the first and only thought that went through my head when I looked up at the intruder who almost attacked me with a baseball bat was *whoa.*

Either that or I had the worst survival instincts on the planet and would absolutely be the first one out of the group to get scary-movie-murdered.

# 2

than

"HULLO?"

My anger boiled over at the sound of her careless and groggy voice, thrashing against my skin in waves of thick, hot lava. I ripped off my scarf, now wet from the melted snow, and threw it onto the floor along with my gloves as the heat traveled up my body. It had taken me three tries to get through to her.

"Alexis," I barked, loudly enough that the body seated on the floor jolted in surprise. "Why is there a person in the Laivimere penthouse claiming they're here because of you?"

"Huh? In the what... where?" I could almost hear the stalling engine of her *teeny tiny* brain slowly turn back on as she processed my question. I waited for a few seconds until, fucking finally, she sucked in a sharp breath. "Wait, sorry, *where* are you right now?"

"In. The. Laivimere. Penthouse." The words slithered out

from in between my clenched teeth, each one stretched out into its own sentence so that maybe, *just maybe*, they would somehow have an easier time making their way into my sister's impossibly thick skull.

"You're in Toronto?"

It was like talking to a goldfish. The snack kind, not the living, swimming creature with a semi-functioning brain kind.

"*Focus*, Alexis. Do you know this person?" *Or do I need to call the fucking police?*

"Yes! I do. Sky's staying there for the next few months."

*Of course he is*. Leave it to my little sister to take in every single stray within a twenty-mile radius. Good to know she'd graduated from pets to humans.

Joel was a saint.

"And you didn't think to tell me?" I was all but foaming at the mouth with rage.

"No, because the place is supposed to be empty until July, remember? Did *you* think to tell *me* that you'd be back in town six months early?"

"*No, because the place is supposed to be empty until July, remember*? We don't keep these apartments around to fill with strays, Alexis. They're not fucking shelters," I snapped back at her. "Of all the stupid, irresponsible shit you've pulled over the years, this one takes the cake. So, congratulations. I almost fucking attacked the guy because I thought he broke in." I quickly glanced back down at my sister's apparent houseguest and my near lawsuit, who'd been smart enough to listen to my instructions and sit still while his breathing evened out.

I couldn't see much of his face in the limited light; he had a sweater on with the hood pulled up, and his floppy hair covered most of his forehead and eyes. But he seemed young. Eighteen or nineteen years young. Or, at least, the naked lower half of his face did.

He was also super thin and frail, even for a kid.

And, honestly, now that I looked a little more closely, his nose and lips were a little feminine... and so was his chin, and his jaw, and...

*Oh.*

*Oh, shit.*

"You *what*? Ethan!" Alexis's alarmed voice tore through the speaker just as my own realization smacked me across the face. I heard the rushed rustling of sheets being thrown to the side on the other end of the line. A dog barked in the background. "And why did you say 'guy'? What guy? Are we talking about the same person? Skylar is a girl, dipshit."

*Yeah, dipshit.*

I didn't answer her, my gaze still glued to the body on the floor. She sat too still, almost entirely frozen in fear with the exception of the heavy rising and falling of her chest, as she watched me back through the strands of short, dark hair that curtained her eyes.

"Hello? Ethan? Why aren't you saying anything—what's going on? Is she okay? Do I need to come over? Hand her the phone or put me on speaker or something!" Alexis was full-on panicking.

The logical thing to do was probably to address the girl directly and ask her if she was okay. But she looked terrified—like she was still waiting to see if I was going to attack her.

I had no idea how to even start explaining myself.

"Ethan!"

"We might need to take her to the hospital or have Dr. Gomez take a look at her. She banged her head pretty hard," I finally managed, my voice scratching punitively against my rapidly drying throat.

"Oh my god. What is the *matter with you*?"

*Everything. Everything is the matter with me right now.*

"How the fuck is this my fault? I came home at midnight to find a person dressed in all black walking around in the fucking dark. What would you have done?"

"The exact opposite of whatever the hell it is you did! And stop talking about her like she's not right there with you. Hand her the phone or something! Poor thing's probably traumatized."

My eyes made their way back down to Skylar, fully aware that she had yet to move a single muscle not attached to her chest. "Traumatized" would barely begin to cover it, judging by the way she was looking at me.

*Fuck.*

"Hold on, I'm putting you on speaker. You'll need to tell her who I am and explain that I'm not a serial killer because I'm pretty sure that's what she thinks," I said, more to the girl on the floor than to Alexis, before slowly squatting down to her level and holding out my phone.

"Skylar? You there? You okay?"

"I-I'm here, yeah. Hi." She barely moved, keeping her gaze locked on me. Her voice was soft, though understandably still a little raspy.

It made me feel like absolute shit.

"Hey, are you okay? Ethan says you hit your head?"

"Yeah, um, I'm alright," she said, rubbing the spot that had made contact with the wall. "A little... uh... confused."

"I can imagine. I'm so, so sorry, Sky. I promise I had no idea Ethan would be there. He's *supposed* to be in Seattle right now," Alexis said, still not having explained who I was. Then again, she'd never been all that great at following instructions.

"Oh... okay. But, uh, Lex?" Skylar asked, hand dropping back to her lap.

"Yeah?"

"Who's Ethan?" She tilted her head a little to the side when she asked. Kind of like a puppy.

I almost smiled. Almost.

"Oh right, yes. He's my brother. And as far as I'm aware, he's not a serial killer... at least, I don't *think*. But, like, if we're being honest, would I be all that *surprised* if one d—"

"*Alexis*," I warned, running very, very low on patience.

I didn't like to give my sister a lot of credit because she normally didn't deserve it, but I'd be the first to admit that her ability to pick the most inappropriate times to make the most inappropriate jokes remained unrivaled. It was one of the few skills she'd managed to master in her twenty-four years.

Skylar, however, actually seemed a little amused by the interaction. The corners of her lips twitched, and she slouched a little, as though some of the tension in her body had been relieved.

"You'll have to excuse him, Sky. What my brother lacks in manners, he also, unfortunately, does not make up for in his nonexistent sense of humo—"

I hung up on her, knowing she had nothing else useful to contribute.

"So," I said after a few moments of silence. "You're not a burglar."

"And you're not a murderer."

"Yet," I grumbled with an exasperated exhale of hot air, standing up. "Jury's still out on whether or not I let my sister live after this one."

I offered her my hand, but she hesitated and chose to stand up on her own instead, using the wall for support.

*Fair enough.*

She was tall, probably around five foot ten or eleven, and the black hoodie and sweatpants she wore both looked to be about three sizes too big for her.

*It wasn't all that unreasonable to mistake her for a guy in the dark*, I tried to justify. But it didn't ease any of the guilt.

I hit Ignore when my phone started to vibrate in my hand. "We should probably get you to a hospital and have you checked out. You could have a concussion."

"Oh... that's okay. I'm fine, just a little shaken, I think." She rubbed at the back of her head again, glancing down and away from me.

I paused, studying her. Technically, I couldn't force her to seek medical attention, but she definitely didn't look "fine." In any sense of the word. "You sure?" I tried again. "The hospital isn't too far from here, and the roads are still okay."

"Yeah, seriously, I'm okay. Not like I broke anything..." She trailed off, shifting on her feet. Like she was double-checking.

"Alright, well, it's up to you. Let me know if you change your mind," I said, slipping off my coat and heading to the bar. "Take a seat, at least. I'll grab you some water."

"Sure, thanks," she said, and then, "So, um, if you don't mind me asking... whose apartment is this? Because up until a few minutes ago, I thought it belonged to Alexis." She sat on the couch and fiddled with her sleeves, mindlessly pulling at a loose thread.

"It's not hers, technically," I said, handing Skylar the glass of water before heading back to the bar. I needed a fucking drink. "It's a spare apartment for the family. We filter in and out as needed, but Alexis has been the only one using this place for the last couple of years."

Skylar's lips parted again, like she was going to say something else, but decided against it.

"Whiskey?" I offered, pouring a glass.

It occurred to me as soon as I'd asked that you probably weren't supposed to drink if you had a head injury, and we weren't entirely sure she *didn't* have a head injury.

"That's okay, but thank you." Her eyes dropped down to where my phone sat on the bar, still buzzing. "Are you going to answer that or just let Alexis suffer all night?"

"Suffer. I'm going to let her suffer. She deserves it," I said, bringing the crystal tumbler to my mouth. Skylar didn't agree, judging by the delicate frown that touched her lips.

I put my phone on silent and took a seat in the armchair closest to her. "Problem solved."

"I think you're being a little too hard on her. This was clearly just a misunderstanding," she tried to reason.

Was she serious? Did she not remember the baseball bat? What if I'd used it? "You sure you're not concussed?"

"I'm just saying, I think it's a little unfair to put all the blame on her."

"I'm a little concerned you're not fully grasping what just happened or what *could* have happened," I said slowly.

"No, I am, but it's not entirely her fault. You scared me, and I tripped and fell... and that's about it. And, you know, like you said, I probably shouldn't have been walking around in the dark."

I eyed her, processing the ridiculousness of the situation and argument we were having. At this point, I was semi-suspicious that this whole thing was an elaborate setup put on by Greyson to undermine me.

*I wonder how many cameras he's got hidden around here.*

The only thing that stopped me from looking around for them was Alexis. She was the biggest hole in the theory because I was pretty sure she wouldn't have been able to feign the level of panic her voice had held on the phone.

I was even more sure she wouldn't team up with Grey. She'd never been a big fan of snakes.

"I'm sorry, are you saying you think this is somehow *your* fault?" I asked, watching her carefully. If she was a hired actress, she deserved an Oscar for her performance so far. "Alexis failed to mention your staying here, I almost attacked you with a baseball bat because I thought you broke in, which caused you to trip and bang your head against the wall... and you think it's your fault?"

"Well, I can't really blame you for grabbing a bat, can I? For all you knew, I could have been deranged and had a weapon. Or something."

She wasn't entirely wrong. "For the record, you could still very well be a deranged weapon-carrying lunatic. *Or something.*" Including, but not limited to, an award-winning actress. "None of that is off the table. I still don't actually know who you are."

The corners of her lips perked up. "Skylar. Twenty-four, design intern at Zilmar Bain," she said, holding out her hand.

"Ethan." I took it, surprised by how soft her skin was. Like velvet. Or... a rose petal. *What the fuck? Did you just compare her skin to a fucking rose petal?* "Thirty. Chief operating officer at Milani Group," I continued, trying my best to shake off what had just happened in my head.

Sleep deprivation was one hell of a drug.

"Oh. Family business?"

I paused before answering, a little taken aback. It seemed strange that she didn't already know. "Real estate development. How is it that you and my sister know each other again?"

"We met in college," she answered with fiddling fingers.

"You went to school in New York?"

"I'm from there. Majored in fashion design... Alexis and I worked on a couple of projects together. She did some photography for me, and I helped out with some of her stuff," she said vaguely, her pale cheeks tinting with a hint of color.

"And now you're here... because you decided after graduation to move *away* from one of the biggest fashion capitals of the world?" I didn't mean for the suspicion to seep into my tone, but I was too tired to actively reel it back.

Her body language and voice turned slightly defensive, and maybe rightfully so. "It's just for three months and for work. Then I'm heading back. Zilmar Bain is one of the most prominent fashion *houses* in the world. It's a really coveted position. He only takes two interns a year," she retorted.

That I knew she wasn't lying about. He was single-handedly responsible for half my wardrobe. The majority of my suits were Bains.

"And just so you know, I'm not a 'stray,'" she continued, sitting up straight as she referred to my earlier slight. "I did have other living arrangements lined up, but they fell through at the very last minute, and your sister was generous enough to offer me this place when they did. Which is why I'm saying you should go easy on her. It wasn't planned. She was just trying to do something nice for a friend."

And maybe she was right—maybe I had been a little overly harsh with Alexis. But I hadn't slept in over forty hours, I was exhausted, and I had come home to what, at the time, seemed like someone who'd broken into the apartment.

I hadn't been thinking clearly. Hell, I probably still wasn't thinking clearly.

"Okay, so then what's your plan now?" I asked, shooting straight for the point. It's not like she could stay here for the next three months. Because, unfortunately, I was probably going to be here for the next three months. And then however long after that.

"I'll go upstairs and pack. I can stay at a hotel or something tonight and then start looking for a place tomorrow."

"It's one in the morning," I said, glancing down at my watch. "You're going to pack up and leave right now?"

"I don't have a lot of stuff." She shrugged, slipping her hands into her pockets. "It shouldn't take me too long."

There was no way in hell I was going to let her walk out of here in the middle of the night with a potential head injury after what had just happened. Alexis would skin me alive with her nails. She was a lot more violent than she looked. "You could stay for tonight since it's already so late. We can figure out new accommodations in the morning."

*We? Did you just say "we"?*

"Are you sure?" she asked hesitantly. "I really wouldn't want to impose..."

"I wouldn't have offered if I wasn't."

"Okay, yeah, that would be great. Thank you," she said, standing up. It didn't escape me that the action was accompanied by a wince or that she tried to cover it up. "And I promise I'll be packed up and out of your hair in the morning."

"Sure." I took one last sip of my whiskey and tapped my phone back to life as she walked away.

The missed calls and messages from Alexis were expected. There were more of them than I'd thought possible, but they were expected. What wasn't was the second name on the screen.

**Grey: Welcome back.**

And, just like that, it was back. The agitation and anger that had been building up over the course of the last two days crept up my spine and coiled itself tightly around my neck.

"Oh, and also, just in case it still wasn't clear... I'm, um, not a guy," Skylar added with a playful smirk before turning around again and walking up the stairs.

*Fuck this fucking day to the ninth circle of Dante's hell and back.*

# 3

## than

"I'm serious, Ethan. She better come down those stairs in one piece," Alexis threatened before plopping herself onto a stool on the other side of the kitchen island.

At least she'd made herself semi-useful and put away some of the groceries I'd had delivered this morning. Per the occupants of the fridge pre-delivery, our houseguest's diet consisted of eggs, toast, and ice cream.

"Why don't you go upstairs and check on her now if you're so concerned?" I asked, topping off my third cup of coffee. Five hours of sleep had, unsurprisingly, not been enough to make up for how much I'd missed this week.

"I already texted her. She said she's just getting dressed and will be down in a bit. Plus, I also need to figure out what's up your butt."

"Meaning?"

"Meaning you're being super grumpy. Even for you," she pointed out, popping a grape off its stem and into her mouth.

"Alexis. I'm *grumpy* because I came home last night to what I thought was an intruder, thanks to you." I turned back to the stove, hoping she'd drop it.

"I don't buy it. You look stressed as hell. And tired. Does it have anything to do with why you're back?"

"No."

"Liar."

"I'm here for a meeting. I've come back for meetings before. It's not unusual," I defended.

"Meeting with who?"

"Who do you think?"

"When?"

"In an hour," I said, stealing a quick glance at the clock on the stove before wiping an escaped drop of hollandaise off the side of the plate with a napkin.

"It's Saturday."

"When has that ever been an issue for her? Or me?"

She clicked her tongue at me disapprovingly. "You're all a bunch of workaholics, and it's so unhealthy. Dad was the exact same way. There *is* more to life than the company and your job, you know. Am I the only person in the entirety of our family who sees that?"

"Good morning," a third voice chimed in, just as I turned back around to face Alexis.

I almost dropped the plate I was holding when our eyes met.

*Striking* was the word that came to mind, but it still wouldn't do her justice. Not even close.

The short, black hair was what gave her away. If it wasn't for that, I didn't think I would have recognized Skylar. Except this morning, it wasn't flopped over her forehead, covering a third of her face. She'd tousled it back, revealing cool, glacier-blue eyes in the daylight, accentuated by sharp, dark eyebrows.

"Skylar!" Alexis jumped out of her seat and cupped her friend's face, bringing it down a few inches closer to her level and angling it this way and that. To check for dents and scratches, I assumed. "You okay? Let me see. What did he do to you?"

"I'm fine," Skylar said with a laugh, playfully swatting my sister's fussing hands away. "I told you last night it wasn't a big deal. I lightly tapped my head. It's all good."

*Lightly* tapped? In what version of reality was that a *light* tap?

"Yeah, but you downplay *everything*. Remember last year when you and Tim got into what you told us was a 'little fender bender,' except the car was totaled, you were hospitalized for two days, and the bruises on your ribs were there for like over a month."

Huh. Maybe I *should* have taken her to a hospital last night.

"Really, it's fine. I'm also packed up, so I'll be out of your hair soon, as promised," she said, throwing a quick, wary glance my way.

"We can talk about that in a bit. Sit down and eat first. Ethan made us breakfast," Alexis chirped happily, sitting down again.

"Oh, wow, for real?" Skylar's eyes dropped down to the plate I realized I was still holding. I hadn't really moved, having gotten distracted when the small silver ring pierced through her right eyebrow caught the light.

*The fuck's the matter with you? Get it together.*

"It's his one redeemable quality. He can cook," Alexis teased with a smile as I slid the plate toward Skylar.

"At least I have one," I bit back, earning myself a manicured middle finger. "And who is *us*? I didn't make you shit."

"What? Seriously?"

"You didn't even tell me you were coming over." Was it me and the lack of sleep, or was she being extra annoying this morning?

"Did, too! I told you what time I'd be here in one of my texts last night."

Oh. Yeah. "I didn't read any of those."

"You really made this? Like, from scratch?" Skylar asked, staring down at the eggs Benedict in front of her.

"They're easier to make than they look." I shrugged. "Think of it as an apology. For last night."

"It's lovely. Thank you," she said, bringing her gaze back up to meet mine.

I couldn't get over her eyes. They were the color of blue ice.

*Contacts, maybe?*

"Don't get used to it. He's never this nice," Alexis chimed in, unprompted. Not a single person had asked. "To anyone. He just feels bad for what he did. Which, not so coincidentally, is also an extremely rare occurrence."

"Do you still need to be here, Alexis?" She was getting on my last nerve.

"You two always like this?" Skylar asked before taking a bite of her food, visibly amused by the back-and-forth.

Alexis opened her mouth to respond but was interrupted by a muffled, incoherent noise before she could say anything.

"Yeah, I told you, he can *cook* cook." My sister laughed, knowing exactly what had incited that reaction.

"This is really, really good," Skylar said to me, a touch of surprise flashing across her features. "But, um, why am I the only one eating? Did you already have some?"

"I'm good. I have to get going soon," I told her, making note of the time.

"He doesn't do carbs," Alexis inserted, once again without prompt, rolling her eyes. Then she turned to me. "Also, we're coming with you," she said without providing any context whatsoever as to why that was something that should happen.

"What?" I said, completely taken aback, at the same time as Skylar asked, "Why?"

"He's going to the office," Alexis informed her friend before turning back to me. "I'm taking her to talk to Ali about an apartment. He's on call for the property management team this weekend, and there's no point in taking two cars when the roads are this shitty."

Skylar shifted in her seat, leaning more to one side. "Oh, Alexis, about that. It's really okay. I—"

"No, c'mon, Sky, let me help fix this. Please? I feel so bad and, like, partially responsible for the whole thing."

"You're fully responsible," I assured my sister. The quip inspired a faint chuckle out of Skylar, which was distracting enough that I didn't see the grape Alexis whipped at my face until it was too late. It hit me square on the nose before I caught it.

"Alright. I'm going to go do some prepping for my meeting," I said, popping the grape into my mouth. "Be ready to leave in twenty."

The last thing I heard was Skylar offering to share her food with Alexis, though I didn't hear my sister's response before the door clicked shut.

~

"Come in," the serene, detached voice commanded as soon as I knocked.

The giant, minimally furnished office was always a few degrees cooler than the rest of the building. Whether that was due to the actual temperature setting of the room or the presence of the white-haired, crimson-lipped woman it belonged to, I couldn't tell.

She was sitting behind a strategically elevated glass desk. Her throne, if you will.

"Good morning, Anita." I greeted my grandmother by her first name, per her requested preference. Alexis was the only one who still called her "Nonna." She was also the favorite grandchild and the only one that didn't work for Anita.

"Ethan." Anita looked up and put down her silver pen. There were only two other items on her desk, a computer and the small, neat stack of papers she'd been reviewing when I walked in. There were very few things my grandmother disliked more than clutter. "Perfect timing. Sit." She motioned to one of the stiff, black leather armchairs facing her desk.

I walked up and onto the grey marble platform and placed a folder in front of her before taking a seat.

"And what's this?" she asked.

"Operations business plan for the expansion," I managed to say in a neutral tone. A miracle. "It's incomplete, obviously, since I only found out about it two days ago and haven't had a chance to meet with the appropriate team leaders. But it's a solid start."

*And it only cost me thirty fucking hours, my sleep, and my sanity to get it done before this meeting.*

"No need," she dismissed without bothering to open it. "Greyson presented a full plan when he pitched the idea, operations included. I'm surprised his assistant didn't forward you a copy."

I could physically feel the blood drain from my veins when her words sunk in. Not only had the fucker gone behind my back to pitch an idea that grossly overstepped onto my turf without so much as a word to me, but he'd done it with a fully developed business plan.

And no, of course his minion hellhound hadn't forwarded me a fucking copy.

"Here, take a look." Anita grabbed a brown leather portfolio out of her desk drawer and handed it to me.

I opened it reluctantly, my jaw tightening as I flipped through it.

It was all there. The predevelopment plan, financial outline, market analysis, feasibility analysis, development phasing, construction, marketing strategies... everything. You name it, it was there.

He'd have to have been working on this thing for months. And I'd had no idea.

Greyson was the CFO. This wasn't his fucking job. And yet he'd done it anyway, gone to her about opening up the first Milani luxury resort. Not only was I the last to know, but I'd been stupid enough to think I could still regain control if I showed up with a plan.

Stupid enough to not realize he'd already have one.

"He wants to get started right away, and I agree with him. But it's a massive undertaking, which is why I've asked you to come back. I want you redelegating all of the projects you're currently overseeing so you can focus on this."

"Really? Because it kind of seems like Grey's got the whole thing under control," I grumbled, throwing the portfolio back onto her desk. It landed with a dramatic slap against the glass.

"I expect the two of you to work together on this, Ethan. My patience with your petty rivalries is running perilously thin," she clipped with a disapproving narrowing of her dark eyes. "And I'd prefer to step down this year without having to worry about my successors behaving like petulant children."

I tensed up at the mention of her retirement, the other bomb she'd dropped over the phone. At this rate, Grey was going to be the one she chose to take over. Because I was starting to suspect he'd timed the reveal of his idea to coincide with her announcement in an attempt to secure his win. A good CEO always had a plan for the company's future.

The timing was a little too perfect, and there was no such thing as a coincidence when it came to my brother.

*I'll act civil when he does*, I opened my mouth to say, just before a movement outside of the glass wall to my right caught my attention. An anomaly in the ordinarily deserted office on a Saturday morning.

It was Alexis and Skylar. I'd asked them to meet me up here once they were done.

They settled in the waiting area, with Skylar stretching her long legs out in front of her and scrolling through the phone she'd fished out of her back pocket, blissfully unaware of her audience. The glass was designed to provide a one-way view only. She couldn't see us.

"And who might that be?" Anita asked, a tinge of curiosity lacing her voice. I looked back at her, surprised to find her inquisitive eyes on me and not the person she was asking about.

I almost heard the *snap* as it happened. As the idea came to me. I don't know how, and I don't know why. It just did.

Maybe it was because I was reminded of last night when, in my sleep-deprived and delirious state, I'd thought she might be an actress.

Hell, maybe I was *still* delirious.

Or maybe I was just backed into a corner and out of options. Because Grey was about to win, and I couldn't just sit back and let him. I couldn't just watch.

"Skylar," I responded before the rational part of my brain

could wake up and stop me. But at this point, maybe it wouldn't have put up that big of a fight anyway. "My girlfriend. Soon to be fiancée."

She stilled in apparent surprise and, for a second, I thought she saw right through me. But then her eyebrows raised slightly, and she turned her head for a closer look at my lie.

What did Anita care more about than business? Her legacy, lineage, and the family's image. Alexis announcing her engagement to Joel was the first time I'd seen her happy and actively smiling in... years, probably. And my brother sure as hell wasn't going to be settling down anytime soon. If ever.

Grey's reputation preceded him in that department. And she hated it.

She hated the countless articles released over the years with his face plastered on the front, *North America's Most Eligible Bachelor* pictured with a different blonde socialite every week.

She hated the media attention, the number of women paid for their silence, the rumors and whispers circulating around him with the clients and industry leaders. His twenties had been a fucking mess, and his reputation never fully recovered. It was barely any better now; he'd just gotten more diligent with getting those NDAs signed.

My grandmother had been on both of our asses about settling down for years, wanting it to happen before her retirement. She wasn't all that impressed with my record, either, but at least I'd managed to keep it on the down-low and out of the public eye.

Bottom line, anyone could come up with ideas and plans, but the CEO was also the face of the company. And Anita wanted a grounded family man representing Milani Group, not a serial philanderer with a tarnished image.

It was the one thing I knew I could one-up him at—his Achilles heel. And he wouldn't see it coming.

It was a stupid, reckless idea. It was also my only one.

# 4

## Skylar

"I'm sure we can still find you something," Alexis mumbled while we scrolled through apartment listings on our phones, waiting for her brother to finish with his meeting. "I'm sorry. I should have told Ali before we came here that you were looking for something furnished. I didn't realize there would only be empty units available..."

"It's okay. Thank you for trying anyway." I sounded almost as deflated as I felt. And for once, I didn't have the energy to fake it. I just kept scrolling and scrolling... and scrolling, even though I couldn't seem to pay any actual attention to the listings, too preoccupied with the stress of not knowing what the hell I was going to do. Almost everything I'd found was out of my price range. Not as bad as New York, but I didn't have any family here to stay with.

"Uh..."

I looked up to find Alexis frowning down at her screen. "What? You find something?"

"No, Ethan just texted me." She paused, confusion curdling her expression. "He said, and I quote, 'Just go with it. Tell Skylar. Explain later.'"

"What does that mean?"

"Your guess is as good as mine..." She trailed off, throwing a nervous glance at the office door to her left.

Before we could exchange theories or I could analyze why the message had made Alexis squirm in her seat, the door opened.

I noticed Ethan first, even though he was the second person to walk out of the room. His brown eyes bounced from me to Alexis and back again. He looked tense, his posture too stiff, jaw too tight.

"Good morning, Nonna!" Alexis chirped, hopping out of her seat with a practiced balletic elegance. Twenty years of dance experience tends to seep into your everyday movements, from what I'd observed from her.

I followed suit and stood up with significantly less grace and much to the dismay of my sore lower back.

"Alexis." The woman, impeccably dressed in a blue pantsuit, offered her granddaughter a gentle kiss on both cheeks. "It's nice to see you, dear."

"You too! I'd like to introduce you to my friend Skylar." Alexis smiled, half turning to face me. "Sky, this is Anita, my grandmother."

Anita's gaze cut to me, assessing. She walked closer to where I stood, coating the air around us in soft Chanel.

I suddenly felt very underdressed in my white T-shirt and black jeans.

"It's lovely to meet you," I said, but not before clearing my throat. There was something very intimidating in the way

Anita held herself. She was at least a couple of inches shorter than me, even in her heels. Yet, somehow, it felt like she was gazing down at me.

"So," she said, shaking my hand. Her skin was cool against mine, her grip firm. "You're Ethan's girlfriend."

I blinked back at her, pretty sure I'd misheard what she'd just said. "I'm sorry?"

"Ethan says the two of you are dating?"

*Um... whosaidwhatnowhuh?*

Alexis's mouth dropped open behind her grandmother's back. But the shock on her face only lasted for about a second before morphing into raw, murderous rage aimed directly at her brother. She looked like she was ready to maul him.

Ethan looked like he might just let her.

"Um, I—I don't..." I kept glancing between the siblings, my tongue tied into a useless, incoherent knot inside my mouth.

That's when things *really* took a turn. Ethan walked to my side, sliding a gentle hand to hover over the small of my back. "Sorry, sweetheart," he cooed, flashing me a charming, lopsided smile. His teeth were insanely white. "I know we said we would keep it a secret for a little while longer."

What the actual fuck was happening?

I stood there, gaping at him like a mounted sea bass.

"She's a little shy," Ethan said to his grandmother with a chuckle, as though *my* behavior was the one that required an explanation. The easy smile he wore was starting to tighten. And I wasn't entirely sure the guy was still breathing.

Was this what he'd meant by the text? Was this what we were supposed to be going along with? Was he a crazy person? Should I have been concerned? Had I hit my head harder than I'd realized? Was *this* the matrix?

*I really need to watch that movie.*

The dull headache I'd woken up with had turned into a

full-blown migraine, protesting against the effort needed to make sense of the situation by pounding against my skull.

It took me another second, but I finally cleared my throat again and looked back at Anita. "Yes, uh, sorry," I said, not sure what the hell else to do. "I thought we were still keeping it under wraps, so I was a little... surprised."

Her scrutinizing gaze glided to Ethan, stayed there for a second too long to be comfortable, then returned to me.

"Well, then. That's quite understandable," she finally said with an expression that could only be described as stoically unreadable. "You'll have to forgive my grandson. I was under the impression that I'd raised him better than that." Her tone had softened a fraction while addressing me, but the bladed glare she cut Ethan could have withered steel. "If you'd agreed to keep the nature of your relationship quiet for the time being, then he should not have said anything until he'd discussed it with you first. Though I'm sure he'll apologize. Thoroughly."

"Right. Yes. I'm very sorry," Ethan responded without pause. "I wasn't thinking. I'll make it up to her."

"You'll also have to accept my own apologies, Skylar," Anita said with a subtle glance at her watch. "I have another appointment to attend to, so I have to cut our introduction short. But I trust I'll be seeing you at the party?"

Ethan stiffened to stone beside me. His sister's eyes were struggling to stay inside the confinements of their sockets.

*Party? What party? What am I supposed to say? Should I make an excuse? Stop taking so long to answer—you're being so suspicious.* "Um, I'm no—"

"Excellent. We'll catch up then," Anita interrupted coolly. "Enjoy the rest of your day." She gave me the faintest hint of a smile before saying goodbye to her grandkids and floating back into her office.

*Mmmmmkay...*

Alexis was the first one of us to move. She stomped forward the second her grandmother's door was closed, an accusing finger pointed at her brother. "*What* did you d—"

"She can see us," Ethan said, maintaining a blank expression. "The glass has a one-way view out of the office. Let's get down to the parkade, and you can scream at me there."

"*Scream* at you? I'm going to fucking *kill* you for this, Ethan," she hissed.

"Great. Do it in the parkade." Then he turned around and started to walk away.

Alexis glared after him, her face and neck painted red.

What was happening now? Why was Alexis so angry? I mean, I understood why she would be angry. But why was she *this* angry?

"Come on," I said, gently grabbing her hand. I really wanted to get out of here. There were too many windows, and the sunlight wasn't helping my headache.

"It's finally happened," she said as we walked, staying far enough from Ethan that he couldn't hear us. "He's lost his goddamn mind."

"You don't think he's got an explanation?"

"I don't *care* if he does. You don't—he can't—" She pursed her lips in frustration and exhaled before starting again. "I don't know what he's thinking. But he shouldn't have pulled you into whatever is going on with him. There's no excuse for it."

I thought the elevator ride down to the garage, filled with tense, unpleasant silence, was the least fun social situation I'd ever been trapped in. Then we got into Ethan's car.

"I can explain," he said as soon as the last door had slammed shut.

"Like hell you can!" Alexis yelled back at him from the

passenger seat. Her voice bounced off the windows and crashed into my head.

"I *can*," he argued. "Anita is retiring this year. She's going to make the announcement at the party."

"*What*?" Alexis snapped back at him. "Are you having a psychotic break? How is that even close to an explanation?"

"Greyson went to h—"

"Oh. My. *Fucking god*. That's what this whole thing is about? The two of you and your stupid freaking competitive bullshit rivalry?"

I had no idea what they were talking about. I couldn't really concentrate; they were being too loud.

I sunk farther into the back seat, rested the side of my forehead against the cool leather, and almost melted in relief.

"Just listen." Ethan had his hands up, an attempt to calm Alexis down. It wasn't working.

"No, *you* listen. You had no right to bring her into this. Especially after last night! What the hell is the matter with you? What were you *thinking*?"

"I was thinking that if I didn't do something, he was going to get promoted to CEO, Alexis. You really want Grey in charge? He wins, and the precious little dance studio you care about so much goes down. That's what you want?"

That seemed to shut Alexis up. But I didn't know why. What dance studio? Who was Grey? What was going on? Why were there so many lights in this stupid garage?

Alexis took a deep breath and shut her eyes. The few seconds of silence that followed were heaven-sent.

"How does you telling Nonna that you're dating Skylar solve anything? It makes no sense," she said with more calm this time.

"Haven't you ever wondered why Dad was the one being groomed to take over instead of Uncle Carlo? Even though he was younger and had less experience? Why, even after Dad died, they didn't bring Carlo back to take over?"

Alexis didn't answer. She just crossed her arms and waited for him to continue.

"Because Carlo's personal life was a huge mess. He had mistresses in most of the major cities we do business in, and it got around. There were so many rumors about him in the industry that it was impossible to keep track. Remind you of anyone?"

"Grey's cleaned up his act on that front, though. Publicly, at least."

"You're missing the point. One brother was a grounded family man, and the other didn't have the word 'commitment' in his vocabulary." He ran a quick hand through his hair. It was a nice color. The same dark chestnut as his eyes. "You know how much she values all that crap. How badly she wants us to settle down."

Alexis sighed. "This is, by far, the dumbest idea you've ever had. And it's not going to work."

"Yeah? Can you think of something better? Because I'm open."

"Why me?" I asked, sitting back up. It was the first time I'd spoken since getting into the car. Both their heads turned in my direction at a speed that made me think they'd forgotten I was even there. "Why did you say we were dating? Why not pick a friend or someone you know better?"

"Not my best improvised moment," he admitted. "She saw you sitting outside, asked who you were, and that's what gave me the idea. So it just sort of... came out. But I can make it worth your while."

"Do you even realize what you're asking?" It was a genuine question.

"Yes, and I have a plan. Or at least the beginnings of one."

He had maneuvered in his seat so that he was almost fully facing me now in the Escalade. "All you'll have to do is attend a few family events with me and pretend we're dating for the three months that you're here. That's it. Then you'll move back to New York, Anita will retire, we'll wait a few more months, and then tell everyone we broke up. We'll say we couldn't make the long-distance thing work and neither of us wanted to move. In exchange, you can stay at the penthouse. And I'll pay you."

*Uh...* "I don't thin—"

"Half a million."

"*Dollars*?" Instant, *instant*, regret. The word violently yanked on my brain on its way out. I hadn't meant to yell.

"Five hundred thousand US dollars," he reiterated, maintaining eye contact. Even Alexis looked perplexed.

"Are you insane? Half a *million* dollars to attend a few family events and pretend you're my partner?" *Pound. Pound. Poundpound. Pound. Pound.*

"Well, that... and I also told Anita that I was going to propose," he said, dead serious. "So we'll have to figure that out. Pick out a ring and everything."

"Wait, sorry, just a sec," Alexis jumped in, holding a hand up. I thought she was going to back me up, echo my thoughts and yell at her brother again for the insanity spewing from his mouth. But she wasn't looking at him. She was scanning me up and down, her brows pulling together. "Are you okay? Why are you so pale?"

Really? *That* was what she chose to focus on in the middle of all this chaos? Were both siblings crazy?

I didn't respond. Quite frankly, at this point, I *couldn't* respond.

So I did the only thing that my body would allow: I opened the car door, aimed for the garage floor, and hurled.

# 5

than

Four hours. It had been four torturously long hours since Skylar had been led through the sickly green double doors of the emergency room.

Four hours of restlessly tapping my foot and looking up concussions as Alexis listed all the gruesomely inventive ways she could dismember me using just her nails.

"What could possibly be taking them so long?" I eventually snapped, on the brink of losing what little remained of my goddamn mind. Because what the *fuck* could have possibly been taking them so long?

"She's probably dead," my sister replied with an entirely straight face, a successful attempt at making me feel worse. The middle-aged man with the patterned eye patch sitting in front of us snorted yet another unnecessary laugh.

I ignored them, whipping out my phone again so I could scroll through my fiftieth head injury article since sitting down, none of which had mentioned anything about the concussion examination process taking four fucking hours.

So, unless it was something more serious, then I didn't understand why—

"*Finally*!"

My head jerked up to find Skylar standing beside us. Still alive. All in one piece. Unattached to a machine. Unaccompanied by a somber-looking medical professional. No wheelchair or lawsuit in visible sight.

"Sorry that took so long," she said, fumbling with the zipper of her jacket. "They had to do a bunch of tests."

Alexis shot out of her chair. "And? What did they say? Are you okay?"

She shrugged. "I'm fine. No internal bruising or bleeding or anything, just a mild concussion. It was the headache that made me sick."

"That's it?"

She nodded, a polite smile tugging at the corners of her mouth. "That's it. I've been given painkillers and told to 'take it easy' and 'rest up' for a bit."

A few of the muscles in my neck that had been intent on imitating a rubber-band ball began to loosen their grip. Alexis let out a relieved sigh.

But only until Skylar bounced on her feet and said, "So, um, if you could do me a favor and take me back to your apartment, I can pack my things and check into a motel or... something..." She trailed off, eyes sliding from my sister's bewildered expression to mine. "What?"

"You're joking," Alexis deadpanned. "Please tell me you're joking."

Skylar's mouth floundered slightly, her silence doing the speaking for her.

My sister's brows jumped, her head jutting forward. "You think we're letting you check into a motel after *that*?"

"I mean... I'm fine. It's not a big deal. I can just—"

"Absolutely not!" Alexis exclaimed, loud enough to attract a few curious looks from patients and staff. "*Absolutely* not, Skylar."

Skylar looked like she wanted to argue but thought better of it. I didn't blame her—she wasn't winning this one.

I cleared my throat, slipping my phone back into my pocket. "If you're not comfortable with coming back to the apartment because of me, I can—"

Her pale eyes flared, cheeks tinting with subtle color. "No, I swear that's not it. I just didn't want to... um, trouble you."

I shrugged. "I don't mind."

It was the least I could do at this point, after everything.

She held my gaze, trying to gauge how sincere I was being. Or maybe I was holding hers, trying to see how many shades of—

"You can come to my place," Alexis intervened. "I think that might be a better idea."

I glared down at her. "*How*? You live in a one-bedroom. With your fiancé."

"We'll make it work," she hissed through gritted teeth, returning my scowl. "Joel can sleep on the couch or go to his parent's house or something."

We both knew that didn't make sense when there were three empty bedrooms available at the penthouse. And so did Skylar, judging by the way she reacted.

"That's *really* not necessary, Alexis. Honestly. I'm fine."

I pushed an impatient hand through my hair. "Let's just go back to the apartment so she can get some rest, and we'll talk about living arrangements tomorrow. I'll pull some strings, make something happen."

They agreed.

It took another eight minutes of pointless arguing, but they agreed.

"SIT DOWN."

"You should—"

"Shut up and sit down."

I sighed, sinking onto my armchair. Skylar was upstairs, doing some of that resting she'd been prescribed. "At least try and keep it down," I said.

Alexis crossed her arms, hip jutted, glare in full murderous tact.

She wasn't going to listen. Never did.

"This is all your fault," she bit out. "All of it."

"I know." I swallowed, head tilting back as I braced myself for the long hour of yelling and scolding that was about to inevitably follow. Not that it really mattered. None of it was going to make me feel worse than I already did.

But instead of raising her voice or smacking me with the particularly oversequined decorative pillow she kept eyeing, Alexis slowly meandered to the couch beside my armchair and dropped onto it with an exaggerated huff.

And, for just a few minutes, there was silence. Sweet, sweet silence.

"When was the last time you slept?" she eventually asked. "And I mean a full seven to eight hours, not a night-time nap."

"I don't know. Why does that matter?"

"I think you should sleep."

"Thanks for the tip."

It was supposed to be sarcasm; it just didn't come out right.

I was too tired to argue or bicker. And I still had so much fucking work to do.

This had been the shittiest day I'd had in a long time. And there'd been more than enough of them lately to compare it to.

Alexis pushed out another breath, allowing her arms to uncross and fall to her sides. "I'm being serious," she mumbled.

"I know."

"You look terrible."

"Thanks."

She paused, nudging my leg with her foot. "It's no fun when you don't bite back."

"Is that why you're not yelling?" I asked. "Or are we just not at that part yet?"

She thought about it before answering. "I think I'll save it for when you don't look like you're on the brink of death by sleep deprivation. Plus, it doesn't seem like Skylar's going to go along with your idiotic plan, so..."

So... I was fucked, and entirely out of ideas.

"Seriously, what were you thinking?" Alexis asked, sitting up straight.

I hadn't been. Not really.

"Does it matter now?" Like she'd said, it didn't seem like Skylar was going to go along with any of it anyway.

"Yeah, it does matter, actually," Alexis claimed. "I'm getting... a little worried about you."

I frowned, tilting my head on the couch so I could look at her. This was new. "What?"

"I said I'm worried about you," she repeated, brows crumpling. "And so is Joel."

"Why?"

"Well... because..." Her hand flopped up and down,

gesturing to all of me. "Because *this*," she said, as though that explained everything perfectly.

I sighed. "I'm not the one that's in need of your concern right now, Alexis. Save it for the girl upstairs sleeping off the concussion I gave her."

"Yeah... I'm definitely more worried about you right now," she argued. "*She's* going to be okay. I'm not entirely convinced you are."

New tension twisted in the back of my neck. "That makes sense. I lose a few hours of sleep, your friend slams her head into the wall and goes to the ER. Clearly, I'm the one you should be worried about."

"That's obviously not what I'm talking about... Are you sure all of this is worth—"

"I'm fine," I cut her off. I'd rather be yelled at than go down whatever conversational path she was leading up to. "Just make sure your friend is and that she doesn't try to hide it again or downplay things if her symptoms get worse."

Alexis huffed in dramatic frustration and slumped back into the couch. There was a full minute of silence before she ruined it and mumbled, "Sky might sometimes downplay her misery, Ethan, but you won't even acknowledge yours."

# 6

**kylar**

I DIDN'T MEAN to eavesdrop on Alexis and Ethan's conversation. But they weren't exactly being quiet, and I was too tired to get out of bed and shut the last inch of the bedroom door.

She was using her worried voice with him, and I could tell she was genuinely concerned, but I didn't hear why. Mostly because of the pesky koala. It kept shoving a churro at my leg and telling me to wear it as my wedding ring, which made no sense. How could a churro possibly pass as a ring? It was way too big to fit on my finger. What an idiot. Not known for their wit, were they, the koalas?

So I did the only thing that made any sense: I looped it around my wrist instead. *There. No one will know the difference.*

"Is that your ring?" Anita had materialized in the park, standing in front of me. She'd grown twelve inches since this morning. A defiant slap in the face of science. But, somehow, I knew it was inevitable; she made more sense like this, towering over me.

Then I noticed the others. Stolen glances from whispering faces I didn't recognize.

Why were there so many people here already? It was the middle of the day! The engagement party wasn't supposed to be for another five hours!! I wasn't even dressed!!! I hadn't even showered!!!! *I wasn't even wearing deodorant*!!!!!

I spotted a massive oak on the other end of the park—the perfect hiding spot—and booked it. No matter how much I ran, though, I couldn't seem to reach the tree. Either it was getting smaller, or the two stone fountains perched in front of it were getting bigger, reshaping as they grew. They were conjoined in the middle by a thick line, which at first glance made it look like two people holding hands. But they kept morphing, expanding until they outstretched the oak behind them, reaching for the blood-orange skies.

I stopped running when I realized what they were. The fountains weren't made from stone like they'd looked from a distance. White paint had chipped wherever the water touched, revealing the decaying wood it'd been tasked with covering up.

But that wasn't what made my throat sprout its own overactive heart. It was the final form the wood had taken. Two familiar-looking heads facing each other, married in the center by their elongated noses. Two liars exposed. Pinocchio and Pinocchio. Ethan and Skylar.

My tongue was cotton, my limbs glass. The wood had started to creak and crack, its warnings louder even than the sound of my lungs. The fountains had grown too big for their frail base. The ground underneath them shook, and the veins spread.

I'd started to back away from the impending disaster, but it was too little too late. The whole thing caved and, in one horrifying moment, came crumbling down on top of me in an avalanche of dust and chaos.

My body shattered, the shriek of breaking glass so loud it suffocated my terror.

And then... nothing.

I assumed I'd died. That's what the darkness must have meant. But what about the smell? Did death smell like... garlic... and tomato sauce?

My eyes opened slowly, blinking away the lingering traces of talking koalas and collapsing fountains before summoning my hands to rub their vision into semi-existence. Okay, so I was still alive. The darkness was due to the lack of sun, not the lack of everything. It was 8:28 p.m.

Another waft of the mystery food hit my nose, inciting an aggressive growl from the pit of my empty stomach. I lay there for a few more minutes, staring up at the dark ceiling and thinking, deciding.

Eventually, I sat up with a groan and forced my stiff body out of bed. The headache had eased up, but my butt was still sore, and my leg muscles had been replaced with bags of soaked sand. It took me forever to make it down the stairs.

"You're awake." Ethan was in the kitchen, dicing... tomatoes, I was pretty sure. My foggy vision was still adjusting to the reintroduction of light, so from a distance, his cutting rhythm was a smooth blur of steel and red.

"Um, yeah. I didn't realize I'd sleep for so long. Should have set an alarm or something."

"How are you feeling?" He was eyeing me as I approached, a small frown creasing his forehead, but the flow of the knife remained consistent. I'd have cut myself seventeen times in the three seconds he'd had his eyes off that board.

"Better. My headache is pretty much gone." I ran a hand

through my hair, smoothing a few of the loose strands back. "Where's Alexis?"

"I sent her home a while ago, before the roads could get worse. It's supposed to keep snowing."

"Cool." I shifted on my feet, unsure of what to say next.

"Are you hungry?" Ethan said, breaking the silence before it could stretch over the conversation and stifle it into a coma.

"Starving. Haven't had dinner since yesterday." I carefully eased myself onto a stool across from where he stood.

The left side of his mouth hooked up. "You like lasagna?"

Is that what the smell was? Excitement whirled up my torso. "It's my favorite," I said, hugging my stomach to muffle the sound of any impending growls. It was bad enough that I was basically salivating on the counter; I didn't need to add *noises* to it. "Can I help?"

"It's almost done. Just needs a few more minutes in the oven. Want something to drink?" He slid the diced tomatoes into a large salad bowl filled with greens.

"Water would be great. Thank you."

A small waft of silence settled between us, providing just enough empty space for the giant elephant to squeeze its way into the room. It stood in the corner, watching me.

I fixed my eyes on Ethan's back, trying to think of what to say, absolutely not noticing the way the muscles in his shoulders rolled to hug the cotton of his charcoal T-shirt when he reached for a couple of glasses on the top shelf. Not that he needed to reach very far, considering his height. And not that I noticed that, either.

"So, um," I started, averting my gaze to the sleeve of my sweater, where it was safe. "About this morning..."

More silence. Liquid pouring.

I inhaled and tried again. "Could you just explain again..."

"You don't have to worry about it," he said, sliding a glass of water to me on the counter. "It was a ridiculous idea. I'm sorry I dragged you into it."

*Oh.* "What are you going to tell your grandmother, then?"

"I don't know yet." A hand through his hair. Everything about him was… clenched. "I'll need to tell her we broke up, but the timing… she's going to ask questions."

"Okay… so the offer isn't on the table anymore?"

A pause. His posture shifted at my tone, unsure. "Do you want it to be on the table?"

I readjusted myself on the stool and sat up a little straighter. "Can I get some more information before I answer?"

"How many tests did they run on your head?" He leaned on the counter, lids narrowing.

"My head's fine. Thank you for your concern."

"You sure?"

"Yes." I almost rolled my eyes.

"And how's your memory? Do you remember the conversation in the car?"

"I don't think I could forget that even if I wanted to."

"You asked me if I was insane."

"That question still stands." I shrugged, holding back a smile. It was mostly a joke. Mostly. "But I didn't say I wouldn't do it."

# 7

## kylar

Ethan might be crazy, but here were all the things I could do with five hundred thousand dollars:

1) Pay off Jo and Peter's mortgage.

2) Pay off my student loans.

3) Move out on my own when I got back to New York.

4) *Pay off Jo and Peter's mortgage.* All of it.

The list had been stewing in the back of my mind every minute I'd been conscious since the painkillers kicked in at the hospital (albeit that only equated to a few hours at this point, but still). And every time I thought about it, I kept circling back to the same conclusion: it would be stupid *not* to do it... right? Or, at the very least, it couldn't hurt to get some more details. I needed to make sure it didn't involve anything extra crazy or, like, illegal.

And I was 99.8 percent sure that wasn't the concussion talking.

...

Okay, make that 99.7 percent. The skepticism in Ethan's eyes wasn't helping. He was scanning my face so intently you'd think my medical records were written on it.

"I'm telling you I'm fine," I insisted, *again*, just as the oven beeped. "Can you just... give me some more details? I feel like there's a bunch of info I'm missing."

He pursed his lips instead of answering, and I was sure he was going to tell me to forget about it again. "Eat first, then we can talk," he said instead.

Okay, he was stalling, but at least he didn't say no.

"Are you sure you don't want any help?" I asked. My stomach purred in anticipation when he opened the oven door. The aroma that filled the room was heavenly.

"I'm sure."

We settled back into silence while he worked. And I went back to not noticing how his biceps—

*Stop ogling, for the love of god. You've seen an attractive man before, yes?*

I tore my eyes away.

That was one of the many (*many*) things I was confused about. Ethan was quite... conventionally attractive, if you will. I didn't know much about his personality, but assuming he was a half-decent human being, I doubted he'd have any issues getting an actual girlfriend. Why hadn't he gone down that route instead? It wasn't like his grandmother was retiring tomorrow. He'd still have time to find someone...

A plate slid into my line of vision on the marble counter, midthought. I blinked at it a few times, trying to register the image.

It was the most picturesque serving of lasagna I'd ever seen in my life. The slice was cut into a perfectly symmetrical square, baked to flawless, golden perfection, garnished with some sort of green leaf, and placed right in the center of the white plate. A couple of clean, deliberate splashes of red sauce occupied one side of the dish, and the colors of a vibrant side salad curved the other.

What the hell? How long had I zoned out?

"What's wrong?" Ethan asked after a few seconds of me just staring down at my food. "You're not hungry anymore?"

I looked up at him, my jaw slack. He was leaning forward again, elbows on the counter and biceps working overtime to support his upper body. Not that I noticed. And not that he caught me noticing. "What line of work did you say you were in again?"

The left corner of his lips curled. "Real estate development."

"Are you sure?" It was a serious question, regardless of what the one side of his mouth thought.

He nudged the plate a little closer toward me. "Eat. Please."

"I don't know if I can… It's too pretty."

Then he did something so unthinkable, so monstrously abhorrent, that I audibly gasped. He took my fork and used it to smother the sauce and messy up the salad. "How's that? Better?"

I gaped at him, eyes wide.

Then, without warning, he moved the silver weapon over the perfect, cheesy square. "Okay, should I do the lasag—"

"No!" I dove for the fork and snatched it out of his hand before he could act on his threat. "Why did you *do* that? It was so perfect!"

I was annoyed for all of about three-quarters of a second, just until the lip curl graduated to a half-smile at my reaction. And then it wasn't annoyance anymore. I didn't know what it was, but it was flip-floppy and somehow worse.

"Eat, before it gets cold."

"Where's your plate?" I asked, realizing only now that he'd just made the one.

"I had dinner already."

*What?* "Then why did you make this?"

"Think of it as an apology."

"I thought that's what the eggs Benedict was for."

"That was for last night. This is for this morning." He nudged the dish closer.

I considered him for a moment. "Don't take this the wrong way, but I kind of hope you keep messing up."

Lip curl. "Your chances are looking pretty good, based purely on my track record."

"Mmm. In that case, you should know I'm also a big fan of green curry."

Half-smile. "Noted."

"What did you eat?" I asked, utilizing my fork to push the leaves back to their side. A futile attempt at righting the mess.

"Grilled chicken and some greens."

That was it? "And you're passing up lasagna now?"

His shoulders danced with a small shrug. "I mostly eat low carb, high protein."

"Oh. That sounds... unexciting."

"When I got here, the only edible items in the kitchen were toast, eggs, and ice cream," he countered.

"You're forgetting the ketchup and hot sauce," I pointed out. "Goes great with the eggs."

"I'll take your word for it."

I took my first bite after blowing the steam away, fully expecting it to taste just as good as it looked, and I *still* wasn't prepared.

"How is it?" Ethan asked, like he didn't already know he'd perfected the dish.

How appropriate would it be if I wept in front of him? Over pasta?

"I mean, it's no eggs and ketchup," I joked instead, taking another rather large bite.

The small, deep chuckle that burst out of him was so unexpected that it made me laugh, midswallow. I choked.

"You okay?" he asked as I coughed into my elbow, residual traces of humor lighting up his voice.

"Yes," I managed to rasp. I reached for my water and gulped the rest down, very much aware of the exact shade of blotchy scarlet my skin had adopted. "Sorry. First time eating."

"Chewing helps, I find," he teased while pushing his full glass to me on the counter.

"I knew I was missing a step." I took a few sips of his offering once the coughing subsided, and a soft lull settled on the conversation.

Then came the realization of how effortlessly it had flowed over the last few minutes. And ironically enough, it was the awareness that made things awkward again. My eyes moved back down to my food, and all of a sudden, I couldn't think of what else to say.

Ethan drew back, and I shoved more lasagna in my mouth so that the not talking would be less weird. It barely worked, but we got away with it for a minute or so. Eventually, though, the silence stretched too thin, and I was running out of food.

"Um, so back to that other thing. Can we talk about it now?" I asked, tentatively poking at a diced tomato.

He let out a lungful of air. "I'm trying to figure out if you're serious, joking, or if it's the concussion. You seemed pretty convinced in the car that the whole idea was insane."

"That's because it *is* insane," I reiterated. "Do *you* not see how crazy it is to hire someone you barely know, for an obscene amount of money, to pretend to be your partner? To lie to your family for a promotion?"

"Desperate times" was his insufficient answer. The playful tone was back, which was kind of surprising. It went very much against my first impression of him.

"Why can't you just get a real one?" I asked, finishing off my plate. I would have licked it clean if he wasn't standing right there.

"A real what? Girlfriend?"

I nodded, mouth full. "Yes," I said once I'd swallowed (successfully this time). "A real person you're dating. That way, you won't have to lie, and you still end up with what you want. Win-win."

He leaned in again and met me at my eye level. I definitely, for sure, did *not* notice the ring of earthy gold circling his pupil. That would have been a very strange and vivid detail to pick up on. "Let's say, theoretically, that in the time allotted I'm actually able to find someone I genuinely like and want to pursue a real romantic relationship with. It would be a little suspicious if I showed up with them on my arm to the next family event, don't you think? My grandmother thinks I'm about to propose. To you."

"You know what would be even more suspicious? Pretending to be in a serious relationship with someone you barely know. People are going to see right through it because, contrary to what romantic-comedy scriptwriters want you to believe, this shit would be a lot harder to pull off than just memorizing a few facts about each other."

"You're overthinking it."

"You're underthinking it," I assured him.

"Then why are you considering it?"

I contemplated my answer before responding. "I think it's crazy, and I'm not convinced it's going to work. But you're offering me half a million dollars to show up to a few events and what? Hold your hand and wear a ring?"

"More or less."

"What's the more part?"

He scratched at the faint shadow of incoming stubble on his jaw. "We'll have to do some prep work. If we did this, we'd need to do it right. Or it won't work. Not with my family."

I pushed my empty plate to the side and leaned in, mirroring him. "And what if we do all the prep work and still get caught?"

"We won't get caught."

"When we get caught, do I still get the money?"

I wasn't sure which part of this conversation was amusing to him exactly because I was being quite serious, but the lingering lip curl had slowly started to morph into a full, lopsided smile. "Granted you keep your end of the deal and don't blow the whistle or let it slip that we aren't really dating, then yes, you'll still get the money. We'll have an agreement drawn up."

"And if we do everything right but you don't get promoted?"

"You'll still get the money. We'll add that in, too. Plus, you'll be compensated for all expenses, like outfits and travel when needed."

"And I'd be living here?"

He shrugged. "If we were in a relationship, it would only make sense that you'd stay with me while you were in town. Anything else might even be suspicious."

I considered that, resting my chin on my palm. "Right. I guess that does make sense. Okay, then I just have two more questions."

"Shoot."

"Firstly, who's Grey?" I asked.

The name had been mentioned in the car, but I had no idea who he was, just that he was also a contender for Anita's spot once she retired.

"Brother," Ethan answered.

And... that was it. That was all he said. I waited for him to continue (older? younger?), but he didn't.

"Um, alright." *Next question, I guess.* "So, last one, then. What was the party your grandmother was talking about?"

"Her birthday. It's in two weeks." Another short answer. The lightness in his posture had flickered, his shoulders visibly firming with tension under his T-shirt.

I bit the inside of my cheek, thinking.

"You don't have to make a decision now," Ethan said, standing back up straight. "Especially in your state. You can sit on it for a few days or a week. See if you have any other questions once you're feeling better."

"Or... what if we did a trial run?" I suggested. It was the best idea I could come up with to test the waters before committing.

He seemed intrigued. "Elaborate."

"Well, we barely know each other. Who knows if we'll be compatible enough to successfully pull something like this off without wanting to rip each other's hair out in the first, like, week. Especially if we're living in the same apartment." Roommate tension hell was real. I'd had friends go through it, and it wasn't something I was interested in experiencing firsthand.

His head tilted, considering.

"So I propose we do a two-week trial run," I went on. "Your grandmother's party will be the test. After that, we can decide if we want to actually commit to doing this for however many months until it's safe enough for us to 'break up' without raising suspicion, after you get promoted. It'll give us both enough time to think it through, get our story straight, memorize whatever facts we need to, et cetera."

Ethan crossed his arms but still didn't say anything. He looked—dare I say—a little impressed.

"Not half bad for someone with a concussion, huh?" I teased. Although, the joke was really on me since the headache was starting to sneak back.

"It's a good idea," he admitted. "It makes sense and would also give us time to iron out the details of the agreement."

"Exactly."

"What about payment?" he asked. "Five percent of the full amount seem fair? Twenty-five thousand for two weeks, but only if you make it to the end and attend the party."

He was asking if twenty-five thousand dollars for two weeks of "work" seemed fair, and he was serious. Bless his heart. Sweet, sweet, sheltered child, living on a whole other planet in a galaxy far, far away. "Mmm, yup, sounds fair to me," I agreed with what I thought was going to be convincing nonchalance. But the sarcasm seeped through, and he caught it with a smooth lip curve. At least he seemed to have a decent sense of humor, contrary to what Alexis had claimed. That would make getting along a little easier. Hopefully.

"So, we have a deal?" He held out his hand.

"On one condition," I said, and it was nonnegotiable. "I'm assuming some sort of nondisclosure agreement will be involved, and I want an exception. I want to be able to tell one person." Someone who was preferably not related to him. Just in case.

He withdrew his hand. "Who?"

"A friend in New York. She doesn't run in the same circles, and I can guarantee her silence."

He wasn't convinced, and I didn't blame him. I was pretty sure verbal vouching wasn't exactly legally binding.

"Will she sign an NDA?" he asked.

I shrugged. "I can ask her. How long will it take to draft one?"

He didn't even hesitate. "It'll be in your inbox by the morning."

"Seriously? How?" How could he possibly make it happen that fast?

"If she signs it, we have a deal," he said instead of answering. His hand extended toward me again.

"Okay. Deal." I took it, not noticing the size difference or anything pertaining to body temperature.

Somewhere out there, in an alternate dimension of forgotten dreams and ignored warnings of the universe, a koala shook its head and called me an idiot.

# 8

kylar

"YOU *WHAT*?"

"Would you shhh! I told you, I don't have my headphones in!" I whisper-yelled at Mikaela's flabbergasted face on the screen. I didn't know where I'd put the damn things.

"You *what*?" she tried again, whisper-yelling back.

This wasn't working. "Hold on just a second." I picked up my laptop and shut myself in the walk-in closet. It was probably a little excessive, but I could tell she was getting riled up, and I didn't want Ethan to overhear. Though I wasn't actually sure he was home. I hadn't left my room yet this morning. I'd woken up, brushed my teeth, and called Mikaela.

"Okay, you may freak out now," I told her once I was settled comfortably on the floor. It was nice and warm in here.

She was looking at me like I'd changed colors and grown a third breast since the last time we'd talked. Although the reality of my situation probably had a higher shock value.

"You've been there for like what? Four, five days? *That's it.* How could this possibly be your life?"

Her guess was as good as mine, honestly.

"Okay, I do feel like it all sounds slightly more dramatic retold than it actually was," I defended.

Her dark eyes narrowed into daggers. She was not having it. "Girl, I know you're not trying to downplay a break-in, a concussion, a trip to the ER, and *agreeing to a contractual fake relationship for which I had to sign an NDA*. All in less than a week, Skylar! What the hell? It's barely even Sunday!"

"It wasn't a *break-in*. That's just what I thought was happening at the time. It's his apartment. Or his family's or whatever. Also, I agreed to a two-week trial, not to the full thing." Yet.

"And you're living with him!" she continued on, like there'd been so many things that she'd almost forgotten about that one. "Unbelievable. Your life is unbelievable."

I could see, in this particular instance, why she'd think that. "It's been a crazy few days for sure."

"I'm glad you're okay, at least." She sighed and leaned back into her purple couch. "You *are* okay, right? You're not just saying that so I won't worry and nag?"

"Yeah, I swear. The headache was terrible that first day, but it's gotten a lot better. My butt's still sore, though." And bruised. It wasn't a pretty sight.

"Okay, so explain... just... what? Why does he need a fake girlfriend, and why did you agree instead of filing a restraining order?"

"From what I understand, it's for a promotion. His grandmother is retiring... at some point. I think he said sometime this year?"

"Are you asking me?" At least she was laughing.

"*Anyways*, grandmother is retiring, and he's up for the

position against his brother. Long story short, he thinks being in a stable relationship will give him the leg up he needs to win. It's a family-dynamic thing. Doesn't make a ton of sense to me."

"Why would you agree to it, then?"

Right. We hadn't gotten to this part yet. "Um, he made me an offer that wasn't exactly easy to turn down."

Her brows perked up. *"Go on,"* they said.

"So, a little background first. Turns out Alexis comes from a pretty well-off family. To put it lightly." I had grazed over the apartment penthouse part of the story. At this point, it was the least interesting thing that had come out of this week, and I'd been in too big of a rush to catch her up on the real tea.

"Okay... didn't we kind of already know that, though? The one time I met her, she showed up to lunch with more than one designer piece on."

"No, Mik. They're like *rich*, rich. Think never having to take public transit and then multiply it by that one cartoon duck that bathes in his gold coins."

"I don't know what you're talking about, but I'm assuming that means he's paying you? How much?"

"Five hundred," I said, slowly for a more dramatic effect, and then, "thousand."

"What?" She leaned in and turned her head like she was sure she'd misheard me.

"Five hundred thousand," I repeated, watching her expression.

Mikaela stopped, eyes and mouth widening as the information processed and then clicked. "*Dollars*?"

That's what I'd said.

"Yeah. The guy's offering me a cool half-mil to pretend to be his girlfriend in front of his family."

"That's *insane*."

I'd said that, too. "I know!"

"Why?"

"Why what?"

"Why that much money? Why the NDAs? What does he want you to do? What does being his fake girlfriend entail?"

"We haven't gone into in-depth detail yet, but it doesn't sound too complicated. I'm mostly supposed to attend family stuff with him and be a convincing romantic partner."

Skepticism swept over her initial look of shock. "Okay, there is no way it's gonna be that easy. I'm calling it right now. Either the guy is bonkers, or he wants you to do something real sketch." She considered it for a second, then added, "Or both. It's the only way that would make sense."

There was a good chance she was right, too. "The only thing I've agreed to at this point is the trial run. And there's no actual commitment, so if things get weird, I can just run."

"Okay, you need to do some serious stealth work over the next two weeks. Ask him questions, make him talk about himself, and try to figure out his level of crazy."

Then she stopped as though reminded of something. And for a second, I thought she might start to tell me that Jupiter's third moon's placement against Pluto in January's Virgo Season made this an unideal time to get into a contractual fake relationship with a practical stranger, because Mercury was on its way back from renegade. Or whatever.

Instead, she said, "He's not a Scorpio, is he? When's his birthday?"

So, I wasn't that far off.

"I dunno," I told her. The stealth-work thing wasn't a terrible idea, though. Like at all.

"I need you to find out and report back so I can look up his chart. If he's a Scorpio, I'm not letting you do this. Or if there's anything weird going on with his moon or Saturn placements. Or Mars. Double whammy if it's a Scorpio-Mars situation."

I had less than zero idea what she was on about. "You're a Scorpio," I pointed out.

She waved off my comment like it wasn't relevant. "Just find out when he was born and text it to me, please."

I would not be doing that. "You got it."

"In the meantime, on a scale of one to serial-killery, what's his vibe?"

I laughed at that. "I don't know, Mik. Two. 'Serial-killery' is definitely not how I would describe him." Minus when I thought he was going to murder me that first night. But, you know, circumstances.

"How would you describe him, then?"

I had to think about that one. "First impressions aside, for obvious reasons, he's got a pretty good sense of humor, I think." I wasn't sure why I felt the need to look away from the screen when I said that, but I did. "Also, he can cook. Like, surprisingly well."

Mikaela eyed me while I fumbled with my shorts. "What does he look like? Is he cute?" she asked.

"Um, I mean, yeah, I guess you could say he's conventionally attractive."

"I see." The words were innocent enough, but she said them in *that* tone.

"What?"

"Nothing."

"No, seriously, what?"

Her lips quirked, and she shrugged. "Nothing. It's just been a while since I heard you describe anyone as 'conventionally attractive.' Or any type of attractive, for that matter."

"That's not true," I said, probably a little too defensively.

"No?"

I opened my mouth again to give her an example, but none came to mind. Not over the last few years, at least. Not since Simon. But I didn't say that out loud. I knew better than to mention him in front of her.

"I can't think of anyone right this second. But there's been guys. Bartenders and stuff." There had been no bartenders. I didn't even know where I got that from.

"Okay."

"I'm serious," I told her.

"I believe you." She definitely didn't. "Anyways, none of this matters if he turns out to be a creepy weirdo murderer. So just keep me updated, okay? I want play-by-play 3:00 a.m. texts as shit's hitting the fan in real time."

"I mean, let's hope that won't be necessary?"

She ignored me and kept going, "What's the Canadian version of 911?"

"911."

"Great, that'll be easy to remember when you send me a 'help, I'm getting murdered by my conventionally attractive fake boyfriend' text and I have to call them on your behalf."

"That's for sure not how that works. You'll just get connected to your local emergency services."

"Ah, well. I'll have tried. Promise me you'll visit?"

"I'll flicker all your lights and haunt your every dream," I vowed.

"It's all I ask."

# 9

**than**

IT HAD BEEN an educational and very amusing ten minutes of trying to get my work done. A few of the key things I'd learned:

1) "Serial-killery" was "definitely" not how Skylar would describe me or my "vibe."

2) Not only did I have a good sense of humor, but I was also "conventionally attractive." A rather rare compliment according to a person named "Mik," who I assumed to be the friend my new co-conspirator had mentioned last night.

3) There was a direct, open vent that connected my home office to wherever their call was happening upstairs. It carried acoustics with beautiful clarity.

The voices muffled to an indecipherable degree when the heat came on and, eventually, were replaced in their entirety by the sound of quick steps running down the stairs.

*I'm about due for a fresh cup of coffee*, I justified as I picked up the half-empty mug and made my way into the kitchen. At least I'd had a chance to catch up on my sleep last night and wasn't dependent on the caffeine to keep me functioning.

Alexis had been right—I felt better. A lot better, actually.

"Hey, good morning," Skylar greeted me when she saw me. She was wearing the oversized black hoodie again, with shorts this time. Also black.

"Morning," I responded, averting my gaze and bringing my mug up to strategically obstruct some of the view when she bent down to grab something from the freezer. Day one of having a female roommate did not need to start with me staring at her bare legs. Regardless of how tempting the view was.

The unsatisfying sip of lukewarm liquid was a reminder of why I'd come to the kitchen in the first place. I dumped the rest of the stale coffee, stuck a fresh pod into the machine, and turned back around just in time to catch Skylar pop a white Popsicle into her mouth.

Except she didn't *just* pop it into her mouth. Her tongue gently grazed the tip first, just before her lips curled around it, and she suc—

I ripped my eyes away from her mouth so violently that my head jerked with them, inadvertently drawing her attention away from her phone and to me.

"What?" she asked, tongue darting across her cream-coated lips.

"It's ten thirty in the morning." And freezing outside.

She arched a pierced brow. "So?"

"A little early for ice cream, don't you think?" A stupid thing to say, even for a panic-induced cover-up. Why the fuck would that be any of my business?

She didn't agree with my statement, nor did she take offense, as was apparent by the way her arctic eyes playfully crinkled in their corners before she answered me. "It's coconut flavored. I'm basically on a health kick and having fruit for breakfast."

I smiled at that. "Ah, my mistake."

"Would you like one? They're really good."

"No, thanks. I've already had my recommended three servings of fruit for the day."

"Bummer. Hate it when that happens." She chuckled and hopped onto the counter, wincing a little when her bottom made contact with the marble. "Anyways, have you had a chance to talk to Alexis yet? About our arrangement?"

"Not yet." I may or may not have been putting it off all morning. I wasn't entirely in the mood to be shrill-yelled at again.

"Okay, I only ask in case you want me to do it? I can warm her up for you. She's probably less likely to get mad and yell at me."

It was like she'd read my mind in between licks of her healthy breakfast fruit.

*You better hope she didn't read all of it, perv. And for the love of decency, stop looking at her mouth.*

"I'm tempted," I said, my disobeying eyes flickering back to her lips at the exact incorrect time. "To let you talk to Alexis, I mean," I clarified, too quickly to not be suspicious. The words all but tripped over one another on their way out.

A light rush trickled up my chest and warmed my skin. To an uncomfortable degree.

Skylar, entirely oblivious to the fact that I was *flustered* like a fucking twelve-year-old talking to a girl for the first time, shrugged. "I don't mind."

"It's fine, I'll deal with my sister. Thanks, though."

"No worries." Then, with the slightest of frowns, she

nudged her chin toward her Popsicle and said, "Are you sure you don't want one of these? You keep looking at it."

*Jesus Christ.*

"Yes, I'm sure. Sorry." I cleared my throat, snatched the fresh cup of coffee that had finished brewing however-long-ago, and walked out.

All the while, that small, inconvenient flush of heat had started to spread into thin flames, lashing and licking—

*Fucking stop it.*

"For what?" Skylar slid down from the counter and followed me out of the kitchen.

"What?" I couldn't remember what I'd said.

"Sorry for what?"

I didn't know. "Nothing. It's a Canadian thing. We apologize for everything."

*You're an idiot. You should apologize for that next.*

"Okay. Anyways, so I know you said you eat low carb and high protein. Does that mean you *never* eat sugar and empty carbs? At all?" she asked, leaning against the doorway of my study. "Feels like that's something I should know as your soon-to-be fake fiancé."

I took a breath and sat down, rotating in my chair to face her. "I try to stay away from them. But, and I know this is going to be near impossible for you to believe, I'm not perfect. So I do cheat. Sometimes."

Her smile widened. "What's your kryptonite?"

"Salted-caramel apple pie, with pecans," I admitted. And a scoop of vanilla ice cream on the side, but we were currently not thinking about, talking about, or looking at any frozen-dessert-related things.

"Wow, go big or go home. I like it."

"What's yours?"

She thought about it, which would have been fine had her

thinking process not entailed a slow, not entirely silent suck of her Popsicle.

I kept my eyes glued to her forehead, threatening to de-socket them if they so much as blinked the wrong way.

"Brownies," she finally answered. "Dessert-wise, at least. No nuts or anything extra added, though. Just plain old-fashioned homemade brownies. Bonus points if they're fresh and warm."

"It's a good choice."

"I know."

There was a short bout of silence, and I thought that our conversation was over and she'd leave, but instead, she lingered and said, "So then, tell me something."

She was... surprisingly talkative this morning. I wondered if this was the "stealth work" she was doing, per her friend's suggestion.

The amount of amusement that followed that theory was also a surprise. "What?"

"If you stick to such a strict diet with limited food choices, how come you're so good at making dishes you don't eat? Where'd you learn to cook so well?"

*Ah... that...*

My hesitation was instinctive, and I wasn't sure where it came from exactly.

"Um, you don't have to tell me if you don't want to," Skylar clarified, peeling her shoulder off the doorway and straightening back up. I must have paused for too long. "I didn't mean to pry."

"No, it's fine. Might be a good idea for you to know stuff like this anyway," I said, rubbing my chin. "We had a private chef growing up, and I basically annoyed her into teaching me. That's how I got started, at least. I helped her make dinner almost every day after school when I didn't have soccer practice."

Her eyes pinched in their corners, like she was resisting a smile. It's possible that her lips had also moved; I wouldn't know.

"And how exactly did you annoy her into it? You kept asking until she said yes?"

"No, it was all her idea. I talked so much as a kid that I'm convinced it was her way of keeping my hands and mouth occupied. I'd head to the kitchen as soon as I got home and talk her head off. She'd give me a snack, help me with my homework if I needed it, then we'd start cooking," I explained. "I eventually learned to enjoy it, so I kept doing it. Even on my own."

Skylar tossed her half-eaten Popsicle into the trash and sat down in the chair facing my desk. "Well, that's sweeter than I was expecting. Do you still keep in touch with her?"

"Couldn't avoid her even if I wanted to."

She brought her knees up to her chest and wrapped her arms around them. "What does that mean?"

"Well, for one, her son is marrying my sister," I revealed, reaching for a small blanket in my bottom drawer and tossing it to her.

She caught it. "Wait, *what*?"

I chuckled at her expression and leaned in, placing my elbows on the desk. "Joel and I are the same age, so Marta would bring him to work with her quite a bit. Especially on the days she was busy and wanted me out of the kitchen. Although, most of the time, it would backfire. We were exceptionally good at getting into trouble together," I said while she spread the blanket over her legs, excited eyes glued to mine. "Alexis developed a crush on him when she was around five and would follow us around every time he came over." And I did mean every time. We eventually had to get creative with how we got rid of her.

Skylar sighed, practically melting on her seat. "That's the cutest thing I've ever heard."

"I personally found it quite annoying." And maybe a little endearing, looking back on it now. But you'd have to pry that admission out of my cold, dead mouth. "What about you? Any irritating little siblings follow you around growing up? Or older ones you trailed after?"

She shook her head. "I wish."

"They're not that great. You've met Alexis."

The joke landed, and she huffed a little laugh. "Except that she is pretty great," Skylar defended. "You're very lucky. I really wanted a sister growing up."

"I'll keep that in mind while she's ripping me a new one over our arrangement," I said with a sip of my coffee. "Speaking of, I should probably call her, then get back to work." The longer I put it off, the worse it would get. I already knew she wouldn't be on board with this.

Then I needed to go over Grey's business plan. Thoroughly.

I suspected Mila would put a same-day meeting or two into my calendar on Monday, and I didn't want to give her—*them*—the satisfaction of showing up unprepared.

The devil had found his perfect minion in her, much to everyone else's dismay.

"Sounds good," Skylar said, reluctantly peeling my blanket off her legs while she stood up.

"You can take that with you if you want," I offered.

She immediately smiled and wrapped it back around herself, seemingly content. "Thanks. And um, yell or something if you need saving," she offered before leaving.

~

"*ETHAN*, I swear on everything you think you believe in—"

"Yes, I know. I get it, Alexis." We were on a voice call, and I couldn't see her face, but I knew the exact glare she'd throw my way for interrupting her. She'd inherited it directly from Anita. In all fairness, I had quite a bit of work to do, and this conversation had already gone on for longer than was necessary.

"Except you don't seem to *actually* get it." She exhaled, frustrated. "And Sky doesn't know what she's getting herself into with this. It's not fair to drag her into it."

"No one's dragging her into anything. She'll have a better idea of what she's in for after Anita's party and can make her decision then. That's what the trial is for."

"So, what? What happens if she changes her mind after the trial? What are you going to tell everyone?"

Honestly, I was really hoping I wouldn't have to worry about that. "If she does, I'll say we broke up."

"Or, you could say you broke up *now*. It isn't too late. You already have a valid excuse—you can tell Anita Skylar didn't appreciate you telling people about your relationship without discussing it with her first. Or something. Literally *anything* will be better than your current plan."

We were going around in circles now. "I'm not changing my mind. Just make sure you don't let things slip on your end."

She tried a different approach. "Me slipping is the least of your worries. Grey isn't going to go down as easily as you think he is," Alexis insisted. "It'll take the tiniest slip between you and Skylar, something most people would brush off as entirely insignificant, for him—*or Mila*—to become suspicious. And if either of them thinks there's even a shred of possibility that you're lying, they're going to rip the whole thing apart. And what happens then?"

She wasn't wrong. I wasn't going to admit it to her, but she wasn't. "Like I said, even if that were to happen, Skylar would still get compensated. Then I'd just... deal with the consequences."

"The money isn't going to be worth dealing with a bunch of emotionally stunted, power-hungry, ruthless vultures for her!" Alexis snapped suddenly, raising her tone.

A small voice in the back of my head called for a de-escalation, but my retort had slipped before I could listen. "Spoken from a place of true privilege, Alexis. Not everyone has the luxury of scoffing off that amount of money the way you do."

"I wish for *once* in your life you would stop brushing me off and just listen to me. You don't know her, you don't know anything about her, and you're not thinking clearly! This isn't a good idea!" she yelled.

This wasn't her normal bickering. This wasn't even a shrill-yelling episode. She was mad.

"Would you calm the fuck down. Even if people find out, the heat will be directed my way, not hers."

"Seriously? Do you really have your head *that* far up your own ass that you think she'll walk away completely unscathed from all this if it falls apart?"

"*Yes*. What's the matter with you today? What the hell do you think is going to happen to her?"

"What's been the matter with *you* for the last two fucking *years*? You've been back home twice in the last sixteen months, both times for work, and you didn't even *tell me* you were coming this second time. You spent Christmas in a hotel, for fuck's sake, because you 'didn't see the point' in flying home for just three days. You rarely ever call or text, and when we do talk, you're short and impatient and—and—now, *this.* What—"

She stopped, taking a breath.

And maybe she was waiting for me to respond with an explanation. Or an apology. But my jaw was locked, and before I could pry it back open, she started again. This time, though, her voice had lowered to a more sobered pitch, the one she normally reserved for her other brother. "You know what, Ethan. Forget it. Do whatever the fuck you want—you never listen anyway. But just so we're clear, I think this is a *terrible.* Fucking. Idea. So if things start to go south and I think for *one second* that Skylar is going to get hurt, I'll spill the beans myself," Alexis threatened. "And that way, according to your own dumb rules, she still gets the money without becoming a discarded casualty in your stupid, selfish game."

Then she hung up.

# 10

## than

I WAS RIGHT. Sort of.

Mila put not one, not two, but three same-day meetings into my calendar within the first hour of me walking into the office on Monday.

It had been the calm before her storm. By midmorning, she'd added thirteen more, all to be held over the span of the next two weeks and in complete disregard for any and all of my scheduling conflicts.

*It's good to be back*, I thought, tempted to reject them all back to her, one by one, with email notifications and "read receipt" requests on. So very tempted.

But I couldn't. The attendees included investors, reps from the architectural firms we were considering for the project, various team leaders, and Anita.

So Jackson, my unfortunate assistant, spent the day scrambling, trying to move my preexisting appointments around to accommodate the new schedule while I begrudgingly sat through seven long hours of meetings, spearheaded by my brother and his shadow, both of whom seemed to love hearing him talk. That was on top of my regular workload for the day.

I wasn't sure when exactly, during the week's chaos, I could start handing off my current projects to other managers. That in itself, with the reorganizing and training, was going to take up a shit ton of time.

Oh, and Alexis wasn't talking to me. She'd gone radio silent, ignoring my calls and texts since yesterday morning. I'd tried her three times in between meetings to no avail. I checked again as soon as I unlocked the apartment door and walked in—still nothing.

As a last resort, I decided to try her more reasonable half:

**Me: Hey. Can you tell Lex—**

"Hey. Didju jus' get home?"

I whipped around and almost dropped my phone at the sight of the slurring, white ghost lurking at the bottom of the stairs.

"Jesus Christ, what is *with* you and walking around in the dark?"

The ghost shrugged, rubbing the sleep from her eye. "You're doing the same thing. Why didn't you just turn on the lights when you came in?"

Fair point. Except I wasn't dressed in a baggy white pillowcase of a T-shirt that was virtually glowing against the moonlight.

"You scared the shit out of me," I told her.

"Makes us even, then, I guess," she said, sounding a little amused. "At least I wasn't holding a baseball bat."

"New house rule," I decided, "no more walking around here at night with the lights off."

"Fine. That's fair."

"Anyways, how was your first day?" I asked, slipping off my jacket and shoes while my heart breathed through its panic attack.

"It was good, pretty standard stuff. Mostly got acquainted with the team and did some training..." She trailed off with a small yawn.

"Did I wake you?"

"Nah, I just came down to get some water," Skylar said, making her way to the kitchen. "How was your day?"

"Long," I answered, heading for the bar. I was also in need of refreshments.

"Were you really at work the whole time?" she asked when she sauntered back into the room with her water.

"Unfortunately."

"It's, like, eleven thirty."

"Yes. Yes it is." I sat down in my armchair with a small glass of bourbon and leaned back. Exhaustion pulled on my eyelids as soon as my head hit the leather.

"Mmm" was her response. Her body half turned as if to walk away, then seemed to change its mind. "Do you always work this much? On evenings and weekends?"

"Sometimes," I admitted. "But it's usually not this bad. This last week has been particularly long and difficult."

An even longer pause this time. "D'you want to talk about it?"

It occurred to me that her inquiry was probably more "stealth work" and not actual curiosity or concern, but I didn't have the energy to humor it this time.

"No. But we do need to talk."

"Uh-oh. Nothing good ever comes out of that sentence," she said, sitting down on the couch adjacent to my chair.

"I was originally planning on scheduling a couple of sessions with you to go over the basic details we need to know about each other ahead of the party. But I don't think I'll have the time I thought I would this week, and I'm not sure what the next one will look like." I reached for my bag, took out a folder, and handed it to her. I'd worked on it yesterday evening after going over Grey's plan, just in case. Turns out, it hadn't been a huge waste of time. "So, I drafted that up. It includes basic information about me and our relationship. It's enough to get us through one party if people were to ask about us. How we met, how long we've been dating, things like that. You'll need to memorize it. I've also included a form for you to fill out with some of your basic background info."

She scanned the first page, tracing a slim finger down the lines as she read through them. "Okay," she eventually said. "I can work with this if you think it's enough."

I took a sip of my drink and leaned forward, elbows on my knees. "You don't agree? That it's enough?"

"I mean, like you said, it's just for one party for now..."

"But?"

She fiddled with the corner of the folder, averting her gaze. "Nothing. I think I may have watched one too many romantic comedies. This should be fine."

I should have ended the conversation there, finished my drink, and gone to bed. But amused curiosity pawed at my chest. "You have to elaborate."

"It's stupid."

"I could use a laugh."

She looked back up at me, her own smile playing at the corners of her mouth. "Fine. I think memorizing all this stuff is great and important, but there's... I don't know, don't you think it won't really matter if we're not, like, comfortable and *in sync*?"

I wasn't entirely sure what she meant, but I knew for a fact that she was overthinking it again. However, this could be kind of fun. "Give me an example. One from a movie."

"I... don't think we should get into it. Seriously. You're probably right—this should be enough for just one party. Plus, we're still in the trial phase and everything..."

"Please?" my curiosity pressed.

It took her a few fiddles of the paper, but she eventually said, "Well, okay. This is *just an example*, so don't take it the wrong way, but in the last one I watched, the couple was basically bullied into kissing each other in front of the guy's family to celebrate their engagement. Except they were so awkward about it that there's no way it would have passed as believable in real life."

She delivered. For what felt like the first time that day, I laughed. "Skylar, I'm not going to kiss you. Especially in front of my family."

One silent second ticked by. Then two. The third was when it finally clicked, and I realized what that must have sounded like. "Wait, that came out wrong—"

"It's totally fine," she interrupted, refusing to meet my eyes. "It, uh, that wasn't what I meant—"

"It's not what I meant, either—" I tried to explain.

"Oh, it's okay, don't worry—"

"I just—"

"Don't worry about it—"

"I think, if we did that—"

"Honestly, you don't have to—"

"You might freeze, and—"

"Explain—" She stopped abruptly, blinking back up at me. "Wait... what?"

"What?"

"You just said you think I'd freeze?"

Oh, that. "Yeah. I don't think we'd be able to pull it off."

And we wouldn't need to; I'd never been overly affectionate with my partners in front of my family. They wouldn't expect it.

"Because you think... that *I'd* freeze." She touched a finger to her chest for good measure, to make extra sure we were talking about the same person.

I really did try to hold back the smile that was attempting to break through in response to her shock; it wasn't going to help my case. "Yes, Skylar, I think there's a good chance that if I kissed you in front of my family, you'd freeze."

Her lips were parted, eyebrows raised, and a finger still glued to her chest. "Are you joking?"

I took another sip of my drink, an attempt at hiding my smile. "Am I wrong?"

"*Yes*, and quite possibly delusional. Also, a little arrogant, I'd say."

Second laugh of the day. "Well, then I apologize."

Her eyes sharpened into icicles. In the limited light of the city and the moon spilling through the windows, they'd turned to a silvery grey. "I'm being serious."

"I know. I take it back. I'm sure you'd handle it with ease and grace." I'd probably sound more convincing if I could push the damn smirk back down.

"I *would* handle it with ease," she argued. "And also grace. Whatever that entails."

I shoved a hand through my hair. "I'm sorry. Yes, I am sure you'd do great. I was just thinking back to Anita's office and how surprised you were—"

"That's a completely different story; there was literally no warning. I wasn't prepared for your crazy," she insisted.

"I did warn you... did Alexis not read you the text?" How was my sister *this* bad at following instructions?

"She did, but 'just go along with it' or whatever isn't exactly specific, is it? Go along with *what*?"

"And what would you have wanted me to type in the three seconds I had to get that message out?"

"Okay, sure, special circumstances. But what I'm saying is that I wouldn't have frozen the way I did had I been properly warned."

I shouldn't have toyed with her, I knew that. I should have just let it go. But this was the most entertained I'd been all day, and I wanted to prolong it for one more minute. Maybe two. "Why are we arguing about this? Are you saying you *want* me to kiss you in front of my family? Or just in general? Because if that's the case, you can just say so."

I could practically see patches of scarlet start to blot her skin. They took on a more purple hue in the dark. She kept her composure, though, crossed her arms, and leaned back. "Obviously not. But I *am* saying that you're wrong. And probably projecting. Because, between the two of us, I don't think I'd be the one to freeze."

It was a quick flip of the switch. The insinuation of her statement—her *challenge*—flamed the air around us. It wasn't how I'd expected her to react. At all.

*Don't do it. Don't do it. Don't do it. Don—*

"Wanna bet?"

# 11

kylar

I'D NEVER BEEN a competitive person. Didn't have a single competitive bone in my body.

I couldn't care less about winning. In fact, if it were up to me, every team would get a trophy. And if there was only one, someone else could have it.

So why the hell was I *this* tempted to say yes to what was quite possibly the stupidest bet that had ever existed in the history of bets? Why did I want to prove him wrong *this* badly? To the point where I could physically feel the overwhelming urge to take it buzz under my skin and bite at my tongue to move and say yes.

I should have just kept my mouth shut about the stupid movie. Mikaela had made me watch it with her over a video call last night, and of course that had to be the scene that stuck with me. The scene I had to use as my stupid example in place of the literal dozen others.

It took a few beats to calm down from the unexpected rush of... whatever it was and ground back into my senses.

Except, just as I got there and was about to turn him down, the smirk that had been plastered on Ethan's face for the last five minutes twitched, and he opened his mouth. "Knew it," he mused softly and ever so arrogantly.

Then he stood up, downed the rest of his drink in one go, and started to walk away, waving a single, lazy hand in the air as a good-night.

*Don't do it. Don't do it. Don't do it. Don—*

"You're on."

He let out another low, airy chuckle and didn't so much as spare me an acknowledging glance as he continued up the stairs.

Like he'd set the trap and I'd willingly pranced into it.

HERE WAS THE THING. I didn't actually know what I'd agreed to with the bet. Well, not exactly, at least. What were the terms? Rules? Or were there no rules? Was he just going to plant one on me at his grandmother's party? Was *I* supposed to plant one on *him* at his grandmother's party? Was that how I would win? Was there even a prize?

Was the bet even on?

I mean, I was *pretty sure* it was on. But he hadn't verbally acknowledged it, had he? He'd just... laughed and sauntered away.

I'd probably be less stressed about it had I actually seen more of the guy this week. But he was gone by the time I made my way downstairs in the mornings and wasn't back until after I'd already gone to bed.

So the bet was just there, drenched in regret and looming

over my week.

I'd heard him come home a couple of times while trying to fall asleep, so I knew he was at least spending nights there. His steps up the stairs were always slow and heavy, then followed by the gentle click of the bedroom door shutting across the hall from mine.

I felt a little bad for the guy, but I wasn't sure if I should. I mean, yeah, it was probably exhausting, but if he—

"Hey, Sky? Look down here for me? Just the eyes—keep your chin up, please."

I reeled my strayed focus back into the studio. Alexis was down on one knee now, camera angled up to my face.

"Also, you're slanting," she noted.

"Sorry." I readjusted myself on the stool and did as I was told, keeping my chin tilted while my lazy gaze lowered down to her lens.

It had been a while since I'd posed for a shoot, and I was more rusty than I think either of us was expecting. It took a while for me to relax and warm back up to the camera. And being distracted didn't help.

Alexis had been as patient with me as always, and there didn't seem to be a time limit as to how long we had the space for, so at least the stress levels were low.

"Perfect," she said through the quick, overlapping clicks of her camera.

She threw out more instructions and adjusted her position again and again. And again. Until she was finally satisfied. "Okay, I think we're done."

I hopped off the stool and ran to my clothes. I'd never been so happy to put on a sweater before in my life. It was freezing in here, especially with just a tank top on, and the little electric heater they'd brought in was barely helping.

Alexis stood and started to flip through her camera, concentrated brows pulled together.

"How'd they turn out?" I asked, heading her way to see.

"Nu-uh," she scolded, pulling the camera away from my line of vision. "You know the rules. No looking 'til they're all done."

I knew what the answer would be, but I tried again anyway. "Come on, please?"

"Nope."

I sighed. She'd always been so stubborn about this. "Okay, well, I apologize in advance if they're not great. It's been a while."

Alexis huffed a playful chuckle. "Like that's even possible with you in front of the camera. You can keep the jeans, by the way. They look fantastic on you."

"We agreed to no payment for the shoot, remember? This is supposed to be *me* paying *you* back for letting me stay in your apartment."

"Yeah, I don't think that's a valid argument anymore. Keep the jeans—it would be wrong of me to deprive the world of you in them."

"Thanks," I laughed, reaching to help her pack up the lighting equipment. "I really love this space, by the way." It had been a great pick for the shoot.

"Yeah, me too," she agreed, looking around with expressive fondness for the exposed brick walls and large, arched windows of the quaint little dance studio she'd chosen.

"I'm surprised they were cool with us being here alone. And for this long. How'd you get in?"

"Oh, I have a key," she said while shoving a few detached metal bars into their designated bags. "I teach here part-time."

"What, really? Ballet?"

"Yeah. Just a couple of times a week, though. And mostly

the little munchkins, unless I'm covering," she said. Her love for it all was more than evident in the way she softened just talking about it. "I'm good friends with the girl that runs it, Jane. She's a few years older than us, but you two would actually get along quite well, I think."

Her reveal pulled at a memory I'd completely forgotten about, something Ethan had said. "Wait, is this the dance studio you guys were talking about in the car?"

"The one and only." Alexis sunk down onto the hardwood and pushed the half-finished packed bags aside so she could spread and stretch her legs. I didn't blame her—she'd been crouched down for the majority of the last hour. "My brother wants to tear it down. The sociopathic one, not the raging grumpster you've had the misfortune of being acquainted with."

I smiled at her exaggerated description of Ethan. Couldn't help it. "Why?"

"Greed." She grimaced a little, like the word left a bitter aftertaste in her mouth. "It doesn't matter, though, because we're not going to let him do it. What I want to know is how things are going with you. What's it like living with the most irritable man alive?"

I joined her on the floor, hugging my knees to my chest. "He's really not that bad," I defended with a chuckle, and it was the truth. It hadn't taken very long to warm up to him. Definitely not as long as I'd been expecting. "Plus, I haven't seen much of him this week, to be honest. He's been working a lot from what I gather."

"Yeah, that checks out," Alexis sighed, her shoulders dampening while she twisted the camera strap she'd been playing with. "Typical of him."

"I mean, as long as he enjoys it and it's fulfilling..." I tried reasoning, but my words faded in response to her deepening frown.

She didn't reply. Just kept wordlessly twisting and twisting until the tension drained all the color from the tips of her fingers. I gave her time, and eventually, she released the coil and mumbled, "I think Ethan hates his job."

I considered her words, trying to fit them into the image of Ethan I had in my head. It wasn't a match. "Really?"

"Yeah. Really. He just refuses to admit it to anyone, including his own stupid, stubborn self. That's my theory, at least."

Well, that made no sense. "So then, why would he—"

"He doesn't," she claimed, letting out another heavy breath. "I don't think Ethan actually wants to be CEO. I think he just wants to beat Grey."

I allowed that to sink in with my chin resting against my knees. All... *this* for a prize he didn't actually want? Just to make sure his brother didn't get it?

Alexis dropped the camera strap and scooched forward, closer to where I sat. "He told me about the two-week trial thing."

I glanced back up at her, at the new tension she was holding in her shoulders. "Are you mad? That I agreed?"

She shook her head. "At you? Not even a little."

"At him?"

Alexis pressed her lips together, letting her eyes roam around my face while she decided on the best way to answer. "You know the day we took you to the hospital?"

I nodded. How could I possibly forget.

"Ethan called me that night. He was worried because you'd been asleep for too long, but he didn't want to come into your room and check on you. He thought it might be inappropriate or make you uncomfortable. So he called me and asked what foods you liked and whether you had any dietary restrictions. And then he swore me to secrecy."

"Wait, so *you* told him about the lasagna?" I thought it had just been a lucky coincidence.

A tiny laugh escaped her. "His plan was to lure you out with it. Based on that response, I'm guessing it worked."

A light flutter circled my chest, once, twice. My arms tightened around my knees.

I almost kind of wished she hadn't told me that.

"I helped him with the groceries that morning, and there was no pasta in those bags, which makes sense, knowing Ethan and his dumb aversion to carbs. So, unless you already had some lying around... he went out in one of the worst storms we've had all winter to buy it. Because I told him lasagna was your favorite."

*Oh no. Oh no, nono.*

Why was she telling me this?

"I'm telling you this because I don't want you to take my warning the wrong way. I don't want you to think Ethan's a bad person, because he's not," she explained, fiddling with her pants in place of the strap now. "But... I think that sometimes, good people make bad decisions. And I think that this is one of those times and that you should know... what to expect before you go into this. So you can be prepared for the types of personalities you're going to be dealing with."

I stayed silent through the pauses that stretched out her sentences, watching as she took another deep breath before continuing. "My brothers are competitive, for lack of a better word. Especially with each other. And... I, um, I won't bore you with my excuses for their behavior, but I will tell you that, at this point, it's pretty much ingrained. It defines their relationship... or lack thereof, I guess. And I will also tell you that when they get like this—when Ethan gets like this—it's tunnel vision on steroids.

"He doesn't see anything else. He just... keeps going. Even if what he's doing is destructive. To the people around him or to himself. It's him and the goal, and he'll do whatever it takes to get to it. Everything else is either a distraction or an obstacle standing in his way.

"Grey operates a little differently. Ethan uses sheer force and determination to get what he wants. He bets on being able to outplay you... because most of the time, he can. Grey is less spontaneous, more tactical, strategic and calculating. I wouldn't bet against either of them, but with Ethan, you... at least see more. He *shows* more, even if it's not always on purpose. With Grey, you only see what he wants you to see. Period. He's a lot harder to read... so be mindful of that when you interact with him.

"The one thing the two do have in common is that neither of them will give up. They... don't know how. I can't stress that enough—they really don't know how. So the game isn't over until it's *over*. Until there are no more moves left to make or the clock runs out. They were always placed on different teams growing up, and I've seen them try to finish physically demanding games with injuries more than once and in different sports. A couple of times, it was painful just to watch them try to keep going. And they *would* keep going if their coaches didn't pull them out. And if they couldn't argue their way back in to finish, which Ethan actually managed once."

"Why, though?" I asked when I could locate my voice. She'd said she didn't want to bore me with her excuses for them... which meant that there *were* excuses. Reasons. "Why to that extent?"

"They weren't always like this. They just..." Large brown eyes dropped down to fiddling fingers, and when they eventually came back up, I could see my reflection in their glass. "Don't you wonder sometimes? How different things might be... what it would have been like to grow up with parents that loved you... unconditionally?"

# 12

kylar

Alexis was kind enough to drive me home.

*"Home,"* I thought, getting off the elevator. It was one of those words. The more you said it, the weirder it sounded.

*Home. Home. Hoooommmme. Who comes up with—*

The lights were on. In the apartment.

I could see them spilling into the hallway, onto my sneakers, while my fingers hovered over the keypad of the lock.

So I… turned around. I went back into the elevator, rode it down, went back outside, and went for a walk in the brisk, late-evening Torontonian winter air. Because why not.

It was refreshing. A little cold, kinda snowy, and maybe somewhat deadly, but refreshing nonetheless. Plus, I needed food. Hadn't had dinner yet, so.

I passed by three, four, five, six, seven, eight, nine, ten, eleven takeout places and stopped for the twelfth because my fingers were in too much pain to keep going. *Not* because it was the only one closest to having low-carb options.

Either way, I got my dinner. So, all in all, super productive. An hour well spent in the polar windchill.

And then I was back to where I started, standing outside the apartment door. Except this time, my fingers didn't hesitate before putting in the code. Though they were shaking a little. Because I was still cold and stuff.

"Hey," Ethan said when I walked in. He was standing in the kitchen, and for a second, I thought I was too late... but I couldn't smell anything. So maybe not.

Or maybe the frost had killed my nose.

"Hi." I slipped off my boots before making my way up to the counter separating us. "Have you had dinner yet?"

"No. I was just about to make some." He raised the empty pan he'd been holding.

*Oh, good.* "Okay. Well, if you don't feel like cooking... I, um, got myself dinner. But I think I might have bought too much. Dinner," I specified, just in case it wasn't clear.

He looked down at the takeout bags in my hand and... frowned. He was frowning at me. *I knew it.* I should have searched up healthy takeout options instead of blindly walking—

"Where are your gloves?" were the words that accompanied his disapproving glare.

"Pardon?"

"Your gloves," he repeated.

"I forgot to pack them," I admitted, unsure of their relevance to the topic at hand. "Why?"

His chin flicked toward the takeout bags. "That place is nine blocks away. Did you walk?"

"It wasn't that bad," I lied, placing the bags on the counter.

Technically, my fingers didn't hurt anymore. They weren't even tingly. Just numb. "Are you hungry or not?"

He eyed me a little but let it go. "What did you get?"

I took off my jacket and started opening the bags. "Chicken, kimchi, kale salad, cauliflower tots, and, um, a baked potato," I declared, pulling out each one individually as I listed them off. I wasn't sure what he liked.

The chicken was fried, but the "healthy" kind of fried with "no breadcrumbs," according to the menu. I didn't know what that meant or how cardboard-esque the taste was going to be.

"You bought... two of each, sans the potato."

"I'm hungry. Skipped lunch."

Ethan's eyes narrowed slightly, and he leaned on the counter, studying me. "You look different."

His hair was damp and freshly tousled, like he'd just gotten out of the shower. I could smell the shampoo from here. And the soap. Sweet and spicy and clean.

"I did my makeup differently today, for work," I said. There was more of it, to be specific. Around my eyes mostly. The camera didn't always pick up on subtleties.

And technically, it had been done by a professional, not me. But these weren't details he needed.

"I thought you said interns got Fridays off."

Okay. So he'd already read the information form I'd filled out and left on his desk, per the instructions in the folder. That was... quick. Considering.

"Different work."

"Is the makeup also what's making you act weird?"

What were the chances I had enough foundation and concealer on to hide the incoming splashes of red? "That's a little rude. Is this your way of thanking me for sharing my food?"

He didn't bite. "Is this about the bet? Are you trying to bribe your way out of it with chicken and kale?"

I'd honestly forgotten about the bet. It had been a busy two hours in my brain.

"Uhm... I mean, it wasn't. But if you want to let me out and admit you're wrong, I won't argue."

Instead of answering, Ethan put a cauli-tater into his smirking mouth. The fact that he was ultracompetitive also explained why he'd been so quick to make the bet in the first place. Kind of wished I'd known about that a tad bit earlier.

"Thank you," he said, taking a seat across from me. "This is actually very nice. And thoughtful."

It wasn't that nice. It's not like I'd found out his favorite food, went out into a storm to buy the ingredients, then made it for him from scratch. Sorry, made it *to perfection* for him from scratch. All because I wanted to make sure he was okay without making him uncomfortable.

*That* would be nice.

This... wasn't even close. It was a little embarrassing in comparison, actually.

"Not a big deal. Like I said, I bought too much... dinner. For just myself."

And then I couldn't meet his eyes anymore, so I lowered mine and went for the food, only to find that my appetite had started to fade and was being replaced by... a different, swirlier sensation in my stomach. And the more I could feel his gaze on me, the worse it got.

Eventually, Ethan followed my lead and reached for a salad. It had been the only thing on the menu with pecans in it.

"Regardless, I appreciate it," he said. And then, before we could settle into a silence that would have been uncomfortably loud, he broke it. “Did you have a chance to go over the document?”

“Memorized it,” I said, grateful for the change in topic. “Did you get mine?” Though I already knew the answer. It was the only way he’d know I didn’t work on Fridays.

“Memorized it.”

My fork froze midstab. There was no way. “All of it?”

“All of it.”

“How? I put it on your desk last night. When would you have had the time?” It hadn’t been a short form, either. And I’d... added to it.

The smirk on his lips remained playful, but something in the way he was looking at me turned... sharp. “You don’t believe me?”

Oh god. “I didn’t say that.”

“Wanna make it into a game?”

“Oh. No, thank you,” I answered, shoving a bunch of greens and goat cheese into my mouth.

The reminder of how much I hated kale was pretty instantaneous. It was a horrid excuse for a vegetable. Didn’t taste edible. *Just keep chewing. Not like you can spit it out in front of him.*

“The rules are simple,” Ethan went on, ignoring my obvious and thorough lack of interest in competing with him in any way, shape, or form. “One question, one answer per round. We keep going until one of us gets one wrong. That person loses.”

“Or, we could just not and say we did—”

“If you win, I’ll let you out of the bet and admit I was wrong.”

“Full admission?”

“Full admission.”

*Worth it.* “Done.”

# 13

**than**

"MY BIRTHDAY," Skylar fired between small bites of her chicken.

Please. Nine rounds in, you'd think she'd go for something a tad more challenging. "April sixteenth. My first pet?"

"Sammy the goldfish. Lived to the ripe old age of ten. Mine?"

"You weren't allowed pets growing up. But you wanted a golden retriever so bad that you saved up your allowance and bought a stuffed one. Her name was Bailey, and you dragged her everywhere with you," I said, wiping the side of my mouth with a napkin. "What varsity team did I play on?"

"Team*s*. Plural—which is ridiculous, by the way. Soccer and swim. How old was I when I broke my wrist?"

"You didn't. You sprained your wrist in the second grade by attempting to rock in a non-rocking chair and falling backwards. The left one. What am I allergic to?"

She huffed a little giggle. "The birds and the bees."

"Bee *stings* and duck feathers," I corrected, pushing back my own smile. She should technically lose for that.

"That's basically what I said," Skylar claimed with a playful roll of her eyes.

Whatever she'd done with her makeup today had given them the gravitational pull of Jupiter. I couldn't stop looking. They were mesmerizing. Trapped bolts of lightning th—

"...Ethan?"

"Sorry," I said, clearing my throat. "What?"

"My top three favorite types of milk."

My lips twitched. "That wasn't a question on the sheet."

"Yeah, but it should have been. Pretty standard stuff, if you ask me. I put the answer in the miscellaneous section."

"There was no miscellaneous section."

"Yeah, but again, there should have been. So I put one in the back."

Keeping my composure was becoming a bit of a struggle. "You didn't put one in the back. You added two full, double-sided pages of only semicoherent nonsense."

"Yeah. *To the back.*" She was practically giddy with mischief. Her lean on the counter matched mine, and her lips were quivering with the effort it was taking to contain her laugh. "Answer the question, Ethan."

I inched a little closer every time she said my name. It was new. I didn't hate it.

"Fine," I caved. "But if I can get this right, then it's an automatic win."

Skylar bit the inside of her cheek before agreeing. "Only if you can get them in order."

*Hah.*

"There wasn't a top three," I said, recalling the words she'd scribbled and stapled to the original document. "There were four, total. And you were very specific in noting that they were listed in *no* particular order. Which is probably why they weren't numbered; you used bullet points. Chocolate milk was the first one listed, dark chocolate milk was number two, hot chocolate was three, and frozen hot chocolate was last." I knew the smirk I wore was cocky. I didn't care. "There were nineteen questions on the added pages; the milk one was number eight. Above it was your least favorite type of clown, to which the answer was a surprisingly well-drawn caricature of a disgraced former American politician. Below it was the best time of day to call you, to which the answer was 'Don't. That's literally why texting was invented.'"

Her soft smile had widened, crinkling around her eyes. "Wow," she purred, voice feathered with amusement. "You *are* good. Didn't think you'd actually read through them."

Multiple times. And there may or may not be a picture of that caricature on my phone. She'd never know. "I skimmed it."

"Alright, I concede defeat. You win," Skylar said, reaching for her empty plate. "That was a little quicker than I'd been expecting."

"Mmm, never had a woman say that to me before."

"Gross." She laughed and chucked her crumpled napkin at my chest before standing up.

The motion sobered down my grin.

I realized, to my own reluctant surprise, that I didn't want the conversation to be over yet. I didn't want her to leave and go upstairs. We cleaned in silence while I racked my brain, looking for an excuse to keep the conversation going.

Skylar beat me to it.

"Hey, do you, um, feel like having a drink? Or something?" she asked into the fridge as I handed her the last box of leftovers to put away.

I did everything I could to stop the giant grin that wanted to break out. I failed. "I do, um, feel like having a drink. Or something," I teased.

"Wow. Instant regret."

I laughed and turned to walk out of the kitchen, toward the bar. "What would you like?"

"I'm good with whatever you're having. Just going to get changed first real quick."

I poured two glasses of whiskey for us, adding a dash of bitters and sweet vermouth, unable, for whatever reason, to keep a small smile off my face.

*At least she's funny and easy to get along with. Makes everything else a little less difficult.*

Skylar ran back down the stairs a few minutes later in what looked to be a much more comfortable outfit. A T-shirt and sweatpants, both the opposite of formfitting. She pulled them off incredibly well.

I handed her a glass once she'd plopped herself down on the couch and took a seat beside her, allowing my body to sink into the soft leather. It had been a long week.

"Thank you again," I said, "for dinner."

"You're welcome," Skylar muttered under her breath, tracing a delicate finger over the rim of her glass.

I couldn't understand why she was being so weird about it... almost like she was embarrassed. It didn't make sense.

What made even less sense was my immediate urge to try and make her feel better. "I can't remember the last time someone thought to bring me food," I said, unsure whether admitting something slightly vulnerable would help or make things worse.

Her finger stilled, and she looked up at me. "Really?"

"Really," I confirmed with a small sip of my cocktail.

"Except Jackson, sometimes, but that doesn't really count. Since I pay him to do it."

It might have worked. She rotated on the couch to face me, bringing her legs up into a cross-legged position. "Who's that?"

"My assistant."

"You have one of those?"

I wasn't sure if it was the words or the tinge of surprised awe they held that was funny. Regardless, I laughed before I said, "Yes. I do indeed have one of those. Why is that so surprising?"

"I'm not sure. You're just so... young, I guess. When I think of COOs and CEOs with assistants, I think of... older people with, like, greying hair and... just... different... looking..." Her cheeks were taking on a new shade of pink with every delayed word, eyes bouncing around as the sentence got away from her.

*Cute,* I thought. "Different-looking, how, exactly?" I pressed, turning so I could fully face her.

More "conventionally attractive," maybe? Like the vents had tattled?

"Why are you smiling like that?" Skylar asked with narrowing eyes.

"I'm not smiling," I assured her, bringing my glass up to meet said smile. After a more generous sip, I went on. "I'm just asking how you think I look different than these CEOs you're imagining. Just so, you know, I can maybe work on looking more the part. Might increase my chances."

She was struggling to keep her own composure now. "Well, firstly, like I said, greying hair. So obviously, you'll need to dye it. Add some salt to the coffee."

"Obviously." And obviously salt, not sugar.

"And, while we're at it, you'll need to restyle completely.

This," she said, gesturing to my head, "needs to be less *GQ*, more dental office."

"I barely know what that means," I confessed.

Biting down her grin, she scooched closer and reached for my hair with her free hand. I didn't stop her. "Most CEOs don't have this much hair, by the way. They lose it all because of the stress. It's science."

"*Is* it science?"

"Straight up biochemical metamorphysics," Skylar confirmed, pushing my hair to the side. She smelled like sweet lemons and vanilla. "You should probably shave it all or just, like, the middle. I can do it for you. It'll show your grandmother you're working so hard you're losing your hair."

"That's a great idea."

"I know. I'm full of those." Finally, once she was satisfied with her work, she sat back and grinned. "I should have been a hairstylist. A shame. It was my third choice, too."

I took out my phone and glanced at her work. I looked like I'd walked straight out of the '50s. Apparently, that's what "dental office" meant. An impressive accomplishment, considering she'd only used one hand and no comb. "Well done. What was your second choice?"

"Tube man."

I chortled on my drink. It burned. "Are you particularly talented at flailing?"

"Yes, it's a gift. *And* I'm the perfect shape to be one." She stood up and presented herself with a small spin, gesturing up and down with her hand. "See? A tube. Paint me green and I could insta-transport Mario."

How had we arrived here? How fast had this whiskey kicked in? "You definitely don't look like a tube."

"That's kind of a rude thing to say to someone, Ethan," she claimed, plopping back down. "I'd never tell *you* you were the wrong shape for chasing your dreams. Only that your hair is wrong. And like your jaw, maybe."

"What's wrong with my jaw?" I asked, rubbing it defensively.

"Nothing. That's the problem. You need more Frisbee in its bone structure, less boomerang."

More and less of what? "Are you high? What was in that chicken?" I reached out and touched her forehead.

"How does you checking my temperature help determine whether or not I'm high?"

I didn't know. Maybe *I* was high. I felt... *something.*

Light. I felt light.

Also, I was still touching her.

"Fever also causes nonsensical speech. It's science," I explained before dropping my hand. It buzzed. My skin was buzzing. I wiped it against my jeans.

"*Is* it science?"

"Straight up biothermodynamical physiatrics."

"Bet you can't say that thirty times fast. And I feel like I'm making perfect sense," she argued. "Maybe it's you, not me. A generational difference in lingo, perhaps?"

I bit back my laugh. "First I'm too young, now I'm too old?"

"Thirty's a weird age. Not that I'd really know. I have years and years and *yeeaaars—*"

"Alright," I said, starting to stand up so I could pretend to leave, but Skylar grabbed hold of my arm and dragged me right back down, giggling.

"Sorry, sorry, don't go," she laughed. "I'll be nice."

"Let's not start making promises we can't keep."

"No, I swear. I'll stop making fun of your disgustingly luscious, non-greying hair and weird, angled, non-circular jaw."

"Oh good, you were starting to really hurt my feelings there. What was gonna be next? My eerily perfect teeth?"

She raised her eyebrows. I'd nailed it.

"You wouldn't have *dared*," I claimed, positively appalled.

"Why are they *so white*?" she asked, flailing her hand around my face like it personally offended her. A perfect demonstration of her tube man skills. "Do you use them to navigate your way in the dark? Is that why you never turn on the lights? Do you have to keep your mouth shut while driving because they're a traffic hazard?"

"It's the only way they'd give me a license," I confirmed. "My card came with a muzzle. They charged me extra for it."

She made a face. "Did they at least let you pick out the color?"

I shook my head, expression grim. "Default beige."

"*Ugh*." Her head rolled right along with her eyes. "That must be so embarrassing for you. The Hannibal look hasn't been in for *years*!"

"It's been tough," I agreed.

"Don't worry. I'll bring it back when I'm big and famous and setting trends. My debut collection will feature a nude restraining mask. I'll call it *The Ethan*," Skylar promised, smiling at me with her eyes. I was starting to think I'd never get sick of their blue, that their novelty would never wear off.

She'd moved closer to me on the couch at some point. Maybe after playing with my hair. Or maybe I'd moved closer to her. Or maybe neither of us had intentionally moved, and gravity had changed directions.

The last option seemed to be the most feasible. It would also explain why my heart didn't know which way to beat.

I cleared my throat and finished off the rest of my drink before asking, "Is that the dream, then? Big-time designer with your own brand?"

She put her empty glass down on the table and hugged her knees to her chest. "No. I mean, it's a goal, but I wouldn't say it's my dream. Maybe a part of it."

There it was again. Curiosity needling restlessly at my chest. Would it be inappropriate to ask her what her dream was? *Guess we're about to find out.* "What is it, then? What's your dream?"

I watched her react to the question, her head tilted to the side under the weight of it, and her blink back at me was at half speed. It took a few moments, but she finally said, "I'll tell you mine if you tell me yours."

*Oh, that's easy.* "I don't really have one."

"What?" she asked, slightly straightening. "Really?"

"Yeah."

"What about becoming CEO?"

"That's not a dream," I said, echoing her words back to her. "It's a goal."

She let out a small "Oh." Then her spine deflated again, bringing her chin back down to her knees. Her brows remained furrowed, like she was trying to make full sense of it.

"It's not weird," I assured her after a while.

"It's a little weird," she argued. "Doesn't everybody have some sort of dream? Even if it's just a small one?"

"I have pretty much everything I want," I told her, standing up. "It's a good life. Not a lot to dream about."

"I mean... I guess..." Skylar muttered, watching as I took our empty glasses to the bar.

"Can you tell me yours now?" I asked, reaching for the bourbon. "Who knows, maybe it'll inspire me."

She didn't take the bait. "No way. It was supposed to be a trade-off, which doesn't work if you don't have anything *to trade*," she explained with both her mouth and her hand. I was really starting to understand the tube man thing. "And also, I can't trust you with my dream knowing what I know now. You're, like, a little dead inside. Probably. What if it's barren in there? And my poor dream just shrivels up and dies?"

I chuckled at the level of feigned concern in her voice. "Can't argue with that, I guess."

"I'm sixty percent serious," she claimed.

"I believe you," I said, handing her a fresh cocktail as I sat back down. "It's fine. You don't have to tell me."

She thanked me for the drink and leaned a shoulder against the leather cushion. "What about when you were little? Five-year-old Alexis was busy chasing Joel around. What about five-year-old Ethan? He must have had a dream."

He absolutely did. "Five-year-old Ethan wanted to be a cape-wielding superhero by day and swim in a giant, pool-size pie by night. Or a giant peanut butter jar. That would have been his dream," I stated, almost certain of its accuracy.

"That's a good one."

"Yeah, I developed a concerning level of obsession with swimming in food when I was a kid," I admitted without thinking. Not like she'd asked. "Once, we tried filling one of the bathtubs with chocolate pudding. Made a massive mess. There were empty pudding cups and spoons and chocolate goo *everywhere*—we were covered in it. One of the maids found us an hour before a bunch of potential buyers were set to arrive since we were trying to sell the house. I've never been yelled at more in my life."

I'd forgotten about that. Felt like a different lifetime.

"Who's 'we'?" Skylar asked. She was leaning in now. We were close enough that my every inhale was filled with her fresh, sweet scent.

It took me a second. "What?"

"You said 'we' tried to fill the bathtub with chocolate pudding. Who's 'we'?"

Oh. "Uh, I don't really remember. Probably with Joel or something," I lied.

Her smile had turned somewhat wistful. "That's a cute story. Do you have any more?"

"Think it's your turn now. What kind of trouble were you getting into as a kid?"

She shifted. Just slightly. "Um, well, I definitely wasn't attempting to fill bathtubs with chocolate pudding. That sounds like a ton of fun."

"What were you doing, then?"

"Drawing, mostly," she said. "I did a lot of that when I was younger. Still do, I guess. Part of my job."

"Come on," I pushed, and maybe I shouldn't have, "everyone has at least one juicy getting-into-trouble story. There has to be one. Did you ever draw on something you weren't supposed to? Alexis did that a bunch."

"No, never. As far as I can remember, at least. Honestly, I was a pretty quiet kid. Kept to myself, mostly," she explained. And it was because of the slight alcohol-induced fog that I'd failed to pick up on the subtle body language sooner. The new forcefulness behind her crafted casual expression, the fidgeting and fiddling of her fingers. "If anything, I might have been too quiet. Actually got into trouble for that at school more than once. Not sure if it counts, though."

"What? Why?" Why would a child get in trouble for that?

Skylar shrugged. "I had a hard time communicating sometimes, and I think a few of my teachers and other adults got a little frustrated with me. Not all that interesting."

She had no idea how much curiosity was gnawing and clawing at my throat, how much worse it got when she glanced down as she spoke.

"I think it's a lot more interesting than you realize," I told her. The truth. But I didn't push anymore.

The corners of her mouth nudged upward at my comment, drawing down my gaze. Her lips were thin and perfectly defined, with a prominent Cupid's bow that looked as though it had been carved by the Roman god himself.

How had I not noticed their shape before? Or the subtle curve of her chin in contrast to the sharpness of her jaw? And how the peaks of her cheeks jutted out, just a little, just enough.

I wasn't sure if it was the bourbon or the skewed direction of gravity that was the culprit behind the way my heart had started to slam forward, slow and heavy, right up against my chest.

Whatever it was turned ten, a hundred, a thousand times worse when my traveling gaze reached her eyes. And the reason as to why I hadn't noticed those other things became so abundantly clear.

They were breathtaking in the inevitable way your lungs stood no chance against icy waters. It was impossible for them not to steal the entirety of your attention so the rest of her snuck up on you slowly, in pieces.

I wondered if she knew the impact they had. If the lingering, lazy gazes were on purpose, to show off the way they'd somehow captured, in their crystallized strokes, so many impossible shades of winter.

"I know I didn't give you any, but will you tell me more stories of when you were a kid?" Skylar asked with slowed blinks, her voice closer to a whisper now. Had I been an inch farther away, I might not have fully heard her.

I could have said no again, insisted on a trade-off, but in that moment, the whiskey would have done anything as an excuse to keep looking. Keep talking. It was the whiskey that complied, told her story after story of pranks gone wrong and self-inflicted haircuts with safety scissors.

And maybe this was more of her "stealth work," but that wouldn't have mattered, either.

I wasn't sure how long we talked and laughed for, but it was long enough for the night to weigh down on our heads. Until we were both leaned into the cushions, fighting sleep.

I eventually lost. I didn't remember it happening, but I must have. Because when I came to, everything was dark. I sat up and looked around, allowing my vision to adjust. But to the whiskey's immediate, irrational disappointment, there were no sneaking burglars or lingering ghosts in limited sight.

The tumblers were also gone, replaced with the pillow my head had been resting on and a blanket covering my body. The same one I'd lent Skylar last week. Maybe that's why I'd dreamed of lemon cakes.

I eventually stood and made my way upstairs, as quietly as my legs would allow. It turned out to be the right call. Skylar's door was left open, just a few inches. Just enough to tug at my lips and chest that she didn't feel the need to shut and lock it. That maybe she felt safe and comfortable here. With me.

*Or maybe she just forgot. Shut up and go to bed—you have a shit ton of work to do tomorrow.*

She was still asleep in the morning when I left, so I put my gloves just outside her door.

That must have also been the whiskey.

## 14

kylar

I DRIFTED in and out of restless "sleep" all night (if you could even call it that), begging, *pleading* for the blender that had taken up unlawful residence inside my stomach to pick any setting other than Crush.

But it was too little, too late.

At one point, in the light of midmorning, I caught myself smiling up at the ceiling like a loon. And then proceeded to not immediately stop. I tried, but the stubborn thing wouldn't leave my face. Not while I showered, or brushed my teeth, or got dressed.

The nerves joined in shortly after I put on pants. They rippled under my skin like I'd chugged a pot of coffee, a little shaky but ready to climb a mountain or three. I'd forgotten what this felt like. About the high-inducing, jittery rush that came with a new crush.

It was very distracting. So much so that I didn't see the

little bundle waiting just outside my door and stepped right on it. The soft, smooth texture of whatever it was didn't match the complaining *crinkle* that accompanied it.

*What...*

I lifted my foot and found myself blinking down at dark brown leather. A pair of gloves, with a folded piece of paper on top.

*Are oversized gloves in? Either way, better than frostbite. (I think? If blackened fingertips are trending, use paint.)*

I read it four times. That didn't include the full minute of just stare-smiling at the piece of paper while my heart adopted an entirely new, uncoordinated rhythm to its beat.

When I was finally able to tear my eyes away, I slipped my fingers into the too-big slots of the gloves. They didn't fit, obviously. Not even a little. They were massive and perfect.

Did this mean he wasn't home, then?

I carefully folded the note back up and ran downstairs, listening for the rustles of another human in the apartment. But I couldn't hear anything...

He wasn't in his study, either. I checked via what I was convinced was a super-casual, nonsuspicious stroll past the open door.

Disappointment pulled at my high when I found the room empty, which was ridiculous. What had I been expecting or hoping for, exactly? Even if he was home, he'd probably spend the majority of the day working, like last weekend.

*That doesn't mean you can't send him a thank-you text for the gloves, though,* my brain justified. *In fact, it would probably be rude* not *to...*

What I didn't see coming was the return of the nerves as soon as I pulled out my phone. How hard should one simple text have been? All I had to do was say something like... like what, exactly? Why was I blanking?

I typed "thank you" a bunch of times and deleted it a bunch of times. Because obviously "thank you," but what else? The two words weren't enough just on their own, yet I couldn't for the life of me come up with what needed to follow them.

I thought about it while the coffee brewed and I watched the eggs cook. Still nothing. Not a single thing until I was mixing the ketchup and hot sauce with my fork. Then I had an idea. A really stupid idea that I was for sure going to regret right away, but an idea nonetheless.

It took a while to set up the scene. I hadn't been anticipating how hard it would be to make a single glove stand on two fingers like a hand man. I had to use fabric tape to hide the pinky and ring fingers, create a little stand out of toothpicks and paper for it to lean back on, then stuff its "legs" and "body" with tissues to make it work. Twenty minutes well spent. Plus another five (okay, ten, maybe fifteen. Drawing the animations on my phone took a bit) to do the rest.

Finally, I got it. A picture of my one-armed, leather monster standing victoriously on the counter, the ketchup-covered fork angled to look like weaponized claws, with my out-of-focus body lying facedown in the background.

His name was Wereglove, and I loved him. He had a snarly little face and a single large fang. I even drew him tiny, curly horns in lieu of the pointy ears usually sported by werewolves. He was supercute if I said so myself. Real lethal-looking, but in a Pixar way.

Did I have to change because I scraped the "bloodied" fork across the back of my white T-shirt a bunch of times to make it look like I'd been attacked by my tiny clawed monster? Yes. Was it worth it? Of course not. Or maybe yes. I wasn't sure whether Ethan would find this funny or really, really stupid.

Scratch that (hah). He was for sure, without a doubt going

to think it was really, really stupid. I sent it anyway, along with a bunch of fang emojis and a message.

**Me: wereglove haTH woneth the bAttle iN Kitchen against punY finger human. alsO, another word with a U in it**

In my mind, Wereglove had a lispy British accent. Quite a posh one, too. The savage.

I sat down to eat my cold eggs, smiling to myself. I expected Ethan was busy and wouldn't respond right away. Or maybe at all. But to my genuine surprise, the small New Message *ding* echoed through the kitchen less than a minute later, casting a swarm of nerves up my chest and through my arms. I reached for my phone right away.

**Ethan: How long did it take you to set that up? Don't lie.**

I huffed a laugh before typing.

**Me: Ethan, please. Time is no object for me**

**Me: Also, you probably didn't catch it because it's so well disguised, but if you look really closely, there's a hidden message in there somewhere. That's all I'm going to say**

**Ethan: Too cryptic. I don't see it.**

**Me: That doesn't surprise me**

There was a small pause before the three dots appeared again.

**Ethan: I can't tell if that was an intentional dig at my intelligence or not.**

**Me: That doesn't surprise me**

**Ethan: I liked you better last week when you were still a little shy.**

**Me: Really?**

**Ethan: No.**

I'd been smiling so much all morning my cheeks were

starting to hurt. I put down my phone and massaged them a little before going back to my eggs.

It wasn't until I'd finished off the plate, cleaned up, and was on my second cup of coffee that my phone dinged again.

**Ethan: Plans tomorrow?**

I blinked down at the screen, trying to make sense of the words. Separately, then together. Plans? Tomorrow? Plans, tomorrow? Why? Why was he ask—

**Ethan: My lawyer has an early draft of an agreement ready. Will be picking up physical copies this aft, we can go over it together if you have time tomorrow.**

*Oh.*

The crash was just as steep and swift as the spike, bringing me back down to reality.

I started to type out my response with shaky fingers. The silly, residual aftermath of my earlier assumption.

**Me: Brunch plans but free after. Let's say 2 pm?**

**Ethan: Perfect.**

I set down my phone, reached for the still-standing monster glove, and started to destuff it.

It was silly and unreasonable, the ball of disappointment rolling up my throat. I forced myself to swallow it back, but all that did was push it down to my stomach, where it had more room to grow.

# 15

# than

The Itch was back.

I'd been sitting there, staring at the desk in front of me, for thirty minutes too long. The glass was covered, end to end, with open screens, paper documents, plans, unread emails, deadlines.

I instructed my hand to move and reach for my pen. But it couldn't hear me and remained white-knuckle clenched.

The Itch had started to bite. At the tips of my fingers, my palms, my ears and my shoulders and my throat and my chest. My eyes. Again and again and again. And a hundred more fucking times, just for good measure. It used to never be this bad, this restless. I could feel it crawling all over my body, bladed tentacles dragging across my skin.

I wanted it off me.

The *swish* of a new message rang against my ears, but my eyes remained fixed on the mess.

Less than a minute before she called. For the third time. I hit Ignore.

It buzzed again, and I snatched the phone off the table, ready to either whip it across the room or tell her to fuck right off. But it wasn't Mila. The missed calls were, but not the text.

Skylar's name flashed up at me from the screen, and my breath hitched in an entirely new way. I opened it to find a picture of... a something. A glove? My glove. The animated version.

How the hell had she managed to make it stand and pose like that? And was that the tip of a fork acting as its oversized claws?

And that wasn't even the best part. His face was. He was ridiculous-looking, with his lopsided horns and crazy eyes. And the longer I stared at that single-fanged, viciously snarling mouth, the funnier it became.

I zoomed into the picture for a closer look at the scene. More specifically, at her. Skylar's comically contorted body was blurred in the background, facedown, elbow-up, with red marks all across her back.

Against all odds, a small laugh tumbled up my chest and managed to escape, leaving in its trail a glowing warmth that relaxed some of my tightened muscles. I smiled as I typed out my reply, and when hers came, I smiled at her quip and the speed of her wit. And when it was over, way too quickly, I wanted to keep it going.

Then it hit me. The sudden, unexpected urge to hear her voice. To the point where my thumb was already hovering over the Call button, but I stopped myself just in time.

Because what the fuck?

I put my phone down and rolled a few feet away from my desk, baffled. Where had that come from?

I'd known her for a week, and suddenly, I wanted to hear

her *voice*? Thinking her eyes were attractive was one thing. Thinking *she* was attractive, or funny, witty, was one thing. I wanted to hear her *voice*? Because I thought it'd make my shit morning a little better?

No, it wasn't just her voice. It was her laugh. I wanted to hear her laugh.

*That's worse, idiot. It's so much w—*

"Is your phone broken?"

Dread snaked through me like a live wire, fast and loose. I looked up to find Mila standing at my door, spine held straighter than the wall beside her.

I'd been so preoccupied and in my head that I hadn't heard the warning *clicks* of her cloven hooves echoing down the hall.

"What?" I asked. Maybe snapped.

Had I thought she was capable of any emotion, including contempt, I'd have sworn she was looking at me like I was every shade of stupid under the sun. "Is your phone broken? Would you like a new one ordered?"

I wasn't even remotely in the mood. "What do you want?"

"Anita would like to see you in her office to go over the preliminary layout plans of the Mahik Island project. She will be flying out to Seattle tonight, so it can't wait until Monday. Grey is already there," she said, her tone curling around the insinuation that, once again, I was holding them up.

*Good*, the bitter voice in my head chimed before I could stop it.

"I'll be there in five," I told Mila. She lingered like she might argue but then thought better of it and left.

I looked back down at my desk, at my phone and the mess that surrounded it, while the *click*s and *snap*s of Mila's steps retreated from my office.

The tension had returned with a vengeance, digging its

nails so deep into my neck I could barely straighten my shoulders as I reached for my phone and started to type.

**Me: Plans tomorrow?**

I didn't need to hear Skylar's voice. I didn't need to hear her laugh. What I needed from her was a signature.

# 16

## kylar

Something was off with him.

Shoulders, maybe? Or did I need to readjust the width of the lapels? Widen them a bit more...

I pulled the desk lamp closer and scanned the sketch again, head to loafers, looking for the detail that was tipping the merlot suit off-balance. *It probably is the lapels*, I thought, releasing the grip my teeth had on the wood of my pencil.

I had my answer sixteen minutes and four adjustments later when I determined that it, in fact, was not the lapels.

*Or maybe I need to move the breast pocket—*

My spine snapped straight with the spirit of a meerkat as soon as the *beeps* of the front door lock went off. Earlier than I'd expected. It was only 5:30.

I bounced out of my chair as the fizz of nervous excitement hit my bloodstream, grabbed the trimmer from its bag, and slipped it into the pocket of my sweater.

Probably the best $28.73 I'd ever spent. I regretted nothing.

I fixed my hair (twice), wiped away the loose mascara flakes from underneath my eyes, then pinched and patted my cheeks to life before trotting downstairs.

He wasn't in the living area or kitchen, and I hadn't heard him come up the stairs, which likely meant...

The door to his office was closed. *So he probably doesn't want to be disturbed*, the small voice in the back of my head noted as my fist raised. I hesitated because maybe it was right.

*I'm for sure right.*

Thus began the internal struggle. I walked away, made it about six steps, then changed my mind and walked back. Then I did it again. It wouldn't hurt to at least knock, right? He could just tell me if he was busy and c—

I jumped a little when the door opened. My feet made it back to the ground right away, but my heart seemed to remain suspended in the air, stuttering at the sight of Ethan in a navy dress shirt. Blue was definitely his color.

As was grey. As was green. As was black.

*Those are literally the only colors you've seen him in so far. Except for, like, white.*

Yes. Right. As was white.

He leaned against the doorway and cocked his head. "What are you doing?"

"Nothing," I said. *Don't be suspicious.* "Just, you know, hanging out."

Brows furrowed over suspicious eyes; the left corner of his lips curled. "Walking back and forth out in the hall?"

"Well, um, I was going to knock." Eventually. Probably.

He didn't say anything, just observed for a few seconds, eyes swimming across my face and leaving splashes of tingling color in their wake.

"Anyways." I cleared my throat, my nervous fingers fidgeting in my pockets. "What's...*up*." The *P* popped from my lips like bubble gum.

The key here was to be super casual, which was a thing I was currently being. Hence the *P* popping. Only casual people did that, I was pretty sure.

"You're up to something," Ethan accused immediately. "What is it?"

I blinked up at him.

"Uhm, I don't know what you're talking about," I attempted to insist. How the heck had he caught on so quick? Had he not *heard* how I'd popped that *P*?

"No?"

"No*pe*," I assured him convincingly.

"You're a terrible liar," he said, smiling just slightly. Like it was forced, but his mouth was too tired to fully commit to the fraud. "But I guess it's better to know that now, ahead of the party." Then he straightened from his lean and walked back to his desk.

I did not look at his butt as he walked away. Nor did my brain make inappropriate comments about its shape.

*Its* perfect *shape. The round, firm—*

*Hush, I'm acting.*

So far, this had not gone according to plan. At all. But at least he hadn't closed the door in my face. So... an invitation?

I took a tentative step inside, looking around.

The furnishings in here gave off a much more traditional and regal feel than anything else in the apartment. It was the Persian carpet, I thought, with the soft creams and muted reds. And all the mahogany wood. The desk, chairs, and bookshelves were all made from the stuff.

But it was cozy, too. Especially now, at night, with only the desk lamp turned on. That recliner in front of the fireplace was a prime sketching spot. There was also a black gym bag perched right beside it, which explained the biceps I may or may not have had at least one dream about. But how the hell did he find the time?

"You can come in," Ethan said, noting the way I was just sort of... awkwardly hovering near the door. "I'm almost done."

"You're still working?"

I didn't know how he did it. How he—or *anyone*—could work this much without burning out. It didn't seem possible to me.

"No, just an email to my lawyer," he said.

*Still...*

I took a seat in one of the chairs facing his desk and started to observe, quietly. Mostly my surroundings. The leather-bound books, floral fixtures... Ethan's tense, concentrated brows...

I pulled my eyes away, up to the crystal chandelier, only to have them rebel and sneak back down, fixating on his jaw and throat this time.

So then I forced my gaze away again.

And... again.

It wasn't entirely my fault, though, was it? How were his eyelashes *so ridiculously* long? It was really, very hard not to stare. Near impossible for absolutely anyone, I'd wager—

"Okay," he said a little suddenly, closing his laptop and pushing it aside. The movement was more aggressive than I'd been expecting.

Also, either I'd been too distracted by his eyelashes to notice when his fingers had moved, or he hadn't actually typed anything... just stared at the screen.

"Spill," he said.

*Um...* "What?"

He was leaning forward now, elbows planted on the desk. "What are you up to?"

*Damn it.* "I already told you, I'm not up to anything?"

Was I asking him? Why had that come out as a question?

*Because he's right, and you're a bad liar.*

*I said hush!*

"You sure?" Ethan drawled.

"Mhhmm." It was fine. This was fine. I could still recover.

"Then what's that?" He pointed right at it. At the spot where my fingers were curled around the trimmer. *Inside* my loose pocket.

Honestly. It would have been easier to pull this off on an actual, literal detective.

I was not impressed. "Why are you like this?"

His chuckle at that was huffy and light. Like the energy it took to muster it had been scraped from the bottom of a near empty barrel.

"I grew up with two siblings and a Joel, Skylar. At this point, I've pretty much seen and done it all."

"And become no fun in the process." Someone had to tell him.

"Seriously, what is it?" he asked again. And I could tell it was morphing into a game for him. A puzzle.

"Well, now you're never gonna know." If I didn't get to have my fun, then neither did he. "Because you're a bummer, and I don't wanna play with you anym—"

I was interrupted by a muffled, thick *bzzzz.*

My thumb had accidentally pushed against the power button of the trimmer when I shifted forward in my seat so I could get up and leave.

So *bzzzz* went the foiled plan against the fabric of my sweater, sounding. Exactly.

Like.

A.

Vibrator.

Ethan's eyebrows shot up.

And I could feel it. My whole body burning crimson. Yet the only thing I could do was stare. One eternity, two eternities, three, four.

Then, a miracle. My thumb received a signal from my last remaining, panicking brain cell and pushed the button again.

The *bzzzz* cut off.

Right then would have been the perfect time for me to explain myself. But instead, even after a long stretch of silence, the best I could come up with was "Um..."

That response, evidently, made Ethan *more* suspicious. His eyes moved from my pocket to my face. Then, he let out a slow "What..."

I took the trimmer out and held it up in lieu of a verbal clarification, thinking that the visual would be the quickest way to explain. But instead of the *aha, that explains it* look I was expecting from him, Ethan's eyes widened with shock, and his mouth silently stuttered with unsteady little movements.

*Why...* I looked at the trimmer in my hand and realized, only then, that with the rounded protective lid on, the stupid thing kinda, sorta, really looked a little bit like a—

"No! Nono!" Because *oh. My. Actual. Fucking. God.* From his perspective, it looked like I, the village lunatic, was maybe proudly shoving a potential vibrator in his *face*. I full-on panicked. "Look it's a thing a thing a one of the a trimmer thing look!"

I ripped the lid off and threw it to the side. "It's a trimmer, hair trimmer, for your hair. See? It was gonna be a joke. Like a stupid, stupid joke. From last night. Remember?"

It took a second. Or thirty trillion. I didn't know. I regretted everything. My timing had been off. He had clearly been in no mood—

Ethan's mouth started to spread into a slow, understanding grin, his hands came up to his face, and he managed a defeated "Jesus fucking Christ" before the chuckles kicked in.

They started slow and soft, almost muted, given away mostly by the shaking of his chest. Emphasis on *started* that way. Because next thing I knew, he was full-on laughing. And laughing.

...

And laughing.

"In my defense, this is, in its entirety, your fault," I grumbled while he practically doubled over in hysterics.

My heart was still jammed in my throat, trying to wiggle its way out. Also, breathing had become a bit of a manual task.

Finally, he was able to gather himself enough to sit upright again and drop his hands.

He was still chuckling, cheeks flushed, brown eyes bright and wet with too much laughter. It was... he looked younger, a little boyish, even.

"Just... your face... I wasn't..." he started, then was overtaken, once again, by a fit of laughter.

"Would you calm down? It wasn't that funny," I pointed out, trying to sound annoyed. It didn't work. My whole chest was practically vibrating with satisfaction. I'd made him laugh.

Not, like, on purpose. It sounded like he was mostly laughing at my face. But still.

Eventually, it subsided enough that he asked, "What could your original plan possibly have been? What were you going to do with the trimmer?"

I felt like the answer to that would have been pretty obvious. A trimmer had a limited number of functions. And I could personally only think of one. "Three guesses," I told him, turning the device on. Purposefully this time.

Ethan's eyes narrowed slowly, but the smile never left his lips. The only thing I took from that was encouragement.

"Skylar." It was a warning.

"Wrong." I stood up. "Two more."

"Skylar." Still smiling. *Encouragement.* "If you come near me with—"

"Nope! One guess left," I said, rounding the desk. "Wow. You really suck at this game."

Ethan's chair had swiveled, allowing him to face me the whole way around, until I was standing not two feet away from him. "If you so much as point that thing in my direction, I'll—"

"I'm afraid that's also incorrect." I tilted my head, feigning stupidity. My brain cell lost its footing against said tilt and tumbled nucleus-first into my skull and died, probably. Because clearly I wasn't thinking anymore. At all. Just moving.

Ethan caught my wrists as soon as I reached forward and held them still. He was laughing again, eyes bright with amusement. "I can't believe my sanity was the one being questioned all of last week. Or that you tricked me into thinking you were at all quiet and shy."

"Shhh. It's okay. Just the middle," I assured him in a gentle, soothing voice. My lips were trembling with the effort it was taking to hold back my own laughter. "Just like we talked about."

"Skylar, if you shave the middle of my head, I'm shaving yours." A promise. We were mock struggling now, my arms gently pushing forward, rebelling against Ethan's grip.

"I have excellent bone structure and would pull off the balding middle-aged man look with *ease*," I informed him proudly, inspiring another chuckle. "And it'd probably come with a raise, so joke's on you."

"You're right. We should do yours first, get you that raise," he offered, generous as he was.

The pushes and tugs of the giggle-filled struggle had moved us closer. My face above his was only inches away, and I could smell the subtle spices of a cologne or aftershave on him. There were tingles and swirls, and half my vital organs had grown wings.

And that was why, just for a second, I forgot what we were even doing. I forgot why we were wrestling, I was so distracted by his everything.

But it only lasted for that one second.

Because then...

I slipped.

My hand slipped. His grip had loosened through his laughter, and my arm was pushing, and I wasn't paying attention.

I heard it first. Because my eyes were locked in a tight, breathless tango with Ethan's.

It was the slightest shift to the tone of the *bzzzz* and lasted less than a quick heartbeat.

We both froze.

It took its time, the small chunk of chestnut brown hair falling onto Ethan's shoulder. Unsuspectingly cavalier, like an autumn leaf swaying in the opening scene of an apocalyptic horror film in which everyone dies a gruesome death within the first three minutes.

*Oh no.*

I turned off the trimmer just as Ethan let go of my wrist and slowly, oh so slowly, picked up the chunk of hair.

Then he looked back at me, gaping expression mirroring mine. And I thought for sure he would be mad. I expected it and was going to apologize and grovel and pay for a haircut to fix it and—

He smiled. And his eyes...

*Ah, crap.*

I ran.

# 17

## Skylar

TWO STEPS. I made it two steps before realizing that Ethan was still holding on to my other arm.

He hadn't expected me to run, though, because I was able to slip out of his grasp with a single pull and book it out of the room.

The squeak of a chair. A deep chuckle. Quick steps behind me.

I laughed as my heart bounced around in my chest, adrenaline pumping my legs faster toward the stairs.

I was probably about to die. Or be balded.

It was the most fun I'd had in ages.

I made it all the way to the top of the stairs before his arms were around my waist and my feet were lifted off the ground.

"*Ooooh*mygod, no, I'm sorry!" I half yelled, half giggled. "I didn't mean to! I swear I didn't mean to! Don't shave the middle of my head—I'll look like a Muppet! A hot one, but still!"

We were in his room now, and he was taking me toward... Oh man. "Ethan, that is *so much worse* than what I did! Have mercy!"

Didn't work. Five seconds later, I was lying on my back, on the carpet, right beside the balcony.

My feet started to scramble in an attempt to shovel me away, but it was too little, too late. I was cornered. And doomed. The glass door had already slid open, and Ethan had already scooped up the first serving of fresh, powdered snow.

"Okay, okay okay okay," I said, putting my hands up in surrender. "Tit for tat. Shave a chunk of my hair off. On the side, like yours."

That didn't work, either. "I'll give you one way out," Ethan said, holding the threat right above my face like a madman. He had a knee planted on either side of my hips. "Take back what you said about my jaw and my teeth."

An unreasonable demand by any standard.

"Absolutely no—*pffftfhps.*" I got a mouthful of the snow ruthlessly dropped right onto my face. Oh, how he laughed.

"Tell me I have pretty teeth," Ethan ordered again.

"No, you weirdo!" I was no lying coward. "They're creepy and straight and white. You're like the Ghost of Toothpaste Commercials Past—" I squealed and giggled as he swept my protective arms away. The next handful of snow went straight onto my neck and holy "*shit* that's cold!"

"Say it!"

"No!"

More snow. Right onto my forehead and eyes.

"On second thought, take your time. I could do this all night." Ethan's elated voice said from above me.

"Bet no woman's ever said *that* to you before, either—" In my mouth again. Two scoops. I spit it out and was laughing so hard by this point that I could barely see or breathe.

I brought a sleeve to my face, and he let me. The fool. So as soon as I'd wiped the tears and melting ice away, I grabbed a fistful of revenge and chucked it right at him.

Nothing could have delighted Ethan more than getting snowballed in the face, apparently, judging by that laugh. He wiped it all away with a single swipe of his arm, and then he... then he...

...

...

*Whoa.*

The gears in my head jammed, unable to churn past that one word as I blinked up at him.

He had both hands placed on the carpet now, one on either side of my head. Laughter had reached his squinting eyes, crinkling their corners with pure, unadulterated glee. And he was smiling down at me.

It was the same boyish grin he'd worn downstairs but entirely free from all the tension he held in... well, everywhere. All the time. Only I hadn't realized just how much of it there was until his features had been wiped clean from it. The difference was... drastic.

Breathtaking, even.

I couldn't stop staring.

"I'd take that back if I were you." His words came out as a low murmur. My stomach clenched. Then other things... clenched.

And suddenly, I was very, *very* aware of the proximity and positioning of our bodies. Of the heat radiating from him, in stark contrast to the frigid air spilling through the open balcony door. And I knew the exact moment the awareness flamed my cheeks because his eyes flickered right to them.

"U-um" was what came out of my mouth when I opened it, the sequence of words orchestrated in my head blocked by the surprised nerves balled in my throat.

I swallowed.

Ethan's eyes fell down, tracing the motion. And there was no way he couldn't see my heartbeat hammering out of my neck.

His grin started to wane, slowly. And if I wasn't in the middle of a cardiac episode of sorts, I'd have been furious with myself for ruining it.

I lay still under his gaze as it traveled up from my throat to my eyes and lingered, then lowered again to lock onto my lips. And I was sure... I was *so sure* he was going to—

A gust of wind stabbed the air around us; I shivered.

Ethan stiffened.

He blinked.

Another blast of freezing air and he was standing, closing the balcony door, and taking steps back.

"I—uh," he said as I sat up. "Sorry."

I took a sleeve to my face and neck, wiping away the residual bits of melting ice. My hands were shaking. "For what?"

He didn't answer, just reached into a drawer, grabbed a towel, and handed it to me.

"Thanks," I said.

And then a silence, coupled with... an awareness of sorts. One that was going to turn things awkward any second now...

*So say something before it does.*

"Um, I'm sorry about your hair," I said. Thankfully, it wasn't that bad, hadn't shaved too close to the scalp and would be a pretty easy fix, but still. "I'm also sorry to be the one to tell you that, unlike me, you would not make a sexy bald Muppet."

It worked. It took a second, but it worked. The corners of his lips twitched, just before it turned into a full smile and, eventually, a chuckle.

Satisfaction whirled in my chest.

"You simply don't have my bone structure," I went on, encouraged. "But then again, who does?"

It was a joke. Clearly, it was a joke. And I expected a retort, a continuation of the playful banter our conversations seemed to naturally fall into. But Ethan didn't say anything, he just... looked.

And looked.

*Should have stopped while you were ahead.* "Um, I wasn't being..."

"Have you had dinner yet?"

I stopped, my mouth falling slightly open. That... had not been on the list of things I thought he'd say next.

"Not yet," I answered, detaching myself from any expectations as to what would come next. I'd learned that lesson already.

"There's an Italian place," he said after a small, considering pause. "It's a bit of a drive, but I've been meaning to try it for a while. Wanna go?"

He was... was he... like, a date?

No, probably not...

Or, like, maybe?

My thoughts ribboned into opposing directions, my fingers fidgeting with my sleeve. "Now?"

The left corner of his lips curled, just slightly. I really, *really* liked it when they did that. "Yes," he said.

The instructions from the voice in my head were crystal clear: Play it cool. Play it cool. *Play. It. Cool.*

Yet my facial muscles barely put up a fight against the loony grin that was pushing its way through. "Okay, sure. I just need to dry my hair and get changed. Meet you downstairs in ten?"

And I could have sworn he was holding back his own smile. "Meet you downstairs in ten."

~

"So, WHERE ARE WE GOING?" I asked as we pulled out of the garage.

"Guelph."

"Cool. Haven't had Italian in a while. Do they have a good low-carb selection?" Or was I going to get to see him cheat and stuff his face with pizza? God, I hoped it would be the latter. Maybe I could figure out a way to convince him...

Ethan glanced over at me, clearly amused. "Guelph is the name of the city we're going to. It's a little over an hour away."

I... wait, what? "We're leaving Toronto?"

"We're leaving Toronto."

Well, that made very little sense. "Isn't there like a hundred Italian restaurants in this city?"

"Maybe more."

"And we're still going to Guelph?"

"Yup."

I narrowed my eyes at him. Mikaela had totally called it. I'd never say it to her face, mostly because I probably wouldn't get to, but she'd totally called it. "Is this a cover? Are you taking me to a remote location to murder me and steal my skin? Is it because I said you had creepy teeth? Because, honestly, you can barely even see their radioactive glow when your mouth is closed."

That made him laugh. *Purr*, went my insides.

"Not quite. I need you alive for at least a few more months," he pointed out. "After that, though, all bets are off."

I smiled and leaned back into my seat, settling in. "I've been warned."

This was going to be fun.

# 18

**than**

"...ETHAN, I'm *telling you*, you're straight up wrong."

"I'm not wrong," I insisted *again*. "It's disgusting."

"You literally *just* said you've never even tried it!" Skylar was sitting up now, spine perked and twisted in the passenger seat to face me.

"That logic is flawed," I said, throwing her another quick glance. "I don't need to lick fish guts off of wet tar to know I wouldn't like it."

"*Ew!*"

"*Exactly*."

"No, not *exactly*, you freaking weirdo!" She flicked my arm with the end of her scarf. "Fish guts on *wet tar* isn't the same thing as pineapples on pizza! What's the matter with you?"

"It's almost the exact same thing."

How had we arrived here? Ten minutes ago, she'd been talking about how woodpeckers wrap their tongues around the back of their brains to protect them from injury when they hammered their beaks against wood.

Then I'd made a joke about a different type of wood hammering, which had surprised even me.

Then she'd tried not to laugh. She'd failed, quickly.

And I wasn't sure how we'd gone from that to this.

I wasn't sure how I'd gone from the shit mood I'd been in all day, to catching her suspiciously pacing outside my door, to her "accidentally" shaving a chunk of my hair off, to me torturing her with snow, to *this*.

To actively having to restrain myself from pulling the car over and Skylar onto my lap, plans and contracts be damned.

I couldn't get my eyes to stop flickering over to her lips every two seconds. Like moths to an irritated, pouty flame. They tinted red when she was riled up. Because of course they did. Of course she was insanely attractive, even while annoyed.

I felt a little punch-drunk.

"And would you keep your eyes on the road?" she complained, nudging her head sideways toward the traffic. "Isn't it, like, moose season up here?"

The laugh escaped before I could stop it, and I didn't miss her satisfied smirk. But I did comply. I peeled my gaze off her and stuck it back on the road for the remainder of the drive.

Mostly.

But she only caught me twice. Glared at me twice. Held back her smile twice. All the while trying to convince me that pineapple on pizza was, in fact, "not a crime against humanity" and I was "the most absurd and unreasonably dramatic person" she'd "ever met" for claiming such a thing, which was "saying a lot" because "I *literally* work in fashion, Ethan."

I couldn't stop smiling. Really, truly, could not stop smiling. Which only seemed to encourage her to keep going.

And going.

And before I knew what had even happened, we were sitting at a small pizzeria three blocks down from the restaurant I'd planned on taking us to. Because she'd dared me. Or it was a bet? Kind of a blur, getting here.

"Eat it," Skylar demanded, shoving a slice of Hawaiian toward my face. "Tell me I'm right."

I leaned away, glaring down at her hand. "I can't believe you convinced me to do this. Do you know how hard it is to get a last-minute table on a Saturday night at the place we were supposed to go to?"

She rolled her eyes, lips twitching. God, they were good lips. I couldn't keep my eyes from zeroing in on them every two seconds.

"I literally just said, 'Hey, Ethan, bet you won't eat a whole slice of pizza with pineapple on it' *as you were opening the restaurant door*, and you turned us around and practically shoved me all the way down here," she claimed. Which was a lie. It couldn't possibly have been that easy. "It was *that* easy. Now, are you going to eat, or do I win?"

I snatched the slice out of her hand and bit into it.

It was abhorrently revolting and inedible, just like I knew it would be. But at the same time, it wasn't that bad. "I hate it," I told her, taking another bite. It was sort of a strange combination... not bad, just strange. And maybe a little good. "You were right, it's not the same thing. I'd rather eat the tar."

A slow, easy smile started to spread across her face, drawing my eyes down. Again. I wondered if she noticed.

"Yeah, looks like you're really struggling through it," Skylar drawled.

"Understatement. You should feel terrible for making me do this." Another bite.

I ate four slices and missed zero of the smirks, eye rolls, and quips.

I was baffled by how increasingly comfortable it was with her. And distracting, effortless, *fun*. She was so much fun. The conversation and banter flowed naturally, and I... started to consider it again, weighing the pros and cons again. Arriving at the same conclusion... again. I needed—

"Ethan?"

I looked up.

I froze.

It took me a long, long second to process what was happening.

Because at first, I thought, *no way*. What were the chances? What were the chances of running into *him*, *here* of all places? While I was with *her*, of all people.

Zero. It had to be zero.

No.

Less than zero. The probability of this was less than zero.

"Ethan... holy shit. You're so... grown-up." The words were stretched and carried too much air, as though *he* couldn't believe it.

It was my turn to say something, I knew that. But shock and disbelief had sewn my throat shut. So I just... I didn't know what I was doing. But there was quite a bit of staring involved.

"You probably don't—uh, it's been a while. You probably don't recognize me, huh?" he went on.

That should have been true. I shouldn't have recognized him. I didn't think Alexis or Grey would. Maybe not even Anita, though I couldn't be sure on that one.

It'd been twelve years; his hair was more salt than pepper now, and there were permanent lines etched into the skin around his eyes. Yet he somehow looked *younger*, softer.

The turbulent mix of stress and exhaustion that used to be so prominent in his features was gone. The consistent, disapproving frown that was near identical to his brother's, gone.

He looked like a different person. Felt like a different person. It'd been a shock, seeing the photos last year. I didn't know what I'd been expecting when I'd searched for them, but it hadn't been... that. It hadn't been *this*.

"Carlo?" I finally managed. I didn't know why the end of his name curled into a question. It didn't need to be.

My uncle's face split into an unfamiliar, goofy grin. One I'd only ever witnessed on him in pictures. The new pictures. From after. "It's nice to see ya, kid."

It was?

I didn't think it would be. I didn't think he'd want to talk to me or to any of us.

But maybe I was projecting.

"It's nice to see you too. How, uh—how've you been?" My voice sounded thick, rusty, unused. I cleared my throat, like it would help.

"Good. Great, actually. A bit hectic around the house with two kids and another one coming, but I wouldn't have it any other way."

My eyes moved to the blonde woman sitting at a booth directly across the room from us and the two six-year-olds with her. One boy, one girl. Lanya, Romeo, Riley.

Lanya smiled when she caught my eye. Smooth and polite.

"Lanya, my wife," Carlo said, tone lifting with pride. "And the, uh, chaotic handful that are Romeo and Riley. Twins." Then he looked at me again, his grin in full, goofy tact. So strange. "What are the odds of that, eh? Both brothers having twins? Though Enzo was quite a bit younger than me when he had you boys. More energy, too, I gather."

That was it. That was how casually he brought up Dad.

With none of the venom or bitterness in his voice that I would've expected.

But maybe that was more projecting on my part.

Before I could wrap my head around... *any* of it, Carlo's attention shifted to my left, then moved back to me expectantly.

*Skylar.*

"Right. Sorry, uh, Skylar, this is my uncle, Carlo." I sounded so ridiculously stiff and robotic. "Carlo, this is my... this is Skylar."

Thankfully, they took it from there. Polite introductions, polite small talk in polite voices, while I gathered my... wits? Brains? Chill?

Whatever would make thinking and talking easier.

"We're here for two more days."

I'd inadvertently tuned out, trying to detangle my thoughts. So it took a moment—and the gentle brush of a knee against mine under the table—to realize Carlo was talking to me again.

"We're visiting Lanya's family, then headed back to Vancouver on Monday morning. We live out there now," he explained.

I nodded like it was new information.

I wondered if Anita knew. That he'd moved across the country, gotten married, had kids. That she'd done him a favor. That they'd both clearly, inadvertently done him a favor.

There was no doubt in my mind that Dad had known. Enzo Milani had kept tabs on everyone, knew everything. How else would he have been able to stay in complete control?

Carlo shifted from one foot to the other, making no effort to hide his hesitation as he took out his wallet.

"I know things between me and your dad weren't great in the end there. Before I left and all. But I, uh, I want you to know that I don't hold any of that against you boys. Or your sister, of course. You were good kids, all three of you." He kept his eyes on the card as he talked, then placed it down in front of me. "If you want to have coffee and catch up tomorrow before we leave, or whenever you're in my neck of the woods, call me."

And then he left. Just like that. Without waiting for an answer. Carlo waved, said goodbye, told Skylar it was lovely to meet her, and went back to his wife and kids.

To his *wife* and *kids*.

*Carlo*.

# 19

kylar

I'd personally never seen a ghost. But—

*Really? Is now* really *the best time to be jinxing your lack of encounters with supernatural entities?*

Mikaela's voice in my head.

My hand curled into a fist and tapped the underside of the wooden table. A ritualistic one, two, three.

Just in case.

Ethan, who wasn't helping by acting like *he'd* just seen a ghost, didn't notice. He was too busy... processing. Which, from the looks of it, meant turning a somewhat concerning shade of perplexed pale and staring down at the white business card in his hand like he was expecting it to hatch any second now.

Carlo sat at a table across the room with his back turned to us, which worked in my favor because he couldn't see my eyes shifting between him and his malfunctioning nephew every few seconds.

"So," I said after a long minute or two of waiting out Ethan's shock. "That's the uncle you were talking about? In the car with Alexis the day we..." I almost said "went to the hospital" but decided against it. "The day we visited your grandmother?"

Ethan tapped the card against the table and muttered his confirmation. "That's the one," he said.

Huh. I mean, obviously, I knew it had to be him because what were the chances Ethan had *two* uncles named Carlo. But still... "I know I was working with a very limited amount of information, but I have to say, he's not how I imagined," I said honestly, watching as Carlo brushed the hair out of his daughter's face. Both of them laughed when the curls fell right back. "Like, at all."

*That* dude was the serial philanderer with a messy reputation and mistresses in every city? The one pulling a purple elastic off his wrist and helping his six-year-old tie her unruly hair back?

"A lot can change in twelve years. Apparently."

I let my gaze settle back on Ethan like it wanted to. Like it *always* wanted to, the insatiable bastard.

In my defense, Ethan constantly had the whole "conventionally attractive" thing going on. *Constantly*. Guy never gave it a rest. So how much of the staring was my fault, really?

Even right now. Why did his shoulders need to be so broad *while* he looked like he was edging the cusp of an existential crisis? Was it really necessary?

And why was his frown so sexy? It made the muscles in his jaw clench all tight, which thinned his mouth into a prim, stubbornly smooth line, *which then* resulted in the subtlest curve of a dimple on his chin.

"You're a twin?" I asked, veering entirely off topic.

Unspoken, inappropriate translation: *"There's* two *of you? Does he also have a tiny chin dimple that only comes out when he's unhappy that I kinda, really wanna kiss? Or do the gods just love you the most?"*

"Fraternal," Ethan explained, eyes drifting back to me. The frown started to slowly morph into soft amusement as he took in my expression. "Barely counts."

"Oh, I think it definitely counts," I argued, and his little smirk jerked. *Encouragement.* "Which one of you is the evil one? And I don't want to hear 'there's no evil twin, Skylar,' because everybody knows there's *always* an evil twin, Ethan."

And I could actually see as it happened. The physical changes as his focus shifted from whatever was going on in his head to our conversation. His shoulders deflated an inch, his eyebrows relaxed, lids lowered to half-mast, and that lopsided smirk I was a little too obsessed with was spreading.

It was more gratifying than it had any right to be when he looked at me like that. It caused a whole bunch of manic fluttering in my chest, like my heart had grown its third pair of uncoordinated baby bird wings.

Ethan's eyes meandered to my heated cheeks, left to right, then lowered down to my lips before coming back up to my eyes. They took their time. Like, they *really* took their time.

I didn't mind.

"I'd like to hear your theory," he drawled. "Which twin do you think is the evil one?"

"And what makes you think I have a theory?" I asked, blinking up at him innocently.

He'd moved closer, gaze latched onto mine.

"The fact that you didn't automatically assume it was Grey implies you definitely have a theory."

I narrowed my eyes at him, unable to push down my smile. "You're too observant for your own good, you know."

"Let's hear it" was what he said. "*This should be good*" was what his tone implied.

"Fine," I caved, preparing for my ramble with a deep inhale. He was probably going to regret asking, but okay. "Grey would be the obvious first guess for any fool, but as you must know by now, *I'm* no fool. I've seen enough movies to know there's a 42 percent chance of a twist coming, where *you* end up being the evil twin. But we're going to round that up to 80 percent due to the *substantial* amount of evidence stacked against you. And by 'substantial,' I mean three."

I held up my fist so my fingers could count along as I listed my irrefutable proof of his villainy. "One: it's always part of the evil twin's plan to *not* tell people he's a twin in the first place. Feels like a pretty pertinent piece of information to leave out of your info sheet, Ethan. Should have been one of the first things listed.

"Two: according to every animated movie ever, villains almost always have weird teeth. It's part of their counterculture. Yours are like Gaston's but on steroids."

"Who's Gaston?"

"I don't answer stupid questions," I told him without pause. A laugh burst out of him, my insides purred, and I kept going. *Encouragement.*

"And three: villains make you sign contracts and agree to things that are untoward all. The. Time. It's probably like the first thing they teach in Villainous Tactics 101 - The Unethics of Menace," I leaned back and crossed my arms with as much arrogance as I could muster, like I'd totally got him, like it *all* made so much sense.

Ethan's eyes were narrowed into thinking slits, his smiling

lips parted. "So... if I'm the villain, do you think *Grey* is the protagonist? Like, is he the good guy?"

"No. *I'm* the protagonist," I said, pressing a finger to my chest. "Grey's like the weird, mysterious side character that doesn't show up 'til halfway through the movie or something. His relevance is still pending—to be determined."

"He has no relevance," Ethan claimed, bringing his arm up to rest on the back of the booth, right against my shoulder.

"TBD," I insisted, leaning into his arm. And there it was again, the soft and spicy scent of his cologne. "Also, don't think I haven't noticed that you're not denying any of this."

He shrugged. "Villains are almost always more interesting than the good guys anyway. Cool backstories, less cookie-cutter, monotonous personalities. More monologuing would be the downside, but I can deal with that. I'll take it."

...

*Damn it.*

"That's actually not entirely incorrect."

"What? You wanna jump over to the dark side? That easy, huh?"

"That depends. Is there an initiation process? And how weird is it? Like, will I have to eat the heart of a sacrificial blobfish while chanting in hieroglyphics under the full blood moon? Or go through an entire fifty-pack of teeth whitening strips in twelve hours like you obviously had to do? Because, honestly, it's not worth it. I'll stick to the boring hero role."

"I..." Ethan had to stop himself for a second and make room for the delayed, airy chuckle. Then he asked, "How exactly does one chant in a logographic system of writing for an ancient language they don't speak?"

I waved a hand at him. "You're overthinking it. This is a *villainous* ritual meant for the bad guys, Ethan. So you'd probably just do the most ignorant and offensive thing and just start announcing the pictures out loud. Like 'standing man pointing,' 'duck,' or 'slug-looking snake.'"

"A... slug-looking snake."

"That's actually a real symbol. It's a horned viper, to be specific. But looks kind of like a slug with the way it was drawn. Also, fun fact, sometimes the snake symbols, viper included, were changed up by scribes in pretty gnarly ways to make sure they didn't come to life and attack the reader. Like cutting them up or stabbing them in the back with multiple knives. In the literal, nonfigurative way."

Ethan was sitting so close now that, even in the somewhat ambient lighting of the restaurant, I could make out every spec of chocolate and honey in his eyes. They were so warm. It was like basking in the sun every time he looked at you.

"And how do you know this?" he asked. Sort of murmured, actually.

*Movies.* "I read and stuff," I claimed. "Also, knowledge of ancient languages? Badass villain skill to have. I'd make such a good bad guy."

Granted, said knowledge was limited to five symbols and the snake thing, but still.

Ethan's lips quirked again. "You know bad guys actually have to be *bad*, right? And do bad things. That's the whole point."

The perfect opportunity to be flirtatiously coy, and yet... "You're underestimating me, Ethan. I do so many things badly. Synchronized swimming, keeping plants alive, *cooking*. I'm a horrendous cook, ask anyone. Ask Mikaela. I poisoned her *once*, just once, like *two* whole years ago, and now she refuses to put anything I make anywhere near her mouth. Which is an overreaction on her part, I'm sure you'd agree."

I'd have been more disappointed in myself for not going down the flirty route if Ethan hadn't laughed the way he did at my answer. Instead, I all but melted right onto his lap like butter.

Simon had always hated when I took our conversations on a tangent, and he never laughed at my stupid jokes. Not once. He didn't think they were funny or entertaining. He didn't think *I* was funny or entertaining.

My ramblings annoyed the hell out of him. Most of the time, he'd roll his eyes and tap his foot until I shut up. Because Simon liked me the way I was at the beginning, quiet and reclusive—an ornament.

But then again, so did my parents. None of it was anything new, so I didn't question it. For the two years I was in that relationship, I thought it was me. For the first twenty years of my life, I thought it was me.

And those were the people I was thinking about at that moment as I watched Ethan laugh. Simon and my parents. So, when his chuckles subsided and he said, "I can't believe you used to be the quiet kid," my filter slipped.

And so did my answer.

"Yeah, well, not everybody can tolerate me as well as you seem to be able to."

I didn't even realize what I'd said until he reacted. Until the smile flickered and confusion strained his brows.

"What does that mean?" he asked.

"Nothing," I said quickly. "Sorry. That came out wrong."

Ethan's frown was back, full force. "I don't... I don't *tolerate* you, Skylar. Is that really what you think? Is that how this is coming across to you?"

Oh god. "*No*. It's not," I insisted. "It was just a poor choice of words. I didn't mean it like that. I swear."

"Okay," he said softly, so I let out a breath. It was premature. "What did you mean by it, then?"

*Damn it.*

I racked my brain for an excuse and came up blank. I couldn't think of a single lie to tell in the moment. Not one.

*You could just tell him the truth.*

*No.*

*Part of the truth.*

*No.*

*Okay, well, then come up with a lie faster. You can't just keep blankly staring back at—*

"Skylar? What did you mean by it?"

I was going to do the denial thing again. I was. I even got as far as opening my mouth, ready to insist that it really was just a poor choice of words. But then, Ethan cheated.

Or, like, his fingers did. The ones attached to the arm that was resting beside my shoulder.

They found the back of my neck and started grazing, gentle as feathers, up, then down.

The sensation caught me so off guard that I inhaled audibly.

He smiled at my reaction. Up and down his fingers went while my deflating brain started to puddle onto the floor of my skull.

"U-um."

"Tell me," he murmured. Up, down.

"I don't know. Nothing."

Up.

Down.

"You sure?" Circle.

*Holy hell.*

*Breathe.*

"You're cheating." Shouldn't have breathed. Too much air. "This is cheating."

"Mmm. Should I stop?" Up. Do*wn*. His pinky dipped beneath the neck of my shirt, and I was pretty sure I made a "no" noise with my exhale. Or some sort of other noise.

I wasn't sure, but I was pretty sure.

The left corner of his lips curled. I wanted to touch it with my mouth.

Up, down.

*Ciiiiircle.*

"Tell me." His voice was such a low, heavy purr that it plunged right down to my core. And he was so close. He was *so* close. Soft, clean spice.

"Nothing to tell." I deserved an award for retaining my ability to speak and hold my ground during... whatever this was. I honestly didn't know. Didn't care as long as it didn't stop.

"You're a bad liar."

"I'm no—mnmnm." Because his thumb got involved, drawing small circles right behind my ear. "This is, um, warfare. Psychological."

His thumb moved down, and I prayed to the planets that he couldn't feel the tangled, clumsy flaps of my heart beating against my neck.

"Villains don't play fair, Skylar. Everybody knows that."

I had to grip the edge of the booth to stop myself from leaning into his palm. And climbing onto his lap so I could have my wicked way with him right then and there.

"I can play unfairly, too, you know," I claimed with false confidence. I doubted there was anything I could do to make him act like a drunk, touch-deprived cat.

"I believe you," Ethan mused lightly. Up, down. "But first, tell me what you meant."

Right. That. The thing we were talking about when there were a hundred *way* better things we could be doing with our mouths.

"Why do you want to know so bad?" Why did it even matter?

"Because you keep not telling me things. About your childhood, your dreams, and now this. And it's starting to drive me a little crazy."

*Oh.* So it was like... a game? He wanted to know because I wouldn't tell him?

"You know more about me than most people," I argued as his fingers adopted new, torturously delicate patterns across the base of my skull. I hated it. I loved it. I hated how much I loved it. "You had me fill out a whole document about myself, remember?"

Something flashed behind the molten brown of his eyes. He hadn't been expecting me to put up this much of a fight.

Was I winning? Is that what felt so good? Or was that still his fingers?

I didn't know; I just kept going, chasing the high. Chasing revenge. "It's not my fault you didn't ask the right questions, is it, *Ethan.*"

I put as much warm honey behind his name as I could manage, letting it roll off my tongue slowly as my eyes trailed down to his faltering smirk. I lingered there. One beat, two beats, three, four. Five.

...

Six.

And then my eyes went back up.

It *worked*. His fingers had slowed to a stop, and he blinked back at me, lips parting. The smirk was gone.

Ha-*hah*! My lungs were filled with helium as I grabbed hold of the reins. It was my turn; I just needed to be brave.

My hand moved to his knee, and Ethan tensed, not having expected the retaliation. I had to suppress a grin.

*Well, well, well, if it isn't the consequences of his own actions.*

"Skylar." A warning. But I was used to those by now, so I let my index finger draw its first circle.

"Told you I could play unfairly, too." *Ciiircle.*

"I never said you couldn't—"

He cut off with a low exhale as my fingers changed course, trailing gentle lines a few inches up his thigh, then back down.

And again.

"Something wrong?" I asked, voice dipped in molten sugar. "What happened to all your questions?"

Up, down.

"This isn't the proportionate response you think it is." His breathing had started to change, both in its pattern and weight. *Encouragement.*

"Mmm. Should I stop?" I murmured the mimic. This was so much fun. He was *blushing*. Only a teeny, tiny bit, but the flush was there.

Uuup, dooown. Ciiircle.

I didn't know what the points system was for this game, but I was pretty sure I was on my way to winning it.

But then he leaned, right down to my ear. His voice was low and smooth, smoked bourbon and honey. "No, Skylar, you don't have to stop. We can keep playing for as long as you want." His hand came down on top of mine, holding it in place against his knee before I could start moving up again. "But not here."

Not wh—

The restaurant. We were still at the restaurant.

The *clink*s and *tink*s of utensils against ceramic and glass, the casual background chatter, all of it came flooding back into focus in a single wave of awareness as I looked around.

Ethan didn't let go of my hand, didn't draw back. "I think a more... private setting might be better suited for our little game. Wouldn't you agree?"

*Yes. Yup. Mhhhmm. This is a great game. We like this game a lot. Agree to that and say yes with your mouth so we can go back to the apartment and keep playing.*

*He smells sooooo good.*

*Shut up and talk!*

"Good thing you're parked on such a quiet street" was what fell out of my mouth.

*I'm sorry... WHAT?*

And I could *feel* it when he smiled.

# 20

than

I WAS GOING to have Jackson track down the inventor of the remote car starter, and I was going to send them a love letter.

The Escalade was almost *too* warm by the time we got there. I felt hot, my chest overly active as I clung onto my breath and opened the door for Skylar. A wordless, seven-minute walk was more than enough time for her to have changed her mind.

But she didn't even hesitate.

I grinned and followed her into the spacious back seat. The door clicked shut, the light went off, and silence followed.

For the first full minute, the only thing I could do was look at her. Let my eyes wander up and down Skylar's face, from the delicate bow of her upper lip to the piercing silver of her eyes in the dark.

She was so intensely beautiful it almost hurt.

I held out my hand for her, palm up. She took it and let me

guide her body forward and over mine until she was straddling me on the seat.

*Much better.*

"This is cozy," Skylar teased, sliding her hands up to my shoulders. The wool of my coat was thankfully thick enough that she probably couldn't feel how much *more* cozy I very desperately wanted us to be. "Can we resume the game now? Are you ready, Player Two?"

Her little smirks were getting so cocky. I fucking loved it.

"Almost," I said, pulling her hips closer. "Game rules first."

"There's going to be *rules*?"

"Just one on my end," I clarified. "Plus whatever you'd like to add."

She lifted a dubious pierced brow. "What is it? And what if I don't agree to it?"

I flicked the zipper of her jacket. Maroon was a nice color on her. "Then we don't play."

She narrowed her eyes some more. "Okay... what's your rule?"

"The controller remains in your hands at all times. If at any point during our games you're not having fun, you're not comfortable with the mechanics or the setting, or you just don't want to play anymore, then we stop," I said, continuing to toy with her zipper. Down an inch, then back up. "All you have to do is tell me, call a time-out, and we stop. Okay?"

At first, she didn't react. At first, the only thing she gave me was a slow, incomplete blink, her lips parting.

Then her chin bobbed, once, twice. But no words came out.

My fingers stopped fiddling. "Skylar?"

A swift dip of her gaze was my only warning before her hands cupped my face and her mouth captured mine.

There was a moment when time seemed to stop, the

ground seemed to tilt, and gravity seemed to forfeit. A moment when the only thing in existence was the soft, lush press of Skylar's mouth against mine.

One moment of suspension, right before lightning struck and lit my whole body on crackling fire.

My hands moved then, one to the small of her back, the other to the nape of her neck, bringing her closer as I deepened the kiss. The tiniest little moan escaped her throat in response, and I died. The sound shot straight to my chest, pierced my writhing heart, and killed me. And it was so, very worth it. But it wasn't enough, not nearly, so I asked for more, coaxing another small noise out of her with soft caresses of my tongue, brushes of my lips. Then another, and another. Little whimpers that could ruin lives and move mountains, crumble them willingly—*happily*—to the ground.

When she drew back for breath, my mouth moved to her chin, her jaw, her neck, peppering her skin with soft nips, licks, and kisses, until she was clutching onto fistfuls of my hair and molding into me as she fought harder for air. Her scent was everywhere; it was everything, eating away at what little remained of my sanity.

I smiled into her neck when I felt it, her pulse bouncing against my mouth with a frantic enthusiasm that rivaled mine. I lingered there, teasing it with my lips and teeth until she pulled back with a tremble and a sigh and claimed my mouth with hers again, this time with more pressure, more heat, more need. This time, her tongue demanded my immediate, undivided attention, her hands moving greedily from my hair to my neck to my shoulders and chest, then back up again.

The fire became an inferno, engulfing my body in thick, insatiable flames. I reached for her zipper and tore it down just as she rocked her hips against mine. Even through the thickness of my coat, the shock of pleasure hit so hard it knocked the air out of my lungs. She did it again, and I was pretty sure I groaned into her mouth.

*More*, I thought as tension and desire coiled every single muscle in my body. My hands moved to the front of her blouse, slipping beneath the fabric—

*Not here.* A thread of reason through the blinding blaze and fog. *Not here, not in the back of a car. Not the first time. Not with her.*

It took everything I had in me and more to ease back until our lips were barely grazing. Neither of us said anything as our breaths tangled, and I tortured myself with another brush of my mouth against hers before I finally pulled back enough to look at her.

Skylar's eyes were as glazed and foggy as my brain felt. Somehow, they were even more enchanting like this. "Whoa" was all she said when she eventually spoke.

And how could anyone resist grinning at that? My whole chest caved, collapsing onto itself in response to that single, sweet word out of her mouth. "Yeah, whoa," I whispered back through the heavy rise and fall of my chest. I leaned in again so I could nuzzle my nose against hers before I scolded, "But you cheated. We weren't supposed to start until you agreed to my rule."

A faint half-smile tugged at her mouth. "I would like to apply for an amendment to the language of your proposed rule before accepting, if I may."

I pressed my forehead against hers as the laugh escaped. I really shouldn't have been surprised. "Okay, which part isn't to your liking, exactly?"

"How about we say that we... share the controller instead of me just having it. Because, you know, just in case *you're* ever uncomfortable and want to stop..."

Amusement wormed through me. It was accompanied by

something else... something buttery and snug. "You're worried about me not having a good time?"

"Not *worried*, per se. We are talking about *me*, after all, Ethan. So of course you're gonna have a good tim—" she squealed her giggle as I bit her neck.

"You're getting way too cocky for your own good," I grumbled into her skin before spoiling it with open-mouthed kisses.

"Mmmm, yup, way too cocky. Punish me some more," she crooned, lifting her chin to give me better access. Her hand went to the back of my head, stroking, and *holy shit*, how did that feel so good?

"Skylar," I warned, my lips refusing to fully separate from her smooth, soft skin despite my orders. "If we don't stop now, there's a good chance we're going to get arrested for indecent exposure." And whatever else. I couldn't think all that clearly in the moment—there wasn't enough blood circulating out of my lower half.

"Mmmm, okay. As long as they wait 'til we're done."

She had no right to be as funny as she was, not on top of everything else.

She kept going, kept teasing. "Maybe they'll let us borrow a pair of handcuffs..."

I was going to die here. Right here. This was it. And I only had one regret.

"...and maybe I'll let you use them on m—"

My mouth caught hers before she could finish. It wasn't all that gentle this time. I couldn't do it anymore. I wanted to rip her clothes off so badly my whole body was shaking. There was no denying it; I wasn't delusional. I wanted her. I wanted her. I wanted her. And I wanted to make sure she knew it.

*"Yeah, well, not everybody can tolerate me as well as you seem to be able to."*

I kissed her harder. Every single cell in my body was switched *on*. And every single one of them was laser focused on Skylar. I hated that word—"tolerate." I hated that she'd used it. I hated that someone had made her feel like she needed to use it. I hated that she wouldn't tell me who it was, that she'd brushed it off.

I hated how desperate I was to know.

"We have to go home," I said when I finally managed to break away from her. My voice was so thick it was a miracle the words came out at all. "Now."

She didn't argue this time, just looked at me like she was as desperate to get rid of our clothes as I was. It didn't help.

I almost leaned in for one more taste, it was beyond tempting, but there was no way I'd have the strength to peel myself away again. So, instead, I opened the door and helped her out of the car.

It was going to be a long drive home.

# 21

## kylar

Fifty-eight minutes. I counted.

Fifty-eight minutes of revved engines and surpassed cars and barely breathing. But somehow, we made it. To the parkade, to the elevator, to the apartment.

The door shut with a *click*. And then... nothing.

Neither of us moved to turn on the lights because neither of us moved. Not me with my back against the door, not Ethan standing two feet away, watching me with his hands in his pockets. My heart had sprouted its own hearts, multiplying until there were hundreds of them running rampant in my chest. Tiny, feverish little birds trying to escape.

Fifty-eight minutes of silence had been a long time to think. So I waited, because maybe he'd changed his mind.

Because, *"When Ethan gets like this, it's tunnel vision on steroids."*

Because, *"He doesn't see anything else. It's him and the goal...*

*Everything else is either a distraction or an obstacle standing in his way."*

Because I couldn't fit him into the ruthless and destructively competitive mold Alexis had painted, so now maybe I just needed to wait for the other shoe to drop. It seemed inevitable, something that was bound to happen, and maybe now would be when it did.

One beat, two beats, three, four.

He moved then, a single step forward, his eyes bolted tightly to mine. And we stood there, mere inches apart.

"You are so insanely beautiful, Skylar. It blows my mind," he whispered down to me, a warm hand coming up to cup my cheek. And when his thumb brushed against my skin, it snagged my breath, and he *smiled*. Because he felt it. He saw how my lashes fluttered at the simple touch, how my cheeks flushed at his words.

Maybe I should have been a little embarrassed; maybe I should have tried to hide it. But I wasn't. I didn't.

Then he leaned down and placed a feathery kiss on my forehead. "And witty," he murmured, mouth moving to my temple. "And charming." Cheek. "Fun."

I was dizzy by the time he reached my ear, barely able to tell up from down. "So, believe me when I say that I don't *tolerate* you. I don't know what that comment was about or who, but just so we're perfectly clear, driving down to Guelph for dinner was only an excuse to extend the evening by a couple of hours. There was nothing special about that restaurant—I just wanted to spend more time with you."

My jaw had started to fall slack, and there was an unexpected clawing at my throat. And before I could even begin to formulate a semicoherent response, Ethan's lips were on mine, and the world was tilting, and I was falling, plummeting upward. His mouth was pure satin and honey, and I didn't understand how someone could taste so good. *Feel* so good.

I didn't understand him at all. I didn't understand his words or why he'd felt the need to say them. I didn't understand why they made my eyes sting the way they did.

*Don't you dare.*

I squeezed my lids tighter together, gripped Ethan's lapels, and pulled him closer. He complied, pinning me against the door with his body. But it wasn't enough, not nearly. We started fumbling with buttons and zippers and scarves until the thick winter layers were discarded onto the floor and our shoes kicked off.

Still not enough. I wanted him stripped. I wanted him on top of me. I wanted him to say more pleasant things. I wanted him. I wanted him. I wanted him. And I wanted him to want me, too.

And I was so out of my mind with it that I would have said it out loud if our tongues hadn't been tangled. He kissed me like there was something sweet to be savored in every single stroke and brush and nibble. It was maddening, tormenting, perfect. And I wanted more. So much more.

And as though he could hear my thoughts, Ethan pushed his hips forward, grinding into me, setting my everything on fire.

"More," I breathed against his lips. "More, please."

And that was all it took. I was hoisted up against him, my arms and legs wrapped around his body, holding on for dear life. Then we were moving, lips and tongues refusing to separate. I was going to eventually pass out from a lack of oxygen, and it was going to be well worth it.

I didn't know how he did it. I couldn't process how he managed to get us up the stairs and to his room without dropping me, but he did. I knew he did because I heard the door shut right before I was on the bed. Right before Ethan was finally, *finally*, on top of me.

Right before he pulled back.

*Nooo.*

"You remember our rule?" he asked, and his voice was so charred and thick I barely recognized it.

I nodded. Couldn't talk. Hoarding oxygen.

"Good," he breathed, brushing a thumb across my cheek. Such a small, gentle gesture, yet I felt it *everywhere*. "Last time I was tested was a few months ago. I was in the clear, haven't been with anyone since."

"Same," I managed, currently incapable of anything even close to a full sentence. "Tested. Clear. Three years."

Good. Great. Responsible adulting done.

I tried to pull him back in. Boulders generally don't budge against normal human strength, though.

"Three *years*?" he repeated. It was actually closer to four, but we didn't have time for any of that now.

My hands moved to the bottom of my shirt, pulled it up over my head, and chucked it away in one swift motion.

Ethan's mouth snapped shut immediately, and his eyes dropped down to the black satin covering my chest.

"Still wanna talk?" I asked.

And, Apollo as my witness, the sun produced less heat than the look he gave me then. It cracked straight through me like lightning. Head to chest to core, jump-starting every nerve ending in my body into standing attention.

As it turned out, he did *not* want to keep talking. His mouth had other plans with my mouth. Hot, urgent, delicious plans. So did his tongue, his hands.

He was everywhere. All over me. He was all I could taste, smell, hear, feel. And it. Wasn't. *Enough*.

I reached for his belt and all but ripped it off him.

He reached for my jeans and all but ripped them off me.

I went for his shirt next, but before I could claw at the buttons, he used his grip on my thighs to ease my legs open beneath him, then moved his hips against me.

And *oh*.

He did it again, and *holy* shit. I gasped against his lips, my fingers digging into his shoulders.

"Fuck, I love your little noises," he groaned, trailing heated kisses across my jaw, down my neck.

Thank everything, because the second the fabric covering my breasts was gone, replaced by Ethan's hand and mouth, I lost any and all control over what sounds my throat produced.

"So soft," he praised, and it was *zing* after *zing* of pleasure cutting through me every time he teased a nipple with a brush of his thumb, swirl of his tongue.

Then his hand moved, dipping between my legs. Featherlight touches and strokes over the cotton fabric.

It built and built and built, tease after tease after tease, until the ache became unbearable, until I was writhing and panting and grabbing at him and, "*Ethan*. Enough. Just. Condom. Where?"

I was about to combust.

And finally (*finally*), he pushed himself back up, reaching for the bedside drawer. My hands didn't waste any time, fumbling with his buttons as soon as they were within reach.

His shirt opened, and he slid it off, and I... wasn't expecting it. I mean, I was expecting it, but I thought maybe I shouldn't have been expecting it. Because, "*How*?" I asked, utterly baffled by the hard muscle carved onto his chest and abs. "Seriously. How could you possibly have time to work out?"

Cocky smirk was cocky. "An hour before work every single morning, no exceptions. It keeps me sane."

I saw my opening, and I took it. I had to. "Good lord. This is you *sane*?"

His laugh was pure serotonin. "Unfortunately," he answered, then brought his lips down to mine again.

Except he was smiling, and I was also smiling. And then I was giggling, and he was chuckling. So we were kiss-smile-laughing, and it was the warmest, loveliest thing I'd experienced in a long time.

Ethan nipped at my bottom lip as punishment when I couldn't pull myself together, then drew away. And this time, when he looked down at me, there was so much affection mixed with the humor in his eyes that I could have drowned in it. I *would* have drowned in it. Jumped in voluntarily. Enthusiastically.

"Sorry," I laughed. "I'm sorry. Sorry, sorry." Still laughing.

Literally *nothing* was funny.

Well, some things were funny. Just not now.

Ethan didn't say anything, just kept watching me, kept grinning. And I couldn't believe I'd gone twenty-four years without knowing that smile. What a waste. What *encouragement.*

I lifted a hand and brought it to his cheek, brushing a thumb over his bottom lip. Then, in the sweetest, most genuine voice I could muster, I said, "Have I told you how much I like your teeth?"

And he *burst* into laughter.

"Fuck," he choked out in defeat before rolling off me, and then we were both in absolute hysterics. Like, the type of uncontrollable laughter that feeds off the other person's uncontrollable laughter.

I was dying, clutching onto my stomach, because *he* was dying, clutching onto his stomach.

It went on for way too many minutes. There were tears

streaming down my face, and I'd somehow ended up on the floor, fighting for air.

"I think we're doing this wrong," I eventually managed, climbing back onto the bed. Ethan was on his back, hands over his face and chest, shaking with a new fit of only semi-audible chuckles. "I mean, I know it's been a while, but I don't think there's supposed to be this much laughing involved."

He lowered his arms and sat up slowly. He was positively *pink* in the cheeks, eyes wet. I crawled over and straddled him, wrapping my arms around his neck. "You're cute when you laugh," I said, because he was.

I thought he might protest against my word choice, but instead, he snaked his arms around my waist and pulled me closer, then kissed me. Gentle and sweet. "I definitely don't think we're doing this wrong, Skylar," he murmured against my lips. "No part of this feels wrong."

There wasn't a single other thing he could have said in that moment to make my insides react in the dangerous way they did. Not one.

I pressed my chest tighter against his, running my hands from the hard muscles of his shoulders up to his neck, his jaw. His breath hitched when my thumbs started to caress his skin, and that little reaction was everything. Knowing I had that impact on him was *everything*.

"You know, you're nothing like I thought you'd be," I admitted. "Nothing like the impression I had of you that first night."

That left lip curl was going to be the end of me. I brushed a thumb over it as he spoke. "I'm going to go ahead and assume that's a good thing."

I pouted and cocked my head. "You sure?"

Ethan's fingers had started to trace delicate lines up and down my back, and I wanted to curl right into his chest. Everything, *every*thing he did felt incredible. Including the way he playfully licked at my pout just then, inspiring a small giggle out of my throat.

We were playing a proximity game with our mouths, not close enough to be kissing, but close enough that every time one of us talked, there was a chance our lips brushed. And every time it happened, every time he drew a new line on my back, a fresh cluster of butterflies spread through my stomach.

"Had I known you were this sweet, I might have signed that contract the first day you suggested it," I teased.

"Mmm, I should have seduced you a lot sooner, then." His lips sealed over mine again, and it—

I froze.

The thought was fleeting at first, a whisper in the back of my mind. But then it found its footing, found a supporting voice, and settled.

Because, *"He doesn't see anything else. He just... keeps going. Even if what he's doing is destructive. To the people around him or to himself. It's him and the goal, and he'll do whatever it takes to get to it."*

There was no way...

I tried to push it away, tried to kiss him back and keep the dread and alarm from seeping in, because I *knew* where it came from. I *knew* it was unreasonable. I *knew* the insecurities that fueled it.

But it was too late. The words were a broken record in my head, lava and ice down my spine.

*"He'll do whatever it takes."*

"Skylar?"

Ethan had broken the kiss and was looking at me with his brows pulled together, and I... suddenly felt very, *very* naked.

Which triggered a small flake of panic.

Which triggered a spiraling avalanche of realizations.

I'd misunderstood this, hadn't I? It hadn't been a date. Not really. Not sincerely.

*"He'll do whatever it takes."*

I pushed myself off him, arms flying up to cover my chest.

That little flake of panic? Snowballing. Fast. Downhill. Headed straight for a cliff.

It made sense, didn't it? This wasn't my insecurities. This wasn't me overthinking. It made *sense*. There was a reason Alexis had warned me. There was a reason the things she'd said didn't match what I'd seen from him. There was a reason he was being so nice to me.

It wasn't that she was wrong about him. It wasn't that he was different with *me*, that *I* was somehow special. I wasn't delusional; I wasn't stupid. I'd known him for less than two weeks; she'd known him all her life. She was his sister. She knew him better. *There was a reason she'd warned me.*

"Skylar?" Ethan said again because I still hadn't answered. He reached forward; I moved back.

"New game," I said because it was the first thing that came to me. "Truth or truth."

And I could see his brain fighting through the daze, trying to play catch-up. Trying to figure out why I'd suddenly switched gears, pushed away from him, reached for a pillow, and used it to cover up. Trying to figure out what he'd done to prompt it.

I almost felt bad. Almost.

"You're shaking" was his response.

My arms tightened around the pillow.

"I'll go first," I said, ignoring the concern in his voice. Not like it was real. Not like he actually cared. "What are we doing right now? What is this?"

And I swear he was looking at me like I was some sort of

overly complex quadratic equation and he was trying to solve for the *y* of it all.

He didn't answer, so I tried again. "Why did you take me to dinner? What was your objective?" The shaking was contagious, apparently, and my voice had caught it straight from my limbs.

Still no answer, but he did stand up and reach for something on the floor. My shirt.

"Wear this first. You're going to catch a cold," he said.

And I *hated* that he insisted on keeping up the act. I *hated* how my chest reacted.

I wasn't cold. If anything, my body temperature was running a few million degrees too high. But I slipped the shirt on anyway, keeping the pillow up as a shield. Not that it mattered—Ethan looked away until my top half was dressed.

I hated that, too.

"Now," he said, keeping his voice too soft, too sweet, too understanding. It was all wrong. "Start from the beginning. What just happened?"

He sat down on the bed, keeping his distance.

"That's not how the game works. You have to answer first. With the truth," I insisted. And I wished so badly that the trembling would stop. It made me sound weak, and I wasn't weak. I didn't want him to think of me that way, that I was someone that could be walked all over, taken advantage of, lied to, manipulated.

I *wasn't*.

Ethan considered me for a few seconds before speaking. "Okay. But if I answer, then so do you, yes? Question for question, truth for truth."

I nodded. "Yes. Fine." As long as he actually told me the truth.

"Alright, then... what's your question, exactly?"

I didn't know whether to be irritated or calmed by the fact that he was playing along so willingly. That he'd just accepted the turn of events and adapted so quickly.

"Why did you suggest we go out to dinner?" I was still hugging the pillow, clutching it tightly enough that my knuckles were throbbing a little.

"I already told you why. I already said I wanted to spend m—"

"The truth," I interrupted because I didn't want to experience him saying it again. My heart hadn't caught up to my mind yet, and I was a little scared at how it was going to react.

Ethan didn't get angry, he didn't get frustrated, he just... kept looking at me like *I* was the puzzle. Like *I* was the one hiding things. "What makes you think that wasn't the truth?" he finally asked.

I opened my mouth again, but nothing came out. Because I couldn't tell him that Alexis and I had talked, that I was putting two and two together. I didn't think she'd want me to share, and I wasn't going to betray her trust. So, I diverted. "You don't get to ask a question yet, remember? Not until you—"

"I already told you the truth, Skylar. There isn't a secret answer or an *objective*, whatever that means. Whether you believe me or not is up to you, but I did my part, and I answered, so now it's your turn. And I want to know why you think I'm lying."

I didn't say anything.

One beat, two beats, three, four.

Ethan let out a frustrated huff of air before standing up. And I thought he'd finally had enough of me and that he was going to leave or kick me out of his room. It's what I would have done. But instead, he walked over to his dresser, slipped on a black T-shirt, then dragged his desk chair to the edge of the bed and sat down, facing me.

"I have all night if that's how long you need," he said.

My knuckles were screaming at me to loosen the death grip I had on Ethan's pillow. It made my jaw clench.

I said nothing.

"Fine. You want me to revise the question? Ask another one?" He leaned forward, elbows resting on his knees. "Why do you think I suggested we go to dinner if it wasn't for the reasons I gave? What's your theory?"

My eyes flickered to the door behind him. It was inadvertent... I didn't... mean to. I meant to talk. I was angry; I should have *talked*. Should have told him exactly what my theory was, that I knew what he was doing. That's what well-functioning adults did—they communicated. But I couldn't do it. My stupid mouth wouldn't cooperate; it was clamped shut. So my eyes flickered to the closest escape route instead.

He caught it. Of course he caught it.

And I watched as the realization set in that he wasn't going to get an answer. I watched as it turned into confusion, then disappointment. I watched as he gave me another minute, just in case. And then I watched him nod his acceptance, stand up, and walk out.

I listened as his steps retreated down the stairs. I listened as they carried him down the hall. And I called it a half second before his office door slammed shut.

Then, only *then*, did my voice decide to make a whispered comeback.

"You're a coward, Skylar."

# 22

## than

I WAS PRETTY SURE the door slammed, but I barely registered it.

It could have shattered off its hinges, disintegrated into sawdust, morphed into a portal leading to another dimension, and I wouldn't have spared it a single glance in that moment.

I was too busy pacing.

I could figure this out; I knew I could. I just needed to *think*, talk it out with myself. It happened too quick for there not to have been some sort of trigger, and if I could figure out what the trigger was, I could probably map out the rest of it.

Because up until I kissed her again, Skylar was fine. More than fine. *Enthusiastic.* She seemed like she was enjoying herself almost as much as I was. All the physical and verbal cues were there, until she just... went rigid on my lap. Flip of a switch.

*Okay, so let's backtrack a little. What happened right before that?*

*We were talking.*

*About?*

*About... she said she felt like we were doing things wrong, that there wasn't supposed to be so much laughter involved.*

*And then?*

*I disagreed. Nothing about what we were doing felt wrong. Nothing about being with her felt wrong.*

*To you.*

*To me.*

*To her?*

*... I don't know. Maybe that's it? Was she just... did it not feel right to her? To be with me?*

I cracked open the balcony door. It was so fucking hot in here. I was sweating.

*Okay. Focus. What did she say after that?*

It took me a second, sifting through the memories of her practically naked on my lap, trying to concentrate on what we'd talked about instead of what we'd been doing. What we'd been about to do. What she'd felt like. What—

*Focus. What did you talk about after that?*

*We talked about... she said that I wasn't like what she'd initially thought.*

*And you assumed that was a good thing.*

*And I assumed that was a good thing.*

*And then what?*

*She pouted.*

*Not relevant.*

*It was sexy as hell. I licked it. She giggled.*

*Stop smiling. What did she say next?*

*She called me sweet. She said that if she'd known it earlier, she'd have signed... the contract.*

*And then what did you say? What did you say right before you kissed her? Right before she froze?*

...

I stopped pacing, stopped moving, stopped breathing as the puzzle pieces slotted into place.

No fucking way. There was no fucking way she actually thought that I'd taken her to dinner or done any of this in an attempt to seduce her into signing the contract. There was *no fucking way.*

*How else can you explain the "objective" thing? What else could she have meant?*

...

Fuck.

Where would she even... why... how... *why*? Why the *fuck* would she ever come to that conclusion? Why would she think I was being serious?

It was slick and hot and heavy, the anger that followed. And I didn't know if it was directed at her or at myself. If it was because she thought so little of me or because I deserved it.

Because it was exactly the type of thing I'd do. It was exactly the type of thing I'd done.

*Remember Darya? Remember what you did when you found out Grey was into her? Remember making out with her in front of him at the Byers party just so you'd get in his head? Remember the things you whispered in her ear when you knew he was looking, sleeping with her just to spite him? Remember not calling her back after that?*

*Remember it was all over a soccer game? A regular game. Not a championship, not even a qualifier. It was all over a stupid, regular game that was so insignificant you can't even remember who won.*

I slammed the balcony door shut, hard. Hard enough that I almost missed the hesitant pitter-patter of steps starting to make their way down the stairs.

I waited, holding my breath.

They were inconsistent and a little flaky, retreating every few steps before changing their mind and coming back, until her shadow finally made it to the office door. I watched as she hesitated, then walked away. Then came back. Then walked away.

And it pulled at my heart a little. Such a small thing that she didn't realize I could see or hear her, but it made my chest do all sorts of floaty, achy tricks. And I started to realize what Alexis had meant when she'd warned me.

When she'd said that I didn't know Skylar or anything about her. That bringing her into this wasn't a good idea. That I was an idiot for thinking she'd walk away from all this unscathed. I understood why my sister was worried that Skylar might get... trampled over all this. It would be so easy, wouldn't it. For her to get crushed.

I leaned against my desk, crossed my arms, and waited with my heart crawling up to my throat as the indecisive little shadow continued to linger at the door.

And eventually, it came, a soft double knock.

"Come in."

She did. Skylar walked in, closed the door, and looked at me with her lips pressed into a flat, determined line. And I realized what had taken her so long; she'd been psyching herself up, building up the courage to confront me with her theory.

I didn't miss what that realization did to my insides. I didn't miss what the sight of her did to me. What I felt when our eyes met. How badly I wanted to go to her, touch her, explain myself. How *desperately* I wanted her to know that she was wrong. I didn't miss any of it. That was the problem.

*One week. You've known her for one week. Eight days.*

"Um, can we talk?"

I let out a lungful of hot air. "Yes, we can talk."

"Cool." Her fingers started to fiddle with the sleeve of the large sweater she'd changed into. And there it was, like clockwork, the urge to reach out and soothe them. I balled my fists tighter, my molars threatening to crack.

"I'd like to start off with an apology," she said and—

Wait. What?

Her throat bobbed with a swallow, her fingers fiddled, but she maintained eye contact when she answered. "I... I sometimes have a hard time communicating. It's something I'm working on, but it's not always... easy. For me. To discuss certain things. Especially if... if they're, um, confrontational or accusatory or anything of that nature." She stopped to take a breath before continuing. "But that's not your fault, and I'm sorry for shutting down the way I did upstairs instead of talking it out. It... and I'm sorry in advance if it happens again in the future."

I just sort of... gaped back at her.

She thought... she thought I was *using* her, right? That was her theory. She thought I had tried to seduce her, get her into bed, that I'd lied to her all night, in order to get her to sign a *ridiculous* agreement that... only led to more lying. She thought all this, and she was standing there, apologizing for not confronting me about it upstairs? When she was half-naked and vulnerable?

Anger whipped at my core. At her, at myself, at everything and everyone. I couldn't tell whether it was justified or irrational. And I didn't care.

"I also owe you an answer," Skylar went on. "Truth for truth. It's only fair. You asked why I think you suggested we go to dinner, right? You asked what my theory was?"

My heart was slamming into my ribs. Hard. Fast. Blood rushed against my ears.

"Will you tell me the truth? If I tell you what my theory is, will you be honest about whether or not I'm right?" she asked, pulling at the loose thread on her sleeve.

I cleared my throat, opened my mouth, but decided on a nod instead, afraid of what I might say if I let myself speak.

"Okay," she said, looking down. "I think... I think that maybe you took me to dinner under false pretenses, to... to influence my decision. Regarding the contract. That all of... what happened in the car and upstairs, and everything you said... might have been insincere... in order to get my signature."

Her words churned in my stomach, shoving and yanking and twisting.

"That's what I think," she finished off, gaze slowly resurfacing to measure my reaction. "Is... um, is that what you were doing?"

Skylar didn't give herself enough credit. Not nearly. Because I didn't think there were many people that would have had the maturity or the guts to do what she just did, to be as honest and open as she just was.

Too bad it was bullshit.

"Ethan...?"

Because I'd been silent, staring.

"No," I finally said. "No, Skylar. That wasn't what I was doing. We didn't go to d—I wasn't about to have *sex with you* for a signature."

I hated that I even had to say it.

I hated the taste the words left on my tongue. It was bitter and sour and stale. I wanted to spit, cleanse my mouth of it.

And I was pretty certain that the gravity of her accusation didn't hit her until that very moment because I saw the tension in her shift. Like she was only now questioning herself.

"Do you believe me?" I asked, because it mattered. It really fucking mattered.

She hesitated. Her chin bobbed once, twice. It was all I needed to know.

"Then we don't have a lot more to talk about."

Her breathing had picked up along with the fidgeting. Her eyes were pools of melted ice. "I—I didn't say no. I don't—I'm not sure."

My knuckles were threatening to desocket.

"I have some work I need to get done now, if you don't mind."

And she finally dropped her hands. "Ethan—"

"Get out. Please."

Her mouth opened. It closed.

She chewed at her cheek. Pulled at her sleeve.

Opened her mouth. Closed it.

She turned around.

She left.

# 23

kylar

I DIDN'T SLEEP.

I just kept replaying the night over and over again in my head. Every single part of it, beginning to end, on a loop.

If Ethan ever made it upstairs, I didn't hear him. But I did hear the apartment door open and shut at 5:29 in the morning.

8:14 was when I forced myself out of bed to get dressed.

8:27 was when I crawled back in.

8:28 was when the loop restarted.

I went over it all in detail again. And again. And again. Everything we did, everything he said, looking for literally *any* indication that he'd been lying or acting or insincere in any way.

But I kept coming up blank. Every time. I couldn't identify a single moment during the night I could point to and say, *"There! That right there was obviously fake!"*

I tried. I really did. Because the alternative was that I'd

accused him of something horrible without proof and didn't believe him when he denied it. The alternative was that I'd started to develop feelings for someone for the first time in years, freaked out, doused the whole thing in propane, and lit it on fire. Like a *crazy* person.

I felt like shit.

I'd been so convinced last night, hadn't I? In that moment, there hadn't been a single doubt in my mind that Ethan was just using me to get the contract signed. Not until I confronted him.

I kind of wished he'd yelled. I think I'd feel better if he'd just... yelled or snapped or said something, anything *remotely* malicious or mean out of anger. Something I could hold on to and hate him for.

*Because he probably, most definitely hates me*, I thought, turning my face into the pillow. *If he really wasn't lying, then he probably thinks I'm insane and dysfunctional and broken. And he's probably thankful that he dodged a bullet.*

And maybe he had. Maybe I was a bullet and he'd dodged me.

I sniffed.

Maybe Alexis had it backward. Maybe she should have warned *him* about *me*. Told him to stay away, you know? Like, "Watch out for crazy Skylar, don't be too nice to her or she'll lose her fucking mind and jump to insane, unfounded conclusions about your intentions at the worst possible time. Like right before you're about to have sex."

My legs flailed, kicking at the duvet and the sheets and the mattress.

*I should give him his gloves back. He won't want me holding on to those anymore.*

*He'll probably want me out of the house, too. I should pack.*

*And honestly, he might even take the deal off the table. If he really was telling the truth, then there might not even be a contract to sign after last night.*

I groaned into the pillow.

We were supposed to go over the agreement this afternoon, so I just had to wait until then. If he canceled, then I'd probably have my answ—

My phone started to buzz on the bed.

I reached for it, heart flipping. But it wasn't Ethan.

My eyes bounced up to the time. How was it 11:03 already? How had I forgotten about Sunday virtual brunch?

I kept looking at the screen, and it kept buzzing. Kept buzzing. And then stopped.

I let out a breath.

It started up again.

*Shit. Okay. It's okay. It's too late to cancel now, but you can do this. You can be normal. You're a* good *liar, Skylar, no matter what anyone says.*

I sat up, cleared my throat, picked up the call, and smiled.

"Heyo," I chirped convincingly.

Mikaela narrowed her eyes at me through the screen. Like, almost immediately. "What's wrong with you? What happened?"

*Smile harder.*

"Just a bit sick," I explained.

"That's not your sick face—that's your lying grin! What's going on?"

My what? "Nothing. I just, uh, forgot about virtual brunch, so I'm a bit... whatever that word is. Rattled, I think. Yes. I am... rattled. Because of not having any food prepared."

My excuse made things worse. She tilted her head at me, then leaned in and started to whisper. "Is this a hostage situation? Blink twice if I need to call 911."

I kept my eyes wide open, overwhelmed by my sudden, urgent need to blink. "I'm not being held hostage."

She leaned in even closer, studying me carefully. Her whisper was so loud she might as well have used her outdoor voice. "That's exactly what a hostage would say."

"Okay. So then, what would a non-hostage say?"

"A non-hostage would tell me the truth." Mikaela straightened, tone normalized. "What happened? Why do you look like you haven't slept at all and like you're trying not to cry?"

I swallowed, but the frog leapt right back up and lodged itself in my throat again. "I'm not. I mean, I'm not not trying to cry."

She didn't say anything.

"I'm not," I repeated because she didn't believe me.

Nothing.

The tears I'd been suppressing all night started to crawl behind my eyes. I blinked, trying to keep them back. They didn't deserve to be shed; I didn't deserve to cry it out or to feel better about this. Not if I was wrong.

I swallowed and blinked. Blinked and swallowed.

Mikaela waited, sympathy softening her features. It only made me feel worse. I didn't deserve that, either. She wouldn't be sympathetic if she knew.

"I don't really want to talk about it, Mik," I mumbled.

Her lips thinned into a contemplative line. "Are you safe?" she eventually asked.

I nodded, wiping a sleeve against my eyes. They were getting ready to spill. "Yes. Yeah. It's nothing... I just... really messed up. I think. I don't know."

"Okay," she said. "And you don't want a second opinion?"

"You're going to get mad at me," I told her. Because she was. "And I don't want any more of that today."

"That's fair," she said, leaning back into her purple couch. "What if I promise no judgment or opinion?"

I considered that. Then I considered it some more. "Really?"

"Cross my heart," she swore, sealing her oath with a line across her chest. "I'm here for support only. All ears. No judgment. No getting mad. No matter what."

I hesitated. "You really swear?"

"*Yes.*"

"Um... okay," I caved, shifting on the bed. Because I really did want to tell her. I told Mik everything, even if it meant facing her wrath. Because, most of the time, she had a point.

I took in a large breath. "So, you know... you know that guy?"

"The conventionally attractive rich fake boyfriend slash potential serial killer you're currently living with up in Winter Mapleland? How could I forget? He can *cook*, after all."

"He also goes by 'Ethan,' believe it or not," I said, unable to hold back my smile. "Anyways." I cleared my throat, fingering the little loose thread on the sleeve of my sweater. "I uh... did something..."

"You had sex with him."

Should have been prepared for that, knowing her. I wasn't. "*Mik*!"

She shrugged. "Didn't you?"

"No," I said right away, shifting my weight again. "Not really. Almost. But no."

"What does that mean? What does 'almost' mean?"

"We were about to," I clarified. "Like we were literally in bed. Um, and then I... ruined it. Everything."

Mikaela didn't respond to that, just hugged a knee to her chest and waited for me to go on.

"I sort of... we'd gone to dinner before that, and I was under the impression that it was maybe a date."

"It wasn't?"

"I don't know." I still didn't. Was kind of hoping she'd be able to tell me.

"But you wanted it to be."

"I..." Nodded.

Her smile was infuriating. "Wow. You *like* him," she teased, seemingly unable to help herself. Even though I was clearly going through a crisis.

"I just said we almost... we were in bed. Feel like it's a given that I like him, Mik."

"Oh, you sweet, innocent, young new soul." Mikaela *tsk*ed at me, even though I was a year older than her. I knew better than to argue. She wasn't talking about my current, physical form. "People who don't like each other have sex all the time. Take me and Luke, for example."

"I'd really rather not."

"Hate the guy. Scum of the Earth. Gum in your hair. Hot as sin. Excellent at sex."

We'd gotten sidetracked.

"He's really not that bad," I defended. Also, I was pretty sure the not liking thing was one-sided. He looked at her kind of... softly sometimes, but only when she wasn't paying attention. I did not say this out loud to her for my own sake.

"He's a garbage goblin wrapped in sexy human skin. You just have a tendency to see the good in people, Sweet Soul."

Funny she should say that. I twisted the thread over my index finger.

"Regardless," Mikaela went on, waving the topic of Luke away with swats of her hand like it were a pesky mosquito. "We're getting distracted. Please continue."

I worried the inside of my lip, unsure of how to go about

this. How to put everything into words. I couldn't... explain the last week properly. I couldn't explain the chemistry I felt with Ethan. How could I when I didn't really understand it myself?

"Hold on, let me switch you over to my laptop. Phone's about to die." Phone was at 17 percent. I just wanted a bit more time.

Three minutes later, I was set up with the laptop on the bed, sitting cross-legged and looking at Mikaela on the screen, blanking.

"You can just tell me where things went wrong, if that helps," she suggested, watching as I struggled for the words. "We can start there and work backwards if you need."

"Okay." I took a breath. Then another. It was probably a good idea to do it this way. Rip it off like a Band-Aid. "We were... we were about to... have sex. And I stopped it."

I had to pause and swallow. Stupid frog lodged in my stupid throat.

"Because I thought that he was just doing it all... he was being nice to me and taking me out to dinner and... the physical stuff not because he wanted to, but just to get my signature. For the contract."

It sounded so much more ridiculous when I said it out loud. I felt like such an idiot. I couldn't even look at Mikaela anymore; I was staring down at the duvet, pulling and twisting at the fabric.

"Sky..."

"And then. And *then* I confronted him about it," I went on, wiping at my stupid eyes, which were brimming with stupid tears. "Because, you know, why wouldn't I? Why would that be a bad idea? I thought that's what I was supposed to do—communicate. Even though I had no proof. None. Because there wasn't a *single* thing he'd done all night to make me believe he wasn't sincere. All he did was make a joke, and it sent me spiraling like a lunatic. A joke and something Alexis had said."

I took a sleeve to my wet cheeks. "And he was so nice, Mik. You don't even know. He wouldn't even kiss me... wouldn't do anything until he made sure I felt safe and that I knew we could stop at any time. And it was the most fun I've had in a long time. He's so fun to be with, to talk to. He didn't... I don't know why I was so convinced last night. I don't know why I didn't believe him when he told me I was wrong. I don't know why I *still* don't really believe him. It just... I don't know."

I stopped, breathed, looked up at the screen. Mikaela was staring back at me, chin on knee, head tilted. I couldn't really decipher her expression. Contemplative, maybe.

"So. Yeah," I said. "I messed up. I think. Right? I messed up. And he hates me, I'm pretty sure. Because he kicked me out of his office really quickly after that, which I can't blame him for. He's probably going to kick me out of the apartment, too. I should... pack. Probably. And look for a new place."

I sniffed.

She stared.

And stared.

Then stared some more.

"Can you please say something now?" I mumbled.

"Sure," she said, as though she'd been waiting for my permission to speak. "Don't pack."

...

"What?"

"Don't pack," she repeated. "He's not going to kick you out. And if he sees those bags, he's going to get the wrong impression, and it's probably going to make things worse."

Oh. I guess that made sense. "How do you know? That he won't kick me out?"

Her lips pressed into a line, and then she said, "A hunch."

"A what?"

"Intuition, instinct, whatever you wanna call it."

"Mikaela, *I accused*—"

"I know. You told me. You upset him and hurt his feelings pretty bad, I bet."

Another sniff. "Not on purpose."

"Mmmm."

My hands dabbed at my face one last time, and then I leaned in. "You're doing that thing where you're not saying stuff but you're thinking them."

"That was our deal. I said I would only listen, remember? Crossed my heart and everything."

"Okay, well, uncross it, please. I need you to tell me what you think. And what I should do because I honestly have no idea. I don't know how to fix this."

She ran a hand across her chest again, in reverse this time.

"Okay," she said as soon as her arm had dropped. "You ready?"

"Lay it on me."

"I think you're right," she said.

It took me a second.

"You think... you think I'm right about what? About Ethan using me?"

"Yeah, I think that's what he was doing." Her eyes sauntered down to her cuticles.

"How do you know?"

She shrugged. "Pretty obvious. Seems like the type."

*What?* "You don't even know him, though."

"The whole premise of your relationship with him is based on a lie," she pointed out.

"That's not fair." I was sitting up straighter now.

"You asked for my opinion."

"Well, yeah... because..." *Because what?*

"I'm just saying, it makes sense."

"It does?"

"Honestly, he might not even have done it for the signature. He might have taken it a step further. Wanted to trick you into an actual romantic relationship, but only because he needs one for his promotion or whatever. That way, he wouldn't even need to pay you. No contract, no payment, no paper trail. No risk of the lie slipping if *you* think it's real. Not if he's the only one 'in the know,' you know?"

I gaped at her.

She kept going.

"Or, like, even *further*. He'll probably propose, just like he told his grandmother he would. Marry you to keep up the lie. He'll shed a couple of tears as you walk down the aisle, just to make it look more believable.

"Add a kid or three to the mix a few years in, maybe a dog, a ferret. Your tenth anniversary will be blessed with a surprise pregnancy. He's been having pretend sex with you all these years to keep up the ruse, faking his orgasms. Your children will grow up, leave the nest; you'll retire in the French countryside, where he makes you breakfast every morning. But also lunch and dinner, because of that one time he let you cook and it almost killed him. It's all part of the con. Every pancake, every sausage.

"And then, finally, the time will come for him to tell you the truth. He'll be on his deathbed, wanting to clear his conscience after a lifetime of deceit. You'll be holding his hand, tears streaming down your face, saying goodbye to the love of your life after fifty years together. He'll look so frail, so weak. Nothing like the conventionally attractive man you once knew. But still beautiful in your eyes, of course.

"He'll cough and say, 'Come closer,' so you will. He'll say, 'Even closer,' so you'll bend down. He'll take one last, rattling breath in preparation for his reveal, one last breath before he rips your world apart. You'll close your eyes, knowing what's coming. You've known all these years, but you thought he'd change, he'd *grow* to love you. You could *make him* love you. But he never did, did he? So you hold your breath, heart breaking as he whispers his dying confession to you, as he uses his very last breath to say, 'You're... a... goof... Skylar.'"

Mikaela's scratchy deathbed voice cut off with a choking sound, her eyes rolled to the back of her head, and she died, tongue and head falling to the side for maximum effect.

I almost shut the laptop on her face.

"I hate you," I told her sincerely. "I hate you so much."

She sprang back up. "And what lessons have we learned from today's story, Skylar?"

I held up three fingers in preparation for the countdown. "One: you're not funny. Two: I need a new best friend. Three: I should stop telling you things."

Had she made me feel better? A little (read: exponentially). But at what cost?

"I'd be more inclined to believe you if you weren't trying so hard not to smile."

I sucked my cheeks back in and bit down on them.

"I'll tell you what we've learned," Mikaela continued. "First of all, we know that you don't *actually* believe your theory. Because when I told you I agreed, you got defensive. Of him. Like, immediately."

Wait a second. "You Jedi mind tricked me?" Was that how it worked? I didn't know. Hadn't seen a Star Wars movie since I was, like, six.

"I don't know those words," she claimed, waving them off impatiently so she could get to her next point. "Second of all, we have relearned what we already knew. That you're a huge goof."

"Not true."

"Skylar. You do this all. The. Time."

That made me pause. And think. "I do?" I did?

"*Yes*, ya goof. Every time a guy is even remotely into you, you're either entirely oblivious to it, deeply in denial, or you find some way to sabotage it."

"Since *when*?" I asked a little defensively. "Name one time I've done that."

"Phillip," she responded without hesitation.

Terrible example. "We were friends."

"He wrote you *poetry*."

"That's not fair. Poetry was just his thing; he wrote it all the time. Plus, it's not like the poem was *about me*. It was about flowers."

She blinked at me slowly, like she couldn't believe just how daft I was being. "It was about irises, Skylar. Not just any flower. *Light blue irises*. He wrote a poem about your eyes for your birthday. *Irises*. Light blue. Do you see what I mean?"

I pulled at my sleeve. "You're reading into that."

"*This*. This right here is exactly what I'm talking about. Even when the evidence is laid out in front of you, clear as day, you still refuse to believe it."

I didn't say anything. I wasn't sure what to say, in all honesty.

Mikaela let out a sigh, then leaned in again. "Skylar, listen to me. I know... I understand where your hesitation might come from and why you might question Ethan's intentions. I don't know the guy, I don't know everything that's happened, but I *swear* to you, on everything I have, that it's not difficult to believe he's already developed real feelings for you. I know you think it is, but it's not.

"You are funny, charming, beautiful, talented, and *kind*. You are so many wonderful things, and I hate that you can't see it sometimes. I hate that you do this to yourself, that you can't see how truly deserving you are of love. Because you *are*. I promise you, you are."

Guess whose throat frog was back, clogging everything up.

I sniffed.

"You wanted to know what I think you should do?" Mikaela went on when I remained quiet. "I think you should talk to him, and I think you should apologize. And then I think you should *go for it*."

"But what if..." Because what *if*.

"There's no way for us to know for sure, Sky. There just isn't. Love is always a risk; it's always a step into the unknown. And it's always going to be. You just have to decide if he's a risk worth taking."

## 24

## than

I COULDN'T REMEMBER who'd won.

I'd been parked outside our office building for an hour, racking my brain, trying to figure it out. Trying to remember a single identifying detail about the game.

Had it been raining? Snowing?

Had I scored a goal? Broken a bone? Had Grey?

One hour turned to two. To three.

Because I couldn't remember who'd won the fucking game. And every time I tried to convince myself that it didn't matter, that I needed to get out of the damn car and go inside, that I had actual work that needed to get done, my fingers would curl tighter around the steering wheel, refusing to comply.

I could remember the party. The feeling of satisfaction, knowing I'd gotten into Grey's head. I could remember how many messages Darya left me after the fact, voicemails and texts. I could remember ignoring them, ignoring her, being a selfish asshole, thinking that she'd served her purpose, that she'd get the hint eventually.

But I couldn't remember who'd won.

I couldn't remember if it had been worth it.

*Is that what you think? That it would have been worth it if it was you? Has any other part of the last thirty years been worth it? Is that why you can't get out of the car? Why you've spent the last two years anywhere and everywhere but here?*

Three hours turned to four.

The fifth one was when I caved, reached into my pocket, pulled out a small, white card, and started to dial.

# 25

## kylar

ETHAN DIDN'T COME HOME.

I waited all day. Worked on my portfolio, cleaned, watched a bunch of movies, and waited.

And waited.

Our 2:00 p.m. appointment came and went, accompanied by complete and utter radio silence.

Which, okay, he was probably angry and needed time to cool down. That was understandable, I thought. So I didn't message him. If he hadn't reached out, it meant he wanted space. I could respect that.

But then, it started to get late.

And then, it started to get *really* late.

My anxiety kicked in at around 11:40. I was in bed, trying to fall asleep, knowing I had to be up early for work. But I couldn't, not while waiting for the small *beeps* of the front door to go off.

By midnight, I was pacing around my room. It had started to snow. *Hard*. And it was already settling on the roads.

I gave up, picked up my phone, and typed out a simple message.

**Me: Hi. Roads are not ideal. Just wondering if you're ok?**

And then I deleted it because it was stupid.

**Me: Hey. It's pretty late, just wanna make sure you're ok?**

That was even worse, wasn't it?

**Me: It's late. Just want to make sure you're safe.**

*What are you, his mother?*

What followed were seven more variations of the same thing until I forced myself to settle on the eighth.

**Me: Hey. Roads are not ideal and it's late... just wondering if you're ok?**

The text didn't go through immediately. It stayed put, pending and pending, and then... the bubble turned from blue to green. *Message Not Delivered*.

Oh.

My first thought was *Don't panic*.

His phone was probably just turned off. Or ran out of battery. Or something.

*Just go to sleep. You have work in the morning. It's not unusual for him to come home late. It's nothing.*

I slipped under the covers, plugged my phone in, and shut my eyes.

...

...

*What if something's happened?*

I squeezed my lids tighter.

*Nothing's happened. Go to sleep.*

...

...

*But what if it has?*

*It hasn't.*

*Are you sure?*

I turned to my side, curled my knees up to my chest, and started counting sheep.

*Sheep number one. White.*

*Sheep number two. Eggshell.*

*Sheep number three. Cotton.*

*Sheep number four. Alabaster.*

*Sheep number five. Ivory.*

*Sheep number six. Charcoal.*

*Sheep number seven. Snow.*

*Sheep number eight. Snow.*

*Snow.*

My left eye opened. Just slightly.

It was still snowing.

*Hush. Go to sleep.*

I tried. I really, really did. Squeezed my lids, counted more sheep, imagined a peaceful river flowing through outer space. But the little voice in the back of my head would. Not. Shut. Up.

*What if*, it kept saying. *What if, what if, what if, what if.*

So I reached for my phone again. 1:05.

Then I put it down. Counted sheep. Gave up. Reached for it again. 1:39.

*What if. What if, what if, what if.*

Rinse, repeat. 2:02.

*WHAT IF. WHAT IF. WHAT IF.*

And then the blankets were kicked off, and I was pacing again. Around the bedroom, out of it, down the stairs, up the stairs, down the stairs, around the living room, around the living room, around the living room.

2:41.

I lost the battle, the war, and sent him another message.

**Me: Hi, it's late and weather is crappy. Really just want to make sure you're okay?**

Green. Undelivered.

Logically—*logically*—there was a pretty good chance he was spending the night somewhere else. But that didn't stop me from checking the accident reports. It didn't stop my anxiety from expanding into my lungs and chest and throat.

Because why had the messages not sent, at least?

*Maybe he doesn't have a charger on him.*

*WHATIFWHATIFWHATIF.*

3:03.

I was sitting on the couch, hugging my knees to my chest, staring at the green, undelivered text bubbles. My thumb hovered over one, trying to decide whether or not resending the message at this hour would seem weird and desperate.

3:16.

I pressed my forehead against my knees.

*You're being silly and ridiculous. Should have just gone to sleep.*

*WHATIFWHATIFWHATIF.*

*He's a grown man. He's fine and probably just spending the night somewhere else.*

*WHATIFWHATIFWHATIF.*

*You've known the guy for less than ten days. It's unreasonable for you to be this worried. Stop it.*

*WHATIFWHATIFWHATIF.*

*You're going to feel really stupid about this tomorrow. And tired.*

*WHATIFWHATIFWHATIF.*

*WHATIFWHAtifwhatif.*

*Whatifwhat if, what if.*

*What if.*

*What if ... if*

...

...

...

"Skylar?"

Me? That was me.

Something nudged my arm.

I lifted my head. Blinked.

"Hey, what are you doing?"

What was I... doing. I was in the living room, on the couch, waiting. I'd dozed off, waiting for Ethan.

Ethan.

He was sitting on the coffee table, facing me. The realization jolted me upright, hands flying to rub the sleep and fog from my eyes.

I looked at him, looked at the time, looked back at him. "It's four thirty."

"Exactly. What are you doing?"

What was *I* doing?

A rush of emotions hit me at once. Frustration. Anger. *Relief*. So much fucking relief. But also *anger*.

"You said we would go over the contract this afternoon. Remember?" It came out sharp-edged. I hadn't meant for it to, but it did.

"Right."

That was it. That was all he said.

My eyes were starting to adjust to the dark, and his features were becoming more crisp, clear. He looked tired, pale, worn down. His hair was disheveled, like he'd run a hand through it one too many hundred times, and a light scruff coated the normally clean-shaven lower half of his face. His shoulders sagged as he leaned forward with his elbows resting on his thighs, like they had the weight of the universe pressing down on them.

Though none of that compared to the complete and utter look of exhaustion that glazed his brown eyes.

They looked... done. Defeated.

My anger vanished.

I moved forward to the edge of the couch so I could get a closer look at him. "Are... is everything okay?"

Which was a stupid question. Clearly, everything was not okay. He looked as though *nothing* was okay.

"I snapped at you yesterday," he said in lieu of an answer. And even his voice was... *off*, wrong. Was he sick? He sounded sick. "You told me that the confrontation was difficult for you. But you were honest with me anyway, and I shouldn't have snapped at you to get out. I feel bad about it. And I'm sorry."

Wrong. Wrong wrong wrong wrong. It was all *wrong*.

I was the one that should have been apologizing. And that's what I wanted to tell him, but he cut me off before I could start.

"But I think," he went on, maintaining eye contact. They looked so, *so* tired. "That, regardless of what you believe my intentions were, it was a good idea for us to stop before things escalated any further. Upstairs. I don't think it was a smart idea... I shouldn't have initiated it."

Oh.

Oh, okay.

I moved back a few inches.

But he still managed to drive the knife in. "And I think it's best if we just stick to a professional relationship."

Right. Because he was hiring me. Trying to. With payment involved.

I didn't miss how finite his wording was, either. He didn't say, *for now*. Didn't leave any room for interpretation. Professional was what he wanted. Professional. Which was the least personal and romantic of all relationship types, I was pretty sure.

So, *"I don't want you,"* essentially. Which, yes. Made sense.

So. Okay.

Loud and clear.

Ethan's eyes dipped down to my lap, and I realized I was wringing my hands on them. I stopped and shoved my fingers under my thighs.

I stayed silent, so he continued to fill in the gap, twist the knife. "I just think things might have gotten messy if we continued... in that direction. And I don't think I have the capacity right now for things to get more complicated than they already are."

Right.

Yes.

He had a lot on his plate. With work and things. Anyone could see that.

And it was messy with me. I. Was. Per last night. And who'd want that?

Not me.

So. Okay.

My brain was really foggy from having just woken up. I tried to push and blink the haze away so I could think more clearly, catch up. I wished we were having this conversation when I was a little less disoriented. Or, better yet, not at all.

"I think it's best to just end it now since we haven't known each other for very long," he went on, twisting and twisting. "Before feelings get involved."

Before feelings got involved. Before feelings. Before.

And then he started to list things off, reasons as to why this was for the best. I missed some of it, my mind reeling through the daze, but the main points stuck.

He said, "Because things at work are delicate right now."

He said, "You're friends with my sister."

He said, "There's an age difference."

So. Right. Yes. Work and Alexis.

And he was older. So. Maturity difference.

Because a thirty-year-old woman probably wouldn't have randomly accused him of trying to manipulate her right before sex without any evidence to back it up. She'd probably be more mature than that.

So. Okay.

Ethan let out a breath. "You're not saying anything."

My initial plan had been to listen to Mikaela's advice and apologize to him for last night. I'd prepared all day for it, readied the speech in my head. Memorized it.

Now, though? Gun to my head, I wouldn't have been able to recall any of it, not a single word.

So I nodded. "Okay." Because what else could I say.

His eyes bounced between mine. One beat, two beats, three, four. And then he nodded. "Okay."

And that was that.

Except neither of us moved. And I didn't know why. All I knew was that Ethan was looking at me, I was looking at him, and neither of us moved.

"Are you going to tell me why you fell asleep down here now?" he eventually asked.

But he already knew why, didn't he.

What I really wanted to do was respond with a smart, funny remark. Because my ego and my pride wanted him to think that I wasn't affected by any of this. At that moment, I wanted to be the strong, quick-witted woman from the movies. The one that could just... brush this off. Like it was nothing. Like he was no one.

I wished I were like her. I really did.

But I was tired. And I was sad.

Even though he said we hadn't known each other for very long, even though he said this was before feelings got involved.

My heart was really, really sad. It had worried for him, stayed up for him, felt relief for him. Because it hadn't known that feelings weren't supposed to be involved yet. That his feelings weren't involved yet.

And the last thing I wanted to do as the hurt curled itself up in my throat, as it sent exhausted, sad, angry tears up to my eyes, was play pretend. So, instead, I stood up and walked away without giving Ethan an answer.

I WAS STILL STARING out at the falling snow when my alarm went off an hour later.

# 26

## kylar

I ALMOST FELL asleep on the toilet.

At work.

Twice.

Everything seemed to drag. Meetings, conversations, coffee orders. I'd never been good with functioning on minimal sleep, ever. So two consecutive nights of no REM was killing me slowly, painfully.

I just wanted to go home.

*Home,* home.

I missed Mik, Jo, Peter.

But at least the apartment was empty when I got there, a discovery that made my entire body sigh with relief. I'd spent the whole day thinking about not thinking about Ethan, all the while fighting sleep. It had been emotionally, mentally, physically draining.

So he was just about the last person I wanted to see today. Or tomorrow. Or the day after that. Or—

*You'll have to talk to him eventually. The party is this Friday.*

I pushed that thought away, changed into the most comfortable sweats I owned, poured myself a glass of red wine, crawled into bed, and started to watch *Pride and Prejudice* on my laptop.

It was the perfect remedy. I was going to finish the movie, drink my wine, then sleep for ten hours. And I was going to feel better tomorrow.

I barely made it ten minutes into the film before passing out. Didn't even touch the wine.

"Alexis, *no*."

"Skylar, *yes*."

"Not a chance." I crossed my arms to show her I was *serious* about this.

"Just try it on!" she pleaded, voice bouncing off the white walls of her studio. She held the garment bag out to me again. "That's all I'm asking. Just put it on."

Nope. No. Absolutely not.

"Alexis, when you said you had a dress that would be 'perfect for me to wear to the party,' I thought you meant, like, something from the mall. Off the rack. Not a *limited-edition Kilarni piece*." In hindsight, I really should have known better. It was the apartment penthouse thing all over again. "That gown costs more than I'm set to make during my internship! The whole three months!"

I didn't even want to touch it without gloves.

"First of all, it *is* perfect. The party's black-tie. What do you think other people are going to show up in?" Alexis argued.

"Second of all, it won't fit me, my waist, my height, *or* my boobs. Or else *I'd* wear it. It's a huge waste, don't you think? To just let it sit in my studio closet, all by its lonesome, pretty little silk self?"

It was almost the exact argument she'd made about the apartment. "I'm not wearing it."

Alexis pointed an unhappy finger straight at my nose. "You used to never be this stubborn—you'd always at least hesitate. This is Ethan's fault. That overgrown, grumpy gargoyle is already starting to rub off on you."

I felt myself flush at the sudden, unexpected mention of her brother, heart leaping in my chest. And then I looked away. But I quickly changed my mind and looked back at her because the looking away had been suspicious, I was pretty sure.

"Uh, what was *that*?" she asked.

"What was what?"

"*That*. Your face. What did your face just do? And why are you turning red?"

"I'm n-not."

*Nice.*

"Now you're turning even *more* red," Alexis accused, large brown eyes widening into saucers before she gasped. "Oh my god. *What did he do*?"

Oh god. "*Nothing*. I swear. My face is normal. This is my regular face," I insisted, even as the color spread down to my arms. I was starting to sweat. Pits and palms.

I could tell by the way she was looking at me that she was trying to decide whether or not she believed me. So I gave her a wide, reassuring smile, like any good liar would.

Her eyes thinned. "I'm calling him right now."

*Fuck*. "No! Don't!"

That... came out a lot louder than I'd intended. So loud, in fact, that it made Alexis jump. She gaped back at me, clutching the garment bag to her chest.

I cleared my throat.

She gaped.

"You, uh, don't need to call him," I said, in my *indoor* voice this time. "He didn't do anything, and I'll... I'll try on the dress."

If I wasn't glowing with the vigorous enthusiasm of a radioactive tomato by now, it would be a miracle. So, before I could make things any worse than they already were, I walked over to Alexis, grabbed the garment bag from her, and practically ran into the closet.

I changed quickly, slipping into the gown without taking the appropriate time to admire its brilliance. I registered the basics: black, silk, straps, slit. That was it.

"Okay, here you go," I said, walking out of the small room. "Tried it on, just like you asked."

Alexis was sitting on a small stool right beside where her camera was set up. Her arms were crossed, and her eyes were... assessing. My face. Not the dress.

I did a little spin, trying to redirect her attention. "What do you think? Good? Bad? Yea? Nay?"

"You look unreal," she deadpanned, and then, "Is something going on between you and Ethan?"

I shook my head. "No*pe*." Which, technically, was not a lie. There wasn't anything going on between me and her brother anymore. "Anyways, don't you think the slit is too high? There's only, like, two inches of fabric between my hip bone and where the cut starts." I pointed a finger to the upper part of my right leg, where the cut began. Another attempt at redirection.

Her eyes remained glued to my face. "No, you have the legs to pull it off. The length is also perfect, just like I knew it would be. There'll be no drag once you're in heels. Are you sure there isn't something you're not telling me?"

"Positive. Do you have a mirror so I can see?"

She nudged her chin in my direction. I turned around and —oh. Oh, my god.

"I told you," Alexis said, walking up behind me. "I *told* you. You look like a Greek goddess of the night or something equally unrealistic. It's absolutely ridiculous."

Holy crap. "I have curves." They were subtle, but they were there. The draping of the fabric made it look like I had curves around my hips.

*Me*. Tube Man Skylar.

The black silk dress was simple, elegant. Two thin straps, A-line cowl neck, and a long (*long*) slit up the right leg. But it was the fabric that did most of the work, lying against my skin in effortless, delicate drapes that hugged and hung in all the perfect places.

"Here are the shoes I had in mind for you. I've only got a few pairs of heels in your size, but I think these ones will go quite well," Alexis said, handing me a box containing black lace-up heels.

The six minutes it took me to get them on was well worth it. She was right—they did go quite well.

"Good lord, your legs," Alexis sighed from beside me. "What I would give."

"Wanna trade?" I teased, nudging her arm. "Your boobs for my legs."

Unlike me, Alexis was not tubularly shaped. She'd been blessed with curves I could only dream of.

"I'd honestly consider it if Joel wouldn't have a meltdown. He's rather attached. Named them and everything."

"Bummer." Not that I blamed him.

"Mmm," she agreed. "Anyways, I'll grab you a bag for all this stuff. Just a sec."

Uh. "Wait, I didn't say I'd wear it. Just that I'd try it on."

"The party's tomorrow. What else are you going to wear?"

"You tricked me, and you know it." I hadn't questioned it when she told me I could borrow an outfit. We'd done enough shoots together for her to know my size, shape, what looked good on me, and what didn't. "Plus, you have other dresses here that'll fit me. I know you do. There's also, like, a hundred malls in this city."

"You're wearing the dress, Skylar. You already said you liked it."

"I'm not wearing the dress, Alexis. Doesn't matter if I like it —it's way too expensive. What if I... I don't know, spill a drink on it or something?"

"Dry cleaners."

"What if it rips?"

"I hear you're pretty proficient at sewing. Almost like you do it for a living."

Wasn't gonna work. "I'm not wearing it."

"You are."

"I can't."

"You will."

"Alexis, *no*."

"Skylar, *yes*."

Thirty minutes later, I got into a taxi with the dress, the shoes, a pair of earrings, a coat, and a budding headache.

She had no right calling me stubborn.

# 27

## kylar

For the first time all week, the lights were on in the apartment when I got there, Ethan's loafers were placed beside the mat, and I could hear the rustling of papers coming out of his open office door.

There were two things wrong with this picture: Ethan always put his shoes away, and he never kept his office door open.

But neither of them registered properly over the rush of adrenaline or the increased heart rate.

I considered beelining straight for the stairs.

*But you're going to have to talk to him eventually. The party is tomorrow night. You don't even know what time you sh—*

A man stepped out of Ethan's office.

Like, some random guy.

He saw me, stopped. I saw him, short-circuited.

"Who are you?" Guy asked, dark brows pulling together.

I—who was *I*?

Closest escape route was behind me. The smart thing was to turn around and run out. But my one brain cell had died a multitude of deaths over the last two weeks, so I just stood there, staring. Because fight or flight or freeze, apparently.

"Why are you in my apartment?" Guy asked again.

Wait a minute, I'd already seen this movie. Different actor, but I could have sworn it included that exact same frown. Like, the *exact* same disapproving frown. There was something so, very familiar about—

Oh.

Oh, my god.

Oh no, oh my god.

Flight.

Wait, no, that didn't seem right.

Fight. You were supposed to *fight* the potentially evil twin.

Wait, no, that didn't seem right, either. He was way bigger than me. Also, I couldn't fight. Didn't know how. Never saw *Fight Club*.

Wait, was Ethan here, too?

*Please, please let Ethan be here.*

"Hello?" Guy took a step forward. "Who are you?"

The movement was what snapped me out of the nervous, nonsensical rambling in my head. Sort of. "I'm, um, I live here. Who are *you*?"

Because I couldn't be 100 percent sure. This would be a lot easier if they were identical.

"You... *live* here," he repeated with another few steps toward me. His hair was a deep, dark brown, like his sister's. And his eyes... those were onyx. It was a rather intimidating color; I couldn't really tell where his pupils ended and his irises began.

He was also tall, like Ethan. Similar build, too. Stupid levels of handsome. Lots of eyelashes.

All in all, I really should have been less focused on his looks and a bit more alarmed, having come home to find a random dude in the apartment. Seriously, I had the survival instincts of an albino possum who liked to play undead in predator territory.

*First one out of the group to get scary-movie-murdered, for sure.*

"I do live here," I confirmed with what I hoped was confidence, slipping a hand into my pocket. The one holding my phone. "You don't, though. So you should probably tell me who you are now."

His eyes flicked down, then up. And then they were absolutely *brimming* with amusement.

Guy put his hands up. One of them was holding a bunch of papers. "I surrender—please don't tase me."

*Don't wh—oh, he thinks you have a weapon in your pocket. A Taser.*

"You haven't answered my question," I said.

"Right." He dropped his hands, then held one out to me casually. "Greyson. Or Grey, if you'd like."

Twin status confirmed. Which... honestly made me more nervous than it would have had he been some random guy.

"You're Ethan's brother," I said, walking over to shake his hand. Though I had to discreetly wipe mine on my jeans first. Because nerves. My heart was beating so fast I was a little scared he'd be able to hear it. Or, like, feel it through my palm or something.

I kept the handshake quick.

"Unfortunately," Grey answered with a smile. This twin was also a Whitestrip fanatic, apparently, but the left corner of his lips didn't overcurl like Ethan's did. Instead, he had a tiny dimple just below that spot but on the right side. "And you are?"

"Skylar."

The grin widened. It was weirdly disarming, his smile. Probably because of the unexpected dimple dot. "It's lovely to meet you, Skylar. I'm sorry for scaring you. I wasn't aware that my brother had taken up... a roommate."

Right. Okay. Acting time. *You can do this*. "Girlfriend, actually."

Pure, unfiltered amusement in his eyes, on his lips. And I realized he'd been teasing. "Yes, of course."

"If you don't mind me asking, why are you here?" Alone. Going through Ethan's things in his office.

Grey held up the stack of papers he'd walked out with. There were red marks and writing all over them. "Came for these."

That didn't explain much.

"Was Ethan expecting you?"

Grey shrugged. "I left him a voicemail. Any idea when he'll be home?"

That... felt like something I should know. It felt like something a partner would know.

So I blurted out a lie without thinking. "Soon, I think. Should be soon."

He grinned. "Perfect. Then you wouldn't mind if I wait here, would you? I'd like to have a word with him."

*Ummmmmmmmmmmmmmmm.*

"Not at all. Please," I said, gesturing to the couch. Because my panic-riddled brain couldn't think of an excuse on the spot to get rid of him. "Would you like a drink while you wait? Tea? Water?"

Grey nudged a chin toward the bar. "I was going to make

myself a cocktail, if you'd like one. My brother owes me a few drinks this week, you see."

I... didn't. But mostly because I wasn't really paying attention, trying to figure out how to excuse myself so I could call Ethan. "Sure, sounds good. Just let me put this stuff away and wash my hands. I'll be right back."

And I had to actively stop myself from Usain Bolting it up the stairs.

My phone was out of my pocket and I was dialing the second both my bedroom and bathroom doors were shut.

*Please pick up. Please.*

Straight to voicemail.

I tried again. And again. Voicemail, voicemail.

*Fuck.*

"Hey, Ethan," I started to whisper after the *beep*, trying to keep my voice from shaking. "So, um, your brother is here. In the apartment. So if you could call me back immediately, that would be really swell, thanks."

And then, just in case, I sent a couple of texts.

**Me: Can you call me back ASAP**

**Me: Grey is here. He's waiting for you. Coming home soon?**

They went through as green. I cursed.

How was his phone off again? Why even bother owning one?

*Okay. It's okay. Here's the plan. You're going to go downstairs, you're going to sit and talk and act normal for, like, fifteen minutes so as to not seem suspicious, and then you're going to pretend like Ethan texted you saying he's going to be home late, which will give you a perfectly good excuse to send Potentially Evil Twin on his merry, villainy way.*

I pointed at myself in the mirror. "And whatever you do, don't freak out."

Grey was sitting in Ethan's brown armchair when I went back downstairs, flipping through the red-marked document. There were two drinks on the table in front of him.

This was fine. I was fine. I could *do* this.

"Hey, sorry about that," I said, taking a seat on the couch. My phone went right beside my leg, speaker pointing outward, unobstructed. "There was a dress in that bag that required an immediate hanging."

"Ah, so you're coming to the party, then." He set the papers aside and reached for his drink. Whiskey something, from the looks of it. Or maybe just whiskey.

And unless Ethan had changed his mind or disappeared off the face of the planet (both of which were very real possibilities at this point), then, "Yes, yeah. I'll be there."

*I think. I'm pretty sure.*

"So, um, what is that anyway?" I asked, gesturing toward the marked papers. My main goal was to keep the rein on the conversation. That way, we'd avoid the more dangerous topics... like my relationship with Ethan.

"A report I've been waiting on," Grey answered with a sip of his drink. "I need it for a meeting in the morning."

Right. Okay. But couldn't Ethan have just... taken it to work tomorrow? Or today? Also, where was he *now*? Was he not *at* work? Couldn't *he* have come to pick up the report?

I wondered how suspicious it would be if I were to ask. Then I wondered if I was overthinking it. *Then* I wondered what, exactly, would be a nonsuspicious, safe topic for us to talk about. Something that required a minimal amount of lying.

Grey beat me to it.

"I won't bore you with the details, since I'm sure you get enough company talk from Ethan," he went on with a polite, understanding smile. "So, tell me, what do you do for work, Skylar?"

Oh this, *this* was a very safe topic. *Stay here for a bit, then do the pretend-text thing, and voilà! Out he goes.*

Some of the tension in my shoulders eased as I gestured toward his white dress shirt. More specifically, to the telltale, little black *ZB* stitched onto the inside band of his open collar. "I'm a design intern. At Zilmar Bain."

The reveal made his eyebrows bounce. "Seriously?"

"Mmhmm."

The surprise reached his dark eyes, brought a light shimmer to them. "And what does that entail, exactly? What does a design intern do?"

I scrunched my nose. "It's a little less exciting than it sounds, to be honest. I mostly just help with sewing and pattern making, running errands, and a bunch of admin work. Oh, and I do, like, three coffee runs a day. Sometimes four."

His eyebrows acted the same way Ethan's did when he was confused. They created a faint little V in their middle, one of them slightly raised. "They can't just have the coffee delivered?"

"They do have it delivered, by me."

Another grin. "Right."

"I do get to assist with a few upcoming photoshoots, though, for the spring and summer collection. So that's pretty neat." I was really looking forward to it, actually. That and the new flagship store opening event.

"And how is it, working for Zilmar? He a good boss?" Grey took another sip of his drink. I hadn't touched mine yet—didn't really want it, still a little nauseous.

I shrugged in response to his question. "I haven't really had a chance to interact with him much. He's a busy man." He'd also been in Paris the majority of the last two weeks.

"Mmm, that he is."

It took me a moment. "How do you know?"

"He's a friend," Grey noted casually. *Casually*. As though he were talking about some dude down the street and not an *international icon of fashion and design*.

My jaw dropped. I blinked. "You're *friends* with Zilmar Bain?"

The corners of his eyes crinkled through his widening smile. "We call him Zee, but yeah."

*Wow*. "How?"

"I play golf with his brother, and he gets dragged along sometimes. Funny guy. Dramatic and neurotic as all hell, but funny."

I grinned because that was in exact line with what I'd heard and observed about Bain.

Then, before I could respond, Grey glanced at his watch and said, "You got any of your sketches here? Can I see them while we wait?"

And that made me pause.

*Ummm, no, that's probably not a good idea. I should do the pretend-text thing now and tell him to get out.*

But *then* he said, "I can put in a good word for you if you want. Next time Zee joins us," just as I reached for my phone.

Wait, really? "You would? Why?"

"Think of it as an apology. For scaring you earlier." He tipped his tumbler in my direction before finishing off his drink. "I feel kind of bad about it."

It was a little weird how unexpectedly alike the brothers were, considering their strained relationship. That seemed like something Ethan would say and do.

It *was* something Ethan had already done. But he'd apologized with breakfast instead.

*It's a bad idea. You should just tell him to leave. Remember what*

*Alexis said about him? With the whole "he only lets you see what he wants you to see" thing?*

*Yeah, but she also warned me about Ethan, and look at how that turned out.*

Plus, the industry was so insanely competitive... and a good word could lead to a good job, which could lead to a good career. Connections were everything. His one word could be everything.

*Don't do it.*

"Okay, just a second," I said and stood up.

Five minutes. That was it. I was going to let him skim through the sketches for five minutes, and then he'd leave.

"Here." I plopped back down on the couch, handing him my black sketchbook. "Not my official portfolio or anything, just what I use for daily drawings and idea purges and stuff."

Grey was mostly quiet as he started to flip through the pages, turning them with gentle care, which I thought was nice.

Maybe there was no evil twin. Maybe the impossible had happened and the movies were wrong.

"I figured you were good, knowing how competitive Zee's internships and positions are in general," he said, eyes glued to a dark teal suit I was particularly fond of. Slim-fit, double-breasted with peak lapels. "But this... I'd honestly wear all of these."

The compliment wormed its way over my lips, forcing it into a small smile, despite all the nervous energy zipping up and down my spine. I had to sit on my hands to stop them from fiddling with anything and everything within reach.

"Could you make them?" he asked, flipping over to a charcoal, hooded blouson. "If someone were to ask? The suits, specifically."

"I could, yeah." And by now, the anxious little voice in the back of my brain telling me to send him away was getting louder, more antsy.

*It's time*, it kept saying. *Pretend to get the text, tell him to go.*

He was almost at the very end of the sketches anyway—a few more flips and he'd hit a blank page. I was going to wait until he got there, but it felt like he'd started to slow down a little, brows pulled together as he silently studied the designs.

*Okay, it's time.*

I grabbed my phone, tapped it to life, and opened my mouth... just in time for the *beeps* of the front door lock to go off.

My whole body whipped around to watch Ethan open the door and enter the apartment. A miracle.

And *oh*, he'd gotten a haircut.

It looked so good, wow.

*Not the time.*

*It looks sooo good, though. With the back sweep and everything.*

*Shut up!*

"There he is!" I blurted, throwing my hands up in excitement since I was pretty sure that's what people did when their partners came home. "*Baaabe*, we've been waiting for you!"

Ethan looked at me like he thought I was maybe having a stroke.

And then...

And then he saw Grey.

# 28

than

AT FIRST, I thought I was hallucinating. Because it didn't make any sense.

Skylar, Grey, scotch.

Skylar, Grey, scotch.

Skylar, Grey, sco—

And then it hit, slick as oil, hot as lava, whipping and slashing through me, coiling around my fists, jaw, neck. It *twisted*, tighter and tighter, suffocating every last ounce of reason I had in me.

Because Greyson—the fucking *cockroach*—was sitting in my living room, drinking my scotch.

With Skylar. With *my* Skylar.

The air in my lungs boiled, and my duffle bag hit the floor with a loud, dull *thud*.

"What. The *fuck*. Are you doing here." The words came out as a low, thundering rumble.

Skylar slowly lowered herself back onto the couch, but Grey didn't pay me any attention. His focus was on a book. Fucking prick.

"*Grey*," I barked.

Skylar flinched.

Slowly, my brother closed the book, pushed it aside, and looked up at me. "Where the hell have you been?"

"That's none of your goddamn business. Tell me what the fuck you're doing in my fucking *apartment*."

I was seething.

What had he done?

How long had he been here?

What had he said to her?

Grey's head tilted. "Since when is this place yours?"

"I *live* here, asshole. You can't just come barging in. You know the rules."

"You want to talk about *rules*? You were supposed to have the Symnoks reports sent to me with your notes and signatures yesterday." He picked up a stack of papers and slapped them back onto the table to make his point. He'd gone through my shit. Of course he'd gone through my shit. "You're not picking up your phone, you haven't been to the office, and you've skipped every single meeting we've had scheduled this week. I came here to make sure you weren't *dead*."

"Sorry to disappoint. I've been working remote and checking emails. You couldn't have sent me one of those?"

"You screen my emails. And Mila's."

"Neither of you ever has anything important to say."

Yet somehow, they managed to send hundreds of emails a week between the two of them. I'd resorted to autoforwarding their bullshit into a separate folder. It did not get checked regularly. When it did, it was not by me.

*I need to give Jackson a raise.*

"If you'd just done your job and sent these to me like you were supposed to, I wouldn't be here," Greyson bit back, standing up.

I glowered. "You didn't *tell me* you needed them yesterday. And even if you had, it sure as hell wouldn't justify breaking into my apartment." And I knew he had because there was no way Skylar would have let him in.

"Is it breaking in if I have the code?" he asked mockingly.

"Is it punching you in the face if I do it with my fist?"

"Charming, isn't he?" The question was directed at Skylar, whose eyes were glued to me. *Good, stay here.*

Grey didn't wait for an answer from her before turning back to me. "And I did tell you I needed the reports early. Last week. Via an email you obviously didn't bother to check."

"Well, you have them now, so *leave*."

"We still need to talk ab—"

"Either get the fuck out right now, Grey, or I'll make you."

His eyes lit up with amusement in response to the threat. Then, he turned to Skylar again.

And he smiled.

He smiled *that* smile. The one with calculated *intent* behind every millimeter of its half curve.

My whole body clenched.

"It was a pleasure to meet you, Skylar. I'm sorry again for our little mishap earlier," he said to her, voice softening three notches too many. "And for my brother's behavior this evening. We'll be in touch about Zee and that suit."

Then the fucker *winked* at her.

What mishap?

What suit?

And what the fuck was a "Zee?"

"It was nice to meet you, too," Skylar said with a small nod, which *nope*. Not a chance. There was no way in hell they were going to be "in touch" about anything. From now until the end of forever. I'd put it in the contract if I had to.

Finally, Grey grabbed his shit and walked to where I was standing near the door. Just a few more feet and he'd be out of it.

My hands were itching to help speed things along.

"She's pretty," he said, voice low enough that only I could hear him. "Freaky eyes. I get it."

I was going to punch him in the fucking throat.

My fist clenched, unclenched. "*Leave*."

And he had the audacity to throw a small, amused smirk my way before slithering out the door.

My attention immediately snapped to a now standing, fidgeting Skylar, but I waited until the elevator outside *ding*ed the all clear. And then, "What. *The hell*."

"Um, I can explain. I think."

"You *think*?"

"In my defense, you didn't pick up your phone."

Not an explanation. "Start from the beginning."

"Um, okay, the beginning. So, I got to the apartment, and the lights were on. I assumed you were home, and I was going to come talk to you about... tomorrow. Details and stuff. But then, some guy I didn't recognize walked out of your office," she said, wringing her fingers. "Which scared me a little bit, to be honest."

"And you didn't think to run? Call the police?" I needed to change the code on the lock. And add a few more digits.

"Well, I guessed who he might be pretty quick," she said. "You have the same frown."

*We what?* "No we don't."

"Yeah you do. It's that one." She pointed at my face. "Literally that exact same one. You're doing it right now."

The muscles in my forehead relaxed instinctively. Skylar's

mouth quirked, and she dropped her finger. "Anyways," she went on, "then the introductions happened, and when he asked what time you'd be home, I panicked and said, 'Soon,' because that's something I would probably know if you were my boyfriend, right?"

The word "boyfriend" zipped right into my chest, and I swear there was *fluttering* involved. An uncomfortable amount of it.

I cleared my throat. "Right."

"Right. Okay, *so then*, he was like, 'You don't mind if I wait here, do you? I'd like to have a word with Ethan.'"

"And you said *yes*? Instead of just kicking him the fuck out?" I started to strip out of my coat, shoes. It was hot in here.

"That would have been so suspicious, though, don't you think?"

"How?" I took a seat on the couch, and Skylar joined me. Lemon. Vanilla.

"Well, because I'd *just* said you'd be home soon. So in my head, saying 'no' felt like saying 'wait outside,' which is *weird*, Ethan. You don't tell your boyfriend's brother to wait outside for him."

It wasn't a flutter this time. It was a tornado.

"Anyways. I told him I needed to put some stuff away, ran upstairs, called you, sent a couple messages. And when you didn't respond, I thought I'd just keep him company for a bit, then pretend like I got a text from you saying you'd be home late and get him to leave without raising any suspicion."

"You could have just told him to leave from the very beginning," I insisted.

"You could have told *me* that if you'd picked up your phone!" she retorted.

I ignored that. "What happened next?"

She shrugged. "I talked to him for about twenty minutes. Then you came home."

"And what, exactly, was said in those twenty minutes of conversation? Word for word, Skylar. What was the 'suit' thing he was talking about? Why did he say he'd be in touch? And why did alcohol need to be involved?"

Instead of answering, she took out her phone, tapped at it a few times, and then offered it to me. "Here, I recorded it."

That... I wasn't expecting that. "You *recorded* the conversation?"

"Just in case," she said. "I had a feeling you'd ask for the specifics to make sure I didn't accidentally let something slip. Since you think I'm a terrible liar and all."

"You are a terrible liar." Also, that had been a fair assumption. And quick thinking. Smart. She was smart.

Her lips twitched. My eyes dipped. Why were we sitting so close? I'd meant to keep my distance.

And why wasn't I more angry with her? Pretty sure I'd walked in on her having a drink with Grey, pretty sure they'd made plans to keep in touch, and I was supposed to be a lot more angry about it.

"D'you wanna listen to it or not?" Skylar asked, nudging my arm with her phone.

I grabbed it and pressed Play.

The recording started off with shuffling and the pattering of steps. Then her voice kicked in. *"Hey, sorry about that. There was a dress in that bag that required an immediate hanging."*

She'd been nervous. Her tone was a tinge higher than usual, her words coming out at a slightly faster speed.

It made me... I didn't like it. That she'd been scared, nervous.

"Gross. I hate hearing recordings of myself," Skylar mumbled beside me.

And either she'd moved closer, or I had. Our legs were touching, arms brushing. *Zip, zap*. Lemon, vanilla.

I had to rewind the audio a bit. Hard time concentrating.

"Did you know? That he was friends with Zilmar Bain?" Skylar asked when we got there.

I shook my head, hit Pause. "No. Have you said anything to anyone at work about your relationship status?"

"Um, yeah, but I said I was taken... when they asked. Because of our trial thing. So we should be good."

*Taken*. My entire being buzzed at that word coming out of her mouth. Even though it wasn't supposed to. We'd *talked* about this. Extensively.

I had to clear my throat again, push the thoughts away again. "Who? Was Zilmar there?"

"No. It was a guy from accounting."

Silence.

"A... guy from accounting," I repeated slowly. "When was this?"

"Um, two days ago." The words were accompanied by fresh color sprinting across her cheeks. I wanted to touch them.

Wait, no. No I didn't.

"He asked if you were single?"

"No... he asked me to dinner."

Oh.

I held her gaze; she held mine. Our limbs were all but tangled on the couch now, we were sitting so close.

Maybe the conspiracy theorists were right. Maybe we were all magnetized. Because how else did this happen every time I was in the same room as her, regardless of how much I told myself *no*? Why else would my skin feel charged every time she was this close?

It had to be the magnet thing.

"Did you want to say yes?" I found myself asking. Because I

was a masochist. Because the thought of some guy asking Skylar out was wreaking havoc on my internal wiring and had detached my mouth from my brain, logic from reason.

Four days of distancing myself, building up my resolve, only to have it melt away in mere minutes.

Why? Because there was a tiny, light brown freckle just above her right eyelid that I'd never noticed before. And now my eyes kept bouncing up to it in awe, like they'd discovered a whole new planet.

*I wonder if she has more.*

Skylar's head tilted, eyes half-mast, pupils dilated. Like she was drunk off the air we were sharing. Or maybe I was projecting. "Does it matter?" she muttered.

It shouldn't have. Except it did. It really fucking mattered. "That's not a 'no,' Skylar."

She bit into her bottom lip. It stopped my heart.

There was a really good chance I was going to accidentally kiss her on purpose, even though I wasn't supposed to.

"Um, Ethan?"

And I was so far gone that her little *um* made my heart stutter. I loved the way she talked, I loved her little fidgets, I loved the way she—

*Stop it.*

I had to clear my throat again. "Yeah?"

"You're... Um, I don't really... have any more room to move back."

She what?

I tore my eyes away from hers, looked down, and realized a few things in agonizingly slow succession:

1) We had not been moving closer to each other. It had all been me. I had Skylar practically pinned to her corner of the couch, with my one arm flung behind her head on the back-

rest, a leg hooked under hers, and a hand on her knee. I didn't even have her phone anymore—it was on the table.

2) Four days away had not made things better. It had made them worse. It had made them a hell of a lot worse.

3) I'd... missed her. I'd *missed* her.

"Oh. Sorry," I said stupidly.

"S'okay," Skylar mumbled as I peeled myself from her and defied gravity all the way to the other end of the couch.

We sat in a dense, strange silence for a minute, and I couldn't really remember what we were supposed to be doing. Or why I wasn't feeling angry anymore. And before I could break through the mental fog, Skylar stood up.

"I'm gonna... I'll just send you the recording," she said, reaching for her phone and the black book on the table. "You can listen to it whenever, and then... I just need to know what time to be ready for the party tomorrow. So if you could... text me... those details..." She trailed off, shifting from one foot to the other.

"Okay," I said simply.

"Okay," she responded. "Alright... bye." Then she turned around and walked up the stairs.

I sat there for a bit, taking inventory, noting the heat that flushed my neck, cheeks.

Some of my limbs felt too heavy; others felt too light. And I was somewhat dizzy, like my brain wasn't getting enough oxygen. Except my lungs were running on rampant overdrive, trying to keep up with my heart.

In fact, my whole chest was a cluttered mess of clumsy movements, and they were starting to mix with the twists and churns of my stomach. It was making me nauseous.

And my hands? Tingling. My flesh was fucking... *tingling.* Like there were tens of tiny goldfish pecking at my skin. Or like I'd smacked something and my fingers were on the tail end of recovering from the impact.

So I kept sitting there, staring down at them, completely and utterly dumbfounded.

I'd *missed* her.

# 29

kylar

MY HEART WAS BEATING at a pace of around ten thousand beats per minute, I was pretty sure. Give or take a hundred or two.

Because what the hell was *that*?

*I'll tell you what that was.* That *was the behavior of a dude who does* not *want to keep things "professional,"* a voice in my head claimed as I shut the door behind me.

It sounded suspiciously like Mik—the voice, I mean—which would make this the second time in a week I'd heard her talking to me without her actually talking to me.

So either I missed being around her so much that my brain was manifesting her voice as a coping mechanism, or Mikaela had somehow (probably through the use of one of those crystals she was always wielding about—an amberchite or whatever) figured out a way to communicate with me telepathically and we needed to have a serious discussion about boundaries.

I leaned back against my bedroom door. Not, like, *my* bedroom door, because this wasn't *my* house or room or whatever. But *the* bedroom door, I guess, of the—

*Would you shut up with the off-topic rambling and focus!*

Except I didn't want to focus on what had just happened downstairs. In fact, I was trying really, very hard to do the exact opposite, hence the off-topic rambling. Because focusing on that would lead to assumptions. And assumptions would lead to hope; hope would lead to disappointment; and disappointment, in this case, had the very real potential of turning into heartbreak. Because, unfortunately for me, Ethan's physical absence from my life this week had done zilch in mitigating my growing feelings for him. *Zilch.*

My whole body had inflated when he walked through that door, which at first I thought was part of the relief, but then... I don't know. It stayed like that the whole time, even after Grey left. And then it felt like... like the sun had risen in my chest, or something equally warm and light and stupid-sounding. I didn't know how to describe it, exactly, because I'd never felt anything quite like it.

So, no, I didn't want to focus on the way Ethan had been looking at me just now. I didn't want to read into why it seemed as though he couldn't keep himself from touching me. Or why he'd care about Ian asking me to dinner. That was dangerous, speculative territory that came hand in hand with an overly long list of "maybes" and "what-ifs."

Like, for example, maybe he'd been looking at me that way because maybe, *just maybe*, he felt the same things I did.

And maybe he kept touching me because maybe, *just maybe*, he'd missed me, too. Since, you know, *I'd* missed *him*. Which didn't make a lick of sense. I barely knew the guy. We weren't even friends, technically. I *wanted* to be friends, but

Ethan couldn't have been more clear about the type of relationship he wanted.

Except, here was the problem: what had just happened downstairs, how he'd acted, didn't entirely match what he'd said. That wasn't how you behaved toward a platonic work colleague that you had no romantic interest in... I was pretty sure.

Or was it all just in my head?

...

*Okay. But what if it's not all in your head? What if he* does *actually feel the same way? What if you haven't fucked this up as much as you think you have? What if there's a chance?*

My chest started rising and falling at a much heavier, quicker pace as I considered that possibility. But the excitement was short-lived.

*He said himself that he wanted to end things before "feelings got involved," remember?* I argued with myself, fully embracing my slow spiral into madness. *Just because you* want *something to be true doesn't mean it actually is.*

And there was no arguing against that, was there?

A ball of disappointment floated up my chest, growing and expanding until it overwhelmed everything else, including the small sliver of hope that had been there moments earlier. So, yeah, maybe I was reading too much into what had happened downstairs. Wishful thinking and all that.

The sting that trailed my conclusion was the exact thing I'd been trying to avoid. It burned at my eyes and nose and throat, which was both stupid and irrational.

So before I could start to wallow in self-pity, I blinked away the fresh dampness of my eyes, threw my sketchbook on the bed, then flopped right onto its covers, not bothering to turn on the lights.

*I should call Mik*, I thought after a few minutes of staring at the dark ceiling. It would be a really good distraction. Plus, I really did miss her. And Jo. And Peter. And they were all probably together right now, playing Catan over brownies and homemade blueberry wine. That's what they—or *we*—did on Thursday nights. There was usually a lot of yelling involved.

Last week, Mik had sent me a picture of the three of them, sitting around the big oak dining table. She'd been beaming up at the camera, lips stained a telling purple. Behind her, Jo, with her grey, frizzy hair tied into a frustrated bun, was pointing an angry finger at Peter as she yelled at him. Her husband, in response, had his hands up in feigned innocence, unruly brows raised in shock at Jo's unfounded accusations.

And then, there was the human-sized stuffed doll dressed in a loose, white T-shirt. It was propped up in my usual seat with what I could only assume to be strands of black licorice glued messily on top of its head. And to top the whole thing off, its face had been replaced by the worst picture of me ever taken, mid-ugly-laugh with my eyes half-closed.

*It's like you never left*, Mik had captioned.

So, yeah, I really, really missed those freaks. So much so that I couldn't bring myself to actually press the call button beside Mik's name, knowing that I would burst into tears at the mere sight of the three of them together and ruin their game night.

And that would have been fine had I then just put my phone down and picked up my laptop or something. But in a moment of total weakness, I did something I hadn't allowed myself to do in almost four years. I opened Instagram and, after a few seconds of hesitation, typed Simon's handle into the search bar.

It was a strange feeling, seeing his face after such a long time. Strange and... a little nauseating, to be honest.

*He grew a beard* was my first thought. *I hate it* was my second.

The rest of him looked the same. Long blond hair pulled into a bun, sharp grey eyes, and that minimalist serpent tattoo peeking out from under the left side of his collar. The only other difference I could see—*aside* from the atrociously kept beard—was the addition of a wedding band on his left hand.

I scrolled.

Nadia Benani was her name. She looked to be my age. Dark skin, darker hair, and one of the prettiest smiles I'd ever seen. And I got to see it from every possible angle, given that she was grinning from ear to ear in every single one of their pictures. They both were. In every documented and captioned dinner, party, date night, lazy weekend, and beach vacation.

I tossed my phone onto the mattress and stared back up at the ceiling.

*So... he's happy. Simon is happy. From the looks of it.*

I didn't know how to feel about that. Or maybe I didn't want to *admit* how I felt about it. That I was still angry. That I didn't think he deserved to feel any of the happiness he was flaunting. I just hoped, for Nadia's sake, that he'd... changed. And that he wouldn't do to her wh—

"Sky?"

I sat up so quick the world spun and sparkled in the dark. "Yeah?"

"Hey, can I come in?" Ethan asked from the other side of the bedroom door.

My heart did a sloppy little leap in my chest, my mind jumping to around a hundred different conclusions as to what he could possibly want before I said, "Yes, yeah, sure."

Ethan opened the door, took one look into the room, and huffed a laugh. "Do you ever turn on the lights? Ever?"

"You're one to talk," I retorted, then nudged a chin toward

the wall of windows to my right. "Plus, the view of the city from here is unbelievable at night. Why would I ruin it by turning on the lights?"

He nodded, leaning a shoulder against the doorway. "Fair enough."

"You needed something?"

Another nod. "Yeah. Right. I just..." He trailed off, slipping his hands into his pockets.

*Uh-oh.* "Did you listen to the rest of the recording? Did I accidentally let something slip?"

Ethan's mouth did that curly thing on its one side as he noted my panic. "You haven't sent it to me yet."

Right. "Sorry. I can do that now." I reached for my phone again, vaguely registering the sound of the door shutting as I tapped away on the screen.

What I *did* fully register was the dip of the mattress shortly thereafter as Ethan took a seat on the edge of the bed.

"It is a nice view," he said. He was facing the windows, hands still stuffed into his pockets.

I finished emailing him the recording—since my texts didn't seem to be going through—placed my phone on the nightstand, then grabbed a throw pillow for my lap. The candy-colored one with the long fringes. My fingers immediately went for them.

My stomach bounced in response to the way the city lights were hitting his features. The same way they had that night, in his room, when he was—

I blinked down, away from him, and started to braid the fringes I'd been twisting, fully aware of how closely their pinks and reds must have matched my cheeks as I tried to reel my mind back into PG territory.

"You're nervous. About tomorrow," Ethan stated after a stretch of silence, clearly misinterpreting my display of nerves.

It was him on my bed that was currently causing my heart to act like a startled rabbit, not the party. At least, not yet. I had a feeling *those* nerves would kick in at around midnight and prevent me from falling asleep.

But he didn't necessarily need to know any of that. So I shrugged, keeping my eyes fixed on the braiding. "You aren't?"

The bed shifted again.

I kept my gaze *firmly glued* to my fingers as Ethan moved closer, and closer, just as he'd done downstairs. He moved until my forehead was mere inches away from his chest, and I was certain that if I were to make the colossal mistake of looking up, we'd be practically nose to nose.

"But I went over your sheet again," I said in what I hoped was an appropriate, professional tone. "So, you know, at least I'm prepared on that front. I think."

"What about the other fronts?" Ethan asked, voice low and smooth.

"Like what exactly?" My fingers moved on to their fourth braid.

"Do you remember our bet?"

I made the colossal mistake of looking up.

We were practically nose to nose.

He was *right. there.* Warm brown eyes, ten billion eyelashes, sharp brows, and spicy soap.

"What?"

"Our bet," Ethan repeated like the problem was my hearing.

"What about it?" I probably should have moved back a little to a more appropriate, professional distance. I didn't, though.

"Are you prepared on that front as well?"

I blinked at him, completely dumbfounded. "You're joking."

His head tilted to the side. "Why would I be?"

"Um, because I pretty much already *won* our bet," I pointed out. Seriously, *where* did the guy buy his soap? Or cologne or whatever. I could sit here and smell him all day.

But, like, not in the weird way.

"I beg your pardon?" He had the audacity to laugh, like I'd just said the most preposterous thing he'd ever heard.

My spine straightened as I met his gaze full-on. "I refuse to believe you're seriously suggesting that the bet is still on. We've already ki—done *that*, remember? And I sure as hell didn't freeze. Ergo, I won."

"Oh, I definitely think you're misremembering things," he insisted, which... honestly infuriated me a little. Not in an angry way, per se. But more in the weird, riled-up way that I seemed to get when we played games. Times ten. Because *what?*

"I assure you, my memory isn't the problem here." I remembered every second of that night with perfect clarity. I couldn't forget any of it if I tried. I knew I couldn't *because I'd tried*.

"Really?" Ethan teased. He had his right hand placed on the mattress now, beside my hip, which allowed him to lean in just a little bit more. "Are you sure?"

"Positive." I couldn't really breathe or, like, think when he was this close. Which was more than a little unfair, if you asked me.

"Tell me, Skylar. What, exactly, was the wording of our bet?"

"Um, you said... that... if you kissed me in front of your family, I'd freeze. So, yeah, technically your family wasn't there, sure, but the point is you kissed me, and I didn't freeze."

"Did I, though?" he said, brows pulling together in feigned confusion. "Did I kiss you first? Or did *you* kiss *me*?"

I rolled my eyes. "You kissed me a whole bunch of times that night, remember? And we never specified firsts or seconds or thirds. It still counts."

He *tsk*ed. "I don't think it does."

Was it just me and the whole getting riled up thing, or was it insanely warm in here all of a sudden? "How could it possibly not count?" I asked, very much aware that this might just be the stupidest argument I'd ever had with someone.

Ethan shrugged like the answer was obvious. "The first kiss in the series is the one that carries the biggest element of surprise. All subsequent ones are almost expected. Of course they wouldn't catch you off guard, so they don't count."

I narrowed my eyes at him. "Are you being annoying on purpose?"

"Yes," he admitted with a lopsided smile that turned my rib cage into bone broth. "But my point still stands: if I were to kiss you first, regardless of the time or setting, you'd freeze."

It was like a fucking sauna in here. "*Ethan*, there is absolutely no way, in this, or any of the other timelines, that I would freeze if you k—"

I didn't get to finish my sentence because—in what was undoubtedly the biggest plot twist in all of history that no one saw coming—Ethan kissed me.

# 30

## kylar

I WAS WRONG.

I didn't remember every single detail of that night with perfect clarity. I'd forgotten what it felt like—what it *really* felt like—when Ethan kissed me.

It was like I was both soaring and plummeting at once. It was the first bite of a warm, freshly baked chocolate chip cookie. It was the excitement of Christmas morning and the promise of New Year's Eve all rolled into one.

It was too much and not nearly enough.

I leaned into it, just a little. Just enough to return the kiss without escalating it, while my fingers clung tighter and tighter onto the pillow in my lap, as though its fringes were my single tether to grounded reality.

Ethan pulled away, just slightly, stealing my breath away with him. He kept his face close as his soft gaze traveled from my mouth to my eyes.

"See?" I managed to whisper eventually. I hadn't frozen. So, we were done. I won, and we were done.

He did a lazy half blink back at me before his eyes slipped down to my mouth again. "No, sorry," he murmured in that low, buttery voice of his. "Show me again?"

And before I could respond, his lips were sealed against mine again. This time, though, he brought a hand up to cup my face, tilting it up so he could deepen the kiss.

A small noise escaped my throat in response, and I tried pulling back a little, tried to hold on to the knowing that this was just for a bet. That it didn't mean anything.

But then, his thumb started to caress my cheek. Once, twice. Right as his liquid tongue skimmed across my lips.

I puddled. The structural integrity of my spine faltered, and I melted right into him with a broken whimper.

I'd been wrong again. This was *way* better than the first bite of a freshly baked chocolate chip cookie. In fact, I'd happily give up chocolate chip cookies for the rest of my life if it meant I could have this instead. I'd give up cookies, period. All kinds. And chocolate. Sugar. Food. Oxygen.

My knuckles dug deeper into the pillow on my lap, my hands begging, *pleading* to let go of the stupid thing so they could play with Ethan instead.

I pulled back. "There," I panted. "There. See?"

But he just shook his head, glassy eyes cemented onto my mouth.

And then he hooked an arm around my waist and pulled me onto his lap in one, effortless swoop. "Just one more," he murmured and kissed me a third time.

I snapped like an elastic band.

The pillow was discarded, and I grabbed his collar and kissed him *back*. With everything I had. Every bit of desire and need and regret. I kissed him back like I should have that night instead of getting into my own head. I kissed him back like I would have if I'd thought for one second that he felt the same things I did and that this wasn't just about a stupid bet.

And Ethan responded. His arm around my waist tightened, pinning my body to his, and when that didn't seem to be enough, his other hand moved from my face to the base of my head, holding me to him as our tongues slid against each other in an erotic wrestling match of sorts.

That's when the fire started, deep in the pit of my stomach, spreading with every lick and bite and nibble and *god* he was so good at this. How was he so fucking good at this?

The ache between my thighs grew until it became unbearable, until I was squirming on Ethan's lap, our mouths moving with increasingly feverish desperation.

I slid my hands down from his collar, slowly, relishing the feel of every inch of hard muscle on his chest, abs. And right as I reached his belt, Ethan groaned, grabbed my hips, and flipped me onto my back.

I gasped with surprise as our mouths separated and I landed on the mattress. And it took a few inhales to figure out what the hell had just happened. I kept trying to pull my thoughts together into anything even semicoherent, but it was a bit like trying to unscramble an egg.

"Fucking hell, Skylar," Ethan panted down at me in disbelief, eyes glazed, cheeks flushed, lips a little swollen, like *I'd* ruined *him* with *my* magic mouth.

He had one hand placed on the mattress beside my head, the other resting on my stomach, like he needed it there to keep our bodies from floating back to each other.

"You started it," I replied through the heavy rising and falling of my chest. I honestly felt a little light-headed.

His brows twitched. "Are you complaining?"

I shook my head. Too quickly, maybe.

Ethan let out a slow, huffy chuckle at my reaction. It made my stomach flutter, and with the sudden and uncomfortable realization that he could maybe *feel* it, I tried to wiggle away from him.

But the second I moved, his palm pressed me back down. "We're not done," he said.

Heat pooled behind my belly button at the firmness of his tone, and a (large) part of my brain wished he'd move his hand just a few inches south.

"You're right," I said in an effort to distract myself. "We're not done. You still haven't admitted that I won our bet. And, more importantly, that you lost."

Amusement twisted the left corner of Ethan's mouth into a very kissable little curve. "Let's pretend like you did win. What do you want as your prize?"

*You.*

The thought darted out of my brain so quick that it almost reached my mouth before I caught it.

"How familiar are you with the Japanese game shows of the early nineties?" I said instead, still panting like I was in the middle of attempting my first half-marathon with absolutely no training whatsoever. "Also, how quickly do you think you can have a lemur delivered to this address?"

There was a slight chance I was delirious from the lack of oxygen and excess of horny hormones. A *slight* chance.

"Scratch that," I interrupted as soon as Ethan opened his mouth. "How quickly do you think you can have a lemur *costume* delivered to this address?" I scanned his shoulders and chest, not daring to look down any farther than that. "And what's your costume size? Also, do you bite?"

He grinned down at me like he found my manic, meaningless rambling positively *delightful*. "Yes. As a matter of fact, I do bite."

How inappropriate and unprofessional would it be to ask him to show me?

I tried to wiggle out from underneath him again but got the same reaction as last time.

"Not done," he said, palm pressing me down. His hand was so warm. "We need to talk."

"About?"

"What just happened."

"We did talk about what just happened. I won, you lost, remember?" I said with another attempt at wiggling away.

Ethan's hand slipped from my stomach and curled around my hip bone. "I really don't think so. You're not going anywhere."

"Wanna bet?" I tried.

"Nope."

I sighed, sinking back into the duvet.

Ethan was grinning down at me, brown eyes gliding all over my face. "You smell like lemon cakes," he said, quite literally out of nowhere.

I blinked up at him. "What... like in a good way or a weird way?"

My shampoo was a lemony-vanilla scent, but I didn't think it was that strong.

Instead of answering me, he leaned down and gently brushed his lips against mine, then placed a small kiss just on the corner of my mouth.

"Like in a 'I've started to dream about lemon cakes because of you' kind of way," he murmured slowly, slipping my bottom lip between his teeth.

My heart slammed into my ribs as his hand moved, sliding under my shirt.

"Like in a 'I've started to relentlessly crave them because of you' kind of way," he went on, mouth moving down to my chin. He smiled into my skin when I shivered beneath him. "Like in a 'I can barely think about anything else, and it's driving me fucking crazy' kind of way."

"What are you doing?" I asked, and my voice cracked a little. Was this still part of the bet?

"Talking," he answered, grazing his lips along my jaw. "I said we needed to talk, remember?"

I went to answer him, but then his attention moved down to my neck, pulling a low moan out of my throat. "I'm going to be so pissed at you if this is still part of the stupid bet," I managed breathlessly. "It's taking it way too far."

"You remember our rule?" he asked in between soft, greedy nibbles of my neck, ignoring my threat.

"Why would I need to for a simple conversation?"

"It's a yes-or-no question, Skylar."

There was a part of me that wanted to prolong this and tease him, but then his hand started to lower to my jeans. Then he hooked a finger through one of the belt loops and lightly pulled down on it.

"Yup," I blurted, trying my best to keep my voice even. "Yes, I remember."

"Good girl."

I made a noise.

It was like the halfway point between a whimper and a gasp, and it was absolutely the first time I'd ever produced anything like it.

Ethan lifted his head and looked down at me with his brows reaching for the high heavens. "Oh. We *like* that."

I flushed.

"Ethan, I swear to every god you could possibly think of, if *any* part of this is still just about the bet, I am going to scary-movie-murder you with a butter knife and safety scissors. It is going to be slow, and it is going to be painful."

The way he was smiling down at me, you'd think this was the most fun the guy had ever had in his life. "There are worse ways to go."

*Jesus Christ.*

I pressed a hand against his forehead.

He grinned. "Not a fever, unfortunately. I'm entirely lucid."

"Are you sure?"

"Positive."

I went to remove my hand, but he caught my wrist and placed a featherlight kiss on my palm.

Butterflies. Butterflies everywhere.

"You know you have a freckle above your right eyelid?" he noted conversationally.

"No." I frowned as he let my hand go—because he let my hand go. Also because I didn't have a freckle there. I was pretty sure.

"You do," he claimed, "It's right... there."

He kissed my eyebrow.

Had I died? Was this the afterlife everyone was always raving about?

"Is it drugs?" I asked him quite seriously.

He laughed. "It's not the bet, it's not a fever, and it's not drugs. Any other guesses?"

"Hundreds," I said immediately, earning myself another highly amused grin. *Encouragement.* "Like, for example, you're not actually Ethan. You're the *other* brother. You know, the triplet everyone thought was consumed by the other two in the womb. You just kinda slipped outta there during the chaotic nightmare that is childbirth, undetected. You murdered Ethan and stole his skin, just like I thought he was going to do to me when I first met him."

"That's a good one."

"It would have made a great plotline for a nineties soap

opera. Like *Passions* or something. Could you imagine? Everyone would see a surprise twin coming, but *no one* would be able to predict a murderer triplet twist. It's gold. I should have been a screenwriter."

I was talking too much. Why was I talking so much?

"*Passions*?" Ethan asked with a laugh. "Aren't you a decade too young to know about that show? I barely know about it."

"Jo owns the entire series on VHS; Mik and I went through them all a few summers back. Ironically at first, but then *un*ironically once we realized just how awesomely ridiculous it was. They actually had a character named Ethan." Who, coincidentally, was also a total babe.

"You call your mom by her first name?" he asked, presumably out of nowhere.

I blinked. "No, why?"

His head did a slight tilt. "Oh. Different Jo?"

And then it clicked. That under the "immediate family" section of the info sheet I'd given him, Jo and Peter had been listed as my mom and dad.

I opened my mouth, then closed it. I could divert. Or just let him think I'd been talking about another Jo. Except I didn't *want to*. I didn't want to divert or lie or let him think something that wasn't true. I just didn't.

"No, it's the same person. But, um, technically speaking... Peter and Jo aren't... they aren't my parents. Technically. And also legally."

I was tempted to avert my gaze, but Ethan was obstructing the majority of my view of anything that wasn't him, so I didn't have a lot of options other than to just look at him while I explained. And so I saw the confusion reach his eyes, slant his brows.

"Okay," he said, a little carefully. "Can you... I'm not entirely sure what that means."

I swallowed, my fingers fidgeting with the bottom of my shirt. "I don't have a relationship with my real—sorry, with my biological parents anymore. Peter and Jo are more my... surrogate parents, I guess you could call them. So that's why... that's why I put them as my answer. On the sheet."

Ethan nodded slowly, like he was processing and trying to decide how to navigate his response. Or maybe he was just surprised by my voluntary offering of all that information.

"Peter was my art teacher. In high school," I explained, needing to fill the silence. "That's how we met. And... you know Mikaela? The girl that signed your NDA? She's his daughter. And Jo's. Biological. And also in every other way. She's a year younger than me, so I didn't meet her until my sophomore year. I would go to the art room every day after school to sketch; she'd go there to read while she waited for her dad to finish work." It had been love at first conversation with Mik. We'd been inseparable within a week, which she later informed me was inevitable. We were soul mates, according to her.

I believed it.

Ethan nodded again but still didn't say anything.

I sighed. "I'm sorry if that constitutes as a lie. Putting Peter and Jo on my sheet. I was going to tell you if and when I decided to sign the contract, but I just... didn't think you needed that level of detail for one party. And I also didn't want to have to explain it all until it was absolutely necessary."

He thought about that for a moment, then said, "So why are you telling me now? You haven't signed the contract yet."

"I don't know. Why don't you tell me what's going on here?" I flapped an exasperated hand between our chests. "I'm trying very hard not to jump to conclusions, Ethan, because the last time we talked, you said that it would be best for us to stick to a 'professional' relationship. But honestly? If my real boss at my real job had me pinned down on a bed, pointing out freckles I didn't know I had, I'd have to have, like, thirty-eight different conversations with HR."

I was talking way, *way* too much. So I clamped my mouth shut before I could say something I'd regret and waited.

And waited.

Ethan was watching me in that soft, careful way he sometimes did. Except this time, it went on for... ever. It went on forever.

"This is the part where you say something," I told him, in case he'd forgotten how conversations worked.

"I don't want to." He said it so quietly it was almost a sigh.

I frowned. "You don't want to... what? Talk?"

"No, I..." He trailed off, pressing his lips together once. "It would be best for us to stick to a professional relationship; in almost every way, that would logically be best. But I don't want to."

Wait, what? "But you were the one that said..."

"I know, Skylar. I know what I said. I've gone over it a thousand times in my head since that night. Every last word. And I —" He cut himself off, huffed a breath, then said, "I take it back. All of it. If you want to keep things 'professional,' if you don't feel anything for me or if you still think that I'm doing any of this because of the contract, then fine. But you'll have to be the one to end it, and you'll have to tell me to leave. I won't do it, because I'm just now realizing how big of a mistake it would be. And I sure as hell don't want to spend the next however many years kicking myself for letting you go. I don't want you to be my next regret. Trust me when I say that I have enough of those already."

My lips had parted, my jaw falling slack as I processed.

"This is the part where you say something," he murmured when I'd stayed silent for about a minute too long.

"Uhm." I stopped, swallowed, needing more time to think. "Okay. So then... what are you saying? What *do* you want, exactly?"

"You."

He answered so fast that it overlapped with the tail end of my sentence. "What?"

"You, Skylar. I want you."

And I swear, it was like my whole chest started to free-fall off a cliff.

Breathing. Breathing was key here. "Like in what way?"

His lips twitched, the humor returning to his eyes. "Like in every way."

I was once again trying really, *very* hard not to jump to any conclusions. "Okay, Ethan, I need you to be, um, *very* clear with me right now as to what that means. Because we are *barreling* toward what could prove to be an extremely catastrophic and unfortunate misunderstanding and I —*mmphn.*"

He was starting to smile again when he leaned down and kissed me.

# 31

than

We weren't done talking. I knew that. But trying to make myself focus on anything other than tearing Skylar's clothes off her body anymore was like trying to fight every known fundamental force of nature, all at once.

I didn't have enough willpower to do it. The more she talked, the harder it became to keep myself off her.

She was *utterly ridiculous*, in the most endearing, funny, and captivating way possible. And she didn't seem to see it. Any of it. She didn't seem to realize how irresistibly charming she actually was or how enamored with her I'd become.

And I didn't want to keep fighting it. Against all logic and reason and knowing all the ways that it could go wrong—knowing all the ways it had *already* gone wrong—I didn't want to fight it. I wasn't going to add Skylar to my tally of regrets. Not willingly, at least.

"Is this a little more clear?" I murmured against her lips.

"Do you believe me yet?"

She shook her head. "Zero percent clear. Show me some more. Or, like, lots more."

I smiled and captured her mouth with mine again.

She let out a small, sweet sigh when I lowered my body and pressed my hips against hers. If she still had any doubts whatsoever as to how badly I wanted her in the physical sense, those should have been put to rest. I was hard as a fucking brick. Had been since I'd pulled her onto my lap and she'd finally let go and kissed me back, *really* kissed me back.

I moved my mouth down to her jaw, her neck, until I got to that one sensitive spot she seemed to have right below her left ear. Sure enough, my nibble was instantly rewarded with a soft moan as Skylar snaked her arms around my neck and pulled me closer.

I kissed her again, and again and again and again. Everywhere I could. Until we were a hot, tangled mess of tongues and limbs and breaths on the bed, fighting to get each other's clothes off.

I wasn't sure how my shirt and her jeans ended up on the floor, exactly, because I knew for a fact that I hadn't allowed my hands to leave Skylar's body for a single second since we'd started this new game, but I definitely didn't miss when she went for my belt again.

Her touch sent a jolt through my lower half, and I groaned, grinding into her.

"It's stuck," she complained, fumbling with my buckle. "Take it off."

I reached down, tore the belt off, and whipped it to the side. It actually felt like I might have ripped into the leather a bit or detached the prong. Not sure.

Skylar's wet, reddened lips curved into a subtle smile as she pulled her shirt off and tossed it in the same direction as my discarded belt, revealing a simple, beige bra paired with her black panties.

It was, hands down, the sexiest thing I'd ever seen. Just the sight of her lying there in black-and-beige cotton underwear.

"You're so fucking beautiful," I said, gazing down at her in awe. "Sky, you're so beautiful. You have no fucking idea."

My words tugged her lids into a slowed blink, and then she raised her arms, wrapped them around my shoulders, and pulled me down again. "Thank you," she whispered, then craned her neck and brought her soft, delectable lips back to mine, where they belonged.

I let my hands roam over the smooth skin of her hips and thighs, teasing at the waistband and seams of her panties, until her movements became increasingly feverish, demanding.

But it wasn't enough. Not even close.

I wanted to see what it looked like for her to unravel completely. I wanted to know what she felt like, how she tasted, what noises she made. I wanted to make her fall apart for me, over and over *and over* again, until my name was a permanent prayer on her lips.

I pushed the black cotton aside, deliberately grazing my knuckles against her silky flesh in the process.

She whimpered.

I died.

"More of that, please," she demanded quietly.

I obliged, gently sinking my teeth into her bottom lip as my index finger slid up her seam and circled her clit once, twice, before dipping back down to tease her soaked entrance.

My dick jumped at the noises she made and the feel of her, so warm and wet and *perfect*. She felt fucking perfect.

I did it again and again, putting more and more focus on her swollen button each time until she was writhing on the bed and biting back moans, and then I inserted a finger, pulling my head back so I could watch her.

Skylar cried out and clenched around me, nails digging into my shoulders, and when I started to move my hand, she met my gaze and tilted her hips up to give me better access. It made my whole body feel like it was doused in liquid fire, having her look at me like that. Like watching me helped her get off.

I added a second finger and palmed her clit, working it with deliberate, pressured kneads until she was a panting, twisting wreck under me.

I swear I almost came in my pants, right then and there, just looking at her gasp and moan, with her mesmerizing eyes all hooded and glazed, cheeks and lips tinted red.

"So. Fucking. Beautiful," I praised again, barely able to hold myself together.

She came undone with a frayed whimper, her thighs clamping shut over my hand, face turning away from me and into the duvet as she shuddered her way through the orgasm.

I memorized every second of it. Every single expression and sound and touch and quiver.

I was so, undoubtedly fucked.

The only sounds echoing in the room now were the heavy clutter of our overlapping breaths. Until I tried to gently remove my hand from in between her thighs. The friction of the movement was met with another shudder and a small whine.

"Sensitive, sorry," she explained, turning her face to mine again. "It's been a while. And that was, um... you're *really* good at that."

I huffed a small laugh as the compliment warmed my chest and let my hand rest where it was, happy to just enjoy the view while she recovered.

Skylar stared back at me for a few moments, then tilted her head slightly and said, "Hey, Ethan?"

"Mmm?" I wasn't entirely convinced I could form coherent words in the moment.

She reached up and cupped my face with her smooth, warm hands. "I think you're really beautiful, too."

My heart stopped beating.

In the literal, nonfigurative sense.

Then she started to stroke my skin with her thumbs, her gaze swimming across my face. "Your mouth does this thing sometimes, where it curls just on the left side. And it—um, makes me a little flustered, to be honest. Pretty much every time it happens.

"And also, you have really, *really* nice eyes. They're like chocolate with the tiniest bit of brown honey in the middle.

"And I also like your teeth and your jaw and your body, just in general. Oh, and also your eyebrows and forearms. And now your fingers. But for different reasons than just aesthetics."

I could feel my smile fade as she talked, her words whirling through my stomach and chest. It felt like I'd been punched in the gut, but in the best possible way.

My jaw had loosened almost completely, and it took some active, concentrated effort to get it to start working again. But even then, the only thing I managed to croak out was an entirely insufficient "Thank you."

Skylar took the tone and inadequacy of my words the wrong way, her hands falling from my face almost immediately. "Sorry, did I just ruin the mood?" she asked, her voice tilting with a slight panic. "I just really like it when you say nice things... so I thought maybe you would, too. I—"

I shook my head, removing my hand from her now relaxed thighs so I could bring her palm back to my cheek, hold it there. She didn't complain this time. "No," I said. "No. You didn't ruin anything."

The mood had shifted, she was right. But not in the way Skylar thought. Something dangerously deep in my core had started to rearrange and slot into place for her. And I wasn't entirely willing to confront what it was yet.

"Thank you," I said again, with more emphasis this time. But I still failed to follow it up with anything that would have been even remotely... *enough*.

She nodded. "I can stop talking now."

I turned my face into her palm and kissed it, then moved on to her wrist, arm, trailing my lips all the way up to her shoulder and neck.

"Just so we're extra clear on this, I fucking *love* it when you talk," I whispered when I reached her ear. She sighed and wrapped her arms around me again.

I started to lose track of the details after that. Lost count of how many times she licked me and I bit her, or how many moans and whimpers and gasps my tongue was able to coax out of her throat. I couldn't recall how we managed to strip out of the last few pieces of clothing or how I was able to fish a condom out of my wallet without separating my mouth from Skylar's skin. And I definitely didn't notice when or how she managed to steal it from my hand, not until her palm pushed at my chest.

I pulled away, and she gave me a little smirk before biting down on the edge of the foil and ripping it open.

Liquid. Fire.

Everywhere.

"Want me to put it on for you?" she murmured in her bedroom voice, gazing up at me with her bedroom eyes, smiling her bedroom smile.

Normally? *Fuck yes*. Right now? I was pretty sure I'd

burst into wet flames if she so much as blinked at me the right way, so, "I got it," I said and pushed myself up to my knees.

Skylar's eyes dipped to my hips and flared, her lips parting as I rolled the latex on. I didn't miss the inadvertent movement of her legs, how they widened just an extra inch.

Had my dick not been weeping at the head with painful, throbbing need, I'd have plunged my mouth in there instead and licked her to orgasmic oblivion. Preferably more than once.

Instead, I dropped back down to my elbows. "Ready?"

Her nods were quick, her breath breaking as I aligned myself with her entrance. I grabbed her hand on the bed, threading our fingers together as I started to ease into her, inch by gloriously tight inch.

The sweet little "*oh*" she produced knocked the wind out of my everything. And then she clenched. *Hard.*

I might have cracked a molar or twelve.

"Relax for me, Skylar," I pleaded through my teeth.

"Sorry." The airy word shook out of her mouth.

I paused, breathed. And when I had somewhat regained control, I looked down at her, trying to focus. It was near-fucking-impossible. "You're nervous?"

Her fingers tightened in between mine, and she swallowed. "No."

Worst liar on the planet.

I frowned, trying to piece it together while my entire body and brain screamed for me to shut the fuck up and *thrust.* Because she hadn't seemed nervous a minute ago when she'd stolen the condom from my hand. So why now, all of a sudden?

"Sky—"

She kissed me, long and deep, and when I tried to pull

back again, her tongue swept across my sanity and wiped the slate clean.

And then her hips moved.

And it nudged me slightly deeper into her.

And my brain melted.

She felt too fucking good. Too perfect. It pulled me too close to the edge, too fast, too soon. My hips pushed forward instinctively; she shuddered and groaned against my tongue, and it cracked my thoughts in half.

I rolled my hips, working myself deeper and deeper until I was fully inside her. Until she was squeezing my hand and asking for more. And more and more and more. Until it turned from smooth, deliberate pushes to deep, hungry thrusts and raspy, desperate pleas.

"So good," I praised down at her, tension coiling in the pit of my stomach. "You feel so fucking good, Sky. It's driving me crazy."

Her reaction was immediate. The way her hips jerked as she tried to pull me closer, the choked whine it earned me.

I smiled. She liked it when I said nice things? I could do that. I could sing her praises all fucking night long. And not a single word of it would be a lie.

So I did. I told her again how good she felt, how pretty she was. I told her she was perfect and that I wanted her all to my greedy, selfish self.

"Mine," I whispered. "Just mine."

She *moaned* my name, and then, in the sweetest little breath, she agreed. "Just yours."

I shut up then. I had to. Because it took every last ounce of my focus and energy to keep a steady rhythm and not slam into her, hard and possessive and greedy. Like that would permanently seal my claim over her.

I'd never been so fucking turned on in my life.

Every single muscle in my body felt like it was vibrating for her. It was physical and spiritual and *primal.*

I wanted her.

I wanted her.

I *wanted* her.

In every fucking way I could have her. Permanently.

I ground out her name, one hand still intertwined with hers, the other fisting the sheets. And, suddenly, I wished I wasn't wearing a condom. Because the primal part of me wanted to empty into her, wanted to watch as I spilled out of her pretty pink—

The image flashed in my mind and *fuck.*

Her thighs had started to tremble, her pants deep and desperate, nails digging into my skin.

"That's it," I encouraged, biting her earlobe. My voice was hoarse, uneven, guttural. "Such a good fucking girl."

She gasped and arched on the bed. Two more thrusts and she was clenching and spasming around me, crying out my name. And it triggered the most intense, explosive orgasm of my life.

My whole body shook with it.

And shook.

And shook.

It kept going; I kept coming, Skylar's relentless squirms and contractions milking me until I was an empty, boneless shell of a former human, drowning in lemon, vanilla, and oxytocin.

"Mine," I whispered, nuzzling her neck. I found her frantic heartbeat, grazed it with my teeth.

It was the only word I was able to produce, the only coherent thought in my mind.

"*Mine.*"

# 32

## Skylar

My mind was empty.

For the first time in my adult life, it was completely, wholly empty. Like the production line of overactive neurons responsible for my thoughts had exploded into... nothing. There was absolutely nothing there.

Ethan had quite literally blown my mind.

The only thing I could do as I lay under him was feel. That was it. And I had absolutely no choice in the matter.

So when he said, “Mine,” it didn’t trigger a never-ending line of questions and doubts.

There was no voice in my head that immediately brushed it off or claimed, *yeah, but people say all kinds of crazy shit during sex. It probably doesn’t mean anything.*

I just... *felt.*

I felt the word wrap around my heart, snuggle it tight. I felt it turn my insides into warm, happy goo. And I felt myself smile against his shoulder when he said it again.

We were still holding hands, our fingers intertwined while he spoiled me with nibbles and kisses.

After a while, the quietness of my brain gave voice to something else, something too obscurely deep and unmapped for me to pinpoint. Mik probably would have had a name for it, but I couldn't even begin to theorize. I simply felt when it spoke.

*Him*, it said wordlessly. *This one.*

"Sky." This voice came from outside of my depths. It was a buttery, smooth purr against my ear.

"Mmm."

"That was incredible."

My whole body smiled. "*Mmmm.*"

I could feel him start to grin against my cheek before he leaned away and gazed down at me.

He really was beautiful. Especially when he smiled. I loved that smile. And his eyes, too. Their chocolate went all soft and melty sometimes when he looked at me. It felt so good.

"Better than incredible," I said. Or my mouth did. I didn't remember instructing it to. He'd set my filter ablaze right along with my thoughts.

And in response, Ethan leaned down again and pressed the softest brush of a kiss just on the corner of my mouth. "Mine," he said.

And I felt it swim through my body, a little tremor of pure happiness and pleasure, like I was exactly where I was supposed to be. Finally.

*Him.*

*This one.*

# 33

kylar

It was pitch-black when Ethan left. I only faintly registered his gentle movements on the bed as he untangled himself from my limbs. And when I mumbled a string of nonsensical complaints, trying to pull him back, he stroked my hair and promised he'd see me tonight.

I fell right back asleep.

"And then what?" Mikaela asked, still munching on a family-sized bag of barbecue chips. Except she called them "crisps." Not because she was British but because she was annoying.

"Nothing. I woke up a few hours later and made the unfortunate mistake of taking my phone into the bathroom with me, then paid the price for it when you called me *seven times* while I was in the shower. *Seven*, Mik." Until I'd finally stepped out of the hot water with conditioner still in my hair and answered the phone, thinking it was an emergency.

It wasn't.

And then she hadn't let me hang back up again. Instead, she'd forced me to keep her on the video call while I rinsed off, all the while yelling her life updates at the ceiling my camera was facing. I couldn't hear any of it because I was literally *in the shower*.

"I missed your face," she said. Which immediately warmed me back up, I won't lie. My spine deflated a little against the couch. "I'm not used to having this much personal space anymore. I hate it, and it's overrated. There's way too much room in our closet now, no one's here to whack me with a pillow in the middle of the night when I snore, I haven't had to scream-wrestle anyone for bathroom time, and not a *single* person has stolen my eyelash curler without permission in the last two weeks and then not put it back. What's the point of even owning one? What am I supposed to do with it? Or all this extra time I have now that I'm not constantly looking for it?"

"You're being a tad bit dramatic," I told her, trying hard to bite back my grin.

"You're never allowed to move away without me ever again. If you get a full-time job with this Zilmar guy, I'm dragging you back here, and you can make the commute from New York to Toronto daily. We're going to be roommates for life." She crunched on another chip, then started waving her hand as she continued. "Plus, I'm tired of having to comfort Mum. It's *constant*, Sky. You know she made lasagna three times last week? Like, in a row. Does she think it'll summon you? Like Beetlejuice?"

"I miss you guys, too, Micky," I whispered quietly, swallowing back the emotion gathering in my throat. What a bunch of dorks.

"*Lies*!" she shouted theatrically, tossing the bag of chips to the side. I saw at least one fly out. She was sitting on my bed, with my pillow resting on her lap. "You're doing fun, mind-blowing sex things with the conventionally attractive fake-but-soon-to-be-real boyfriend who can *cook*. Which, by the way, we are not done talking about."

Mik clap-wiped her hands together, dusting them off. Again, she was sitting on *my* bed, not hers. I watched as tiny red dust flew off her hands and floated down onto my sheets. "Does this mean there's no need to sign the contract? Have you talked about it yet?"

I sucked the inside of my cheek before admitting, "Not yet."

"Do you know what you're going to tell him?"

"I'm kind of hoping he takes the reins on this one," I admitted.

"Why's that?"

I shifted on the couch. "Because how embarrassing would it be if I suggested we… I don't know. I honestly don't even know what I'd suggest."

"Yeah you do."

Yeah I did.

"What if he says no?" I asked. "I don't think you get how intense the brothers are about this CEO thing, Mik. Even if he does want to pursue this, chances are he's still going to want an agreement in place, just in case. And then… don't you think that would be weird? Like the money and the lie would taint the actual relationship? How would that even work? His grandmother thinks we're, like, weeks away from getting engaged. Oh, and unless I get a full-time job with Zilmar, I'm supposed to move back in two—"

"Okay, I'm gonna stop you right there," she said, holding up a finger, "because your left nostril is doing that rapid flaring thing, which usually means you're a half breath away from a full spiral, and we can't have any of that energy today. I'm all out of sage."

I took a breath and sunk back into the couch. "Sorry. This is just... getting to be really complicated. Like, way more than I was expecting."

"Mmmm. It's almost like it would be a good idea to get ahead of it and just tell him what you want before everything goes to shit," she said, reaching for the chips again. "But you're welcome to sit there and make some more assumptions about how he'll react and what will happen. That's fun, too, I guess. Not like they're just a bunch of made-up excuses, smoke and mirrors to hide the fact that you're scared. Not because you think he's going to reject you, but because you know he won't. It's what happened last week; things started to get real, and it freaked you out."

...

...

*Cruuuunch.*

I tilted my head. "You know what I hate about you?"

"The fact that I'm always right?"

Well, now I just didn't want to admit it. So instead, I said, "I'm eating powdered donuts all over your bed next time I visit," I vowed. "Two words, Mik: Ant. Infestation." Because she was terrified of them.

She grinned, mouth full of chomped-up chip bits.

It was so gross. I loved her so much.

ALEXIS MIGHT HAVE BEEN stubborn and generous to a fault, but she was also right. The dress was *gorgeous*.

The silk looked liquid with the effortless way it clung onto my hips and flowed around my heels when I walked. And the color was such an intense, vibrant black you almost expected it to bleed onto your skin if you touched it. Yet all you *wanted* to do was touch it, to see if it really was as lush and luxurious and soft as it seemed. (Which, impossibly enough, it was.)

I'd kept everything else simple, polished. My hair was swept away from my face in smooth, deliberate tousles, my jewelry limited to a pair of small diamond studs (another forced courtesy of Alexis), and I'd kept my makeup neutral, elegant, making its primary focus the black liner that winged my eyes.

I scanned the mirror one last time, still convinced that the slit ran a few inches too high, but there wasn't anything I could do about it now. The fabric looked like it would mar at the mere sight of a pin. There was no way I'd risk it, not even with tape.

So, before I could continue to procrastinate or find something else to needlessly obsess over, I grabbed the long, black wool coat Alexis had shoved into my arms against my will and finally forced myself to leave my room. Ten minutes late.

I couldn't tell which echoed louder as I made my way downstairs: the tapping of my heels against the marble steps or the blood pounding in my ears. Even the air around me felt like it was rattling with nervous energy.

Ethan had come home around two hours ago, knocked on my door while I was in the middle of getting ready, and argued with me for way too long about wanting to be let in. He'd lost. Not because I didn't *want* him to come in, but because I thought it might be a tad too early to let him watch me pluck my eyebrows with half my limbs covered in wax strips while I waited for the blue slime in my hair to work its moisturizing magic.

He'd complained. A lot.

I had to suppress a smile and wipe my nervous palms

against my coat before raising my fist to knock on his office door. Except I didn't get to do the actual knocking part because the door swung open before my knuckles could hit the wood.

He was wearing a black tux.

Ethan, with his new haircut, was wearing a black tux. And a bow tie.

"Hey," I said, trying to keep my voice even. A *bow tie*. "You look nice."

Understatement. Criminal understatement.

I wanted to jump his bones.

He blinked, lips parting slowly as his eyes moved. Down, down, down. Up, up, up. And a small (read: extremely large) part of me felt a tinge of... satisfied pride at his expression.

"What do you think?" I said, smoothing down the silk at my hip. "The slit runs a little long, but other than that..."

"You don't even look human," Ethan said before I could finish.

I had to swallow a laugh. "What... like in a good way or a weird way?"

I saw the amusement flash in his eyes a split second before his arm was around me. It should have been embarrassing, the squeal-like giggle that escaped as I was swept off my feet and carried inside. It wasn't, though.

Ethan placed me on his desk, leaning in close.

"Like in a 'there's no way I'm going to be able to keep my hands off you all night' kind of way," he teased. His eyes were warm and brown and all *melty*.

"Then don't," I said, sliding my hands up his lapels. "Touch me all you want."

His chest hitched under my palms, and then I was the one who was all *melty*.

It was impossibly satisfying, having him respond to my

words and my touch like that. I could experience it a million times, and it probably wouldn't be enough.

When had I become so greedy?

Ethan's grip tightened around my waist. "Should we skip the party?"

I laughed, sliding my arms around his neck. "I think you might regret it if we did. Diabolical plans and all."

He smiled. "Diabolical plans were before you decided to wear that dress and tell me to touch you all I want."

I was grinning so wide my cheeks felt like they might burst. Ethan moved his hands down to my thighs, spreading them so he could move me closer.

"You look fucking incredible," he whispered, brushing his smiling lips against mine.

"Thank you." I was practically vibrating out of my skin with pleasure. "So do you."

He kissed me then, soft and sweet, neither of us able to push down our smiles.

And then he pulled away, hands caressing the silk around my hips. "We should talk. About us, the contract, everything."

My heart bounced. And I wasn't sure whether it was in a good way or an anxious way.

"Okay," I said, my fingers curling around his lapels. "How about tomorrow... after breakfast."

Because a part of me still wanted to prolong it. Just in case.

"Tomorrow," he agreed, nuzzling my nose. "After breakfast."

# 34

kylar

THE PARTY WAS BEING HELD four blocks away from the apartment, at a five-star hotel with a name I couldn't pronounce. Because it was, like, eighteen stupidly difficult syllables long, and they were all tied together in a way that made the whole thing sound backwards.

"My tongue doesn't bend that way," I told Ethan when he insisted I try saying it for a fourth time. He'd had way too much fun with my first three attempts. His eyes were all wet, cheeks colored as he pulled up in front of the valet.

French was the worst.

Except when Ethan spoke it.

It was *really* sexy when Ethan spoke it.

Which was exactly what I told him while we were alone in the elevator of said hotel. He reacted in an extremely unprofessional manner, even though I reminded him that we were technically at work; it was very inappropriate, very unprofessional, and *very* French.

"You have lipstick all over your mouth," I scolded, readjusting my dress as we walked out into the hallway.

He swiped his thumb over his bottom lip. "And whose fault is that?"

"*Yours.*"

He laughed, sliding his fingers in between mine. "Worth it."

I pulled him into a mini hallway that branched off the main one and pressed him against a wall.

The grin he wore was blinding. "*Miss Gage*. I didn't know you had that in you."

"Shut up," I laughed, trying to dig a napkin out of my clutch. It would have been a lot easier if he'd let my hand go.

He peeled his back off the wall. "Do it again. Harder this time."

"Are you going to be like this all night?"

"Yes."

My cheeks were starting to hurt. A lot.

"Hold still for a sec." I gave up on the napkin thing and decided to just use my thumb instead.

He obliged, tilting his chin down slightly to give me better access as I started to gently wipe at the faint smudges of mauve around his mouth. He made absolutely no attempts to hide the enjoyment he was getting out of the attention, hand moving to my lower back, pulling me close as his warm, smiling eyes slid up and down my face.

"Stop looking at me like that," I chided quietly. It was making my insides swirl.

"No." He grabbed my hand just as I started to pull it away and brought it back to his face, placing the sweetest kiss onto my inner wrist.

I was going to go into cardiac arrest because of this man.

"We should go in now," I said, even though my body had started to lean into him. "We're already pretty late."

"Okay." But instead of letting me go, Ethan lowered his lips to mine, arms snaking around my back.

We stayed there for a long time, kissing, teasing, giggling, until the music and chatter of the ballroom grew too loud to ignore.

"We *really* should go," I eventually whispered. We were going to be the last ones to arrive from the sounds of it.

He didn't answer right away.

And then he didn't answer at all.

"Ethan?" I pulled a few inches away so I could look at him properly.

He opened his mouth, then hesitated and closed it again, a line of tension worming through his jaw.

I frowned. Because it was almost as if— Oh.

Oh. Did he... not want to go?

*Ohhh*. He didn't want to go.

"Do you know what," I said, pulling away so I could bring a hand to my stomach. "I don't really feel so good."

The concern on Ethan's face lasted less than a second before it morphed into understanding. I guess I really was a bad liar.

"I don't think I can go inside," I went on with a deep, exaggerated sigh. Might as well go all out. "I feel weak and light-headed and nauseous and feverish and disoriented. And my memory. It's gone. Amnesia. I think I need to lie down. At home. In my own bed. Or yours. But those are the only two options, I'm afraid."

The left corner of Ethan's mouth twitched. "You don't need to—"

"Ethan? Is that you?" I said, blindly grabbing at his face. "I can't see. It's *spreading*."

He bit my thumb.

"And now I'm *bleeding*," I wailed hysterically. This was so much fun. You couldn't blame me for getting carried away.

"*Shhhh*," he tried, chuckling through the sound.

"I think it might be malaria, in all honesty. Mixed with a fresh strand of mad cow. Sprinkle in some dengue—" Ethan whipped us around, pressing me to the wall as his mouth crashed into mine.

I smiled against his lips.

"You're so ridiculous," he murmured, sucking on my bottom lip. "I fucking love it, Sky. So much. I swear, it's like my brain purrs every time you open your mouth."

And there it was, the cardiac episode I'd been worried about earlier.

Then he cupped my face, pressing his forehead to mine. "New plan," he said. "We can't not show up—it's not an option. So we go in and stay for dinner, *just* dinner. It's the first item on the itinerary and should start in about twenty minutes.

"Then we sneak out. We go home. And I'll take you up on that offer of yours, to touch you all I fucking want. In and out of that dress. Deal?"

My panties might as well have just melted right down my leg.

"Only if I get to do the same to you. In and out of that bow tie."

He grinned. It was a dazzling, wicked thing.

I sighed. "You have lipstick all over your mouth."

~

I COULD BARELY FOCUS.

And by barely, I mean not at all.

There must have been two hundred guests in the romantically lit, lavishly adorned ballroom. And that didn't include the string quartet or the tens of uniformed, champagne-equipped servers effortlessly weaving their way between the tables and chairs and scattered groups of chattering gowns and suits.

Two hundred people, and I was introduced to at least thirty of them in the span of about fifteen minutes.

There were investors, lawyers, former prime ministers and current premiers, and lots of middle-aged men with abbreviated job titles (a disproportionate number of whom were named Steve, which I would have found somewhat interesting had I not been so distracted.)

Alexis and Joel had been the first ones to spot us when we'd walked in. She'd *tsk*ed about our tardiness before shoving a champagne flute into my hands. "You're going to need that. And, like, fifteen more," she'd said.

She hadn't been wrong.

Just... not for the reasons she'd thought.

Ethan's fingers grazed the back of my neck for a torturous fifth time since we'd walked in, and he bent down to my ear, informing me of yet *another* way he was going to use his tongue to make me beg when we got home. His first two proposed methods were whispered to me literal seconds before we'd walked up to his grandmother. I'd flushed, blubbering my way through the greeting and birthday wishes, much to my embarrassment and Ethan's amusement.

He chuckled lightly as I downed my second glass of bubbles, then casually turned us around and introduced me to the Chief-Something-Officer of Something-Or-Other Industries and her wife.

I'm sure they were lovely people. Though I couldn't tell you a single thing about them. Nothing. I didn't so much as register their names, too busy picturing Ethan's face in between my thighs.

"I'm going to make you pay for this," I informed him seriously once it was just us two again.

He smirked in that smug way of his. "Promises, promises."

I swallowed my laugh. He didn't need the encouragement.

"When d'you think they'll call us for dinner?" It felt like we'd been here for ages. And I was really looking forward to leaving.

"Few minutes. Shouldn't be much longer."

"Okay. I'm just going to run to the ladies' room. I'll meet you at our table in a bit?"

He placed a small, tender kiss on my temple before letting me go, and I felt it linger there as I made my way out of the ballroom and down the hall. Then it morphed into a loony smile that I couldn't push back down, no matter how hard I tried.

And I *tried*. Bit down on my cheeks and everything. But then *that* turned into a small giggle. Because I'd lost my mind.

Ethan had kissed my temple, and it had somehow wormed its way through my skull, into the pleasure center of my brain, and messed up the wiring responsible for any sort of moderation.

The result was an absurd amount of giddiness bubbling up my spine. And for the first time in a long time, I was starting to feel... content. Like things in my life were finally starting to come together perf—

"Having fun?"

I jolted.

"Sorry," Grey said with a suppressed smile. "Didn't mean to startle you. Again."

It took me a second to reel back to the present and realize that I'd already gone to the washroom, washed my hands, reapplied my lipstick, and walked out.

"It's okay," I said. "I was just on, um, autopilot, I think. A little distracted."

"I can see that."

I smiled politely. He did the same. And then it was just a bit awkward, so I pointed a floppy finger down the hall. "I'm just gonna, um—they're about to serve dinner, so..."

"Right. Yes, of course."

But then, just as I'd started to walk away, he stopped me. "Hey, actually, can I ask you something before you go?"

I paused for a noticeably long second before nodding.

Grey slipped his hands into his pockets, leaned a shoulder against the wall.

"You date your sketches," he said.

And then... that was it.

I waited to see if he was going to get to the question part of the sentence, but he didn't, so I just said, "I do. Yes."

All of my designs had my signature and the date scribbled in the bottom right corner. It was pretty standard practice in my field. Common enough to be entirely... uninteresting.

"And how long have you and Ethan been together?"

"Um, a little over eight months," I answered, per the timeline Ethan had noted in his info sheet.

I tried to swallow back the small ball of nerves that had started to roll up my chest.

Something felt... weird. And off. A bit.

And also, what did my sketches have to do with how long Ethan and I had been "together"? Or were they unrelated?

I kind of really couldn't wait for the dinner part of this whole night to be over. And also, this conversation. I couldn't wait for this conversation to be over.

And I didn't really know why.

"Was that your question?" I asked. It was kind of warm in here.

"No, not quite." Grey cocked his head. The movement was almost... mocking? "I'm just wondering, if you and my brother have been together for eight months, why did you only start sketching him over this last week?"

*I... what?* "What are you talking about?"

The corners of his dark eyes pinched, amused. "The models, Skylar. Why is it that the models in your sketchbook only started to look like Ethan over this last week?"

I paused. It took a few seconds for the realization to start spider-crawling down my spine. "Wh—uh—sorry, what?"

He smiled, then tapped the left corner of his mouth. "Some of them have his little indent from the golfing accident when we were kids. Others have his hair. From the exact shade of brown to the few loose strands that fall over his forehead. And a few of them mimic his posture."

He stopped then, waiting to see if I had anything to say in response to that. I didn't.

"To be honest, it normally wouldn't have raised a question, because it makes sense for you to draw inspiration from the people in your life. But it was just so strangely... sudden.

"Your designs in that book go back almost three months, and all of your models used to be the same. Every single one was generic and faceless, with black hair. But then, eight days ago, it changed. Why?"

My lips had parted, my mind racing to come up with an excuse, *any* excuse that would make even an iota of rational sense. "I... um—"

"If you've been dating for eight months, why is it that when I asked my grandmother about you this morning, she said she only heard about you two weeks ago? Why is it that you only popped up a couple of days after Ethan was informed about her retirement plans?"

*Oh god.*

My eyes darted to the end of the hallway. And a small voice in the back of my brain told me to make a run for it. Walk away.

I didn't.

I should have.

"You want me to help you out?" he asked.

Because he knew.

He *knew*. For sure, he knew. It was in the taunting edge of his voice, the imperfect twist of his too-perfect smile.

My palms had started to sweat.

"I'll take your shocked, deer-in-the-headlights look as a 'yes,'" he said, straightening back up so he could take a few steps forward. I took two back. "Let's see... according to your slight accent and a quick internet search, you're from New York. Studied there. Came here for the internship with Zee and met Ethan through Alexis, who you knew from school. You're the same age, graduated the same year, similar fields of study, and you're featured more than once in her online portfolio; it makes sense.

"Then, Ethan, in a final act of desperation after finding out about Anita's retirement plans, offered you a pretty significant amount of money to pretend to be his partner. And you accepted. Because it's probably enough to cover your student loans, allow you to afford an independent life in New York, plus whatever other excuse you could come up with to justify lying to a bunch of people you've never met and inserting yourself into a situation you know nothing about. Blindly. Without weighing the risks and thinking about the potential consequences."

The black of his eyes had started to spread like crude oil,

spilling into the outskirts of my vision. I was so shocked I couldn't move.

"Did I miss anything?" Grey asked when I remained entirely silent. "We're kind of on a time crunch with dinner being served soon, so that's the TLDR version. But I think I hit most of the main points, no?"

I... I didn't...

"Okay, great," he said, clapping his hands together once. "Now, the fun part: all of those consequences you didn't bother to think about."

# 35

than

ALEXIS: **She's not here.**

I frowned down at the screen.

**Me: What do you mean, she's not there?**

**Alexis: I mean she's not here. The bathroom is empty.**

I slipped my phone back into my pocket as discreetly as I possibly could, ignoring the disapproving glare of my grandmother. "Excuse me for a moment."

It took active effort to keep my steps slow and calm against the uneasy feeling crawling through my stomach.

Alexis was standing around the corner, arms crossed unhappily. "Are you *sure* she said she was just going to the bathroom?"

"Yes. Are *you* sure she's not actually in there?"

"It's completely empty, but you're welcome to go in and look for yourself."

Instead of doing that, I took out my phone again and tried calling her. It rang all the way through to voicemail.

"She's not picking up," I said, shifting on my feet.

"Maybe she realized how terrible of an idea this whole thing was and decided to leave," Alexis offered unhelpfully.

I ignored her, shooting off a few quick texts to Skylar.

The messages I'd missed from her earlier this week popped up all at once, and my eyes and chest snagged on the ones asking me if I was okay.

I needed to apologize for that later.

"Can you try her?" I said, tension coiling through my shoulders.

She frowned. "Just let her go. If she doesn't want to do this—"

"Alexis." I could hear the slight hint of desperation in my voice, but I couldn't find it in me to care.

Skylar had been gone for thirty minutes and wasn't where she'd said she'd be. That was enough of a reason for me to worry.

*You're overreacting. She's going to turn the corner at any second now, and you're going to feel like an idiot.*

*She wouldn't have just left.*

*There's no way she would have just left.*

Alexis eyed me for a second, her frown shifting from unhappy to unhappy and... inquisitive. "What's with you two?"

"What do you mean?"

"I mean... *this*. Why are you acting like this?"

"I'm not acting like anything."

"Yes you are. You're acting weird as hell. And so was she. Not to mention the two of you walked into the party all... *giddy*. And touchy-feely. And it didn't seem fake. It seemed like... like..." Her eyes thinned slowly.

*Fuck's sake.* "Just give me your phone."

She jerked her hand out of my reach, eyes flaring. "Oh my god. You *did* hook up with her! I knew it! I *told* Joel you looked—"

"Now's not the time."

She smacked my arm with her purse. Hard. And then she smacked it again.

"*Ow*, what the fuck is on that thing? Why is it spiked?"

Her glare had turned lethal. "Are you out of your goddamn mind? This whole nightmare wasn't enough of a mess for you already? You had to complicate things *more* by sleeping with her? I can't believe you!"

"It's not what you think!"

"Oh bullshit, Ethan," she snapped.

"We can talk about this later. Give me your—"

"What's going on?"

Our heads both turned at the same time to watch Joel turn the corner. Alexis immediately stomped to his side.

"I *told you* something was going on with the two of them!" she exclaimed, pointing an accusatory finger at my face.

I swatted her hand away. "We can't find Skylar."

"Okay, well, they're starting to ask questions in there, and Anita sent me to check on you. So what do you want me to tell them?"

I glanced back down at my phone in case a message had come through without me noticing. "I don't know. Just buy us a bit of time. She's got to be around here somewhere."

"She probably just left," Alexis chimed in, entirely unprompted.

"Did you try calling her?"

"She's not picking up."

"Okay... Did you try calling the Laivimere front desk to see if she's gone back like Lex says?"

The tension had spread from my shoulders to the back of my neck. "She wouldn't have left without telling me," I said, sounding more defensive than was probably necessary. It irritated me that they both thought she would. And that a small part of me did, too.

Alexis rolled her eyes, then finally decided to unlock her phone. She didn't call Skylar, though.

"Hey, George, Alexis Milani here. Yes, hi. Question for you: remember the guest I brought in a couple of weeks back? Skylar Gage?" She paused for a moment, nodding as George confirmed. "Yes. Yeah. Any chance you've seen her come through the lobby in the last half hour or so? She was wearing a long black dress—you wouldn't have missed her." A longer pause this time. More nodding. "Uh-huh. Okay. Okay. Yes, that's all I needed, thank you so much! Yes, thank you. You too. Bye."

She hung up, looking entirely unsurprised. "Told you. He saw her go up ten minutes ago."

My stomach sank.

But that... didn't make any sense.

"I—uh..."

She'd ditched me?

The smug little smirk Alexis was wearing faltered. "Ethan?"

Why? Had I done something?

Joel nudged my arm. "You good?"

"Was he sure?" I asked. My voice sounded off. Maybe because my throat was so dry. "Was he sure it was her?"

Alexis threw Joel a look before answering. "I mean... he sounded pretty confident. And she would be kind of hard to miss in a full gown."

I glanced back down at my messages.

Sure enough, the little "Read" mark flashed underneath the most recent one. Still no reply, though.

Had I *said* something?

There was a long stretch of silence as I racked my brain, trying to figure out why... just *why*.

Had something happened? Was she sick?

I sent another text as Alexis and Joel stood there, staring at me.

**Me: You left?**

It only took a few seconds for the "Delivered" flare to switch to "Read." And a few more for the three little dots to make a momentary appearance.

Then... nothing.

"Lex, why don't you try calling her," Joel suggested, nudging her arm.

She did. Skylar didn't pick up.

"I'm leaving," I said after her second failed attempt.

"What, like *now*?"

"Tell Anita that Skylar was sick and I had to take her home."

"Wait— But. *Wait*, we're not even halfway through dinner yet," Alexis pointed out, following me down the hall. "You said Nonna is supposed to do her retirement announcement tonight. Don't you need to be here for that?"

I did. She was going to be doing it over the toast, which was why I'd wanted to stay for dinner.

"One of you can fill me in tomorrow," I said, slamming my finger down on the elevator button three impatient times. The doors slid open right away.

Something was wrong. It had to be. She wouldn't have left me here if it wasn't.

The last thing I saw before stepping into the elevator was my sister's mouth dropping halfway open.

# 36

kylar

It was a mess.

My clothes were scattered all over the place. On the floor, the bed, hanging over chairs and open drawers.

I'd taken them out of the closet and thrown them everywhere *except* where they were supposed to go: inside the empty suitcase that sat open in the middle of the room.

I grabbed a pair of jeans with shaky hands, rolled it up in my lap, and.... left it there.

I couldn't do it. I *physically* couldn't bring myself to put it inside the suitcase, even though I knew I had to.

The beeps of the front door went off, and I braced myself, fingers digging into the rolled-up denim. Ethan was going to take one look at this, and... well, I didn't really know how he was going to react. But a small part of me hoped it would be with anger. Because maybe that would make this easier.

"Skylar?"

I held my breath.

"Are you here?"

His steps up the stairs were quick, and his voice sounded worried and breathy when he called for me again, like he'd been running. "Sky? Are you in... he...re."

I kept my eyes pinned to the blurry floor, my jaw clenched so tight it hurt. But I deserved it.

There was a really long stretch of silence. I assumed he was looking around, trying to process the chaos, trying to figure out why I was here, why I'd never gone back to the party.

*"Is this what you meant when you said you'd meet me at our table in a bit?"* he was going to say.

Then he was going to ask what I was doing, why I'd left without saying anything. Why I hadn't picked up any of their calls or replied to any of his texts. And, finally, he was going to ask about the suitcase.

And I wouldn't be able to give him any real answers.

I'd lie, he'd get frustrated, confused, angry. And eventually, he'd get tired of me and storm away.

Because from his perspective, this was the second time I'd done a crazy-person one-eighty on him in the span of a week. And at the worst possible time. First in bed, right before we were about to have sex, and now at his grandmother's birthday party. At the *one* event I was supposed to keep my shit together for. It was literally my job, what he'd hired me to do.

So, yeah, he had every right to be angry and annoyed. To be done with me. He had every right to storm out that door and to decide he never wanted to see me or talk to me or deal with my bullshit again.

It would have been reasonable, and it would have been understandable. Because no one would want to put up with this.

*And that will be the best-case scenario,* I tried to tell myself through the painful tightness in my throat. *If he ends this, it means you won't have to.*

After what felt like an eternity, Ethan stepped into the room. Tentatively.

I could feel him looking around, silently taking in more of the clutter. He stopped a few feet away from me and the empty suitcase. My chin dipped farther down, my shoulders tightening in preparation for the conflict I assumed was about to happen.

"What..." He trailed off before trying again. "What are you doing?"

I didn't answer.

"Sky. Why are you— Are you *packing*?"

My throat had grown spikes; they scratched when I swallowed.

*Put the jeans into the suitcase.*

My arms wouldn't move.

"Skylar?"

And this time when I didn't answer, he knelt in front of me and reached for my face. I pulled away before he could touch me.

"What's... going on? Did something happen?" He kept trying to lower his head so he could look at my face. "Why did you leave without saying anything? Why are you packing?"

The rising level of concern in his voice was torture. I would have preferred the anger. I *deserved* the anger.

"Did I do something?" he asked quietly.

My lower lip wobbled at that. Then my hands went limp against the denim, my shoulders slumped, and when he reached for me again, I didn't have the strength to pull away. "Talk to me. Please?" he pleaded, tilting my jaw up.

Meeting his gaze was a mistake. Because the second I saw

the mixture of worry and hurt and panic in his eyes in place of the anger I'd been anticipating, I cracked in half. The tears started spilling hard and fast, and I tried—I *really* tried—to hold the rest of it in. But then I opened my mouth to breathe, and the first sob fell out.

Ethan's whole body stiffened in response, his expression widening with shock. But that only lasted for a split second because next thing I knew, I was in his arms, which was the exact opposite of what was supposed to have happened. I was supposed to be putting *more* distance between us, not less.

But I didn't want to let him go. I didn't want to lie to him. I didn't want to fight. I didn't want to leave. I didn't want to end this.

How big of a waste would that be. He'd said last night that ending this would be a mistake, and I knew that in my soul. I knew how much I'd regret leaving. Especially like this.

I didn't want to. I didn't want Ethan to be the one that got away.

"Whoa, okay," he breathed as I cried into his neck. My fingers were digging into his coat, clinging on for dear life. "What the fuck happened?"

But by that point, I couldn't have said it even if I wanted to.

Ethan tried to comfort me as best he could, rubbing my back, telling me everything was going to be okay, even though it wasn't. It wasn't going to be okay. I knew that for a fact.

And it was all my fault. I couldn't believe I'd been so stupid. And if Ethan knew, he'd be a hell of a lot less comforting and sympathetic.

I cried for what felt like an eternity. Until my breaths were stuttering, my eyes were swollen and sore, and my muscles were liquid. Until I'd practically gone limp against him. Somehow, though, my fingers still hadn't let go of his coat.

"Sky, you need to tell me what's going on," Ethan murmured, gently massaging the back of my neck.

Except I couldn't. I wasn't allowed to.

"What time is it?" I whispered instead, surprised I still even had a voice.

"Nine thirty."

The car would be here in an hour and a half. I wasn't even close to being packed.

"I need a drink."

His fingers slowed, and he hesitated before he said, "I'm not sure that's the best idea right now."

I swallowed. It burned a little. "Please?"

Ethan sighed, then slowly peeled me off him. My fingers took more convincing than the rest of me.

"Come on." He helped me stand, waited for me to take off my heels, then held my hand and led me downstairs.

I sank into the couch, the entirety of my body feeling like deadweight, as Ethan made his way to the bar. "What do you want to drink?"

"Bourbon," I said. My voice practically creaked it was so hoarse. "Neat. Please."

He eyed me for a few seconds before reaching for the rich amber bottle, then poured us two glasses.

"Here."

I immediately gulped it down. All of it. Before he'd even had the chance to sit.

It burned and stabbed the whole way.

Ethan took the empty glass from my hands as I coughed and choked, and then he sat down beside me and started to pat my back.

He might have cursed a couple of times, but I barely registered it.

"Can I have some more?" I eventually croaked. I needed it to be able to get through this.

He frowned. "You're going to pass out if you—"

I grabbed his drink and downed it.

Ethan pinched his lips together, and by the time I'd finished the second round of coughs, his body was all but curled protectively over mine, arm slung on the couch behind me, eyes searching my face.

"You okay?" he asked when my breathing had somewhat evened out.

I shook my head, then swallowed, my eyes welling up with a fresh bout of tears that had nothing to do with the whiskey. "I need to... um..."

God, this was so fucking hard.

"Just tell me," he whispered.

*Just do it.*

*You know you have to do it.*

*Rip it off like a Band-Aid.*

But I couldn't. I physically couldn't get the words out. Every time I opened my mouth, my lips wobbled uncontrollably, and my throat felt blocked.

I couldn't follow Grey's script. I couldn't end things with Ethan like this.

But I also couldn't tell him the truth.

So I just sort of... sat there, hands wringing on my lap as I tried to figure out what I was going to do.

"You know, um, how we said we were going to talk about us and the contract tomorrow? After breakfast?" I asked in an effort to buy myself a little more time.

Ethan nodded slowly, refusing to take his eyes off mine.

"Can we do that now?"

If he was surprised by my diversion, he didn't show it.

Instead, he reached up and brushed a strand of hair away from my face. "Okay. Where do you want to start?"

I let out a breath, relaxing into his touch as the whiskey started to work its warm magic through my stomach. "Just... can you just tell me what you're thinking, please? And what you want to do?"

Because, technically, I hadn't even made it to the end of the trial.

"I already told you what I wanted, Sky. You. Just you."

"And the contract?" I asked, heart zigzagging in my chest. He brushed my hair back again. It felt nice.

"Just. You."

I leaned into his arm on the couch. He moved closer.

"There won't be an agreement unless you insist on one," he went on, voice low and comforting. "It'll only get in the way. I'll give you the five hundred thousand dollars, as promised, and then we just—"

"I don't want your money." It was an automatic response. It was also the truth.

I didn't want any of it anymore.

"We had a deal. And I'm the one breaking it, so it's only fair—"

"Ethan. I don't want your money." For the first time since this whole nightmare started, my voice was firm, unwavering.

His fingers continued to play with my hair, like it was the most natural thing in the world. It *felt* like the most natural thing in the world. "So what is it that you do want?"

*You.*

*You you you you you you you.*

*Just. You.*

But how was I supposed to tell him that and then leave?

I stayed quiet for a beat too long.

"Skylar... in order for this to work, we need to be able to

communicate with each other. You need to tell me what you want, and you need to tell me what's wrong."

"I know," I said quickly. "I know. You're right. But this isn't..."

I trailed off with a tight sigh, about to lose my goddamn mind. Because this wasn't me not *wanting* or *being able* to communicate. But he couldn't know that.

"I know I said I have a hard time communicating sometimes," I went on. "And that's true. I do. But this isn't... *that*."

I was honestly a little scared he wouldn't believe me.

Ethan's brows pulled together. "What do you mean?"

My lips pursed, my fingers fidgeting as I glanced at the clock. One hour, fourteen minutes.

"I mean... I, um..." I watched the big handle tick once, twice, as the whiskey swirled in my stomach, warming my skin.

Ethan shifted in his seat, and I wondered if he was starting to lose his patience with me yet. But then he said, "If you can't tell me, can you... show me?"

My eyes shot back to his.

He twirled a piece of my hair around his finger, tapped his forehead lightly against mine. "Show me," he said again. "Or at least give me a hint. I'm going a little crazy here, Sky. You left me at the party without saying anything, wouldn't pick up your phone or respond to my messages, and I came home to find you packing your things before you broke down and started crying. I don't know if you're leaving... or what's happening. How would you feel if you were me?"

I'd be going a little crazy, too.

And I probably wouldn't be handling it with nearly as much patience and understanding as he was.

But in all fairness, who would?

Honestly, *who would*?

"Stay here," I said. "I'll be right back."

Then I ran upstairs to grab my sketchbook with my heart crawling up my throat.

I wasn't going to let him go.

*Who would?*

# 37

**than**

SKYLAR SPRINTED BACK down the stairs so fast she was a little out of breath by the time she sat down, clutching a black book in her lap.

Her face was blotchy, eyes slightly swollen, and there were traces of dark makeup running down her cheeks. Somehow, though, she was still beautiful.

She swallowed hard, glancing at the clock as she started to fiddle with the edge of the black book.

I gave her the time she needed, doing my best to seem calm. Like I wasn't losing my fucking mind over this whole thing. Like my heart hadn't tripped all over itself at having come home to find her packing her bags. Like it hadn't squeezed and sliced when she'd broken down and cried into my neck, clutching onto me like she was scared I'd let her go.

I didn't know what the fuck was going on or what could have possibly happened when she'd gone to the bathroom to upset her this bad. And it was driving me out of my goddamn mind. Because if I didn't know what was wrong, I couldn't fix it.

What I did know, though, was that I wasn't going to let this go until I knew exactly what was going on. Until she finally opened up and talked to me.

This wasn't going to be like the last time. We would be here all night if need be.

If she had a hard time communicating sometimes, that was okay. We'd work on it; she'd get better. It wasn't likc I was perfect.

Because I'd already made up my mind about her. I knew what I had, and I wasn't going to let her go. Not like this. There was no way I was going to let her leave like this.

So I gave her time. Let her breathe, think, until she finally decided on how she was going to start.

"Okay, I know... some of this is going to seem off topic, but just... stick with me for a bit, okay? I just need you to listen until the end."

I nodded, and she inched closer, leaning a shoulder against my arm again.

It took active effort not to scoop her right onto my lap.

"Do you remember how you asked me what my dream was?"

My brows ticked. That wasn't the direction I'd expected her to go. "I do."

"Okay, well, um, it's a family," she said, eyes dipping to her fidgeting hands. "I know that's a little simple and maybe even silly, but my dream is to eventually have a happy, stable family and home life. Like with a partner and kids and a golden retriever and everything. It's kind of what I've always wished for because I never really had it growing up."

She paused, bit the inside of her cheek as my heart wiggled restlessly inside my chest.

"I wasn't exactly... planned. Or wanted, for that matter. And my parents never really let me forget it. My mom never let me forget that the pregnancy was the sole reason her acting career never took off because it happened just as she was being considered for her breakout role. It was down to her and one other actress, and she always said that it was because the casting director found out about her pregnancy that he decided against her. And she always sort of held that over my head. Like it was somehow directly my fault.

"It also didn't help that the actress that *did* get her role went on to have a pretty successful career. She's been in a bunch of TV shows and a couple of movies. Her name's Lilla Abbot—not sure if you've heard of her." Skylar's lips twitched up and down, like she couldn't decide whether she found the whole thing sad or funny. "I always knew when my mom was in a particularly bad mood because I'd come home and one of Lilla's shows would be on. Sometimes she'd get drunk and yell at the TV about how much of a better job she could have done in that episode or movie or whatever. And how it was supposed to be *her* on the screen.

"My dad wasn't any better. He never wanted to be a father and had very little patience for kids in general. He told me to 'be quiet' a lot and never wanted anything to do with me. He found me annoying and too talkative, from what I recall. Until I learned to fix that part.

"They separated when I was seven." Skylar paused, eyes still on her lap, visibly hesitating before she continued. "I would, um, hear them fighting. About which one of them would be stuck with me after the divorce."

There was a tight tug at my chest, a sour burn in my throat

as I watched her voice grow quieter, her shoulders slouch, like she was trying to make herself smaller.

"My mom lost, so I stayed with her. Mostly because my dad just up and left one day. Moved to a different state. And then things got... somewhat worse after that. Because then I was also being blamed for their divorce. And I tried so hard, really I did, even when my dad was still there. I did everything I could to get them to love me. Because that's all I wanted obviously; that's what any kid wants. To be loved and wanted by their parents.

"I'd figured out pretty quickly that the quieter I was, and the less I asked for things, the less negative attention I earned from them and the more they seemed to be able to... tolerate me. And by the time my dad left, I was so scared that my mom would also get sick of me and leave that I sort of stopped... communicating.

"It got to the point where my teachers would barely be able to get a word out of me. Which, um, got me into trouble a couple of times. Like once, in second grade, I got sick behind the Reading Couch in class and didn't tell my teacher because I thought she'd call my mom. But of course, that ended up backfiring and being a whole thing..."

The tugging in my chest had intensified to an uncomfortably painful degree, my heart tangling with my stomach as I listened to her speak. Every single part of me wanted to reach for her, pull her into my arms, and comfort her, but I knew it wasn't the right time. That she needed a bit of space to get to where she needed.

So I kept my hands to myself and listened.

"I did end up growing out of the quiet phase eventually. Sort of. I was still shy and kept mostly to myself through middle school and the first year of high school, but it was... better. And then I met Mik." The corners of Skylar's mouth jerked at the mention of her friend, the tension around her brows softening slightly as her crystal-blue eyes finally came back up to meet mine. "She was... honestly, she was, and still is, the absolute best thing that's ever happened to me. And I tell her that all the time. She's adamant that we're soul mates, and I'm not particularly spiritual, but I'm genuinely inclined to believe her.

"She pulled me out of my shell without even really trying. We were inseparable within a week, and eventually, I was spending more time at her house than mine. Which worked out well; my mom was ripping through boyfriends at the time, and it was weird to come home to a new, random guy sitting on the couch all the time, so..."

Skylar let out a breath, head slanting to the side like it was suddenly too heavy to hold up. The whiskey had already started to color her nose and cheeks, pull on her lids and lengthen her words.

"It was like that for a few years, and my mom seemed just as happy with the arrangement as I was. I'd stay at Mik's for days at a time without letting her know, and she'd never call or say a word about it." Her fingers continued to fiddle with the book in her lap while she talked, her eyes bouncing to the clock every few minutes. "And then, um, when I turned seventeen, I was scouted at the mall by this modeling agent. I honestly didn't think much of it and wasn't going to pursue it since I thought it was probably a scam or something. But then she saw the agent's card on my nightstand, and... it was like a switch flipped with her.

"For the first time in my life, she showed an interest in what was going on with me. She asked me questions, encouraged me to meet with the agency and do some test shots. And I was so... overwhelmed by the attention and encouragement that I went along with it. All of it. I did the test shots, created a portfolio, and signed with the third agency we met with. And she was there every step of the way."

Skylar stopped, letting out a heavy breath. "It felt nice, you know? It felt like… I finally had a *mom*. A parent who cared about me, who wanted to spend time with me and was proud to have me as a daughter. Because the part of me that wanted to be loved by her parents had never really gone away; I'd just accepted that it was probably something I'd never have. So when I felt like it was finally starting to happen… there wasn't very much I wasn't willing to do to keep it. My boundaries were wide open, and, um… I think she knew that. And… that she took advantage of it.

"Anyways, the modeling thing ended up kind of taking off. Though I never really enjoyed it, to be honest, being put in front of a camera… having every inch of my body openly scrutinized at casting calls, but I went along with it because I was afraid that if I stopped, then things would go back to the way they used to be. Which I know might sound… stupid—it's not like she was a good mother to me growing up. So maybe I should have been too bitter and angry to care by that point. But at seventeen… and even eighteen, nineteen… you're really still just a kid. You still have… hope that people can change. Or at least I did.

"So it didn't matter that I couldn't eat the things I wanted to or that I wasn't entirely comfortable with some of the photoshoots my mom would agree to on my behalf." Skylar swallowed, a muscle in her jaw squirming with the motion. "It didn't, um, matter that I hated the way the industry made me feel about my body, the impact that it had on my self-esteem. Or that my mom was spending the majority of the money I was earning on herself. On designer clothes and ridiculously expensive wines, then openly lying to me about putting it in a savings account for my college education. I didn't care about any of it because, sometimes, we'd go to brunch, and she'd sneak me sips of her mimosa and tell me she was proud of me. And that was enough."

Skylar sniffed, fingers continuing to fiddle with the top right corner of the black book on her lap. It had started to bend and tear and discolor. She didn't seem to care.

"Sorry. I know this all seems... irrelevant and kind of stupid, but I needed you to... just... um, I needed you to know... why I'd..." She bit down punishingly on her bottom lip out of frustration, hard enough for it to leave an angry dent. "I just think the background will help with the rest of this."

I'd stayed entirely silent while she talked, listening and watching with my heart lodged in the base of my throat. Because I felt like that was what she needed. Space and time to get everything out uninterrupted.

But I couldn't take it anymore, so I reached up and swiped my thumb against the bite mark on her lip. "It's not stupid. *Nothing* about what you just told me is irrelevant or stupid, Skylar."

She looked at me for a long time before nodding, whiskey-hooded eyes rimmed red. "You're gonna be, um, a lot less nice to me when we get into this next part."

"I highly doubt that," I said, continuing to stroke her skin. She leaned into my touch but gave me a look that said she didn't believe me. At least now I was starting to understand why.

And then she said it.

"Any chance you ever finished listening to that recording?"

My thumb slowed. "What?"

She swallowed, blinking slowly. "The recording. From last night. Did you ever finish listening to it?"

My heart dislodged from my throat and plummeted to the pit of my stomach.

*Grey.*

"I haven't listened to the rest of it, no," I said, trying to maintain a reasonable level of calm in my voice. I failed miserably.

I was going to kill him.

If he'd so much as *breathed* in her direction, I was going to kill my brother.

Skylar sniffled. I started brainstorming murder weapons in my head.

"Okay, well, um, now might be a good time for you to... do that."

...

*Fuck.*

# 38

than

EVERY MUSCLE in my body was clenched tight as I reached for my phone, rewound the recording, and pressed Play.

I should have finished listening to it last night. Should have gone over it at least twice to make sure there hadn't been a slip in their interaction.

What the fuck had I been thinking?

I started listening from the beginning, paying closer attention than I had the first time.

But it was fine. She'd handled it well. They were mostly talking about her work, which was a safer topic than most.

And then he asked, *"You got any of your sketches here? Can I see them while we wait?"*

Skylar instantly stiffened beside me.

I cut off their voices.

"You showed him your designs?"

I couldn't believe how much I hated even the thought of that. That he'd seen them first. That he'd seen them at all.

That *Grey*, of all people, had gotten to know something about her before I did. Which I fully realized was petty and maybe even a little immature, but the awareness didn't make the jealousy go away.

Instead of giving me a verbal answer, Skylar tentatively offered me the black book on her lap.

I opened it.

They were remarkable. But of course they were. She wouldn't have gotten the internship at Bain if she wasn't insanely talented.

Sky stayed silent as I flipped through the sketches slowly, lingering on a few of the suits I found particularly appealing. I was bouncing between being endlessly impressed by her and stressing over what—

My hand and brain stuttered at the same time.

I flipped back a page, then forward, my heart jumping straight into my mouth.

Was that... was that *me*?

...

I stared at the model, my lips parting.

Because *holy shit*, that looked just like me.

He didn't have a full face, exactly; none of her models did. But he had my hair and the scar from the time Grey had "accidentally" whacked me in the face with a golf club after I'd won the game. The scar she'd commented on last night, except I didn't think she realized that's what it was.

I traced a finger over the figure. He was dressed in a merlot suit, and he looked *good*. The handsome devil.

I flipped to the next page.

Then the next one.

Then the next.

They all looked like me. There was absolutely no question about it. She'd drawn *me*.

"Sky... this is..."

And that was when I noticed the date. The signature and the date.

The date.

I went back to check when the change had happened.

*Oh.*

*Shit.*

Skylar visibly deflated. "What would you do..." she said quietly, "if you were the evil twin and you saw this... what would you do next?"

The high of seeing myself reflected in Skylar's work collapsed as I realized what path I was being led down.

The signature was legible. And it contained her full name.

"What would you do next?" she pressed when I took too long to answer.

I was starting to really hate this game.

"I would look you up," I admitted. It wouldn't be the only thing I'd do, but it would be the first.

She stood, went into my study, and came back with my laptop.

The images were what popped up first. Runway shots, portraits, and advertisements featuring a younger, poutier Skylar with much longer hair. Some of the brands I recognized; a couple were household names.

Then there was her model profile (which listed her as "currently inactive"), her social media accounts (all set to private), and a couple of interviews she'd done a few years back.

The only other thing of note was the second name that kept popping up through the pages of results alongside hers. Simon King. A twenty-five-year-old photographer based in Brooklyn.

I ignored it the first few times. But after the fourth or fifth appearance of his name, in addition to a picture of the two of them in rather... close proximity, my curiosity got the better of me.

I looked him up.

His website was clean. A minimalist black, white, and grey design. His style of photography seemed to follow the same aesthetic.

Skylar leaned a shoulder into my arm on the couch, peeking at the screen. She hadn't protested or attempted to redirect me away from going to this guy's website, so I assumed I was at least somewhat still on track.

I navigated straight to his portfolio, then to the list of models he'd worked with, scrolling until I found her: Skylar Ainsley Gage.

These photos were more... boudoir than the others I'd seen of her so far. I wasn't sure if that was the right word, but it was what came to mind to describe the tasteful black-and-white images of Skylar, sprawled across white bedsheets in black cotton underwear, covering her bare chest with an arm.

Skylar, topless, lying on her stomach. Hair perfectly disheveled as she looked at the camera with the most enticing "fuck me" eyes I'd ever seen.

Skylar on her knees, her half-hidden face smiling at the camera as she hugged a massive pillow to her fully naked body.

And it kept going. Pages and pages of a mostly undressed Sky teasing the camera with shy smiles and bedroom eyes. I spent more time scrolling through them than was necessary. But there wasn't a single person on the planet that could blame me.

She was enchanting. Truly.

Had we not been in the middle of a crisis of sorts, I'd have thrown her over my shoulder, carried her upstairs to my bed, stripped her down to her underwear, just so I could—

Wait, who actually was this guy? Just a photographer she'd worked with? Why had she only done these types of photoshoots with him?

Before I could even question whether or not I was still on track, I'd clicked on one of his social media links.

Skylar sucked in a sharp breath. Because there it was. Right there, in his status update from last night.

**Simon K:** Here's a non-hypothetical for y'all. Some random hits you up in the middle of the night asking about your ex. Offers you a cool 5k for all the dirty deets. You just got married and the wedding was expensive as hell. WWYD + AITA for saying yes? (Sorry Star. Kind of. But not really.)

The blood seeped from my veins. Slowly.

All of the responses he'd interacted with were pinned just beneath the status.

**StinkyStocks:** lol wtf why

**Simon K:** idk. I heard 5k and stopped asking questions.

**Peter P:** My ex is a dickhead so yeah, I'd do it.

**Simon K:** My ex didn't give my dick head. Does that count?

**Jillybean:** LMAO did u explain the nickname to them?

**Simon K:** It may have come up...

**Jillybean:** Dead. YTA 100%.

I stopped scrolling.

"He's lying," Skylar mumbled in a small voice. "He's such a liar. About the head thing. I..." She trailed off, her cheeks burning crimson. The alcohol had started to mend her words together, blur her *l*'s and *r*'s. "I don't want you to think I have a problem with—"

"The only thing I'm thinking right now is that your ex sounds like an ass."

It was an understatement. My blood was boiling.

I didn't know which I was more angry at, the fact that my brother had gone to this extent or that this asshat had agreed to reveal personal details of his relationship with Sky for financial gain, then openly boasted about it on social media and *mocked her*.

I ground my molars, stubbornly putting off the inevitable. Skylar didn't urge me on this time. I didn't think she was looking forward to what needed to happen next, either.

"Just so we're clear on this... the next part involves me calling your ex to figure out what him and Grey discussed because you still can't tell me," I eventually said, needing to make absolute certain we were on the same page about this.

Skylar dipped her chin into a quick nod before sinking a little deeper into the couch, her eyes meandering down to her fiddling fingers. "Just... please make sure you don't lose your cool with him... no matter what he says. He has... a bit of an ego, and... trust me, if you bruise it, he's going to be a lot less likely to cooperate with you. And he might, um—just promise me."

The mere fact that she'd thought to warn me meant I'd probably regret agreeing. But it wasn't like I had much of a choice. "Okay."

"And keep him on speaker, please. I want to know what he's saying."

I knew in my gut that wasn't a good idea. But, again, it wasn't like I had much of a choice.

My nerves twisted and curdled, my heart thumping louder as I snatched Simon's number off his website and typed it into my phone.

I was going to make Grey pay for this. Every last agonizing bit of it.

# 39

kylar

THE WORLD HAD STARTED to soften and blur around the edges.

I blinked, trying to bring the furniture back into full focus. It didn't really work, but I did it again anyway. And a few more times after that.

And I was so distracted, trying to get my eyes to focus, that I forgot to tell my brain to do the same. So I inevitably missed when Simon picked up the phone.

"And how much is that information worth to you?"

It wasn't the words that pulled me back. It was the tone. I hated that tone. The arrogant, mocking one. The one he used with me all the time. I hated, hated, *hated* that tone.

Ethan's eyes shot to mine as I bristled. "I'll match what he paid you. Five thousand dollars to tell me what the two of you talked about."

There was a lengthy pause on the other end of the line. "What's going on? Why all the sudden interest in Skylar? She's been inactive for years, and even when she was at her peak, she wasn't worth all this fuss."

"I'll make it six if you stop asking questions and adding unnecessary commentary," Ethan fired back, tone crisp. A small muscle in his jaw twitched.

"Dude... seriously?"

"Seriously."

"Uh, alright, fine. But send me half now so I know this is legit. That's what the other guy did."

Ethan complied, putting Simon on hold as he did the transfer.

"Okay, what do you want to know?" Simon asked, sounding more than a little chipper about this whole thing.

"Everything. Tell me every single thing you told him, beginning to end."

"Alright, sure. He was mostly just interested in the details of the relationship and wanted to know if there was any bad blood between us still and, like, if I had any dirt on her or anything. The deal was that I don't leave anything out, and I didn't. So... just wanna make sure you know what you're asking about. I definitely didn't sugarcoat anything."

My gaze fixed on Ethan as the alcohol settled under my skin, warming it with a numbing buzz. He wasn't looking at me anymore; he was staring down at his phone with the tightest, unhappiest frown I'd seen on him yet.

"Yes. That's fine." His clipped tone very much implied that it was *not* fine, but Simon didn't seem to notice.

"Okay, so, first thing we talked about was how Skylar and I met, which was during a photoshoot I did with her for a mid-tier brand pretty early on in both our careers. She walked in, and I was pretty—uh, I don't know if you actually know her or have met her, but her eyes are, like, freakishly light. It's wild. She gets them from her dad's side of the family, I think. I'd never really seen anything quite like them before, so... after the shoot, I asked if she'd be interested in posing for me again. Not for an ad or a brand or anything commercial, just for my own stuff.

"She said yes, obviously—or her mom did, I guess. Deb acted as her manager for all intents and purposes back then. Sky just sort of went along with it, but that's also just her default. She doesn't have much of a backbone."

*"Doesn't."* Present tense.

That little muscle in Ethan's jaw jerked again. It made me want to reach out and soothe it. Simon wasn't worth his anger.

"Anyways, we ended up working together again pretty soon after that, and a few months later, I asked her out." He let out a long breath, like he was already tired of talking about me. "Honestly, I wasn't looking for anything serious with her, just something casual. She was cute. Super quiet and shy initially. But that obviously didn't really go as planned. She was a lot slower to put out than I expected. Should have taken that as a warning, but I'm too stubborn for my own good, so I took it as a challenge instead."

I lifted a hand and brushed my fingers across the unhappy little tic in Ethan's jaw. He threw me a tortured glance before shoving a rough hand through his hair. There was a pretty good chance he was having a worse time than I was. Poor guy didn't have any alcohol numbing his feelings. *Tsk.*

"But that then somehow turned into a whole relationship, without me even really realizing what was happening. You know how it goes. How they trap you like that."

I almost laughed.

He'd asked me to be his girlfriend after our third date. I'd said I'd think about it. He'd then proceeded to bombard me with texts and flowers and chocolates and love notes until I caved a week later.

"Anyways, that's how the whole thing with us started. Lasted around two years. And then, uh, the other guy and I talked about the problems in the relationship and some of the issues I had with her. Which, other than the fact that she could be a little childish and annoying at times, the main thing was the sex—"

I sunk a few inches deeper into the couch, my hands and eyes falling back to my lap. This part wasn't as funny. Even the whiskey didn't think so.

"—it was mediocre at best. That's actually how she got her nickname 'Star.' I initially told her some bullshit about how it was related to her name, like she was the sole star in my sky or something equally stupid. I can't even remember. But she happily bought it... until she caught a snippet of a group chat I had going on with some friends.

"Long story short, 'Star' was short for 'Starfish,' which is, like, slang for a woman who just kind of lies there while you're having sex. Doesn't do much other than spread her legs, you know?

"And I know that sounds a little douchey or harsh or whatever, but in my defense, it was mostly supposed to be a joke; she just had no sense of humor about it. That was our biggest fight for sure. It was around the year-and-a-half mark. She still didn't leave me, though." Simon snickered proudly. It was a throaty, violating sound that made you want to cut off your ears and feed them to rabid cannibals just so you'd never have to hear him do it again. Or maybe that was just me. "That should tell you all you need to know about her and her self-worth. You could fucking—"

Simon's voice cut off abruptly, and I looked up to find Ethan clutching his phone to his ear. His *entire* body was clenched, every visible muscle strained. It looked like he was about to combust. His skin was flushed a fuming crimson, his fingers were bleached with how tightly they gripped his phone, and there was an alarming amount of twitching going on in his jaw and neck. It looked like he was trying really, very hard not to reach through the phone and strangle Simon to death.

Not that I could blame him. I'd had my own strangulation fantasies about my ex. And not, like, in the sexy way.

I pulled at Ethan's sleeve, wordlessly asking him to put Simon back on speaker. None of the stuff he was saying was new... or anything I couldn't handle. But I *did* need to know what he was saying so I could point out the lies and defend myself where necessary.

Ethan ignored me at first, no doubt trying his best to protect me from whatever degrading bullshit Simon was spewing on the other end of the line. But with enough tugging and silent pleading, he eventually caved.

"—she really didn't want to do them at first. Wasn't comfortable with being semi-nude in front of the camera. But Deb was still making all her career decisions, even though she was twenty years old by then. Skylar would have done pretty much anything to make her mom happy, though, so we were able to convince her to pose for one. Which turned to two, to three, and so on. And eventually, I got her to do a fully nude shoot with me. It took a shit ton of coaxing and bribing, but Deb and I were able to convince her," Simon boasted, sounding entirely too smug.

I didn't really know whether I wanted to punch him in the fucking mouth or throw up.

Maybe both.

Probably both.

"So anyways, those were in my possession for a while. She wanted to buy the rights after we broke up, but I wouldn't sell them to her. She wouldn't have been able to afford them anyway; Deb still had control over most of her finances, which, uh—yeah, that was its own mess.

"But either way, I held on to the photos. Didn't intend on doing anything with them, to be honest with you—I just liked having them in my possession. Mostly because I knew how much it bothered her. And man, did I make the right decision on that front. Because the dude that called me up last night paid a shit ton more for them than they'll ever be worth. But that's between you and me."

Then he *laughed.*

The air around Ethan cracked. There was a long, shocked moment of silence, then, "You *sold them to him*?" Thunder. Ethan's voice was a growling, rumbling thunder.

"Yeah. Why? Is that what you wanted, too?" Simon asked, completely misinterpreting Ethan's tone. All traces of humor had evaporated from his voice. He sounded disappointed, like he wouldn't have accepted Grey's offer so hastily had he known there would be a bidding war. "I mean, man, like... the professionally done nudes are gone—it was just the one shoot. But I've got some candid nudes of her I could sell you if you're interested. And they're definitely more provocative if that's what you're looking for."

Never in my life had I seen genuine murder in a person's eyes before that moment.

"Listen to me carefully, you—" Ethan cut himself off with a strangled exhale, clenching his fist a few times as he attempted to pull himself back together before speaking again. "You're going to receive a call from my lawyer within the next hour. Her name is Nora Cheung. I want exclusive rights to every single picture of Skylar you currently have in your possession, regardless of their nature. Nora will do the negotiations with you and draft up the agreements for you to sign."

"What—like *all* of them? Even the random ones—"

"Every single picture you have of or with Skylar. I'll purchase the exclusive rights to every single one of them, on the condition that all copies on your end are deleted as soon as the deal's done."

Simon paused for a long moment, and when he spoke again, his voice was unsteady with excitement. Like he simply couldn't believe his luck. "Yeah, okay. You got it. I have no use for them anymore anyway. And, uh, just... thanks, mate. You're actually doing me a solid. Work's been slow lately, and I just got married, which was unbelievably exp—"

"Is there anything else you discussed with Greyson that we haven't covered?" The words barely made it out of Ethan's mouth his jaw was clenched so tight.

If Simon was taken aback or offended by the interruption, he didn't show it. I guess the ego didn't bruise so easily when a bunch of money was involved.

"Really, the only other thing that we talked about was the breakup, which... I don't know how relevant that is now, if what you were after was the pictures."

"Assume everything the two of you talked about is relevant."

I shrunk a little more, trying to breathe through my rising panic. I didn't realize they'd talked about the breakup. I should have, but I didn't.

I was tempted to nudge Ethan and wordlessly signal for him to end the conversation. He'd gotten to the main points already—there was no need for them to go into anything else. He knew Grey had the photos; he could piece together the rest of—

"You're a little intense, man. Anyone ever tell you that?" Simon huffed another easy laugh. It made me nauseous. "But alright, yeah. So, he was super curious about what led to the breakup after I told him she was technically the one who ended it. I guess he was surprised it was her, especially after everything we'd talked about. And, uh, full disclosure... I'm definitely the bad guy in this scenario. But everyone makes mistakes. We learn and we grow, you know? I'm definitely a better human than I was back then. Worked a lot on improving myself."

There was a really tight, knotted ball of barbed wire burning in my throat.

I shouldn't have made Ethan put him back on speaker. I shouldn't have let him make the call. It had been a mistake. It had been a really big, catastrophic mistake.

I should have... I should have... I didn't know what I should have done.

I didn't know what I was supposed to do *now*.

"But yeah, I'm gonna just come out and say it. I cheated and got caught, plain and simple," Simon went on. His tone was so casual, like he was discussing the weather. No trace of remorse in there whatsoever. "Sky'd gone on a road trip with some friends and came back a day early. Not sure why—she never ended up telling me. Anyways, she—uh, kind of walked in on me... with Deb."

I'd been fine up to this point. Really. Mostly.

Everything Simon had talked about so far had been at least bearable, nothing I couldn't handle.

But this... Even after all these years, even after all that therapy, this part felt like a sucker punch to the gut. It knocked the air right out of me, hunched my shoulders, and made me wish I were a lot less alive.

My palm slammed against my mouth. I held it there as I clutched my stomach.

It was a mix of the alcohol and the searing barbed wire in my throat and the fact that the furniture was spinning and

Simon's laugh and the image of walking in on them. The sounds. The *sounds*.

"So yeah. I fucked her mom, and I guess that was her limit. But in my defense, Deb is a—"

I didn't protest this time when his voice cut off.

# 40

than

I THOUGHT I KNEW ANGER.

I thought I knew hatred.

I thought I'd experienced both.

I didn't. I hadn't.

Not until that conversation. Nothing—*nothing*—I'd ever experienced compared to the white-hot, all-consuming rage I felt toward Simon King fifteen minutes after being made aware of his pathetic, wretched excuse of a rotten existence.

I was going to ruin him. His career. Reputation. Relationships. Life.

And after I was done with that disgusting maggot, I'd move on to *her*. Deb. Or my lawyers would, at least. Until she paid. Literally. Every last penny she'd stolen from Skylar.

I couldn't see beyond it. Couldn't think. I didn't even know how I ended the conversation. How I got Simon off the phone.

Or how I managed to have a coherent discussion with Nora afterward.

Then there was Skylar.

For a good while after I hung up with Nora, I couldn't look at her. Couldn't speak. And when I did eventually manage to gather up the courage and glance in her direction, it devastated me.

She'd gone completely still. She wasn't moving or fidgeting or speaking. Just staring blankly down at her lap, arms wrapped loosely around herself.

It all made sense.

Her freak-out.

Her sudden bout of nerves before we were intimate.

Her reluctance to believe me when I told her I wanted her.

Her desire for verbal affirmations.

Her comment about me "tolerating" her.

Of course she'd freaked out in bed. Of course she'd taken my joke the wrong way. Who wouldn't have? After being surrounded by deceptive leeches, used by the people who were supposed to love and care about her the most.

Of course she'd been nervous when we were about to have sex. After having her confidence shredded by a worthless piece of shit.

Of course she liked hearing me say nice things to her. Of course she had a hard time believing me. Of course she had a little trouble communicating sometimes.

Everything made sense. Including why Alexis had warned me so profusely about bringing her into this.

I wasn't sure how much of this my sister was aware of, but it was enough for her to know how... *fragile* things were.

And I should have listened to her.

I should have listened.

Skylar released a shaky breath when I reached for her, but

she didn't push me away. Not when I pulled her onto my lap or when I wrapped my arms protectively around her.

And then I simply held her, waiting until her rigid body slowly warmed and melted into me.

"I'm going to take care of it," I vowed, my arms tightening around her as she buried her face into my neck. "Grey's not going to do anything with those pictures. I'm going to take care of it. All of it. I promise."

"He's sending a car to pick me up," she said quietly. "It's going to be here in eight minutes. Supposed to take me to a temporary apartment until I can figure out a living arrangement."

I pressed a cheek to her temple. "That's not happening."

She sniffled. "I'm sorry about all of this. I—"

"Don't." My voice cracked. I had to clear it before I continued. "No apologizing for any of this. *None* of it is on you."

This wasn't her fault. It was mine.

And I was going to fix it.

~

"HE'S IN A MEETING. You can't—"

I stormed into his office, ignoring Mila. The door crashed shut behind me.

Grey barely looked up.

"I'm going to have to call you back," he said, twirling a pen between his fingers. "My next appointment is early."

"You went too far this time," I snapped.

"Good morning. Nice to see you finally show up to work," he mocked, putting his phone away. "Granted, it is a Saturday, but I'll take it."

I threw the blue folder I'd walked in with onto his desk.

He didn't so much as glance at it.

"You called her ex and *threatened* her with photos he'd taken of her? Are you that fucked in the head?"

"I didn't threaten her with them, no," he said simply, leaning back in his chair. "It was a bribe. I told her they were in my possession and that I'd be happy to transfer the rights to her if she followed my instructions. Which she clearly didn't."

There were two ways to handle this.

I could lunge across the desk, tear out his fucking throat and shove it down his eye socket like I so desperately wanted to, or... I could stick to the plan.

I took a seat.

Grey's brows twitched, the corners of his mouth twisting in condescending amusement. "Here to talk business, are we? This is new."

I let it roll off my back. The anger simmered, but I kept it from boiling over. It wasn't the right time.

"You went too far this time, Grey. Even you know you did."

He clicked his tongue. "Well, that's simply a matter of opinion. Some might say I went too far; others might say hiring someone to pretend to be your partner in an attempt to cheat your way into a promotion you haven't earned is going too far. But, you know, who's to say who's right and who's wrong."

I slid the blue folder closer to him. "I'm willing to cut you a deal."

He grinned. "I don't think I'm in a very cooperative mood this morning."

I leaned back in my chair, fingers intertwining on my lap. "You're going to want to open that up. See if it helps change your mind."

"Let me guess instead, that'll be more fun," he insisted, clasping his hands behind his head. "Let's see... what would you want to threaten me with? Is it my sex tape with Lisa? Or the one with Ava? Anita really doesn't want those to get out, so it would be a pretty good place to start. Albeit a little boring and predictable."

Lisa was Dad's old assistant.

Ava was her sister.

They'd threatened Grey with the tapes once they'd figured out he was sleeping with them both. He claimed he didn't know he was being filmed. No one believed him.

Anita and the lawyers had eventually stepped in. The sisters were both paid off handsomely, and the videos were then destroyed. With the exception of two copies my grandmother didn't know still existed.

I was in possession of both.

But, "No. It's not the sex tapes." That wouldn't be enough. "I'll give you a hint, though. You're not the subject of the folder's contents."

Here was the thing with my brother: he was notoriously difficult to read. Not in the sense that he showed *no* emotion, but that he *only* showed the emotions he wanted you to see. Period.

But every once in a while, he cracked.

The smile remained in perfect, casual tact, but his eyes gave him away. They hardened noticeably for the slightest of seconds before he blinked it away.

But it was enough.

The game was on.

"I didn't threaten her with the photos," he repeated. "Like I said, I told her they were in my possession and offered to give her the rights if she followed my instructions and kept her mouth shut. It was a bribe, not a threat. If she took it as one, that's on her."

"But there was an actual threat if she didn't comply and if she told me what was going on. What was it?"

"That she'd lose her job. I'd call her boss and tell him about your deal. It would be more than enough for Zilmar to fire her. He's not a fan of liars," Grey said, picking his pen back up. "And neither is Anita, I'm afraid. But my meeting with her isn't until later this morning, and I was going to tell her regardless."

"There's no agreement. You have no proof the relationship was, or is, fake. It would be your word against ours."

"There's no official, signed contract that I'm aware of, no... but there is *other* legal documentation that references the true nature of your relationship. One with both of your names on it that she signed."

I tapped an impatient finger against the back of my hand. "You hacked my email?"

He cocked his head. "Is it hacking if you're stupid enough to use your company email to send her the NDA, knowing IT has full, unobstructed access to that account?" He leaned in then, placing his elbows on the desk. "It's almost like you *wanted* to get caught. Like this whole thing got to be too much, you couldn't see a way out, so you subconsciously created one."

I didn't react.

His smile turned a tinge more sinister than he usually liked to show. "And it's *almost* like you've been traveling constantly, volunteering to oversee projects outside of Toronto, because you've wanted to be anywhere but here. Almost like you burnt out last year, haven't been able to find your way back, and are too tired and jaded to keep trying. But you don't *have* to keep trying if Anita finds out you lied to her about Skylar, not if she fires you over it."

"If I wanted out, I would have quit," I said simply.

He *tsk*ed. "Ah, but you really can't, can you? Enzo didn't raise us to be quitters."

"I coped with my burnout by running away, you coped with yours by rotating a never-ending string of leggy blondes on and off your dick and making an intentional mess of your reputation." I leaned in then, mirroring him. "You think I didn't notice when you stopped making your affairs so public?" I asked. It was my turn to mock him. "You think I didn't notice the difference in you, your work, and your behavior after she started? How quickly she managed to pick you back up and dust you off?"

I paused, smiled. "You want to know why I didn't walk in here with a folder full of shit on you, Grey? Because no one hates you more than you do. But Mila... she's an entirely different story, isn't she? *Her* life actually matters to you. Not that she'll ever know."

Nothing.

He didn't flinch, didn't recoil, didn't blink. His face remained relentlessly amused. "*That's* your theory? You think I'm secretly in love with my assistant?"

I nudged my chin at his desk. "I've spent the last four years gathering dirt not only on her but her entire family. Turns out, unbeknownst to Mila, not all her extended relatives are here all that... *legally*. And that's just the tip of the iceberg. Think of it as a little teaser, an appetizer if you will."

"And everyone always thinks I'm the bad guy," he mused lightly.

"Here are the terms of the deal: you're going to leave Sky alone, give her the rights to those pictures, and *apologize*. And you're not going to breathe a single word about any of this to anyone, including Zilmar and Anita."

"Or what? You'll turn Mila's uncle over to Immigration?" he scoffed.

"Or I'll rip her life to fucking shreds while you watch."

Silence.

For a long time, there was nothing but silence.

It was supposed to be an empty threat. I was never planning on using the information against her; it was always meant to be something I'd be able to hold over Grey's head if need be.

Somehow, though, when I said it, it felt uncomfortably real. It also left a rancid, sour taste in my mouth.

I hated it.

And in that moment, I hated myself.

"You're just like him, you know," Grey finally said. "You don't want to admit it, but you are. A carbon fucking copy. So, congratulations."

I swallowed. Everything was bitter. "Yeah, well, so are you. That was the point."

He nodded once, in both acknowledgment of my statement and acceptance of my offer.

We had a deal.

# 41

## than

I DIDN'T FEEL BETTER.

I thought I would, but I didn't. Everything was still shit.

My chest felt too heavy. My legs too slow. My head too crowded. My bones too... tired.

I was so fucking tired.

Mila was sitting at her desk, flipping through a bunch of paperwork, when I walked out of Grey's office. She didn't feel the need to acknowledge my presence.

Until I stood there for a half second too long.

"Did you need something?" she asked coolly, keeping her eyes down, like I wasn't worth the energy or time it would take for her to glance in my general direction.

She irritated the shit out of me. Always had.

Thing was, though, that no matter how much I disliked her, she didn't deserve to be pulled into our mess.

She didn't deserve to have me dig up dirt on her. And she

certainly didn't deserve to have me *use* that dirt to make threats about her and her family behind her back. She just didn't.

Because at the end of the day, the only thing she'd ever done was her job. She was innocent in all this. Just like Skylar had been. And Darya. Sophie. And every other person we'd dragged into our bullshit mess over the years. Whether they were aware of it or not.

I shook my head, stuffing my hands into my pockets. "Nothing. I just—uh..."

That, at least, earned her undivided attention. She frowned up at me, no doubt wondering why I'd suddenly malfunctioned.

"I just wanted to say I was sorry," I finally admitted.

Mila blinked, looking stunned. Well, stunned for *her*, which essentially meant a slightly raised dark brow and nothing else. "Come again?"

I cleared my throat, bouncing on my feet. "I said I was sorry."

"For what, exactly?"

"Everything. The insults, the nicknames. And how I've treated you over the last few years. Just... everything."

She observed me for a few moments before moving her attention back to her paperwork. "It's fine. I never took it personally."

"Great."

"But since we're doing this, I guess I'll apologize, too," she said, just as I'd started to walk away.

"For what?"

"The insults. The nicknames."

I frowned. "What are you talking about?"

Because, technically, Mila had never actually insulted me to my face. And there were no nicknames I was aware of.

She didn't respond, but I could have sworn I caught the tiniest glimpse of a smile just before she turned her head.

"... And he wants to raise her rent, *again*! She obviously can't afford it! He knows she can't! Which is *why* he's doing it—"

My sister's exasperated huffs cut off as soon as I knocked on the open door, her head snapping in my direction.

"Ethan," Anita said, sounding mildly surprised by my unannounced visit. "What are you doing here?"

"There's something I need to talk to you about."

"We're not done," Alexis snarled at me. Her neck and chest were stained a drastic red, claws digging into her own palms. She was on a warpath.

"Alexis, dear, I've heard everything you have to say. I will have a word with Greyson. However, the last time we spoke about this, he stated that he was simply providing Jane with the market rate. I'm sure we'll be able to give the studio a discount for another year, but eventually, they'll will have to think of something."

"Right, but—"

Anita waved her off while simultaneously motioning for me to sit. "We'll finish our discussion after my meeting with Grey later this morning."

Her scrutinizing gaze followed me all the way from the door to the set of uncomfortable black chairs facing her desk.

Instead of leaving, Alexis crossed her arms and took a seat beside me, her jaw set with stubborn determination. She wasn't done. And she wasn't going to be done until she got what she wanted.

"How is Skylar doing?" Anita asked me, tone uncharacteristically sympathetic. "Joel mentioned something about her feeling ill last night after the two of you disappeared."

"Right. Yeah." I wiped my damp palms against my jeans. "She's still not feeling that great."

My grandmother's head slanted to the side, eyes surveying me. "Have you spoken to Dr. Gomez? She may benefit from a quick house visit."

And instead of answering her, I said, "I flew out to visit Uncle Carlo this week."

I'd never seen her eyebrows arch so high. Ever. "I beg your pardon?"

"I stayed with him for a few days. It was... eye-opening."

All of the color had drained from my grandmother's face. Not that there'd been much to begin with.

"He's happy," I said. My throat felt charred. "Has a wife, kids, a couple of dogs. They own a little cafe right by their house in the suburbs. It's... quiet. And green, with lots of sunflowers planted around the property."

Lanya loved sunflowers. So he'd started planting them everywhere for her.

She woke him up every morning with a cup of coffee and a kiss.

He was happy.

Alexis slowly turned to look at me. I continued to stare straight ahead.

"I'm tired," I admitted eventually. Quietly. It was the first time I'd say it out loud. "I'm *tired*. He's been dead for five years, and we're still fighting."

Anita pinched her lips together. "I never agreed with the way your father chose to raise you boys, but—"

"But you never stopped him," I interrupted, making no effort to keep the bitterness from spiking my voice. "You never said anything. No one did. You let him..." I trailed off, teeth clenching. "You complain *constantly* about my relationship with Grey and how you wish we would at least be civil. Everybody does. But nobody wants to talk about how we got here or whose fault it was."

I was tired. I was angry. And I was tired of being angry.

"No one wants to talk about what it was like before he intervened. No one wants to talk about how Grey and I were inseparable from the day we were born until the day *your son* decided that our friendship was a weakness. That it would keep us unambitious, uncompetitive, *soft*."

Because heaven forbid his sons turned out *soft*.

"We were *six*, Anita. We were helpless, but you could have done something. When he stopped letting us share a room, when he put us in different schools, different teams, when he went out of his way to make sure our schedules clashed so much that we rarely ever got to see each other, no matter how much we begged and cried, you didn't do anything. No one did."

I was so fucking tired.

"You stood back and watched when he started to keep track of our games and grades, and when he started rewarding whichever one of us outperformed the other with gifts, attention, and time. You watched him ignore and neglect the child that 'lost.' You watched him pit us against each other, weaponizing parental love so he could manipulate and mold us into *this*," I spat, my voice growing louder. "*You watched* my relationship with Grey turn bitter and resentful. *You watched* Enzo encourage our fighting and hostility. He wanted us to be just like him, and he succeeded because you let him. And so did Mom and every other adult that sat back and did fuck all to stop him."

I'd worshiped my dad. I would have done anything —*anything*—to gain his approval when he was alive, regardless of who I hurt in the process. Regardless of what I became in the process.

Because that's exactly what he'd wanted.

I understood where Skylar had come from, why she'd done everything her mother had asked of her, why she'd missed the red flags. And I didn't blame her for it. None of it had been her fault.

"Carlo left because of him, and again, you did nothing but watch. Dad planted enough spies around him that the poor guy didn't know who he could trust. He spread rumors about him, destroyed his reputation and relationships, drove him fucking insane until Carlo finally burned out. All because Enzo wanted all of this to himself. And you didn't do anything about that, either. Brushed Carlo off when he tried to tell you what was going on.

"And you want to know what I honestly think? I think that the two of you did Carlo a favor. Put him out of his fucking misery."

I was spiraling, but I couldn't find it in me to care anymore.

"I'm angry, and I'm tired. All the time. It's all I've felt for the last two fucking years, and the *second* I found a semblance of relief from it, she was almost ripped away from me. Because he's been dead for five fucking years, and *we're still fighting*." My throat and eyes were burning; my voice had started to shake. A part of me was afraid that the "almost" in that sentence wasn't needed. And that when I got home, Skylar wouldn't be there. That she'd decided this whole thing was way too fucking much for her.

Nobody would blame her if she left, least of all me.

"Ethan," my grandmother started, her hands clasped tightly in front of her. "I understand your frustration. However, you should know that... a few of us *did* try. We spoke to your father numerous times about his treatment of you boys, but—"

"It wasn't enough."

"No," she said after a momentary pause. "You are correct. It clearly was not. And for that, I'm sorry."

That wasn't enough, either. Her apology wasn't what I'd wanted. Needed. This wasn't about her. Or blaming her. I didn't know why I'd even gone down that route. It wasn't even... I wasn't...

I couldn't...

I couldn't.

"I'm done. I quit."

Alexis gasped. And up until that point, I'd forgotten she was even there. Never in her life had my sister ever been this quiet for so long.

Anita said something, but I'd stopped listening.

I couldn't do this anymore. I hated this job. I hated this... *life*. I was fucking miserable, and I couldn't keep going like this. I didn't want to do it anymore.

It wasn't worth it.

"I'm done," I said again, heart pounding, blood rushing.

My grandmother had stood up, rounded the desk. She was talking.

Talking and talking and talking.

I didn't hear any of it. Not a single word. It didn't matter.

I was done.

I was *done*.

So I stood up and walked out.

# 42

## kylar

I WAS A NERVOUS WRECK.

I'd been pacing around the living room since Ethan left two hours and twelve minutes ago, unable to calm the fuck down enough to do anything other than twist and bend my fingers in ways they weren't meant to twist and bend.

Because what if it was too late? What if Grey had already called my boss? It would be impossible for me to find a job with any reputable designer if Zilmar fired me. The industry was small. People talked.

Or what if he'd done something with the pictures?

I mean, *technically*, he hadn't threatened me with those. But the fact that he even had them in his possession scared the shit out of me. Because maybe he didn't plan on doing anything with them yesterday, but what if he woke up this morning and, like, changed his mind or something?

Was that what was taking Ethan so long? Had Grey already

done something with the photos? Had he already called Zilmar?

Or what if... what if he hadn't, but Ethan wasn't able to get him to change his mind? What if everything was falling apart and I just didn't know it yet?

Grey had instructed me not to tell Ethan anything, and I hadn't. *Technically*, he'd figured most of it out on his own. And last night, with all the champagne and whiskey in my system, I'd somewhat convinced myself that I'd be able to get away with that. This morning? When I was fully sober? I was a lot less confident.

*Oh god.*

And just as I was about to start brainstorming all the different ways my life was undoubtedly over, the door finally unlocked.

My heart leapt into my throat, my feet freezing in place as Ethan stepped into the apartment.

"Hey," I said, my voice two octaves too high.

A mixture of surprise and relief flooded his features as soon as he saw me, which was kind of strange, but I brushed it off.

"Hi," he said.

I waited, fidgeting impatiently with my insides twisting as he stripped out of his jacket and shoes. Then he walked over to where I stood and offered me a brown envelope. "This is for you."

I opened it with shaky fingers, and... there it was. The exclusive licensing agreement for my photos. My lungs emptied, my eyes stinging as I read the document over a couple of times.

"All you have to do is sign it," Ethan said softly. "The paperwork for the others has been emailed to you. Nora did the deal with Simon last night, and I had her draft the paperwork to get them transferred to you this morning. I was afraid he wouldn't sell their rights if he knew they would end up in your hands, so me acting as the middleman was the work-around. And... your job is safe as well. Grey won't be contacting Zilmar about any of this."

"Really?" I said, relief rushing through my body. So much fucking relief. It softened half my muscles into goo. "You're sure?"

He nodded. "Really. I can promise—"

I threw my arms around him. "Thank you," I breathed into his neck. "Thank you, thank you, thank you."

His arms wrapped around my waist slowly, pinning my body to his. "Sky. You have no idea how s—"

Someone banged on the door.

*Loudly.*

"Why is my code not working?" Alexis whined from out in the hall. "I know you're in there. I followed your car. Open up!"

Ethan sighed. "Just ignore her."

"I can hear you, idiot! Open the door!"

I laughed as he begrudgingly let me go, grumbling all the way to the door.

Alexis barged right into the apartment, chucked her bag onto the floor, then lunged at her brother.

I moved to separate them on instinct because she'd gone for him so aggressively that it looked like an attack. But then, I realized what was actually happening.

She was *hugging* him.

And I honestly didn't know which one of us was more shocked, me or Ethan.

"Uh... what are you doing?" he asked her, arms still up. He'd raised them as soon as she'd pounced, readying himself for the fight.

"Holy shit," she squealed, letting him go so she could smack his arm as she hopped on the spot a few times. "Holy *shit!*"

"What's going on?" I asked, sliding the envelope behind a pillow on the couch. I really didn't want to explain everything to Alexis if she asked. Not today.

She grabbed her brother's face, yanked it down more than a foot to her level, then started squeezing his cheeks. And not, like, in a gentle way. "I'm so proud of youuuuuu."

The skin under Ethan's right eye started to twitch, his brows nudging closer as he forced his face out of her grasp, rubbing at his blotted cheeks. "Why are you always so *violent*?"

She shrugged. "It's my love language," she claimed before pointing at me. "Have you told her yet?"

"Told me what?" I was so confused.

Ethan shook his head. "Not yet. I was going to, but then you happened."

"Okay, do it now," Alexis demanded excitedly.

He let out a frustrated breath, pushing a hand through his hair. Then he looked at me and said, "I quit my job."

Alexis burst into another delighted squeal, clapping her hands together rapidly.

"You what?" I said, my head jutting forward in disbelief.

He cleared his throat. "I quit my job."

My mouth fell open.

Because, okay, yes, there had been signs. It wasn't *completely* out of the blue. Especially after last night, with how hesitant he'd been about going into the party. But I didn't think he'd arrived... *here* yet. To this point.

I wanted so badly to go over there and embrace him, but I couldn't really do that in front of Alexis. Because she still didn't know.

And just as I was about to come up with something casual

and generic to say, like, *"Congratulations, buddy. I wish you the best,"* Ethan started walking toward me with his hands held out.

I took a step back, shoving my hands behind my back as my flaring eyes darted to his sister.

She waved her hand dismissively. "Oh, I already know about you guys," she claimed casually. "That's also something we need to talk about because honestly, Sky, I think you can do better."

The quirk of her lips told me she was kidding. But Ethan... oh, poor Ethan.

"*Alexis*," he barked, whipping back around to glare at her.

She paid him absolutely no attention. "I wish you'd told me you were dating again. There are *so many* guys I could have introduced you to who are, you know, closer to you in age, attractive, and most importantly, *employed*. With, like, benefits and vacation pay and stuff. Not that it's too late—you don't have to settle. We could go out tonight—"

She yelped as Ethan picked her up, walked her to the door, placed her outside of it, then slammed it on her evil, cackling face.

"Wait, wait, I'm sorry!" Alexis laughed, banging on the door again. "I was kidding, mostly! We're not done—I have so much more to say! I need to know what your plans are! And there are so many more unemployment jokes to make! Let me back in!"

"Come with me," Ethan said, reaching for my hand so he could pull me into his study and shut the door.

It was quieter in here.

"I quit my job," he repeated.

"So I heard," I said, leaning back against an armchair. "How are you feeling?"

"Tired," he said. "Relieved. And... a million other things."

I bit the inside of my cheek, watching him.

"Sky, I am... *so* sorry, about everything. I can't—" He cut off, took a shuttering breath. "I'm so fucking sorry. I'm sorry."

And then he repeated it ten more times as I walked over and embraced him.

"You have no idea," he whispered, crushing me against him. "You have no idea how sorry I am. You have no idea what you did."

My arms around him tightened, and I was never going to let go. I was *never* going to let him go.

"I'd forgotten what it felt like to *want* to come home at the end of every day, until you," he murmured, and I died a little. "I'd forgotten what it felt like to miss someone. I'd forgotten how to play, to laugh, to just *be*. Until you."

He placed a gentle kiss on my temple. "And I'm sorry. About this. About Simon and your mother, about your dad, all of it. And I swear to you—*I swear*—we're going to take care of them, too. My lawyers are already in the loop, we'll be meeting with them later this week. But for right now, just know this: *they were wrong*."

I bit down on my lip, stuffing my face into his neck.

"They were wrong. They were so fucking wrong. Because you're everything. You're *everything*, baby. And I'll tell you that a thousand times if that's what it takes for you to believe me—"

I was kissing him.

I had him by the collar, and I was kissing him.

It wasn't gentle or soft or reserved. It was every single thing I felt in that moment, everything I couldn't have possibly put into words.

"You," I panted after I broke away, still clinging onto his shirt. I was never letting him go. "You asked me what I wanted yesterday. It's you, Ethan. I want you. You, you, you—"

And then he was kissing me.

He had me hoisted up, crushed against the wall, and he was kissing *the hell* out of me.

"Say it again," he demanded, entirely out of breath. "Say that again."

I pressed my forehead to his, smiling as I slowly repeated myself. "I want you," I said, sliding a gentle thumb across his bottom lip. Because if I liked nice words, Ethan liked nice touches. And sure enough, his breath did a little backflip in response.

I loved that.

I fucking loved it.

My fingers moved to his chin, jaw, tracing gentle lines all the way down his throat and back up, feeling him shudder in response.

"I want you," I repeated softly. "So badly, Ethan. I want you."

"You have me," he murmured before pressing his lips to mine again.

I melted.

I'd never really enjoyed kissing, never understood what all the fuss was about. Not until Ethan. Not until our make-out session in the back of his car. Not until I understood what it was like to feel a kiss in your bones, the tips of your fingers and toes.

It had woken me up after a long, *long* slumber. That's the only way I could describe it.

Because for years after Simon, I'd lost any and all interest in being physically intimate with someone else. Like... that fire was *out*, doused, dead. No matter how hard I tried to force it back, how many guys my friends tried to set me up with, how many times I tried to put myself out there. There was just...

nothing. I'd meet a perfectly nice, attractive man, we'd have a good conversation, and... nothing.

My therapist had assured me that it would just take time, that I was healing. But after a while, I kind of thought that maybe that part of me was broken and that I'd never get it back again.

Until Ethan.

That night had been the first time in years that I'd felt that fire. And in hindsight, I should have paced myself, taken it slow. Maybe that would have prevented the freakout. But I'd been so excited for it to be back, so shocked at how intensely my body had responded to him, that I'd jumped in, headfirst.

One day, I'd explain it to him. And I'd properly apologize for everything.

But right now... right now, I just wanted this. Him. I wanted to play and forget everything that had happened last night.

I groaned when he toyed with the button of my jeans, slick tongue sliding against mine.

The button came undone.

And so did my zipper.

"Tell me what else you want," he murmured, lips and teeth skimming across my jaw.

"You made me a whole bunch of promises last night," I reminded him, half heaving for air. He'd moved down to my neck.

Ethan hummed.

"Touch me," I breathed, heart hammering. "Let's play. I don't want to be sad or anxious anymore today. I've cried enough over Simon and my mom and... I'm trying really hard to move on. So let's just play. We'll talk about everything else tomorrow."

"Play it is." He nipped my skin before putting me down and taking two steps back.

I frowned. "Um, that's the opposite of what I meant."

His lips twisted into a wicked hint of a smirk, his eyes darkening. "Take your shirt off."

And. Okay. With the way my entire lower body reacted to that, Bossy Ethan could *very* quickly become a kink of mine.

I smiled, stripping out of my shirt before throwing it to the side. Which left me in the jeans Alexis had gifted me after our shoot and a black cotton bra.

He took more steps back, hungry eyes roaming up and down my body. Which was, like, *way* more exhilarating than it had any right to be.

I leaned back against the wall, waiting for his next command.

The left corner of his mouth twitched, and ladies and gentlemen, we had a new game.

"Jeans," he demanded next. "Slowly."

I hooked two thumbs underneath the waistband, slowly peeled them down, stepped out of them, then stood back up.

Ethan cursed.

His cheeks were officially flushed, eyes hazy as he took me in. For several minutes, he just observed. It sent a shiver of satisfaction up my spine and back down. Never in my life had anyone made me feel as attractive and desirable as he did.

"Underwear."

I got rid of those, too, throwing them beside his feet. Then I leaned back again, putting my hands behind me, watching, waiting.

His jaw was set tight, his gaze half-drunk, half-feral. Though that little curl of happiness never left the side of his mouth.

Then he walked over to where I stood again, and I had to tilt my head up to maintain eye contact.

"Do you have any idea how beautiful you are?" he said, brushing a piece of hair away from my face. "What you do to me?"

I shook my head. "Show me."

It was supposed to be a sex thing. Where he'd *show me* by giving me a hard, passionate kiss or bending me over one of the armchairs or something.

Instead, he took my hand and pressed my palm against his chest. Right over his heart.

It was hammering. Running rampant and wild. Just like mine.

"Every time I so much as glance in your direction."

And... I died.

It killed me.

I was gone.

And very, *very* wet.

"Ethan..."

But before I could finish the thought, his lips were sealed over mine again. And only after he'd coaxed out a long moan from my throat did he break away and start sinking to his knees, trailing kisses down my chest and stomach on his way down.

My whole body lit up.

"Spread your legs for me," he ordered softly, lips brushing against my stomach as his hands wandered up and down my thighs.

My heart leapt, bouncing all over the place. Because, "Um, just—one quick thing before we start. I've never technically... ever... done that."

Ethan looked up at me, brows rising. "*Really*?"

He said that like it was the most interesting thing he'd ever heard in his life.

I hummed my confirmation.

He gaped up at me, looking like he couldn't decide whether to be shocked or positively *ecstatic* about the unexpected turn of events.

"You wanna try?" he asked.

*Yes, please, so much.*

I nodded, way more enthusiastically than was necessary. "Okay."

He grinned in that wicked way of his. I should have taken it as a warning. I didn't.

"Spread."

This time, I complied.

Ethan took his time, skimming soft kisses across my abdomen, hands grabbing and squeezing my curves, until I was panting, unable to stand still.

Then he spread my lips with his thumbs and planted a small, gentle kiss right onto my swollen bundle of nerves.

I bit back a moan.

"So pretty," he praised, the heat of his breath making me clench. "So perfect."

And then he licked me. Barely. The very tip of his tongue *just* barely grazed my clit.

My knees wobbled, and I made a noise halfway between a whine and a beg.

"Don't be mean," I pleaded.

He grinned up at me, maintaining eye contact as he licked me again. *Thoroughly* this time.

I gasped as the shock of pleasure bolted up my spine, my hands landing on his muscled shoulders for support. And before I could fully recover, he did it again, and again.

And again.

And, "Oh god, that feels—"

He sucked on my clit, and I almost fell down. Would have had Ethan not been holding on to me.

He let out a tortured sound, and before I knew what was happening, I had a leg over his shoulder and his head fully stuffed between my thighs, working me at a steady, dizzying rhythm with his mouth.

He dipped his tongue inside me a few times, groaning with pleasure. Like I tasted so fucking good he couldn't help himself. It was, hands down, the hottest thing I'd ever experienced.

And then, his hands got involved.

He sucked and licked me relentlessly, sliding one finger inside, then two. In, out. In, out. Then... *oh. Oh god oh fuck oh.*

His tongue flicked across my clit as his fingers scratched that deep, *deep* itch.

I didn't stand a chance.

I cried out, one hand digging into his shoulder, the other fisting his hair as my spine contorted and bent forward. I was gasping for breath, trying to keep up with the all-consuming waves of pleasure as Ethan worked me at an agonizingly perfect pace.

It was sensory overload. Too much for me to actually process. Deal with. Handle.

I couldn't do it.

I couldn't...

I...

The earth shattered. My knees caved. My vision starred. My lungs collapsed. And I crashed.

Except Ethan didn't let me go. His mouth continued to work as I spasmed and trembled and clenched until I was panting and whimpering pleas for a break.

Then he let me fall, slowly, right into his arms. Done. Empty. Depleted.

My entire body was liquid. I had no bones or muscles left to speak of, and every few seconds, a new tremor would run through me, making Ethan chuckle.

It took a long time for me to get my voice back, and when it finally did happen, the only thing I could manage was a simple but accurate "Whoa."

He laughed, placed a kiss on the top of my head as he continued to stroke my back. "Yeah, whoa."

I brought my wobbly hands to his hard chest, pushing away enough to be able to look at him.

Ethan offered me a slow, affectionate smile, melted-chocolate eyes looking at me with so much warmth I could have come undone again right then and there. Just in a different way. "Feel better?"

*Better* wasn't even close to describing how I felt. How full my heart was. How my stomach was starting to melt all over again just gazing into those eyes.

I cupped his face, caressing his cheeks. "We should go upstairs."

I wanted to make him feel as good as I did. Desperately.

Over and over and over again.

And then a few more times after that.

Ethan grinned, then leaned in and kissed me one more time. "Mine," he whispered.

"Yours," I promised.

*Him. This one.*

# 43

than

Two Months Later

"Eat it!" Skylar demanded, shoving the fork toward my face.

"You way overcooked it!" I accused, swatting her hand away. "The yolk isn't supposed to have the consistency of *rubber*, Skylar. How did you even manage to do this? And why are parts of it green?"

"Stop being such a food snob and just try it! You promised you would!"

I had to grab her wrist to stop her from shoving the atrocity into my mouth. "You didn't even use salt!"

She rolled her eyes like I was being overly dramatic and unreasonable, as per usual. "The hot sauce we mixed into the ketchup has salt in it. Why would you need to add more to the eggs? That literally makes no sense."

*Jesus Christ.*

"I'm breaking up with you." I let her hand go so I could point to the door. "Please take your toothbrush, your cute butt, and your rubbery, saltless eggs and leave my apart—"

She shoved the fork into my mouth.

I almost gagged.

"That's assault," I told her, my eyes watering as I started to chew. And I mean really *chew*. Something crunched in my mouth, and I had to simply hope and pray that it was just a rogue piece of shell.

"Canadian law isn't real and doesn't apply to Americans," she deadpanned. "I can't be arrested or held accountable for my actions up here."

Then she tried to give me *more* of the ketchup-soaked abomination.

I grabbed her wrists, pinning them behind her back as I pressed her to the counter with my body.

She giggled, bright blue eyes crinkling playfully. I fucking loved those eyes. That laugh. Her sense of humor.

All of it. All of her.

I loved all of her.

Something must have shown on my face because her smile started to wane, and she blinked up at me slowly. "What?"

I shook my head. "Nothing."

She didn't really look like she believed me, but instead of pushing, she said, "Okay, well, here's something... we haven't really talked about what will happen tomorrow... if they don't offer me the job."

Tomorrow was the last day of her internship at Bane and the day she was supposed to find out whether or not they were keeping her on as a full-time junior designer.

She'd come home bouncing with excitement when the

position had opened up last month, and we'd stayed up half the night, going over questions and brushing up her resume.

Not that she'd really needed it. Zilmar had personally asked her to apply for it, all the while heavily implying that the process was simply... a formality.

I hoisted her up onto the counter, pulling her close. "That's because I don't really have any doubt that you'll get it."

She glanced down at her nervous fingers. "Ethan, seriously... what will we do if I have to go back to New York? Would you be willing to do this long-distance?"

She worried the inside of her bottom lip, brows pulling together.

Was she kidding?

"Hell yes, I would be willing to do this long-distance," I told her, nudging her chin. "But I *promise* you, we won't need to."

Her eyes darted up to mine, the corners of her lips hooking up. She'd grown more... observant over the last couple of months. Or maybe it was the opposite. Maybe I'd learned from her, become easier to read.

"What does that mean?"

I sighed. "What if... I told you that I've been thinking about opening up a restaurant. Italian."

Her mouth popped open. "*Seriously*?"

I nodded, unable to hold back my grin. "And what if I told you that I've been looking at spaces in both Toronto and New York?"

Her mouth curved into a slow, seductive little smile. "You'd be willing to move for me?"

I pressed my forehead against hers, sliding her hands into mine. "I'd be willing to do a hell of a lot more than that for you, Sky."

It was true.

The last two months had been incredible. Skylar and I were more compatible than we had any right to be, in almost every imaginable way. I couldn't really make sense of it, and I'd stopped trying.

Because I was *happy*. For the first time in my adult life, I was genuinely happy. And a whole good chunk of it was thanks to her.

This was it for me. She was it.

She just didn't know it yet because I thought maybe it was too soon. And maybe it would freak her out.

"I'd be willing to do anything for you," I told her.

Her eyes flared.

"*Almost* anything," I corrected immediately.

She thought about that, her excitement somewhat dampening. "Define 'almost.'"

"Nothing too illegal or life-sentence-worthy. No exotic animals, no murdering murderers, stealing people's body parts—*including their eyelashes*—or eating any more of your eggs. And absolutely *nothing* involving nunchucks."

I'd learned that last one the hard way.

"So... nothing. You'd be willing to do *nothing* for me, then."

"I'm not stealing my brother's eyelashes for you, Sky. It's not happening."

"Grey doesn't deserve them!" she exclaimed dramatically, like it was the biggest injustice in the world. "They're *wasted* on him, Ethan!"

I chuckled and leaned in for a kiss.

She melted right into me, hands sliding out of mine so they could inch up my chest, making my heart skip every other beat for her. But before I could take things any further, she pulled back.

"Hey... Ethan?"

"Yeah?"

And then she took a big breath, looked me right in the eyes, and said, "I love you."

I stopped breathing. "What?"

"I love you," she repeated, like it was the easiest thing in the world for her to admit.

I thought my heart was going to burst out of my chest.

"I, um, have felt it for a while, I just... didn't want to freak you out," she said, fingers twitching restlessly against my shirt. "Are you freaked-out?"

I shook my head, cupping her face. I was for sure, without a doubt, going to burst. "No. I'm not—" I cut myself off as my lips spread into a wide grin. "I love you, too, Sky."

That smile. Oh, that smile.

I'd lied to her. I *would* do anything for that smile.

I'd raise orphaned capybaras with her in South Africa.

I'd murder every person on her "Murderers I Would Murder if I Were on my Deathbed" list.

And I'd steal Grey's eyelashes. Hell, I'd steal the prime minister's eyelashes for that smile. Those eyes.

"You sure?" she teased. "Even though I don't put salt in my overcooked, ketchup-soaked eggs?"

I stopped, thought about it. "No, sorry, you're right," I said, pushing myself away. "As previously discussed, please take your toothbrush, your cute butt, and your rubbery, saltless eggs—"

She laughed and pulled me back by my collar, sealing her sweet mouth possessively over mine.

"Say it again," she murmured. My demanding little vixen.

"I love you," I repeated, brushing my lips lightly against hers. Once, twice.

And I'd say it as many more times as she needed me to.

"I'm never letting you go," she whispered. "I hope you know that. You're mine, and I'm never letting you go. You're mine in this life, and probably the next million, depending on if Mik can convince my spirit guides to set that up. Apparently, they chat on a monthly basis."

I smiled, my heart swelling.

"Promises, promises," I teased.

Though to her credit, she kept it. In this life, at least.

***The End***

# AFTERWORD

Yay, you made it! Thank you so much for reading *Fool Them Once*. I had such a blast writing about Skylar and Ethan, and I hope you enjoyed reading about their journey as well.

If you'd like to stay with some of these characters for a little while longer, *Half-Hearted* **(Alexis and Joel's novella)** is now available exclusively for my newsletter subscribers!

I'd also be incredibly grateful if you would take a minute and leave a quick review of this story on Amazon, Goodreads, Bookbub or wherever else you like. Every single one goes a long way to helping other readers discover the book.

Wishing you the happiest of ever afters!

Until next time,

Kyra

## ALSO BY KYRA PARSI

In Love And War

> Enemies to lovers

> Office romance

> Forbidden love